PRAISE FOR *THE LAST LETTER*

"Yarros's novel is a deeply felt and emotionally nuanced contemporary romance…"

—*Kirkus Reviews*, starred review

"Thanks to Yarros's beautiful, immersive writing, readers will feel every deep heartbreak and each moment of uplifting love in this tearjerker romance."

—*Publishers Weekly*, starred review

"*The Last Letter* is a haunting, heartbreaking and ultimately inspirational love story."

—*InTouch Weekly*

"I cannot imagine a world without this story."

—Hypable

"A stunning, emotional romance. Put *The Last Letter* at the top of your to-read list!"

—Jill Shalvis, *NYT* bestselling author

"This story gripped me from start to finish. *The Last Letter* is poignant, heartfelt and utterly consuming. I loved it!"

—Mia Sheridan, *NYT* bestselling author

"*The Last Letter* is so much more than a romance. It's a testament to the strength of bonds forged from trauma and loyalty. It's an exploration of motherhood and the importance of family. But above all, it's a story of survival, forgiveness, and the healing power of unconditional love."

—Helena Hunting, *NYT* bestselling author

THE LAST LETTER

REBECCA YARROS

Entangled Publishing, LLC
10940 S Parker Rd
Suite 327
Parker, CO 80134
rights@entangledpublishing.com
Visit our website at www.entangledpublishing.com.

Amara is an imprint of Entangled Publishing, LLC.

Edited by Liz Pelletier
Cover design by Bree Archer
Cover images by
K_Thalhofer/GettyImages
Johncairns/GettyImages
Leekris/GettyImages
Michael Lane/GettyImages
Interior design by Heather Howland

Mass market ISBN 978-1-64063-823-5
Trade paperback ISBN 978-1-64063-533-3
ebook ISBN 978-1-64063-534-0

Manufactured in the United States of America

First Edition February 2020

AMARA

ALSO BY REBECCA YARROS

FLIGHT & GLORY SERIES

Full Measures
Eyes Turned Skyward
Beyond What Is Given
Hallowed Ground

THE RENEGADES SERIES

Wilder
Nova
Rebel

OTHER BOOKS BY REBECCA YARROS

Great and Precious Things

To the kids who
wage war with cancer:

To David Hughes,
who beat his 10 percent chance
with 100 percent heart.

And for those like Beydn Swink,
whose souls were immeasurably
stronger than their bodies.
You are never forgotten.

CHAPTER ONE

Beckett

Letter #1

Dear Chaos,
  At least that's what my brother says they call you. I asked him if any of his buddies needed a little extra mail, and yours was the name I was given.
  So hi, I'm Ella. I know the whole no-real-names-in-correspondence rule. I've been writing these letters just as long as he's been doing what he does...which I guess is what you do.
  Now, before you put this letter aside and mumble an awkward "Thanks, but no thanks," like guys do, know that this is just as much for me as it is for you. Considering that I'd be able to have a safe place to vent away from the curious eyes of this tiny, nosy town, it would almost be like I'm using you.
  So, if you'd like to be my ear, I'd be grateful, and in return, I'd be happy to be yours. Also, I make pretty awesome peanut butter cookies. If cookies didn't come with this letter, then go beat my brother, because he's stolen your cookies.
  Where do I start? How do I introduce myself without it sounding like a singles ad? Let me assure you, I'm not looking for anything more than a pen pal—a very faraway pen pal—I promise. Military guys don't do it for me. Guys in general don't. Not that I don't like guys. I just don't have time for them. You know what I do have? Profound regret for writing this letter in pen.

I'm the little sister, but I'm sure my brother already told you that. He's got a pretty big mouth, which means you probably know that I have two kids, too. Yes, I'm a single mom, and no, I don't regret my choices. Man, I get sick of everyone asking me that, or simply giving me the look that implies the question.

I almost erased that last line, but it's true. Also, I'm just too lazy to rewrite the whole thing.

I'm twenty-four and was married to the twins' sperm donor all of about three seconds. Just long enough for the lines to turn pink, the doctor to say there were two heartbeats, and him to pack in the quiet of the night. Kids were never his thing, and honestly, we're probably better for it.

If pen pal kids aren't your thing, I won't take offense. But no cookies. Cookies are for pen pals only.

If you're good with single parenthood in a pen pal, read on.

My twins are five, which, if you did the math correctly, means they were born when I was nineteen. After shocking our little town by deciding to raise them on my own, I just about gave it a coronary when I took over Solitude when my grandmother died. I was only twenty, the twins were still babies, and that B&B was where she'd raised us, so it seemed like a good place to raise my kids. It still is.

Let's see…Maisie and Colt are pretty much my life. In a good way, of course. I'm ridiculously overprotective of them, but I recognize it. I tend to overreact, to build a fortress around them, which keeps me kind of isolated, but hey, there are worse flaws to have, right? Maisie's the quiet one, and I can usually find her hiding with a book. Colt...well, he's usually somewhere he isn't supposed to be, doing something he isn't supposed to be doing. Twins can be crazy, but they'll tell you that they're twice the awesome.

Me? I'm always doing what I have to, and never what I really should be, or what I want to. But I think that's the nature of being a mom and running a business. Speaking of which, the place is waking up, so I'd better get this box sealed up and shipped.

Write back if you want. If you don't, I understand. Just know that there's someone in Colorado sending warm thoughts your way.

~ Ella

Today would have been a perfect time for my second curse word.

Usually, when we were on full-blown deployments, it got really *Groundhog Day*. Same crap, different day. There was almost a predictable, welcoming pattern to the monotony.

Not going to lie, I was a big fan of monotony.

Routine was predictable. Safe, or as safe as it was going to get out here. We were a month into another undisclosed location in another country we were never *in*, and routine was about the only thing comfortable about the place.

Today had been anything but routine.

Mission accomplished, as usual, but at a price. There was always a price, and lately, it was getting steep.

I glanced down at my hand, flexing my fingers because I could. Ramirez? He'd lost that ability today. Guy was going to be holding that new baby of his with a prosthetic.

My arm flew, releasing the Kong, and the dog toy

streaked across the sky, a flash of red against pristine blue. The sky was the only clean thing about this place. Or maybe today just felt dirty.

Havoc raced across the ground, her strides sure, her focus narrowed to her target until—

"Damn, she's good," Mac said, coming up behind me.

"She's the best." I glanced over my shoulder at him before training my eyes on Havoc as she ran back to me. She had to be the best to get to where we were, on a tier-one team that operated without technically existing. She was a spec op dog, which was about a million miles above any other military working dog.

She was also mine, which automatically made her the best.

My girl was seventy pounds of perfect Labrador retriever. Her black coat stood out against the sand as she stopped just short of my legs. Her rump hit the ground, and she held the Kong out to me, her eyes dancing. "Last time," I said softly as I took it from her mouth.

She was gone before I even retracted my arm to throw.

"Word on Ramirez?" I asked, watching for Havoc to get far enough away.

"Lost his arm. Elbow down."

"Ffffff—" I threw the toy as far as I could.

"You could let it slip. Seems appropriate today." Mac scratched the month of beard he was rocking and adjusted his sunglasses.

"His family?"

"Christine will meet him at Landstuhl. They're sending in fresh blood. Forty-eight hours until arrival."

"That soon?" We really were that expendable.

"We're on the move. Meeting is in five."

"Gotcha." Looked like it was on to the next undisclosed location.

Mac glanced down at my arm. "You get that looked at?"

"Doc stitched it up. Just a graze, nothing to get your panties in a twist over." Another scar to add to the dozens that already marked my skin.

"Maybe you need someone to get her panties in a twist over you in general."

I sent a healthy shot of side-eye to my best friend.

"What?" he asked with an exaggerated shrug before nodding toward Havoc, who pulled up again, just as excited as the first time I threw the Kong, or the thirty-sixth time. "She can't be the only woman in your life, Gentry."

"She's loyal, gorgeous, can seek out explosives, or take out someone trying to kill you. What exactly is she missing?" I took the Kong and rubbed Havoc behind her ear.

"If I have to tell you that, you're too far gone for my help."

We headed back into the small compound, which was really nothing more than a few buildings surrounding a courtyard. Everything was brown. The buildings, the vehicles, the ground, even the sky seemed to be taking on that hue.

Great. A dust storm.

"You don't need to worry about me. I've got no trouble when we're in garrison," I told him.

"Oh, I'm well aware, you Chris Pratt-looking asshole. But man"—he put his hand on my arm, stopping us before we could enter the courtyard where the guys had gathered—"you're not...attached to anyone."

"Neither are you."

"No, I'm not currently in a relationship. That doesn't mean I don't have attachments, people I care about and who care about me."

I knew what he was getting at, and this wasn't the

time, the place, or the *ever*. Before he could take it any deeper, I slapped him on the back.

"Look, we can call in Dr. Phil, or we can get the hell out of here and move on to the next mission." Move on, that was always what came easiest to me. I didn't form attachments because I didn't want to, not because I wasn't capable. Attachments—to people, places, or things—were inconvenient or screwed you over. Because there was only one thing certain, and it was change.

"I'm serious." His eyes narrowed into a look I'd seen too many times in our ten years of friendship.

"Yeah, well I am, too. I'm fine. Besides, I'm attached to you and Havoc. Everyone else is just icing."

"Mac! Gentry!" Williams called from the door on the north building. "Let's go!"

"We're coming!" I yelled back.

"Look, before we go in, I left you something on your bed." Mac rubbed his hand over his beard—his nervous tell.

"Yeah, whatever it is, after this conversation I'm not interested." Havoc and I started walking toward the meeting. Already I felt the itch in my blood for movement, to leave this place behind and see what was waiting for us.

"It's a letter."

"From who? Everyone I know is in that room." I pointed to the door as we crossed the empty courtyard. That's what happened when you grew up bouncing from foster home to foster home and then enlisted the day you turned eighteen. The collection of people you considered worthy of knowing was a group small enough to fit in a Blackhawk, and today we were already missing Ramirez.

Like I said. Attachments were inconvenient.

"My sister."

"I'm sorry?" My hand froze on the rusted-out door handle.

"You heard me. My little sister, Ella."

My brain flipped through its mental Rolodex. Ella. Blond, killer smile, soft, kind eyes that were bluer than any sky I'd ever seen. He'd been waving around pictures of her for the last decade.

"Gentry, come on. Do you need a picture?"

"I know who Ella is. Why the hell is there a letter from her on my bed?"

"Just thought you might need a pen pal." His gaze dropped to his dirty boots.

"A pen pal? Like I'm some fifth-grade project with a sister school?"

Havoc slid closer, her body resting against my leg. She was attuned to my every move, even the slightest changes in my mood. That's what made us an unstoppable team.

"No, not..." He shook his head. "I was just trying to help. She asked if there was anyone who might need a little mail and, since you don't have any family—"

Scoffing, I threw open the door and left his ass standing outside. Maybe some of that sand would fill up his gaping mouth. I hated the *F* word. People bitched about theirs all the time, constantly, really. But the minute they realized you didn't have one, it was like you were an aberration who had to be fixed, a problem that needed to be solved, or worse—pitied.

I was so far beyond anyone's pity that it was almost funny.

"All right, guys." Captain Donahue called our ten-member team—minus one—around the conference table. "Sorry to tell you that we're not headed home. We've got a new mission."

All those guys groaning—no doubt missing their wives, their kids—just reaffirmed my position on the attachment subject.

"Seriously, New Kid?" I growled as the newbie scrambled to clean up the crap he'd knocked off the footlocker that served as my nightstand.

"Sorry, Gentry," he mumbled as he gathered up the papers. Typical All-American boy fresh out of operator training with no business being on this team yet. He needed another few years and way steadier hands, which meant he was related to someone with some pull.

Havoc tilted her head at him and then glanced up at me.

"He's new," I said softly, scratching behind her ears.

"Here," the kid said, handing me a stack of stuff, his eyes wide like I was going to kick him out of the unit for being clumsy.

God, I hoped he was better with his weapon than he was with my nightstand.

I put the stack on the spare inches of the bed that Havoc wasn't currently consuming. Sorting it took only a couple of minutes. Journal articles I was in the middle of reading on various topics, and— "Crap."

Ella's letter. I'd had the thing almost two weeks, and I hadn't opened it.

I hadn't thrown it away, either.

"Gonna open that?" Mac asked with the timing of an expert shit-giver.

"Why don't you ever swear?" New Kid asked at the same time.

Glaring at Mac, I slid the letter to the bottom of the stack and grabbed the journal article on top. It was on new techniques in search and rescue.

"Fine. Answer the new kid." Mac rolled his eyes and lay back on his bunk, hands behind his head.

"Yeah, my name is Johnson—"

"No, it's New Kid. Haven't earned a name yet," Mac corrected him.

The kid looked like we'd just kicked his damn puppy,

so I relented.

"Someone once told me that swearing is a poor excuse for a crap vocabulary. It makes you look low class and uneducated. So I stopped." God knew I had enough going against me. I didn't need to sound like the shit I'd been through.

"Never?" New Kid asked, leaning forward like we were at a slumber party.

"Only in my head," I said, flipping to a new article in the journal.

"She really a working dog? She looks too...sweet," New Kid said, reaching toward Havoc.

Her head snapped up, and she bared her teeth in his direction.

"Yeah, she is, and yes, she'll kill you on command. So do us both a favor and don't ever try to touch her again. She's not a pet." I let her growl for a second to make her point.

"Relax," I told Havoc, running my hand down the side of her neck. Tension immediately drained out of her body, and she collapsed on my leg, blinking up at me like it had never happened.

"Damn," he whispered.

"Don't take it personally, New Kid," Mac said. "Havoc's a one-man woman, and you sure as hell aren't the guy."

"Loyal and deadly," I said with a grin, petting her.

"One day," Mac said, pointing to the letter, which had slid onto the bed next to my thigh.

"Today is not that day."

"The day you crack it open, you're going to kick yourself for not doing it sooner." He leaned over his bunk and came back up with a tub of peanut butter cookies, eating one with the sound effects of a porn.

"Seriously."

"Seriously," he moaned. "So good."

I laughed and slid the letter back under the pile.

"Get some sleep, New Kid. We're all action tomorrow."

The kid nodded. "This is everything I ever wanted."

Mac and I shared a knowing look.

"Say that tomorrow night. Now get some shut-eye and stop knocking over my stuff or your call sign becomes Butterfinger."

His eyes widened, and he sank into his bunk.

Three nights later, New Kid was dead.

Johnson. He'd earned his name and lost his life saving Doc's ass.

I lay awake while everyone else slept, my eyes drifting to the empty bunk. He hadn't belonged here, and we'd all known it—expressed our concerns. He hadn't been ready. Not ready for the mission, the pace of our unit, or death.

Not that death cared.

The clock turned over, and I was twenty-eight.

Happy birthday to me.

Deaths always struck me differently when we were out on deployment. They usually fell into two categories. Either I brushed it off and we moved on, or my mortality was a sudden, tangible thing. Maybe it was my birthday, or that New Kid was little more than a baby, but this was the second type.

Hey, Mortality, it's me, Beckett Gentry.

Logically, I knew that with the mission over, we'd head home in the next couple of days, or on to the next hellhole. But in that moment, a raw need for connection gripped me in a way that felt like a physical pressure in my chest.

Not attachment, I told myself. That shit was trouble.

But to be connected to another human in a way that wasn't reserved for the brothers I served with, or even my friendship with Mac, which was the closest I'd ever gotten to family.

In a move of sheer impulsivity, I grabbed my flashlight and the letter from where I'd tucked it into a journal on mountaineering.

Balancing the flashlight on my shoulder, I ripped open the letter and unfolded the lined notebook paper full of neat, feminine scroll.

I read the letter once, twice…a dozen times, placing her words with the pictures of her face I'd seen over the years. I imagined her sneaking a few moments in the early morning to get the letter written, wondered what her day had been like. What kind of guy walked out on his pregnant wife? *An asshole.*

What kind of woman took on twins and a business when she was still a kid herself? *A really damn strong one.*

A strong, capable woman who I needed to know. The yearning that grabbed ahold of me was uncomfortable and undeniable.

Keeping as quiet as possible, I took out a notebook and pen.

A half hour later, I sealed the envelope and then hit Mac in the shoulder with it.

"What the hell?" he snapped at me, rolling over.

"I want my cookies." I enunciated every word with the seriousness I usually reserved for Havoc's commands.

He laughed.

"Ryan, I'm serious." Whipping out the first name meant business.

"Yeah, well, you snooze, you lose your cookies." He smirked and settled back into his bunk, his breathing deep and even a few seconds later.

"Thank you," I said quietly, knowing he couldn't hear me. "Thank you for her."

CHAPTER TWO

Ella

Letter #1

Ella,

You're right, your brother outright ate those cookies. But in his defense, I waited too long to open your letter. I figure if we actually do this, we should be honest, right?

So one, I'm not good with people. I could give you a bunch of excuses, but really, I'm just not good with them. Chalk it up to saying the wrong thing, being blunt, or just not seeing the need for mindless chatter or any other number of things. Needless to say, I've never written letters to...anyone, now that I think about it.

Second, I like that you write in pen. It means you don't go back and censor yourself. You don't overthink, just write what you mean. I bet you're like that in person, too—saying what you think.

I don't know what to tell you about me that wouldn't get blacked out by censors, so how about this: I'm twenty-eight as of about five minutes ago, and other than my friends here, I have zero connections to the world around me. Most of the time I'm good with that, but tonight I'm wondering what it's like to be you. To have so much responsibility, and so many people depending on you. If I could ask you one question, that would be it: What's it like to be the center of someone's universe?

V/R,
Chaos

I read the letter for the third time since it came this morning, my fingers running over the choppy handwriting comprised of all capital letters. When Ryan had said there was someone in his unit he was hoping I'd take on as a pen pal, I thought he'd lost his mind.

The guys he served with were usually about as open as a locked gun safe. Our father had been the same way. Honestly, I'd figured when weeks had passed without a reply, the guy had snubbed my offer. Part of me had been relieved—it wasn't like I didn't have enough on my plate. But there was something to be said for the possibilities of a blank piece of paper. To be able to empty my thoughts to someone I would never meet was oddly freeing.

Given his letter, I wondered if he felt the same.

How could someone make it to twenty-eight without having…someone, anyone in any capacity? Ry had said the guy was tight-lipped and had a heart as approachable as a brick wall, but Chaos just seemed… lonely.

"Mama, I'm bored." Maisie said from next to me, kicking her feet under the chair.

"Well, you know what?" I asked in a singsong voice, tucking the letter away inside my purse.

"Only boring people are bored?" she replied, blinking up at me with the biggest blue eyes in the world. She tilted her head and screwed up her nose, making wrinkles at the top. "Maybe they wouldn't be so boring if they had stuff to do."

I shook my head, but smiled, and offered her my iPad.

"Be careful with it, okay?" We couldn't afford to replace it, not with three of the guest cabins getting new roofs this week. I'd already sold off twenty-five acres at the back of the property line to finance the repairs that had been long coming and mortgaged the property to the hilt to finance the expansion.

Maisie nodded, her blond ponytail bobbing as she swiped the iPad open to find her favorite apps. How the heck a five-year-old navigated the thing better than I did was a mystery. Colt was a wiz on the thing, too, just not quite as tech savvy as Maisie. Mostly because he was too busy climbing whatever he wasn't supposed to be.

My gaze darted up to the clock. Four p.m. The doc was already a half hour late for the appointment he'd asked *me* for. I knew Ada didn't mind watching Colt, but I hated having to ask her. She was in her sixties and, while still spry, Colt was anything but easy to keep up with. She called him "lightning in a bottle," and she wasn't far off.

Maisie absentmindedly rubbed the spot on her hip she'd been complaining about. The complaint had gone from a twinge, to an ache, to the ever-present hurt that never quite left her.

Just before I was about to lose my temper and head for the receptionist, the doc knocked before coming in.

"Hey, Ella. How are you feeling, Margaret?" Doctor Franklin asked with a kind smile and a clipboard.

"Maisie," she corrected him with serious eyes.

"Of course," he agreed with a nod, shooting me a slight smile. No doubt I was still five years old in his eyes, considering Dr. Franklin had been my pediatrician, too. His hair had more gray, and there was an extra twenty pounds around his middle, but he was still the same as he was when my grandmother brought me to this office. Nothing much changed in our little town of Telluride. Sure, ski season came, the tourists flooding our streets with their Land Rovers, but the tide always receded, leaving behind the locals to resume life as usual.

"How's the pain today?" he asked, coming down to her level.

She shrugged and focused on the iPad.

I tugged it free of her little hands and arched an eyebrow at her disapproving face.

She sighed, the sound way older than a five-year-old's, but turned back to Dr. Franklin. "It always hurts. It hasn't not hurt in forever."

He looked over at me for clarification.

"It's been at least six weeks."

He nodded, then frowned as he stood, flipping the papers on the board.

"What?" Frustration twisted my stomach, but I bit my tongue. It wasn't going to do Maisie any good for me to lose my temper.

"The bone scan results are clean." He leaned against the exam table and rubbed his hand over the back of his neck.

My shoulders sagged. It was the third test they'd run on Maisie and still nothing.

"Clean is good, right?" she asked.

I forced a smile for her benefit and handed the iPad back to her. "Honey, why don't you play for a sec while I sneak a word with Dr. Franklin in the hallway?"

She nodded, eagerly getting back to whatever game she'd been in the middle of.

I met Dr. Franklin in the hall, leaving the door open just a smidge so I could keep an ear on Maisie.

"Ella, I don't know what to tell you." He folded his arms across his chest. "We've run X-rays, the scan, and if I thought she'd lie still long enough for an MRI, we could try that. But in all honesty, we're not seeing anything physically wrong with her."

The sympathetic look he gave me grated on my last nerve.

"She's not making this up. Whatever pain she's in is

very real, and something is causing it."

"I'm not saying the pain isn't real. I've seen her often enough to know that something is up. Has anything changed at home? Any new stressors? I know it can't be easy on you running that place by yourself with two little kids to take care of, especially at your age."

My chin rose a good inch, just like it did any time someone brought up my kids and my age in the same sentence.

"The brain is a very powerful—"

"Are you suggesting that this is psychosomatic?" I snapped. "Because she's having trouble *walking* now. Nothing has changed in our house. It's the same as it has been since I brought them home from this very hospital, and she's not under any undue stress in kindergarten, I assure you. This is not in her head; it's in her hip."

"Ella, there's nothing there," he said softly. "We've looked for breaks, ligament tears, everything. It might be a really bad case of growing pains."

"That is not growing pains! There's something you're missing. I looked on the internet—"

"That was your first mistake." He sighed. "Looking on the internet will convince you that a cold is meningitis and a leg pain is a giant blood clot ready to dislodge and kill you."

My eyes widened.

"It's not a blood clot, Ella. We did an ultrasound. There's *nothing* there. We can't fix a problem that we don't see."

Maisie wasn't making it up. It wasn't in her head. It wasn't some symptom of being born to a young mom or not having a dad in the picture. She was in pain, and I couldn't help her.

I was completely and utterly powerless.

"Then I guess I'll take her home."

I savored the walk from the county road back to the main house. Getting the mail this time of year was always my own little way of sneaking out, and I enjoyed it even more now that I had Chaos's letters to look forward to. I was expecting number six any day now. The late October air was brisk, but we were still a good month away from the slopes opening. Then my small moments of serenity would be swallowed by the torrent of bookings.

Thank God, because we really needed the business. Not that I didn't enjoy the slower pace of fall after the summer hikers went home, but it was our winters that kept Solitude in the black. And with our new, painful mortgage payments, the income was necessary.

But for now, this was perfect. The aspens had turned gold and were beginning to lose their leaves, which currently covered the tree-lined drive from the road to the house. It wasn't far, only a hundred yards or so, but it was just enough distance to give visitors that feeling of seclusion they were looking for.

Our main house held a few guest rooms, the professional kitchen, dining room, and game rooms, plus a separate, small residential wing where I lived with the kids. It always teemed with life when someone wanted company. But Solitude got her name, and her reputation, from the fifteen secluded cabins that dotted our two hundred acres. If someone wanted the convenience of luxury accommodations and proximity to civilization, while still getting away from it all, we were the perfect spot.

Now if only I could afford the advertising to get the cabins booked. You could build it all day long; people only came if they knew you existed.

"Ella, you busy?" Larry asked from the front porch.

His eyes danced under bushy gray eyebrows that seemed to curl in every direction.

"Nope. What's up?" I fidgeted with the mail as I walked up the steps, pausing on a board that might need to be replaced. The thing about rebranding yourself as a luxury resort was that people expected perfection.

"There's something waiting for you on the table."

"Waiting?" I ignored his grin—the man was never going to be a poker player—and headed inside.

I kicked off my boots and slid them under one of the benches in the foyer. The newly refinished hardwood was warm under my feet as I crossed in front of the receptionist's desk.

"Good walk?" Hailey looked up from her phone and smiled.

"Just got the mail, nothing special." I gripped the stack of letters in my hand, prolonging the torture for a few more moments. Besides, that top envelope was a bill from Dr. Franklin, which I wasn't in a hurry to open.

It had been almost a month since I'd taken Maisie to see him, and there was still no diagnosis for her worsening pain. This was just another bill to remind me that I'd dropped us to the lowest insurance premiums possible to get us through this year.

"Uh-huh. You're not looking for a letter, are you?" Her brown eyes were wide with mock innocence.

"I shouldn't have told you about him." She was never going to let me hear the end of it, but I honestly didn't mind. Those letters were the one thing I had just for me. The one place where I could be open and honest without judgment or expectation.

"Hey, it's better than you living vicariously through my love life."

"Your love life gives me whiplash. Besides, we're just writing. There's nothing romantic. Ryan needed a favor. That's all."

"Ryan. When is he coming home again?" She sighed that dreamy sigh most of the local girls let out whenever my brother was mentioned.

"Should be a little after Christmas, and seriously, you were what? Twelve when he left to join up?"

Hailey was only two years younger than me, but I felt infinitely older. Maybe I'd aged ten years per kid, or running Solitude had prematurely shoved me into middle age, but whatever it was, there was a lifetime between us.

"Stop dawdling!" Larry urged, nearly jumping up and down.

"What's the big deal?"

"Ella, get in here!" Ada called from the dining room.

"Both of you are after me now?" I shook my head at Larry but followed him into the dining room.

"Ta-da!" Ada said, waving her arms in a flourish toward the dark farmhouse-style table.

I followed her motions, finding the magazine I'd been waiting for sitting there, its bright-blue cover standing out against the wood.

"When did it get here?" My voice dropped.

"This morning," Ada answered.

"But…" I held up the stack of mail.

"Oh, I just left all that in there. I wasn't going to deprive you of your favorite time of day."

A few quiet, tense moments passed while I stared at the magazine. *Mountain Vacations: Colorado's Best of 2019. Winter edition.*

"It's not going to bite," Ada said, scooting the magazine toward me.

"No, but it could make or break us."

"Read it, Ella. Lord knows I already did," she said, pushing her glasses back up her nose.

I snatched the magazine off the table, dropping the pile of mail in its place, and thumbed through it.

"Page eighty-nine," Ada urged.

My heart pounded, and my fingers seemed to stick on every page, but I made it to page eighty-nine.

"Number eight, Solitude, Telluride, Colorado!" My hands shook as I took in the glossy photographs of my property. I knew they'd sent someone to review us but hadn't known when.

"We've never been in the top twenty, and you just landed in the top ten!" Ada pulled me into a hug, her larger frame dwarfing mine. "Your grandmother would be so very proud. All the renovations you've done, everything you've sacrificed. Heck, I'm proud of you, Ella." She pulled back, thumbing the tears from her eyes. "Well, don't just stand there blubbering, read!"

"She's not the one blubbering, woman," Larry said, coming around to hug his wife. These two were just as much Solitude as I was. They'd been with my grandmother since she'd opened, and I knew they'd stay with me as long as they could.

"'Solitude is a hidden gem. Nestled in the San Juan Mountains, the unique resort boasts not only a family feel in the main house, but over a dozen newly refurbished luxury cabins for those unwilling to trade privacy for proximity to the slopes. Only a ten-minute drive to some of the best skiing Colorado has to offer, Solitude offers you just that—a haven from the tourist-heavy Mountain Village. This B&B feels more like a resort and is perfect for those seeking the best of both worlds: impeccable service and the feeling of being alone in the mountains. It is the pure Colorado experience.'"

They loved us! We were a top ten Colorado B&B! I clutched the magazine to my chest and let joy wash through me. Moments like this didn't come every day, or even every decade, it seemed, and this one was mine.

"The pure Colorado experience is what exists when

the tourists go home," Larry muttered but grinned.

The phone rang, and I heard Hailey answering it in the background.

"I bet the reservations are about to book solid!" Ada sang as Larry danced her around the perimeter of the table.

With a review like that, it was a sure bet. We were going to be slammed, and soon. We'd be able to pay the mortgage and the construction loan for the planned cabins on the south side.

"Ella, the school's on the phone," Hailey called out.

I dropped the magazine with the other mail and headed for the phone.

"This is Ella MacKenzie," I said, prepping to hear whatever Colt had done to aggravate his teacher.

"Mrs. MacKenzie, good. This is Nurse Roman at the elementary school." There was more than a tone of worry in her voice, so I didn't bother to correct her on my marital status.

"Everything okay?"

"I'm afraid that Maisie is here. She collapsed on the playground, and her temperature is at 104.5."

Collapsed. Temperature. A deep, nauseating feeling that could only be described as foreboding gripped my belly. Dr. Franklin had missed something.

"I'll be right there."

CHAPTER THREE

Beckett

Letter #6

Dear Chaos,

Here's another batch of cookies. Hide them from my brother. No, I'm not kidding. He's a shameless thief when it comes to these. It's our mother's recipe, well, really our grandmother's, and he's an addict. After we lost our parents—our Father in Iraq and Mom to a car accident a month later, I'm sure he's told you—these were always in the kitchen, waiting after school, after heartbreaks, after football game wins and losses. They're pretty much like home to him.

And now you have a piece of my home with you.

You asked me something in your first letter, what was that? A month ago? Anyway, you asked what it was like to be the center of someone's universe. I didn't know how to answer then, but I think I do now.

I'm not the center of anyone's universe, honestly. Not even my kids'. Colt is fiercely independent, and he's pretty sure he's been put in charge of personally seeing to Maisie's safety—and mine. Maisie is confident, but her quietness can be mistaken for shyness. Funny thing? She's not shy. She's a ridiculously good judge of character and can spot a lie a mile away. I wish I had the same ability, because if there's one thing I can't stand, it's a lie. Maisie has incredible instincts about people that she definitely didn't get from me. If she's not talking to you it's not because she's a wilting wallflower, it's because she simply doesn't think you're worth her time. She's been like that since she was a baby. She likes you or she doesn't. Colt...he gives everyone a chance, and a second chance, a third...you get the picture.

I guess he gets that from his uncle, because I can admit that I've never been able to give second chances when it comes to hurting the people I love. As embarrassed as I am to admit, I still haven't forgiven my father for leaving us—for the look on my brother's face, or that easy lie that he was just going TDY for a few weeks... but then never coming back. For choosing to divorce my mother instead of the army. Heck, it's been fourteen years and I still haven't forgiven the officer who gave the order that got him killed—for breaking my mother's heart a second time. I really hate that about myself. Yeah, Colt definitely gets his soft heart from my brother, and I hope he never loses it.

At five years old, my kids are already better people than I will ever be, and I'm ridiculously proud of them.

But I'm not the center of their universe. I'm more like their gravity. Right now I've got them locked down tight, their feet on the ground, their path obvious. It's my job to keep them there, close to everything that keeps them safe. But as they get bigger, I get to loosen up just a little, stop tugging so hard. Eventually, I'll get to set them free to fly, and I'll only reel them in when they ask, or they need it. Hell, I'm twenty-four and sometimes I still need to be reeled in. I honestly don't want to be the center, though. Because what happens when the center doesn't exist anymore?

Everything…everyone falls out of orbit.

At least, that's what happened to me.

So I'm good with gravity. After all, it controls the tides, the motion of everything, and even makes life possible. And then when they're ready to fly, maybe they'll find someone else who keeps their feet on the ground. Or maybe they'll fly with them.

I hope it's a little bit of both.

So do I get to know why they call you Chaos? Or is that as secret as your picture?

~ Ella

"Chaos, you wanna share?" Williams asked over comms, nodding toward the letter.

"Nope." I folded letter number six and slipped it inside my breast pocket as the helo carried us to the op. Havoc was still between my knees. She wasn't a huge fan of helicopters, or the rappelling we were about to have to do, but she was steady.

"You sure?" Williams teased again, his smile bright against his camo-darkened skin.

"Absolutely." He wasn't getting the letter or a cookie. I wasn't sharing any part of Ella. She was the first person who had ever been only mine, even if it was just through letters. That wasn't a feeling I wanted to part with.

"Leave him alone," Mac said from next to me. He glanced to my pocket. "She's good for you."

I almost blew him off. But what he'd given me was a gift, not just in Ella but in the connection to more than just the guys, the mission. He'd given me a window to normal life outside the box I'd confined myself in for the last ten years. So I gave him the truth.

"Yeah." I nodded. That was all I could give him.

He slapped my shoulder with a grin, but he didn't say "I told you so."

"Ten minutes out," Donahue called out over the comms.

"What's it like? Telluride?" I asked Mac.

His eyes took on that wistful look I used to roll my eyes at. Now I was oddly desperate to know, to picture the tiny town she lived in.

"It's beautiful. In the summer it's lush and green, and the mountains rise up above you like they're trying to take you closer to heaven. In the fall, they look dipped in gold when the aspen turn…like right now. In winter, it's a little busy because of the ski season, but the snow falls around Solitude, and it's like everything is blanketed in new starts. Then spring comes, and the roads turn muddy, the tourists leave, and everything is born again, just as beautiful as last year." He let his head drop back against the UH-60's seat.

"You miss it."

"Every day."

"Then why are you still here? Why did you leave?"

He rolled his head toward me with a sad smile. "Sometimes you have to leave so you can know what it is you left. You don't really value something until you've lost it."

"And if you never had it?" It was more of a clinical question. I'd never been attached to a place or felt a sense of home. I'd never stayed anywhere long enough for that feeling to take root. Or maybe I wasn't capable of having roots. Maybe they'd been sliced from me so often that they simply refused to grow.

"Tell you what, Gentry. You and me. Once this deployment is over, let's take some leave, and I'll show you around Telluride. I know you can ski, so we'll hit the slopes, then the bars. I might even let you meet Ella, but you'll have to get through Colt."

Ella. We only had another couple of months on this QRF detail. Then it was goodbye to Quick Reaction Force and hello to a little downtime, which I usually despised but now felt mildly curious about. But Ella? That curiosity wasn't mild in the least. I wanted to see her, talk to her, find out if the woman who wrote the letters really existed in a world that wasn't paper or perfect.

"I'd like that," I answered slowly. He'd offered countless times, but I'd never taken him up on it.

His eyebrows rose as his wide grin became almost comical. "Want to see Telluride, or Ella?"

"Both," I answered truthfully.

He nodded as the five-minute warning came over the comms. Then he leaned in so only I could hear him, not that the others had a shot over the rotors anyway.

"You'd be good for each other. If you ever let your feet stand in one location long enough for something to grow."

Worthless. You ruin everything.

I shoved my mother's words out of my head and focused on now. Slipping into *then* was a disaster waiting to happen, so I slammed that door shut in my head.

"I'm not good for anyone," I told Mac. Then, before he could dig any deeper, I ran a check on Havoc's harness, making sure she was clipped in tight so I didn't lose her on the way down.

Gravity could be a bitch.

Ella's comments on that subject ran through my head. What would it be like to have someone ground you? Was it comforting to feel that safety? Or was it suffocating? Was it the kind of force you relied on or the type you fled?

Were there really people who stuck around long

enough to be considered that dependable? If there were, I'd never met one. It was why I never bothered with relationships. Why the hell would you sign yourself up to invest in someone who would eventually say you were too flawed, too complicated, to keep around?

Even Mac—my best friend—was contractually obligated to be in the same unit I was, and even his friendship had limits, and I made sure to never test those lines. I knew in the pit of my stomach that he'd burn anyone to the ground who hurt Ella.

Ten minutes later we touched down, and that was the only gravity I had the time to think about.

CHAPTER FOUR

Ella

Letter #6

Ella,

Thank you for the cookies. And yeah, your brother stole them while I was in the shower. You think he'd be three hundred pounds by now.

I thought about what you said about gravity.

I've never really had that—anything tethering me anywhere. Maybe when I joined the army, but really that was more about my affinity for the unit than it was for anywhere or anyone. Until I met your brother, and they started pushing us through selection. Unfortunately, I am overly fond of him, as is most of our unit. It's only unfortunate because sometimes he can be a real pain in the rear.

Why do they call me Chaos? That's a long, unflattering story. I promise I'll tell it to you one day. Let's just say it involves a bar brawl, two really angry bouncers, and a misunderstanding between your brother and a woman he mistook for a prostitute. She wasn't.

She was our new commanding officer's wife. Whoops.

Maybe I'll make him tell you that story instead.

You mentioned in your last letter that Maisie wasn't feeling well. Did the docs get to the bottom of it? I can't imagine how hard that has to be for you. How is Colt doing? Did he start

those snowboarding lessons yet?
    Gotta go, they're rounding us up, and I want
to make sure I get this in the mail.
    Catch you later,
    ~ Chaos

The only sounds in the hospital room were the thoughts screaming inside my head, begging to be let free. They demanded answers, shouted to find every doctor in this hospital and make them listen. Knowing Telluride wasn't going to look any deeper, I'd brought her an hour and a half away to the bigger hospital in Montrose.

It was almost midnight. We'd been here since just after noon, and both the kids were fast asleep. Maisie was curled in on herself, dwarfed by the size of the hospital bed, a few leads sending her vitals to the monitors. Thank God they'd turned off the incessant beeping. Just seeing the beautiful rhythm of her heart was enough for me.

Colt was stretched out on the couch, his head in my lap, his breathing deep and even. Although Ada had offered to take him home, he'd refused, especially while Maisie had a death grip on his hand. They never could stand to be separated for long. I ran my fingers over his blond hair, the same nearly white shade as Maisie's. How similar their features looked. How different their little souls were.

A soft click sounded as the door opened only enough for a doctor to poke his head in.

"Mrs. MacKenzie?"

I put up one finger, and the doctor nodded, backing away and closing the door softly.

As quietly as I could, I moved Colt off my lap, replacing my warmth with a pillow and my jacket over his little body.

"Is it time to go?" he asked, snuggling deeper into the couch.

"No, bud. I need to talk to the doctor. You stay here and watch over Maisie, okay?"

Slowly, glazed-over blue eyes opened to meet mine. He was still more than half asleep.

"I've got this."

"I know you do." I grazed his temple with my fingers.

With sure steps and very unsure fingers, I got the door open and shut behind me without waking Maisie.

"Mrs. MacKenzie?"

I scanned the guy's badge. Doctor Taylor.

"Actually, I'm not married."

He blinked rapidly and then nodded. "Right. Of course. My apologies."

"What do you know?" I pulled the sides of my sweater together, like the wool could function as some kind of armor.

"Let's go down the hall. The nurses are right here, so the kids are fine," he assured me, already leading me to a glass-walled area that looked to serve as a conference room.

There were two other doctors waiting.

Doctor Taylor pointed me to a seat, and I took it. The men in the room looked serious, their smiles not reaching their eyes, and the guy on the right couldn't seem to stop clicking his pen.

"So, Ms. MacKenzie," Doctor Taylor began. "We ran some blood tests on Margaret, as well as drained some fluid from her hip earlier, where we found infection."

I shifted in my seat. Infection...that was easy.

"So antibiotics?"

"Not exactly." Doctor Taylor's eyes shot up toward the door, and I glanced over to see a woman in her midforties leaning against the doorframe. She was classically beautiful, her dark skin as flawless as her

French twist updo. I was suddenly very aware of my state of dishevelment but managed to keep my hands off my no-longer-cute messy bun.

"Dr. Hughes?"

"Just observing. I saw the girl's chart when I came on shift."

Dr. Taylor nodded, took a deep breath, and turned his attention back to me.

"Okay, if she has an infection in her hip, that would explain the leg pain and the fever, right?" I folded my arms across my stomach.

"It could, yes. But we've found an anomaly in her blood work. Her white counts are alarmingly elevated."

"What does that mean?"

"Well, this is Dr. Branson, and he's from ortho. He'll help us with Margaret's hip. And this…" Dr. Taylor swallowed. "This is Dr. Anderson. He's from oncology."

Oncology?

My gaze swung to meet the aging doctor's, but my mouth wouldn't open. Not until he said the words his specialty had been called in for.

"Ms. MacKenzie, your daughter's tests indicate that she may have leukemia…"

His mouth continued to move. I saw it take shape, watched the animations of his facial features, but I didn't hear anything. It was like he'd turned into Charlie Brown's teacher and everything was coming through a filter of a million gallons of water.

And I was drowning.

Leukemia. Cancer.

"Stop. Wait." I put my hands out. "I've had her at the pediatrician at least three times in the last six weeks. They told me there was nothing, and now you're saying it's leukemia? That's not possible! I did everything."

"I know. Your pediatrician didn't know what to look for, and we're not even certain it is leukemia. We'll need to take a bone marrow sample to confirm or rule it out."

Which doctor said that? Branson? No, he was ortho, right?

It was the cancer doctor. Because my baby needed to be tested for cancer. She was just down the hall and had no clue that a group of people were sentencing her to hell for a crime she'd never committed. Colt… God, what was I going to tell him?

I felt a hand squeeze mine and looked over, my head on autopilot, to see Dr. Hughes in the seat next to me. "Can we call someone? Maybe Maisie's dad? Your family?"

Maisie's dad had never so much as bothered to see her.

My parents had been dead fourteen years.

Ryan was half a world away doing God-knew-what.

Ada and Larry were no doubt asleep in the main house of Solitude.

"No. There's no one."

I was on my own.

The scans began in the morning. I pulled a small notebook from my purse and began to jot down notes of what the doctors said, what tests were being run. I couldn't seem to absorb it all. Or perhaps the enormity of it was simply too much to take in.

"Another test?" Colt asked, squeezing my hand as the doctors drew more blood from Maisie.

"Yep." I forced a smile, but it didn't fool him.

"We just need to see what's going on with your sister, little man," Dr. Anderson said from where he stood perched at Maisie's bedside.

"You've already looked in her bones. What else do you want?" Colt snapped.

"Colt, why don't we go grab some ice cream?" Ada asked from the corner. She'd arrived early this morning, determined that I not be alone.

I could have been in a room with a dozen people I knew—I still would have been alone.

"Come on, we'll grab some for Maisie, too." She held out her hand, and I nodded to Colt.

"Go ahead. We're not going anywhere for a while."

Colt looked to Maisie, who smiled. "Strawberry."

He nodded, taking his duty with all seriousness, then gave Dr. Anderson another glare for good measure before leaving with Ada.

I held Maisie's hand while they finished the draw. Then I curled up next to her on the bed and switched on cartoons, holding her small body against mine.

"Am I sick?" She looked up at me without fear or expectation.

"Yeah, baby. I think you might be. But it's too early to worry, okay?"

She nodded and focused back on whatever show Disney Junior was airing.

"Then it's good that I'm in a hospital. They make you better in hospitals."

I kissed her forehead. "That, they do."

"It's not leukemia," Dr. Anderson told me as we stood in the hallway later that night.

"It's not?" Relief raced through me, the physical feeling palpable, like blood returning to a limb too long asleep.

"No. We don't know what it is, though."

"It could still be cancer?"

"It could. We're not finding anything other than the elevated white counts, though."

"But you're going to keep looking."

He nodded, but the sheen of certainty he'd had in his eyes when he'd thought it was leukemia was gone. He didn't know what we were dealing with, and he obviously didn't want to tell me that.

Day three and four passed with more tests. Less certainty.

Colt grew restless but refused to leave his sister's side, and I didn't have the heart to make him go. They'd never been separated for more than a day in their lives. I wasn't sure they knew how to survive as individuals when they thought of themselves collectively.

Ada brought clean clothes, took Colt for walks, kept me up to date on the business. How odd it was that my obsession with Solitude had been my number three priority behind Colt and Maisie for the last five years, but at this moment felt utterly unimportant.

Days blended together, and my fingers were damn near raw from the internet searching I'd done since Dr. Anderson dropped the *C* word. Of course they'd told me to stay off the net.

Yeah, right.

I couldn't remember a damn thing they said half the time. No matter how hard I tried to concentrate, it was as if my brain had shields up and was only taking in what it thought I could handle. Using the internet filled in the gaps that my memory and my notebook couldn't.

On the fifth day, we gathered in the conference room once again, but this time I had Ada next to me.

"We still don't know what's causing it. We've tested for all the usual culprits, and they've come back negative."

"Why doesn't that sound like a good thing?" Ada asked. "You're saying you haven't found cancer, but you sound disappointed."

"Because there's something there. They just can't find it," I said, my voice turning sharp. "The same as Dr. Franklin. Maisie said she hurt, and she was sent home with a diagnosis of growing pains. Then they called it psychosomatic. Now you're telling me that her blood says one thing, her bones say another, and you're just out of ideas."

The men had the good sense to look embarrassed. They should be. They'd gone to years and years of school for this very moment, and they were failing.

"Well, what are you going to do? Because there has to be something. You're not going to send my little girl home."

Dr. Anderson opened his mouth, and I *knew* from the set of his face, the next excuse was coming.

"Oh, hell no," I snapped before he could get a word out. "We're not leaving here until you give me a diagnosis. Do you understand me? You will not wash your hands of her, or me. You will not treat her as a mystery you simply couldn't solve. I didn't go to medical school, but I can tell you that she's sick. Her blood work says it. Her hip says it. You *did* go to medical school, so figure. It. Out."

Silence roared louder than any excuse they could have given me.

"Ms. MacKenzie." Dr. Hughes appeared, taking a seat next to Dr. Anderson. "I'm so sorry I haven't been here, but I split my time between this hospital and Denver Children's and just returned this morning. I've seen your daughter's test results, and I think I might have one more thing we can test for. It's incredibly rare, especially in a child this old. And if it is what I think it might be, then we need to act quickly." A clipboard appeared in front of me with yet another consent. "One signature is all I need."

"Do it." My name scrawled across the paper as my hand moved, but it wasn't a conscious effort. Nothing felt like a choice at the moment.

Two hours later Dr. Hughes appeared in the doorway, and I stepped out, leaving Colt and Maisie wrapped around each other in front of Harry Potter.

"What did you find?"

"It's neuroblastoma."

Ada followed in my car, Colt strapped into his car seat behind her as we made our way through the curves and bends of I-70 toward Denver. I'd never been in the back of an ambulance, not even when I went into labor with the twins. Now my first trip in one lasted five hours.

They took us immediately to the pediatric cancer floor at the Children's Hospital. There was no amount of festive cartoon murals on the walls that could have possibly lightened my mood.

Colt walked beside me, his hand in mine, as they wheeled Maisie down the wide hallway. Little heads peeked out of the doors or raced by, some bald, others not. There were kids dressed as superheroes and princesses, and one very charming Charlie Chaplin. A mother with a cup of coffee gave me a tentative, understanding smile as we passed where she sat.

It was Halloween. How had I forgotten? The kids loved Halloween, and they hadn't said a single word. No costumes, no trick-or-treating, just tests and hospitals, and a mom who couldn't remember what day it was.

I didn't want to be here. I didn't want this to be happening.

But it was.

The nurse who checked Maisie into her room made sure we had everything we needed, including a pullout bed that she said both Colt and I were welcome to sleep on.

"Do you have costumes?" she asked, too chipper to like and too kind to dislike.

"I...I forgot it was Halloween." Was that my voice? So small and wounded? "I'm so sorry, guys," I said to the twins as they looked up at me with a mix of excitement and disappointment. "I forgot your costumes at home."

Just another way I'd let them down.

"I've got them, no worries," Ada said, plopping a duffel bag onto the couch. "Wasn't sure how long we'd be away, so I grabbed what I could think of. Colt, you're our resident soldier, right?" She handed Colt the plastic-wrapped costume I'd purchased a few weeks ago.

"Yes! Just like Uncle Ryan."

"And Maisie, our little angel. Want to put these on now, or wait?" Ada asked.

"They're welcome to get dressed. We actually do a little trick-or-treat around five, so they'll be all set," the nurse said. I couldn't remember her name. I barely remembered my name.

I nodded my thanks as the kids opened their costumes. Such an ordinary thing in extraordinary circumstances.

Ada wrapped her arm around my shoulders, pulling me in tight.

"It feels more trick than treat," I said quietly so the kids didn't hear me. They giggled and changed, trading pieces so Maisie wore Ryan's Kevlar helmet and Colt had a sparkly, silver halo.

"These are rough days we have coming," Ada agreed. "But you've raised a pair of fighters right there. Maisie won't give up, and Colt sure won't let her."

"Thank you for the costumes. I can't believe I forgot. And everything with Solitude, and gearing up for the season—"

"Stop right there, missy. I've been raising you since you came to Solitude. It's always been you and Ryan, and Ruth, Larry, and me. Ruth was strong, but she knew it would take all of us to pull you kids through after you lost both your parents. Don't you worry about a thing back home. Larry has it under control. And as for the costumes, you have bigger things in that beautiful head of yours. Just let me feel useful and remember the little ones."

So many scans. CT. PET. The letters ran amok in my head while she was in surgery. They called it minor. The tumor they found on her left adrenal gland and kidney was anything but.

Another conference room, but I wasn't sitting down. I was taking whatever news they had for me standing up. Period.

"Ms. MacKenzie," Dr. Hughes addressed me as she walked in with a team of doctors. I was grateful for whatever arrangement she had with Montrose that allowed her to be here, to have the same face, the same voice with me.

"Well?"

"We performed the biopsy and tested both the tumor and the bone marrow."

"Okay." My arms were crossed tightly, doing their best to hold the rest of me together.

"I'm so sorry, but your daughter's case is very aggressive and advanced. In most neuroblastoma cases, the symptoms present much sooner than this. But Maisie's condition has been progressing without any outward signs. It's likely been advancing undetected for years."

Years. A monster had been growing inside my child for years.

"What are you trying to tell me?"

Dr. Hughes walked around the table to take my hand where I stood rocking back and forth like the twins were still babies in my arms in need of soothing.

"Maisie has stage four neuroblastoma. It's taken over 90 percent of her bone marrow."

I kept my eyes locked on her dark brown ones,

knowing the moment I lost that contact, I'd be drowning again. Already the walls felt like they were closing in, the other doctors fading from my peripheral vision.

"90 percent?" My voice was barely a whisper.

"I'm afraid so."

I swallowed and focused on bringing air in and out of my lungs, trying to find the courage to ask the obvious question. The one I couldn't force past my lips, because the minute it came out and she answered, everything would change.

"Ella?" Doctor Hughes prompted.

"What's her outlook? Her prognosis? What do we do?"

"We attack it immediately and without mercy. We start with chemo, and we move forward. We fight. She fights. And when she's too tired to fight, then you do what you can to fight for her, because this is an all-out war."

"What are her chances?"

"Ella, I'm not sure you want—"

"What are her chances?" I shouted with the last of my energy.

Dr. Hughes paused, then squeezed my hand.

"She has a 10 percent chance of surviving."

That roaring returned to my ears, but I shoved it away, concentrating on every word Dr. Hughes said. I needed every ounce of information.

"She has a 10 percent chance of surviving this?" I echoed, needing her to tell me that I'd heard wrong.

"No. She has a 10 percent chance of surviving the year."

My knees gave out as my back hit the wall. I slid, paper crumpling behind me as my weight took down whatever had been there. I landed on the floor, unable to do anything but breathe. Voices spoke, and I heard but didn't understand what they said.

In my mind, they repeated one thing over and over. "10 percent chance."

My daughter had a 10 percent chance of living through this year.

Which meant she had a 90 percent chance of dying, of those angel wings she refused to take off becoming very real.

Focus on the ten. Ten was better than nine.

Ten was…everything.

I pulled myself together. Chemo. PICC Line. Appointments in Montrose and Denver. Aggressive cancer meant an aggressive plan. Binders full of information, notebooks with scribbles. Planners and apps and research studies became my every waking moment. My life changed in those first few days.

I changed.

As if my soul had caught fire, I felt a burning in my chest, a driving purpose that eclipsed all else. My daughter would not die.

Colt would not lose his sister.

This would not break me, or my family. Holding it together was my second priority only to Maisie's survival.

I didn't cry. Not when I wrote the letters to Ryan and to Chaos. Not when I told Colt and Maisie how sick she was. Not when she started vomiting after that first session of chemo, and not when a month later, during her second week-long session, her beautiful blond hair fell out in clumps the day before her sixth birthday. I nearly lost it when Colt showed up from the barber with Larry—his head as shiny and bald as his sister's—but I just smiled. He'd refused to be separated during their birthday, and as much as I didn't want him to see what she went through during chemo, I was incredibly thankful to be with both of them, not to be in a constant state of worry about one while I was caring for the other.

I didn't break down.

Not until New Year's Eve.

That's when the uniforms came to the door and ripped my strong facade to shreds with a simple sentence: *We regret to inform you that your brother, SSG Ryan MacKenzie, has been killed in action.* Due to the nature of their unit, that was all I could know. The details—where he'd been, what had happened, who he'd been with—that was all classified.

When there were no more letters from Chaos, I had at least one of those answers.

They were both gone.

I broke.

FOUR MONTHS LATER

CHAPTER FIVE

Beckett

Beck,

If you're reading this, blah, blah. You know the last-letter drill. You made it. I didn't. Get off the guilt train, because I know you, and if there were any chance you could have saved me, you would have. If there were any way you could have changed the outcome, you would have. So whatever deep, dark hole of guilt you're wallowing in, stop.

I need one thing from you: Get your ass to Telluride. I know your ETS date is right with mine. Take it.

Ella's all alone. Not in the alone way that she has been, but really, truly alone. Our grandmother, our parents, and now me. It's too much to ask her to endure. It's not fair.

But here's the kicker: Maisie is sick. She's only six, Beck, and my niece might die.

So if I'm gone, that means I can't get home in January like we'd planned. I can't be there for her. I can't help Ella through this, or play soccer with my nephew, or hold my niece. But you can. So I'm begging you, as my best friend, go take care of my sister, my family. Do whatever you can to save my little Maisie.

It's not fair to ask; I know that. It's against your nature to care, to not accomplish a mission and move on, but I need this. Maisie and Colt need it. Ella needs it—needs you, though she'll fight you tooth and nail before she ever admits it. Help her even when she swears she's fine.

> *Don't make her go through it alone.*
>
> *I'll save you a seat on the other side, brother, but take your time. Take every single second you can. You are the only brother I would have wished for, and my very best friend. And just in case no one ever told you—you're worthy. Of love. Of family. Of home.*
>
> *So while you're searching for those things, please make sure Telluride is where you look. At least for a little while.*
>
> *~ Ryan*

The mountains rose up above me, impossibly tall considering I was already at almost nine thousand feet. Sure, the air felt thinner, but it was also somehow easier to breathe.

Havoc rested her head on the leather console between our seats as I drove my truck through downtown Telluride. It was Norman Rockwell perfect. Bricked and painted storefronts, families strolling with children. Not quite the tourist haven I was expecting.

It looked like a hometown was supposed to.

It just wasn't *my* hometown.

It was Ryan's. Mac was buried here, at least that was what I'd been told. They'd only sent back Captain Donahue and a couple other guys for the funeral. I'd been kept in the field with the rest of the unit, too valuable to be given leave.

I knew the truth: it wasn't me—at least not with the state I was in then. It was Havoc. They needed her, and she would only listen to me.

I rubbed the top of her head, promising her silently that she'd have a peaceful life from now on. That as quickly as we'd both been given terminal leave, she deserved a little peace.

Me? I lived in a hell of my own making. One that I more than deserved.

I stopped to fill the tank before heading out of town, following my GPS to the address online for Solitude.

Solitude. How fitting. *Alone.*

I was alone.

Ella was alone.

And we'd remain that way, because we'd never be together. I'd seen to that when I'd stopped writing the day Ryan died.

But I could do this. For Ryan. For Ella. But not for me. Thinking it was for me implied there was some kind of redemption that I was worthy of.

There wasn't. What I'd done was beyond any redemption.

My jaw flexed, and my hands tightened on the wheel as I approached the private drive. I made the turn, my gaze catching the mailbox that hung at a haphazard angle on the post. How many times had she gone there looking for my letters? How many times had she found one and smiled? Twenty-four.

How many times had she made the walk without one? Wondered what happened to me? Maybe she thought I'd died on the op with Ryan. Maybe it was better that way.

I wasn't sure I wanted to know.

I drove up the asphalt drive, under the budding aspen trees that lined the way. Ryan would have said there was something fitting about arriving in spring, during the period of rebirth, but that was a load of crap.

There was no rebirth for me. No new beginning. I wasn't here to watch life begin; I was here to help Ella if it ended for Maisie. If Ella even let me near.

The pit in my stomach was entirely too familiar, reducing me to that skinny, quiet kid I'd been twenty years ago, showing up at yet another family's house, hoping this one wouldn't find a reason to make him someone else's problem. Hoping this time he wouldn't pack his stuff in another garbage bag when he accidentally broke a dish or some rule he hadn't known existed, then be labeled "troubled" and shuffled to another, stricter home.

At least this time I already knew what rules I'd broken and was more than aware that my time here was finite.

I pulled up to the circular drive in front of the main house, which matched the pictures I'd seen online. It looked like a log cabin, except huge. The style was modernized rustic, if that was even a thing, and somehow it spoke to me, reminded me of a time when men harvested entire trees to build houses in the wilderness for their women.

When they built things instead of destroyed them.

My feet hit the ground, and I paused, waiting for Havoc to jump down before shutting the door.

I threw the signal for heel, and she came right to my side. We climbed the small staircase that led to a wide porch, complete with rockers and a porch swing. The boxes that lined the porch railing were empty, cleaned out and ready for planting.

This was it. I was about to meet Ella.

What the hell was I going to say? *Hey, I'm sorry I quit writing you, but let's face it, I break everything I touch and didn't want you to be next? I'm sorry Ryan died? I'm sorry it wasn't me? Your brother sent me to watch out for you, so if you could just pretend that you don't hate me, that would be great? I'm sorry I ghosted you? I'm sorry I couldn't bring myself to read any of your letters that came after he died? I'm so sorry for so many things that I can't even list them all?*

If I said any of that, if she knew who I really was—

why I'd stopped writing—she'd never let me help her. I'd get a boot in the ass and sent on my way. She'd already admitted in her letters that she didn't give second chances to people who hurt her family, and I didn't blame her. It was a torturous irony that in order to fulfill Ryan's wish to help Ella, I'd have to do the one thing she hated—lie…at least by omission.

Just add it to the growing list of my sins.

"Are you thinking about going in? Or are you just going to stand out here?"

I turned to see an older man in his sixties coming toward me. Those were some crazy eyebrows. He dusted off his hand on his jeans and reached for mine.

We shook with a firm grip. This had to be Larry.

"You our new arrival?"

I nodded. "Beckett Gentry."

"Larry Fischer. I'm Solitude's groundskeeper." He dropped to his haunches in front of Havoc but didn't touch her. "And who might this be?"

"This is Havoc. She's a retired military working dog."

"You her handler?" He stood without petting her, and I immediately liked him. It was rare that people respected her personal space…or mine.

"I was. Now I think she's mine."

His gaze narrowed a bit, like he was searching for something in my face. After a prolonged silence, which felt like an inspection, he nodded. "Okay. Let's get you two settled in."

A bell chimed lightly as we entered the pristine foyer. The interior was as warm as the exterior, the walls painted in soft hues that looked professionally designed to give it a modern farmhouse look.

Yeah, I'd seen way too much HGTV in the last month. Stupid waiting rooms.

"Oh! You must be Mr. Gentry!" a chipper voice called from behind the long reception desk. The girl looked to be in her early twenties, with a wide smile, brown eyes, and hair to match. High-maintenance but pretty. *Hailey.*

"How would you know that?" I took out my wallet, careful not to dislodge the letter in my back pocket.

She blinked at me rapidly before dropping her eyes.

Shit. I was going to have to work on softening my tone now that I was a civilian—well, almost a civilian. Whatever.

"You're our only check-in today." She clicked through her computer.

I'd be checking out if Ella realized who I was. Then I'd have to find another way to help without her filing stalking charges. Although I'm sure Ryan would have gotten a kick out of that one, he wouldn't be laughing if I couldn't help her.

"Any preference for your cabin? We've got quite a few open now that the season is finally closed."

"Whatever you have will be fine."

"Are you sure? You're booked for—wow! Seven months? Is that right?" She clicked quickly, like she'd found a mistake.

"That's right." I'd never stayed in one place for seven months in my life. But seven months took me to the anniversary of Maisie's diagnosis, so it seemed prudent to book out a cabin. It wasn't like I was buying a house here or anything.

She looked at me like I owed her an explanation.

Well, this was awkward.

"So if I could get a map?" I suggested.

"Of course. I'm sorry. We've just never had a guest stay that long. It caught me off guard."

"No problem."

"Wouldn't it be cheaper to get an apartment?" she asked quietly. "Not that I'm implying that you can't pay. Shit, Ella's going to kill me if I keep offending guests."

She mumbled that last part.

I put my debit card on the counter in hopes that it would expedite the process.

"Run the entire amount. I'll cover incidentals as I go. And yeah, it probably would." That was as much of an explanation as she was going to get.

A ridiculous transaction amount later, I put my wallet away and thanked my younger self for saving like a poor kid determined to never go hungry again. I wasn't poor anymore, or a kid, but I would never wonder where my next meal was coming from ever again.

"Is that…a *dog*?" an older woman asked, her tone soft but incredulous.

"Yes, ma'am." The woman seemed to be the same age as Larry, and by the look of her, had to be Ada. I had the weirdest feeling of stepping into a reality show that I'd only ever watched. I knew who each of them were from Ella's letters, but to them I was a complete stranger.

"Well, we don't *have* dogs here." Her gaze locked onto Havoc like she might immediately grow fleas and infest the place.

Shit. If Havoc went, so did I.

"She goes where I go." My standard answer flew out of my mouth before I censored myself.

Ada gave me a look I'm sure must have sent Ella running when she was younger. I gritted my teeth and tried again.

"I wasn't aware of that policy when I made the reservation. My apologies."

"He's paid up through November!" Hailey said from behind the desk.

"November?" Ada's mouth dropped open.

"Don't worry, love." Larry walked over to his wife and put his arm around her waist. "She's a military working dog. She's not going to ruin the carpet or anything."

"Retired," I corrected him as Havoc sat perfectly still, reading the atmosphere.

"Why was she retired? Is she aggressive? We have small children here, and we can't have anyone bitten." Ada wrung her hands—actually twisted them. It was plain to see her conflict. I was paid through seven months, most of which were in their off-season. I was guaranteed income.

"She retired because I did, and she wouldn't listen to anyone else." I'd been her handler for six years and couldn't imagine my life without her, so it worked out. "She'll only bite on my command or in my defense. She's never peed on the carpet or attacked a child. That I can promise you."

She wasn't the child-killer in the room.

I was.

"She'll be fine, Ada." Larry whispered something into her ear that made her peer a little closer, wrinkling the fine skin of her forehead. Then they had a wordless conversation full of raised eyebrows and head nods.

"Okay, fine. But you're on your own for feeding her. Hailey, put him in the Aspen cabin. That one is due for new carpet next year anyway. Welcome to Solitude, Mr...."

"Gentry," I supplied with a slight nod, remembering to force a quick smile that I hoped didn't look like a grimace. "Beckett Gentry."

"Well, Mr. Gentry. Breakfast is served between seven a.m. and nine a.m. Dinner can be arranged, but you're on your own for lunch, and so is..."

"Havoc."

"Havoc," she said, her face softening when Havoc tilted her head at the mention of her name. "Well, okay then. Larry, why don't you show him to his cabin?"

Larry whistled as we walked out. "That was a close one."

"Seemed like it," I agreed, opening the truck door. Havoc leaped inside in a single, smooth motion.

"Wow. She's got some jump in her."

"You should see her take a wall. She's incredible."

"A Lab, huh? I thought all those dogs were shepherds and stuff. A Lab seems too soft for that kind of work."

"Oh, trust me, her bite is way sharper than her bark."

A few minutes later, I drove the truck along the tight, paved road that wove through most of the property. The Aspen cabin was on the western side, near the edge of a small lake. Havoc would be in heaven. Having studied the area, I knew there were acres between the cabins, the property designed to give visitors what the place was named for—solitude.

Havoc and I climbed up the front porch steps, and I turned the key in the lock. No electronic cards here. It fit with the cabins, the mountains, the seclusion. Larry waved to me from his Jeep as the door swung open, and then he pulled away, leaving us to explore our temporary home.

"This is not a cabin," I told my girl as I stepped into a small foyer complete with hardwood floors and one of those bench things where shoes were kept in baskets. To the left was a mudroom that was no doubt the hub of ski season, and on the right, a half bathroom.

The walls were painted in the same soft hues as the foyer of the main building, the floors dark and welcoming, the rugs clean and modern. The kitchen appeared on the right as I walked farther inside, a welcoming combination of light cabinets, dark granite, stainless-steel appliances.

"At least we can cook," I told Havoc as I glanced over at the dining area that sat eight.

Then I looked past the kitchen to the living room and my jaw dropped.

The living room was vaulted to the second story in a classic A-frame and ran the width of the cabin. Floor-to-ceiling windows brought in the afternoon light as it filtered through the trees and reflected on the lake. The mountains rose above, the snow marking the tree line at the peaks.

If I'd ever imagined somewhere I could make a home, this might have been it.

I'd never seen a more beautiful sight.

"Knock, knock!" a sweet, feminine voice called out from the front door. "May I come in?"

"Sure," I called, walking to the center of the cabin where the hallway led straight to the door.

"I'm so sorry," she said, shutting the door and coming into view.

My heart just about stopped. *Ella.*

Scratch that—*she* was the most beautiful sight I'd ever seen.

Her face was thinner than the pictures I had, the circles under her eyes a little darker, but she was exquisite. Her hair was piled on her head in some kind of knot, and she wore a blue Henley—the exact bright blue of her eyes—under a darker blue vest. Her jeans molded to her body perfectly, but it was easy to see that she'd lost weight since…everything. She wasn't taking care of herself.

Her smile didn't quite reach her eyes, and I realized she was still talking to me.

"Hi, I'm Ella MacKenzie, Solitude's owner. I heard Hailey put you in this cabin, and we've had an issue with the stove that she'd forgotten about, so I wanted to offer you another cabin if you don't want the hassle of a repair team in here tomorrow."

An awkward moment passed before I realized that I needed to respond.

"No, it's fine. I'll be out tomorrow most of the day,

anyway. They won't be in my way. Or I can look at it myself."

"I wouldn't dream of you doing that." She waved me off, looking around the cabin in a quick inspection. "Is everything else okay with your cabin?"

"Very. It's beautiful."

She nodded as she glanced toward the lake, not realizing my eyes were on her. "This one is my favorite."

Havoc shifted at my side, drawing Ella's attention.

"And what do you think about the cabin?" she asked.

Havoc tilted her head and studied Ella. First impressions were everything with her, and if she didn't like Ella right off the bat, there was little hope of recovering.

"May I?" Ella asked, looking up at me.

I nodded stupidly, like I was a junior high boy locked in a room with a girl he crushed on. How the hell was I going to lie to her? Hide who I was? How had I gotten this far without a plan?

She rubbed Havoc behind her ears and immediately won her over.

"You don't mind her being here? There was a miscommunication when I made the reservation." My voice was gruff, my throat tight with everything I wanted—needed—to say to her.

She'd kept me alive.

She'd given me gravity when everything went sideways.

She'd opened the window to show me another life was possible.

I'd destroyed her world and abandoned her, and she had zero clue.

I was just a stranger to her.

"Not at all. I hear she's a service dog?" One last rub, and Ella stood, coming up to just about my collarbone.

I'd always been big, but something about how fragile she seemed made me feel huge, like I could put my body in front of the storm headed her way and protect her...even if the storm was of my own making.

"She's a retired military working dog."

"Oh." A dark look crossed her face before she blinked that fake smile back into place. "Well, as soon as my son figures out you have a dog, you might have a visitor. He's been after me to get one, but now...well, it's just not in the cards, or in my schedule, to train a puppy."

Colt. A jolt of anticipation raced through me at the thought of finally getting to meet him.

"They can be quite the handful," I said, running my hand over Havoc's neck.

"Were you...are you her handler?" Ella asked, studying my face.

God, I could look into those eyes forever. How was Maisie? What treatment was she in now? Was the tumor shrinking? Was it almost operable?

"I was and am. We served together, and now we're out together—on terminal leave, actually. It's not official for another eight weeks. We're both working on the whole domestication thing, and I promise neither of us will pee on the carpet."

The smile that flashed across her face was brief but real.

I wanted it back. Wanted to see it every day. Every minute.

"I'll keep that in mind. So she's trained in explosives, I'm guessing? Were you EOD?"

Here it was, the moment that would define my entire purpose here. Her smile would fade, and I'd no doubt get a well-deserved hand across my face.

"She's trained in explosives and scenting people. She's only aggressive on command and really loves anyone who will throw her favorite toy."

"Explosives *and* people? That's rare, right?" Her forehead puckered, like she was trying to remember something.

"For most dogs, yeah. But Havoc was a special operations dog, the best of the best."

Ella's features flattened, and she stepped back, bumping into the raw wood support pillar that separated the dining area. "Special ops."

"Yes." I nodded slowly, letting her put the pieces together.

"And you just retired? You're really young to get out, knowing what adrenaline junkies you all are. You just…quit?" She folded her arms under her breasts, her fingers rubbing her bicep in a nervous tell.

"My best friend died." My voice was barely a whisper, but she heard the truth of it.

Her eyes flew impossibly wide, the blue even more startling against the sudden sheen of tears I saw gather there before she blinked them away. She glanced at the floor, and within a millisecond her spine straightened and she had walls up twelve feet high.

She wasn't just guarded. She was shut down.

"And that's why you're here."

I nodded again, like I'd turned into a bobblehead since she walked in.

"Say it. I need you to say the words."

My call sign is Chaos. I miss you and your letters so damn much. I crave your words more than oxygen. I'm so sorry about Ryan. I don't deserve to be here. He does.

The options played through my head. Instead, I steered to the safest truth I could give her without ripping her to shreds or blowing the most important mission of my life.

"Ryan sent me."

"I'm sorry?"

"Mac...Ryan. He sent me to watch over you." The way it came out, I could almost believe that I was here as the guardian angel, the one who would sweep in and save her from the shit I had no control over. I couldn't cure her little girl's cancer. I couldn't bring her brother back. In that regard, I was actually the demon.

She shook her head and turned away, making a beeline for the front door.

"Ella."

"Nope." She waved me away—the second time since I'd met her—and reached for the door handle.

"Ella!"

Her hand paused on the handle, the other bracing against the door's trim.

"I know it's too much. I know I'm the last thing you expected." *In every single way.* "If you don't believe me, I have the letter he left me." I reached into my back pocket, pulling out the envelope I'd folded and unfolded so many times that the creases were marked.

She turned slowly, leaning back against the door. Her eyes were wary, her posture tense. She wasn't a deer in the headlights. She was a wounded, cornered mountain lion, all sleek lines and knowing eyes, ready to fight me to the death if I got too close.

"Here." I walked closer and offered her the letter.

She didn't even look at it.

"I don't want that. I don't want any part of it, or you. I don't need a walking, talking reminder that he's gone. I'm not weak, and I don't need a babysitter."

"I'm so sorry he's not here." My throat tightened, nearly closing on the emotions I kept on tight lockdown.

"Me, too." She opened the door and left, and I raced after her like the idiot I was.

"I'm not going anywhere. You need anything, and it's yours. You need help? You've got it."

She let loose a mocking laugh as she descended the

steps.

"I don't want or need you here, Mr...." She opened the door to her SUV and pulled out a paper. "Mr. Gentry."

"Beckett," I answered, desperate to hear her say it. My real name.

"Okay, Mr. Gentry. Enjoy your vacation and then head home, because like I said, I'm not in need of a babysitter or anyone's charity. I've been taking care of myself since Ryan ran off and joined the army after our parents died."

I wanted to grab her, to hold her against my chest and block anything that wanted to harm her. My hands ached to sweep down the line of her back, to take away any of her suffering that she'd let me. I'd known this would be hard, but seeing her wasn't anything I could have prepared myself for.

"It doesn't matter if you want me, because I'm not here on your wishes. I'm here on Mac's. This is all he asked of me, so unless you're going to kick me off your property, I'm going to keep the promise I made."

Her eyes narrowed. "Okay. Anything I need?"

"Anything."

"When Ryan died—"

No. Anything but this.

"—he was on an op, right?"

Could she see the blood drain from my face? Because I sure as hell felt it. I heard the rotors. Saw the blood. Reached for his hand as it limply fell off the stretcher.

"Yes. It's classified."

Her hand gripped the open doorframe.

"So I've heard. I need..." She sighed, looking everywhere but at me for a second before straightening her shoulders and meeting my eyes. "I need to know what happened to Chaos. Was he there? When Ryan died? You were in the same unit, right?" Her throat moved as she swallowed, and her eyes took on a desperate plea.

Damn it. She deserved to know everything. That I wasn't the man I wanted to be, that she needed. That I was the piece of shit who made it back with a beating heart while her brother came home draped in a flag. I needed her to know that I'd chosen to stop answering her letters because I knew that the only thing I could bring her in this life would be more pain.

I needed her to know that it was only Ryan's letter that got me here, and the knowledge that it was the least I could do for my best friend. That I never meant to hurt her, never had the intention of smashing into her life like the wrecking ball I was—not when she lived under such breakable glass.

"Well? Was he?"

But what I needed didn't matter.

I've never been able to give second chances when it comes to hurting the people I love. Letter number six.

If I told her those things, she'd shut me out, and I would fail Mac for a second time. I could tell myself that it was her choice, but really, it would be mine. I was the guy people looked for an excuse to get rid of, and truth was a gift-wrapped reason to kick me to the curb. There were two distinct paths ahead of me: the first, where I told her who I was and what had happened, and she promptly walked out of my life, and the second... where I did everything I could to help her, no matter what the cost.

Path number two it is.

"He was there," I answered honestly.

Her lower lip trembled, and she bit onto it, like any sign of weakness had to be quashed. "And? What happened?"

"That's classified." I was a bastard, but an honest one.

"Classified. You're all the same, you know that?

Loyal as anything to one another and nothing left for anyone else. Just tell me if he's dead. I deserve to know."

"Knowing what happened to Mac...to Chaos...none of that would do you any good. It would hurt a hell of a lot more than it already does. Trust me."

She scoffed, shaking her head as she rubbed the bridge of her nose. When she looked back up, the fake smile was in place, and those blue eyes had gone glacial.

"Welcome to Telluride, Mr. Gentry. I hope you enjoy your stay."

She climbed into the SUV and slammed the door, throwing the vehicle into reverse to get out of the drive.

I watched until she disappeared into the thick forest of trees.

Havoc brushed against my leg. I looked down at her, and she stared back up at me, no doubt knowing that I was an imbecile for what I'd just let happen.

"Yeah, that didn't go so well." I looked up at the cloudless Colorado sky. "We did a number on her, Mac. So if you've got any pointers on how to win over your sister, I'm all ears."

I opened the tailgate of my truck and started to unload my stuff.

It might be temporary, but I was here for as long as Ella would let me stay. Because somewhere between letter number one and letter number twenty-four, I'd fallen in love with her. Fallen for her words, her strength, her insight and kindness, her grace under impossible circumstances, her love for her children, and her determination to stand on her own. I could list a thousand reasons that woman owned whatever heart I had.

But none of them mattered because, even though she was the woman I loved, to her, I was just a stranger. An unwelcome one at that.

Which was more than I deserved.

CHAPTER SIX

Ella

Letter #17

Ella,

The pace is picking up here, which is half blessing, half curse. I'd rather be busy than bored, but busy comes with its own unique set of problems. We keep getting pushed back for redeployment, but hopefully we'll get the okay soon, and I'll be able to keep that date we set for a Telluride tour, if you'll still have me. Warning, I'm bringing your brother, and lately, he smells.

At least the time is going faster, same as these letters. I find that I don't even wait to get one from you before I'm writing again. Maybe it's the simple act of putting pen to paper, of not seeing you react to what I'm writing that makes it so easy, almost effortless.

You asked where I'd settle down if I ever wanted to quit being...what was it you called me? A nomad? I don't know, honestly. I've never found a place that called to me in any way that I could see as special. There were houses, apartments, barracks. Cities, suburbs, and one farm. I've been around the world, but traveling with this crew means that I only see the parts of the world that hurt the most.

I guess I want somewhere where I feel connected. Connected to the land, the people, the community. A place that sinks its hooks into me so deep that I have no choice but to let the roots grow. A place where the earth touches the sky in a way that makes me feel small without feeling insignificant or claustrophobic. Cities are out— remember, I'm not a people person—so maybe a small town, but not so tiny that you can't get away from the mistakes you inevitably make. I'm a pro in the mistake category and have learned that people generally find it easier to kick me out than forgive.

As for the name thing, how about this: on the day I show up in Telluride to get the Colt- approved tour, I'll tell you my full name. I've never hated an OPSEC policy as much as I do right now, but in a way it's a little fun. I'll be able to introduce myself to you, and in the meantime, you'll wonder if every stranger who comes to your door might be me. One day, it will be.

And seriously. Christmas is in less than a month. Buy the kid a puppy. And hug Maisie for me. Let me know how chemo goes this month.
~ Chaos

"Who the hell does he think he is?" I snapped as the door slammed shut behind me. Maybe I slammed it. Whatever.

I let the anger flow through me, hoping it would

overpower the grief welling up in my throat. Chaos had been with Ryan. A part of me had known already—seeing as his letters had stopped when Ryan died—but guessing and knowing felt incredibly different.

I lost Ryan and Chaos and had been handed Beckett Gentry like some kind of messed-up consolation prize with a hero complex.

For God's sake, Ryan. You know I never needed saving.

"Who?" Ada asked, popping her head out of the kitchen.

I kicked off my muddy boots and headed toward Hailey, whose eyebrows would have been in her hairline if she could have jacked them up any higher.

"Gentry!"

"That is one giant bite of man candy, even with the one-word answers," Hailey said, flipping another page in her *Cosmo* magazine.

I snorted, half at her opinion and half at the fact that she still read *Cosmo*. That she was still in a phase of life where *Cosmo* held the secrets of the universe. I'd moved on to *Good Housekeeping* and *Professional Women's Magazine*, where there were no quizzes on how to tell if he was into you.

I was twenty-five with six-year-old twins, one of whom was in a fight for her life, and I owned my own business, which took up every spare minute of my time. No guy was into me. I tugged on Ryan's dog tag, the one that had come back with his things, moving it up and down the chain in nervous habit.

"What? He is. Did you see that scruff of beard? Those arms?"

Yes and yes.

"What does that have to do with anything?"

She looked over the pages of her magazine. "If I have to tell you that he looks like he's about to take

Chris Pratt's role in the Marvel universe, then you're way far gone, Ella. Those eyes? Unh." She leaned back in the chair and stared dreamily at the ceiling. "And he's here until November."

November. That man was going to be on my property for the next seven months.

"He has that whole super-strong, broody, secret pain kind of look. Makes a woman want to pull him close and—"

"Don't finish that sentence."

"Oh, give the girl a break. That boy is something to look at," Ada agreed, leaning against the reception desk. "People skills could use some work, though."

"That boy is special ops." I said it like the curse it was.

"And how would you know that? Because of his dog? I still have my reservations about having a dog on property, but she seemed well behaved, and Labs can't be that aggressive, right?" Ada looked over the desk to see what Hailey was reading.

"One, Labs can absolutely be that aggressive, hence why she's a special ops dog, or was. Whatever. He's her handler."

"Don't be jumping to assumptions just because you feel a little awkward that there's an attractive, single man within walking distance," Ada warned, flipping the page of the magazine herself.

"I'm not—how would you know he's single?" Had they already Facebook stalked him? Did guys like him have Facebook? Ryan never did. He said it was a liability.

"No one checks in for seven months with only their dog if they're not single."

"Yeah, well, it doesn't matter. Ryan sent him."

The magazine hit the desk in a flutter of pages as both women stared at me. Ada was the first to react, sucking in a shaky breath.

"Talk."

"I guess Ryan wrote one of those death letters and asked him to come to Telluride and watch over me. Seriously. Ryan's been dead three months, and he's still giving me his opinion on the men I should have in my life." I forced a laugh and shoved the emotions back in the neat little box they belonged in.

The worst thing about going through so much in such a short time? You can't afford to feel anything about…anything, or you end up feeling it all. And that's what got you into trouble.

"You're sure?" Hailey asked.

"I didn't read the letter or anything, but that's what he said. Given the way he looks, the dog…the way he moves." He'd assessed me from top to bottom within seconds, and it hadn't been sexual. I'd seen him categorize the details in his brain as clearly as if he'd actually had a computer open. "He moves like Ryan. His eyes scan like Ryan's…like my father's." I cleared my throat. "So hopefully, just like my father, he'll get bored and move on quickly." That's what men did, right? They left. Ryan had been honest about his intentions, whereas Dad had lied through his teeth. Jeff had been no better, spinning pretty little stories to get what he wanted and running the minute he'd realized there were consequences. The lies had always been worse than the leaving.

At least Gentry had been up-front and honest about the fact that Ryan sent him here. Honest, bad choices, I could handle. Lies were intentional, inflicted pain for selfish reasons, and unforgivable.

"What are you going to do?" Hailey leaned forward like she was front row to her own soap opera.

"I'm going to ignore him. He'll leave soon enough, once he feels like he's done his duty to Ryan, and I can shut that door on…everything." *On Chaos.* "And in the meantime, I'm going to pick up Maisie from school, because we're supposed to be in Montrose in two hours for her scans. That's what matters right now. Not some Chris Pratt look-alike who has a huge guilt complex."

I was almost back to my office—I needed Maisie's treatment binder—when I heard Hailey laughing.

"Ha! So you *did* notice!"

"I said it didn't matter. I didn't say I was dead." Binder in hand, I raced back through the foyer, grateful we were empty this Monday with the exception of Mr. Gentry.

"And those eyes? Just like emeralds, right?"

Seriously, Hailey had reverted to junior high.

"Sure," I said with a nod, shoving my boots back on. "Ada, will you grab Colt after school? Crap. He's got that cell art project due tomorrow, too. It needs another layer of paint on the edge, can you—?"

"Absolutely. Don't worry. Go take care of our girl."

"Thank you." I hated this, leaving them with everything, walking out on yet another thing that Colt needed. But needs came in seasons, right? This was simply the season that Maisie needed me more. I just had to get her through this, and the next time Colt needed me, I'd be there.

Checking the time on my phone and cursing, I raced down the porch steps, nearly missing the last one. I grabbed ahold of the wooden railing, my momentum sending me spinning around the base of the steps and straight into a very tall, very solid figure.

One with massive arms that not only caught me, but also saved Maisie's binder and my phone from landing in the mud.

"Whoa." Beckett steadied me and then stepped back.

I blinked up at him for a moment. The guy's reflexes were insane. *He's special operations, moron.*

"I'm late." What? Why the heck had those words

come out instead of thank you, or something else that could even pass as social?

"Apparently." There was a slight turn to his lips, but I wouldn't call it a full-out smile. More like mild amusement. He handed over the binder and my phone, and I took them in what felt like the most awkward exchange in the history of awkwardness. Then again, the guy was literally saving me when I'd just said I didn't need saving.

"Was there something you needed?" I hugged the binder to my chest. Maybe he'd taken my words to heart and was getting out of Telluride, or at least off my property.

"I think there's a key I'm missing. The gate to the dock?" He shoved his hands into the pockets of his jeans.

"I guess that means you're not leaving."

"Nope. Like I said, I made the promise to—"

"Ryan. I got it. Well, feel free to…" I waved my arm out toward the wilderness, like the end of the sentence would magically appear through the aspens. "Do… whatever it is you're going to do."

"Will do." His mouth did that quasi-smile thing again, and there was a definite sparkle in his eyes. Not the response I was going for. "So, you're late?"

Shit. I flipped my phone over. "Yes. I have an appointment for my daughter, and I have to go. Now."

"Anything I can help with?"

Holy crap, he looked sincere. I was torn between bewilderment that he'd really shown up here to ask questions just like that and annoyed as hell that a stranger automatically assumed I couldn't handle my life.

The fact that I really couldn't definitely wasn't on the table for consideration.

Clearly, annoyance won out.

"No. Look, I'm sorry, but I don't have time for this. Ask Hailey for the gate key, she's at—"

"The front desk. No problem."

And he'd noticed who Hailey was…perfect. That's exactly what I needed, a lovesick receptionist who would inevitably get her heart broken when he left.

"I so don't have time for this," I muttered.

"So you keep saying." Beckett stepped to the side.

Shaking my head at my own inability to stay focused, I walked past him, opened the door to my Tahoe, and tossed the binder onto the passenger seat. I started the engine, plugged my phone into the jack to charge, and then put the car into gear.

Then I slammed the brakes.

Being annoyed was one thing. Being an all-out bitch? That was quite another.

I rolled down the window as Beckett reached the front door.

"Mr. Gentry?"

He turned, and so did Havoc, who felt more like a shadow, more an extension of Beckett than a separate entity.

"Thank you…for the steps. Catching me. The binder. Phone. You know. Thanks."

"You don't ever have to thank me." His lips pressed in a firm line, and with an indefinable look and a nod, he disappeared into the main house.

An emotion I couldn't name passed through me, racing along my nerve endings. Like an electric shock, but warm. What was it? Maybe I'd simply lost the ability to define emotions when I'd turned them off a few months ago.

Whatever it was, I didn't have time to focus on it.

Ten minutes later, I pulled up in front of the elementary school and parked in the "school bus only" lane. Sue me, the buses weren't due for another three hours, and I needed every minute I had to get to her appointment on time.

I opened the doors to the school and scrawled my name on the clipboard at the window, signing Maisie out.

"Hey, Ella," Jennifer, the receptionist, said as she smacked her gum. She was a little older than I was, having graduated with Ryan's class. "Maisie's back here; I'll buzz you through."

The double doors buzzed, the universal sign of acceptance for entry, and I pushed through, finding Maisie sitting on a bench in the hallway with Colt next to her and the principal, Mr. Halsen, on her other side.

"Ms. MacKenzie." He stood, adjusting his Easter-print tie.

"Mr. Halsen." I nodded, then turned my attention to my oldest by three minutes. "Colton, what are you doing here?"

"Going with you." He hopped off the bench and tugged at the straps of his Colorado Avalanche backpack.

My heart crumpled a little more. Heck, the thing had been so battered over the last few months I wasn't even sure what normal felt like anymore. "Honey, you can't. Not today."

Today was scan day.

His face took on the stubborn set I was all too used to. "I'm going."

"You're not, and I don't have time to argue, Colt."

The twins shared a meaningful look, one that spoke volumes in a language I could never hope to speak or even interpret.

"It's okay," Maisie said, hopping off the bench and taking his hand. "Besides, you don't want to miss fried chicken night."

His eyes threw daggers straight at me, but they were

nothing but soft for his sister. "Okay. I'll save you the legs."

They hugged, which had always seemed to me like two pieces of a puzzle fitting back together.

They shared another one of those looks, and then Colt nodded like a tiny adult and stepped back.

I knelt down to his level. "Bud, I know you want to go, just not today, okay?"

"I don't want her to be alone." His voice was the softest whisper.

"She won't be, I promise. And we'll be back tonight, and we'll fill you in."

He didn't bother to agree, or even say goodbye, just turned on his little heel and walked down the hall toward his classroom.

I let out a sigh, knowing I'd have damage control to do later. But that was the problem. It was always *later.*

Maisie slipped her little hand in mine. She couldn't even be promised now, which meant that as much as I hated it, Colt had to wait.

"Ms. MacKenzie—" Mr. Halsen wiped invisible dirt off his thick-rimmed glasses.

"Mr. Halsen, I was a kid in these halls when you first took over. Call me Ella."

"Ella, I know you're on your way to yet another appointment—"

Breathe in. Breathe out. Do not snap at the principal.

"But when you get back, we need to discuss Margaret's attendance. It's impacting the quality of her education, and we need to have a real discussion about it."

"A discussion," I repeated, because if I said what was actually on my mind, it wouldn't reflect well on my kids.

"Yes. A discussion."

"On Maisie's attendance." Like I gave a crap about kindergarten attendance. She was fighting for her life, and the man wanted to discuss if she'd missed the day where they'd discussed the virtues of *K* being for kangaroo?

"Yes, a discussion on Margaret's attendance."

For an educator, I would have thought he'd have another word.

I looked down at Maisie, whose forehead puckered in her trademark *whatever* look that I recognized all too well...since it was mine. In sync, we looked back to Mr. Halsen.

"Yeah, we'll get right on that."

After chemo. And scans. And nausea and vomiting. And wiped-out blood counts. And everything else that came with a kid whose own body had turned against her.

Two hours later, we sat in the San Juan Cancer Center, me pacing at the end of the exam table while Maisie kicked her legs back and forth, battling whatever iPad app she'd chosen for the day.

I was too keyed up to do anything but wear out the floor. *Please let it be working.* My silent prayer went up with the million others I'd sent. We needed the tumor to shrink, to get small enough that they could attempt a surgery to take it out. I needed all these months of chemo to have been for something.

But I also knew how dangerous the surgery would be. I glanced at my tiny daughter, her hot-pink beanie with matching flower standing out against the white walls. The panic that had been my constant companion these five months crept up my throat, the what-ifs and what-nows attacking like the sanity-stealing thieves they were. The surgery *could* kill her. The tumor certainly *would* kill her.

"Mama, sit down, you're making me dizzy."

I took a seat next to her on the wide side of the exam table and placed a kiss on her cheek.

"Well?" I asked as Dr. Hughes came in, flipping through something on Maisie's chart.

"Hi, Doc!" Maisie said with an enthusiastic wave.

"Nice to see you, too, Ella." She raised her eyebrow. "Hiya, Maisie."

"Sorry. Hi, Dr. Hughes. My manners have run away screaming lately." I rubbed my hands over my face.

"It's okay," she said, taking the spinning stool.

"What do the scans say?"

A soft smile played over her face. My breath caught, and my heart slammed to a stop, awaiting the words I'd been longing to hear and yet was terrified of since this all began five months ago.

"It's time. Chemo has shrunk the tumor enough to operate."

My little girl's life was about to be out of my hands.

CHAPTER SEVEN

Beckett

Letter #7

Chaos,

I'm sitting in the hallway of the Children's Hospital of Colorado, with a notebook propped up on my knees. I would tell you what day it is, but I honestly can't remember. It's been a blur since they said cancer.

Maisie has cancer.

Maybe if I write it a few more times, it will feel real instead of this hazy nightmare that I can't seem to wake up from.

Maisie has cancer.

Yeah, still doesn't feel real.

Maisie. Has. Cancer.

For the first time since Jeff walked out, I feel like I'm not enough. Twins at nineteen? It wasn't easy, and yet it was as natural as breathing. He left. They were born. I became a mother, and it changed me in the very foundation of my soul. Colt and Maisie became my reason for everything, and even when I was overwhelmed, I knew that I could be enough for them if I gave them everything I had. So I did, and I was. I ignored the whispers, the suggestions that I give them up and go to college, everything, because I knew that there was no better place for my kids than with me.

I might have a few issues, but I always knew that I was enough.

But this? I don't know how to be enough for

this.

It's like the doctors are speaking a foreign language, throwing around letters and numbers like I'm supposed to understand. Labs and scans and treatment possibilities and the decisions. God, the decisions I have to make.

I've never felt more alone in my life.

Maisie has cancer.

And I don't know if I'm enough to get her through it, and she has to get through it. I can't imagine a world where my daughter isn't here. How can I be everything she's going to need and give Colt any sense of normalcy?

And Colt…when the genetics came back, they told me Colt and I had to be tested for the gene mutation. He's okay, thank God. We both are, and neither of us carry it. But those moments waiting to hear if losing them both was a possibility? I could barely breathe at the thought.

But I have to be enough, right? I don't have a choice. It's like the moment I saw those two heartbeats on the monitor. There was no option to fail. And there's no way I'm going to fail now, either.

Maisie has cancer, and I'm all she has.

So I guess it's down the rabbit hole I go.

~ Ella

I stepped onto the dock that reached into the small lake just behind my cabin, testing my weight. Yeah, this thing was going to need to be rebuilt. No wonder they'd kept the gate locked.

The sun stretched just overhead, cutting through the brisk morning. I'd been in Colorado for almost two weeks, and I'd learned the key to the weather here was layers, because it might be snowing in the morning, but it was almost seventy by dinner. Mother Nature had some serious mood swings around here.

A light fog rolled off the lake, lingering around the shores of the small island that rested about a hundred yards away in the center of the lake. I knew eventually I'd have to use the little rowboat that was tied up at the end of the dock and row myself over.

Mac was buried there.

It had nearly killed me when I wasn't allowed leave to come back and bury him, and yet there was an overwhelming relief that I wouldn't have to face Ella, to see her expression when she realized what I'd done — why I was alive and her brother wasn't.

Havoc bounded over and shook the water from her coat and dropped the Kong at my feet, ready to take off into the water for the twentieth time or so. She was restless lying around all day these last couple of weeks, and I was, too.

I dropped down to my haunches, rubbing her behind her ears in her favorite spot. "Okay, girl. What do you say we get you dried off and go find a job? Because I'm going to go stir crazy if we stay here much longer like a pair of dead weights. And honestly, I'm kind of expecting you to start talking back at any moment, so some human contact might be needed."

"It's okay that you talk to your dog," a small voice came from behind me. "It doesn't make you crazy or anything." His tone suggested otherwise.

I looked over my shoulder and saw a boy standing on the other side of the gate, dressed in jeans and a Broncos tee. His hair was shorn to the scalp, or rather, had been, and was growing back in a slight sheen of blond fuzz. His full eyebrows were drawn together over crystal-blue eyes, as he gave me a thorough once-over.

Ella's eyes.

This was Colt. I knew it in the very marrow of my bones.

I did my best to soften my tone, well aware that I didn't know the first thing about talking to kids. I assumed not scaring him was a good place to start. "I always talk to Havoc."

She wagged her tail as if in answer.

"She's a dog." His words were at odds with the yearning in his voice and the way his eyes locked onto Havoc like she was the best thing he'd ever seen.

I stood to face him, and he straightened his spine and stared me down. Kid didn't scare easily, which meant I had half a chance here.

"It's not when you talk to them that you have to worry about insanity," I told him. "It's when they start answering you back."

His lips puckered for a second, and he stepped forward, peeking over the half gate to look at Havoc. "So are you crazy?"

"Are you?"

"No. But you have one of our cabins for six months. No one does that. Except crazy people." His expression flickered back and forth between judging me and coveting Havoc.

He'd begged Ella for a dog, and she'd nearly relented—then Maisie's diagnosis came down. But I wasn't supposed to know that. Wasn't supposed to know that he wanted to play football, but Ella was too worried about concussions and pushed him toward soccer. I shouldn't have known that he was supposed to take snowboarding lessons this year, or that he'd shaved off all that hair on his birthday because his sister had lost hers.

I wasn't supposed to know him, but I did.

And it was hell to not be able to tell him that.

"Actually, I rented it for seven months. And you look a little short to be judging people." I crossed my arms.

He mirrored my pose without hesitation. "That makes you even crazier. And I don't let crazy people around my mama or my sister."

"Aah, you're the man of the house."

"I'm not a man. I'm six, but I'll be seven soon."

"I see." I bit back a smile, well aware that he wouldn't be seven for another eight months. But time was all relative at that age. "Well, I'm not crazy. At least *she* doesn't think I'm crazy." I nodded toward Havoc.

"How do you know? Because you said if she talks to you, that means you're nuts." He stepped forward, resting his hands at the top of the gate, which came to about his collarbone. I needed to sand it down so he didn't get splinters.

Man, did he have some lovestruck eyes for Havoc.

"Do you want to see her?"

He startled, his gaze flying to mine at the same time he stepped back. "I'm not supposed to talk to strangers, especially guests."

"Which I totally respect. However, that didn't stop you from coming out here." I glanced behind him, seeing the blue, kid-sized quad that was parked haphazardly behind my cabin. At least there was a helmet resting on the seat.

I had a feeling that wouldn't save him from Ella.

"No one's ever stayed this long, and never with a dog. Not unless they work here, or they're family. I just…" He gave a melodramatic sigh, and his head hung.

"You wanted to see Havoc."

He nodded without looking up.

"Do you know what she is?" I walked forward slowly, like he was a wild animal that I'd spook if I moved too fast. Once I reached the gate, I unlatched the metal closure, letting it swing open.

"Ada says she's a job dog. But not like a special needs dog. There's a girl in my class who has one of those. He's cool, but we can't touch him." His eyes slowly rose, his conflict so open and expressed in those eyes that my heart flopped over in my chest.

"If you back up a little, I'll bring her to see you."

He swallowed and glanced from Havoc to me, and then nodded his head like he'd made his choice. Then he walked backward, giving us enough room to get off the dock and onto solid ground.

"She's a working dog. She's a soldier."

He quirked an eyebrow at me and then skeptically looked at Havoc. "I thought those had pointy ears."

My smile slipped free. "Some do. But she's a Lab. She's trained to sniff out people and…other things. Plus, she plays a mean game of fetch."

He stepped forward, sheer longing in his eyes, but he looked at me before getting too close. "Can I pet her?"

"I appreciate you asking. And yes, you may." I gave Havoc a little nod, and she padded forward, tongue lolling out.

He dropped to his knees like she was something sacred and began to pet her neck. "Hiya, girl. Do you like the lake? It's my favorite. What kind of name is Havoc?"

And boom. I was done for. The kid could have asked me to deliver him the moon and I would have found a way. He was so like Ella in expression, and like Ryan in the way he held himself. That confidence was going to serve him well as a man.

"Now look who's crazy, talking to dogs." I clucked my tongue.

He glared at me over Havoc's back. "She's not talking back."

"Sure she is." I dropped down next to him. "See how

her tail wags? That's a sure sign she likes what you're doing. And the way her head is leaning into where you're scratching? She's telling you that's where she wants you to scratch. Dogs talk all the time, you just have to speak their language."

He smiled, and my heart did the flop thing again. It was like pure sunshine, a shot of unadulterated joy that I hadn't had since...I couldn't even remember when.

"You speak her language?"

"Sure do. I'm what they call her handler, but really, she's mine."

"You handle her?" He didn't bother looking up at me, clearly having way too much fun checking out Havoc.

"Well, I used to. We're both retiring, though."

"So you're a soldier?"

"Yeah. Well, I used to be." I ran my hand down Havoc's back out of habit.

"And what are you now?"

Such an innocent question with an impossibly heavy answer. I'd been a soldier for ten years. It had been my way out of foster care hell. I'd been the best soldier possible because failure wasn't an option, not if it meant going back to the life I'd come from. I promised myself I'd never give them a reason to kick me out, and for ten years, I'd eaten and slept the Army, the unit. I'd earned my place.

"I don't really know," I answered truthfully.

"You should figure that out." The kid threw me some serious side-eye. "Grown-ups are supposed to know those kinds of things."

A chuckle rumbled through my chest. "Yeah, I'll get to work on that."

"My uncle was a soldier."

My stomach hit the floor. What was the line here? How much were you supposed to tell a kid who wasn't yours? What would Ella want him to know?

Luckily, I didn't have to ponder long, because her SUV came tearing down the dirt drive next to my cabin. She threw on the brakes, and a dirt cloud puffed up around the tires. My heart lurched with anticipation. What the hell was I? Fifteen?

"Crap. She found me."

"Hey," I said softly.

He met my gaze, his nose and mouth all scrunched.

"Don't swear."

"Crap's not a bad word," he mumbled.

"Close enough. There's always a better word to use, and I have a feeling your mom makes sure you're educated enough to find them. Make her proud."

His expression straightened, and he nodded solemnly.

"Besides, from the look on her face, you're already in trouble," I whispered.

"Colton Ryan MacKenzie!" Ella shouted as she strode toward us. "What on God's green earth do you think you're doing out here?"

I stood, and Havoc immediately backed to my side.

"Yeah," Colt agreed, standing on the other side of Havoc. "Middle name means I get grounded," he finished in a whisper.

Ella walked the rest of the path to the dock, fury emanating from her in waves. But on top of that fury was an ice-cold fear. I felt it as surely as if she'd brought a snowstorm with her. Her blond hair was loosely woven into a side braid that fell just over her vest, and those jeans...

I snapped my gaze back to hers, which was currently boring a hole into Colt.

"Well? What do you have to say for yourself? Taking your quad? Not telling anyone? Sitting here with a stranger? You scared me half to death!"

God, she was beautiful angry, which was about the only emotion I'd seen from her since I'd gotten here. Every time I'd bumped into her, she'd simply quirked up an eyebrow at me and said, "Mr. Gentry." At least her anger was directed elsewhere at the moment.

"I have been background checked, security clearance and all," I told her.

She shot me a glance that snapped my mouth shut and made me almost glad I'd never had a real mom. That look was the stuff of horror movies.

Colt's eyes went impossibly wide, and he puckered his mouth to the side.

"Colt," Ella warned, crossing her arms.

"He has a dog," Colt said.

"And that gives you the right to not only intrude on a guest's space but put yourself in danger? When I expressly told you not to bother Mr. Gentry?"

Ouch. Guess that explained why it had taken two weeks to meet Colt.

"He didn't mind. He told me that she's a job dog and she used to be a soldier. Just like him. You know, like Uncle Ryan."

Ella's face fell, a veil of sadness clouding her eyes. In that moment, I saw the weariness she'd written to me about. *Sometimes it feels like the world is caving in, and I'm the only one in the center, my arms outstretched trying to brace it. And I'm just so tired, Chaos. I can't help but wonder how long I can hold it before we're all crushed under the weight.* Letter number seventeen. I saw the woman who'd written the letters, who had captured me with nothing more than her words.

My fingers flexed with the need to pull her to me, to wrap my arms around her and tell her that I'd brace the world for as long as she needed. That was the entire reason I was here, to do whatever I could to ease her.

But I couldn't say that, because while she may have

let Chaos do that for her, may even have accepted his love, she wouldn't let Beckett. And if she knew why I kept that secret…well, she'd probably bury me out there next to Ryan. God knew I'd already wished that fate upon myself a hundred times.

"And I'm sure he told you that he worked with Uncle Ryan?" Ella asked, her gaze flying to mine briefly with disapproval.

Ah, that was why she'd put me on the no-visit list.

Colt's mouth dropped open, and he looked at me like I had some kind of superhero cape. "You did? You knew my uncle?"

"I did. He was the closest thing I had to a brother." It was out before I could censor myself. "And no, I didn't tell him, because I didn't know if you'd want him to know," I told Ella.

Her eyes slid shut for a second, and she sighed, so similar to Colt's earlier motion, but not nearly as dramatic.

"I'm sorry for assuming," she said softly. "And for his intrusion on your space. It won't happen again." That last part was aimed right at Colt.

He kicked slowly at the dirt beneath his feet.

"He didn't bother me. In fact, it was an honor to meet you, Colt. If it's okay with your mom, you're always welcome to come visit Havoc. She really does love to play fetch, and I'm not sure if you noticed, but I'm getting kind of old to be throwing for her all the time."

He rolled his eyes. "You're not old." He cocked his head to the side. "But until you know what you are, I'm not sure you're a grown-up, either."

"Colt!" Ella sputtered.

I laughed, and she looked at me like I had two heads.

"It's okay," I assured her. "I told him, since I'm retiring, I'm not really a soldier, and I'm not sure what that makes me at the moment besides a permanent vacationer."

"I'm still surprised you're getting out. In my experience, special ops guys serve until they kick or carry you out."

"Well, I'm on terminal leave, so in forty-five days it will be official."

Her guard dropped for a moment, her shoulders softening. She looked at me like it was the first time she'd really seen me, and it was there again, the thickening of the air between us, the connection we'd shared since our first letters.

But I knew what it was, and she didn't.

"You're getting out because…" Her head tilted, so much like Colt's.

"You know why."

She stepped toward me unconsciously, her eyes scanning mine, searching for something that I was desperate to hand over but couldn't. "You said you left because your best friend died. You got out for Ryan," she concluded.

"For you." The moment it was out of my mouth I wanted to suck it back in, erase the last five seconds in a do-over. "Because of what he asked," I tried to clarify, but the damage was done.

She retreated, her shoulders tense. Those walls came back up, cramming miles of distance in the few feet that separated us.

"I think we've bothered you enough today. Colt, say thank you to Mr. Gentry for not being a psycho kidnapper, and let's go."

"Thank you for not being a psycho kidnapper," he repeated.

"Anytime, bud. Like I said, if it's okay with your mom, you're welcome to come see Havoc again. She likes you." *And it would probably do a little good to get him out of the house every now and then.*

Hope lit up his face like Christmas morning. "Please, Mom? Please?"

"Seriously? You're already grounded from your quad for this stunt, and now you'd like privileges to come spend time with a stranger?"

His gaze flickered sorrowfully to his quad, then back to Ella. "He's not really a stranger, though. If Uncle Ryan was his brother, he's kinda family."

And there went my heart for the third flop.

Family was a word I didn't use and didn't have. Family meant commitment, people whom you depended on — who could depend on you. Family was an utterly foreign concept, even with the unique brotherhood within our unit.

"We'll talk about this later, Colt," Ella said, rubbing the soft skin between her eyes.

"Later you're leaving!"

Well, if that didn't abruptly change the mood.

"I'm not leaving until the day after tomorrow. Now, get in the car, Colt. We'll—"

"Okay!" He gave Havoc another pat and then stomped off toward the truck.

"He seems a lot older than six."

"Yeah. Until this year, the twins were only really ever around adults. A few kids here and there with guests, but they're both basically six going on sixteen. I probably shouldn't have sheltered them so much, but…" She shrugged.

I'm ridiculously overprotective of them, but I recognize it. Letter number one.

"They definitely give their teacher a run for her money. I'm sorry you had to see that." She stared off at the island. "It's been a rough few months…losing Ryan, and everything with Maisie…"

"How are her treatments?" I asked, stepping my toe into waters I had no right to.

Her head snapped toward me. "You know."

"Ryan." Mac and I had talked about it at length, so it wasn't exactly a lie.

She shook her head in exasperation and started walking back to the truck.

"Ella," I called after her, quickly catching up. After almost two weeks of running six miles in the morning, I was finally adjusted to the altitude. Not that we hadn't been dropped into similar elevations in Afghanistan, but I'd been at sea level for two months before getting out here.

"You know what?" she fired back, spinning to face me.

"Whoa!" I gripped her shoulders to keep from smacking into her, then abruptly dropped my hands. That was twice I'd touched her since I'd been here, and the contact was too much and not enough.

"I hate that you know things about me. I hate that you probably knew Colt was my son, that you know about Maisie's diagnosis. You're a stranger who is privy to intimate details about my life because of my brother, and that's not fair."

"I can't change that. I'm not sure I would even if I could, because that's the reason I'm here."

"The reason you're here is buried out on that island!"

In so many ways.

"We can go round and round. But I'm not leaving. So I will make you this offer. You can ask me any questions you want"—I held up my finger when she opened her mouth, knowing she'd ask about Mac's death again—"that I'm allowed to answer, and I'll tell you anything I can about me. You're right. It's not fair that I know so much. It's incredibly creepy for me to know about your kids, your life…you. But Mac loved you, and he talked about you all the time. You, them, this place was the home he so badly wanted to come back to, and when he talked about you, it was like he had this tiny moment of reprieve from the hell we were living. So, I'm incredibly sorry that your privacy has been violated. You have *no* clue how sorry I am, but I can't go back in time and ask him not to overshare, and if I had that magical time button, I'd use it for something far better, like saving his life. Because he should be here. Not me. But I'm the one he sent, and I'm staying." I clenched my jaw. What was it about this woman that killed whatever semblance of a filter I had? Whether it was reading her letters, or staring into her eyes, she had a power over me that was worse than a bottle of tequila for loosening my tongue. She made me *want* to tell her everything, and that was dangerous to both of us.

"If Ryan wanted so badly to be here, he could have gotten out when he was up for reenlistment. But he didn't. Because guys like Ryan—like you—don't stay home, don't put down roots, don't stay, period. I can accept that I'm your…mission, or whatever, for the time being, but don't act like you're not temporary."

I fought every instinct in my body that screamed to declare differently, but I knew she wouldn't believe me, and I'm not sure I would have, either. It was only a matter of time before she realized who I really was and what I'd done. And my feelings for her wouldn't buffer that fallout. A nuclear shelter couldn't.

"I'm sorry," she said quietly after a few moments of silence passed between us. "I can't imagine what you've gone through, if you were really that close to Ryan. And you must have been to uproot your entire life to come here."

"I thought I didn't have roots," I teased.

A tiny smile ghosted across her face, but it was sad. "Like I said, I'm sorry. But imagine if I showed up in…

wherever it was you guys were, and I knew everything about you, and you didn't know the first thing about me. Unsettling, right?"

A raw, grating pain scraped across me, because she did know everything about me. In a way. I'd left out the physical details of my life while I basically pulled my soul out of my body and put it on paper for her. She might not have known *what* I was, but she knew *who* I was, more than anyone else on the planet. I'd let her in and then shut myself out, and I missed her with a ferocity that was terrifying.

"Yeah, I can see how that would be a ten on the weird scale."

"Thank you. And really, it's an eleven." She headed back up the path to her Tahoe, where Colt had the back hatch open and was waiting with his quad.

This apparently wasn't the first time he'd been grounded from it if he was that aware of the routine.

"I got it, Colt," I told him. Then I lifted it into the back of the SUV, thankful there was a rubber lining in the back. When I turned around, Ella was staring at me, her mouth slightly agape. Well, staring at my arms. I made a mental note to get a gym membership. I liked that look.

"Anything else?" I asked, shutting the hatch.

She shook her head quickly. "Nope. Nothing. Thanks for…you know…"

"Not being a psycho kidnapper?"

"Something like that." A blush stole across her cheeks.

"I was serious about the background check. If you would feel more comfortable—"

"No, of course not. I don't make a habit of background checking my guests, and I'm not going to start now."

"You should," I muttered. If I had been a psycho kidnapper, Colt would be dead. Actually, these woods were secluded enough that she could harbor a serial killer and never know.

She rolled her eyes at me and climbed up into the driver's seat.

"Hey, Mr. Gentry?" Colt called from the back seat.

Ella rolled down the window, and I leaned in to see him strapped into a tall, thin car seat that sat beside an empty one.

"What's up?"

"I've decided that, since you're Uncle Ryan's brother, that makes you family." He said it with the seriousness of an adult.

"Have you?" My voice softened. The kid didn't know what he was offering, or how much it meant to me, because he'd always had a family. It was simply a given. "Well, thank you."

I met Ella's eyes in the rearview mirror, and she let out a small sigh of defeat.

"And you're not crazy," he added. "So I guess you can stay."

I smiled so wide my cheeks hurt. This kid was amazing. "Thank you for your approval, Colt."

"You're welcome," he said with a shrug.

I stepped back, and Ella closed her door, then leaned out her open window. "Don't forget that there are meals in the main house. Ada said that she hasn't seen you there, and she gets nosy."

"Noted. I didn't want to bring Havoc in with Maisie there, too." I wasn't an expert on kids with cancer, but I knew enough that she didn't need me bringing extra dander in.

"Oh, that's…really thoughtful of you. But you're okay. After she went neutropenic the first time—that's when—"

"Her white cells drop to where she's susceptible to every infection known to man?" I finished.

"Yeah. How did you know that?"

"I read about neuroblastoma. A lot."

"For Ryan?"

For you.

"Yeah, something like that."

She ripped her gaze away from mine, like she felt our connection, too. But where I embraced the intensity, she apparently did not. "Right. Well, after that, I moved the kids out of the residence wing and into a cabin that we could keep—"

"Wrapped up like a bubble," Colt called out from the back seat.

"Pretty much," Ella admitted with a shrug. "We're actually your neighbors. If you walk about two hundred yards that way, you'll find us."

"Then I guess I'll see you around."

"Then I guess you will."

They drove up the wide path next to my cabin. There must have been a small boat launch here or something to have a path like that cleared.

Havoc sat back on her haunches and cocked her head at me.

"I think that went better, don't you?" I asked. Her tail thumped in agreement. "Yeah. Now let's go find a job before Colt takes away our grown-up card."

Three hours later I was officially the newest part-time member of Telluride Mountain Rescue. Scratch that. Havoc was. She was all the talent, anyway.

CHAPTER EIGHT

Ella

Letter #9

Ella,

First off, I'm speechless. I can't possibly find adequate words to express my sadness at Maisie's diagnosis, or my awe at how you're handling it.

Jeff is an ass. Sorry, I'm sure he must have some redeeming qualities, because at one time you felt him worthy enough to give him your heart and even marry him, but he is. And I say is in the present tense on purpose, because he's still making you feel like you're not enough when you prove over and over again that you are.

You are enough, Ella. You're more than enough. I've never met a woman who has your strength, your determination, your absolute loyalty to your kids. So I included a little something. Take it out when you need it to remind yourself that you can do this, because I know with absolute certainty that you can.

And yeah, I know you're a good mom without ever having "met" you. Mostly it's because I know what it's like to have a bad one, and you are anything but that.

What do you need? I can't bring dinner by, but I can order a mean pizza. Is there anything I can have shipped to you? I know that what you probably need is the support of people, and in that arena, my hands are tied, and I'm sorry. I know I can't do much through these letters, but if

I could, I'd be there, or I'd send your brother home to you.

You're enough, Ella.
~ Chaos

I rolled my neck, trying to dislodge the seemingly permanent knot that had formed between my shoulder blades. Hours hunched over spreadsheets and bills did that to a girl.

I stifled a yawn and checked out the clock. Yeah, eight thirty p.m. was way too late to hit up the coffee. I'd be awake until dawn.

So iced tea it was. I took a sip from my glass and went back to sorting bills. We were in trouble, and it was the kind I didn't know how to get myself out of. The kind that was going to really hit home when Maisie had surgery in three days.

Ada popped her head into the makeshift office we'd put together in the cabin. "I left some muffins for the morning. Is there anything else you need?"

I forced a smile and shook my head. "Nope. Thank you, Ada."

"You're family, dear. No need to thank me." She gave me an ultra-hard once-over and then pulled out the armchair from where I'd shoved it against the wall, sinking into it and placing her hands in her lap.

That was code for Ada-wasn't-letting-up.

Crap.

"Tell me. And don't you dare hold back."

I relaxed in my office chair and almost lied. But the woman mom-stared me, which was pretty much the equivalent of a detective sweating you out under a light.

"What?" I asked, fidgeting with my pen.

"Tell me."

I didn't want to. Voicing the concern to someone else

meant I couldn't handle it myself, meant that it was all too real.

"I think I might be a little financially strained." I was already there emotionally, physically, and mentally, so what did it matter to add one more thing to the ever-growing pile? You can't over-drown a person. Once they're underwater it doesn't matter how much is above them if they can't swim upward.

"How strained? You know, Larry and I have a little tucked aside."

"Absolutely not." They'd worked with my grandmother all their lives, given everything they had to our family, our property. I wasn't taking a dime from them.

"How strained?" she repeated. "Like newborn twins strained?"

Ah, the good old days while I was trying to feed them, clothe them, and pay for online courses while working here at Solitude. Good times.

"Worse."

"How much worse?" There wasn't a line in the woman's body that led me to believe that she was even remotely stressed.

"I think I might go broke," I whispered. "I bet everything on the renovations."

"And you put us on the map. Our reservations are fully booked starting right around Memorial Day. You know this is just the off-season. No one wants to trudge through the spring sludge. It's snow or pure sunshine to make a difference around here."

"I know." I glanced at the stack of bills and shoved another smile forward. Grandma had never mortgaged the property, and even though I'd felt like I was somehow betraying her by doing it, we'd transformed Solitude. "And it's going to pay off. We knew it would be a sacrifice for a few years to pay that mortgage, but with the renovations and constructing the five new cabins this year, it's the best business decision we could have made. But I cut a personal corner this year with the insurance. I figured the kids never got sick, and even if they did, the costs were relatively low at the doctor's, so I moved us to the program that had the lowest premium."

"And what does that mean with all that you're going through?"

"It means that I'm paying a lot of money. Some of her treatments are covered, some aren't; some are only partially covered. Any time we go to Denver, we're out of the network, and then I pay even more." I was hemorrhaging money at a rate that was simply unsustainable. And it wasn't just the treatments. We'd had to hire another employee to stay nights at the main house since I was living here now, and all of the extra expenses that came with traveling to Maisie's appointments added up to money that was flowing out but not in.

"Oh, Ella." Ada scooted forward and put her weathered hand on my desk. I took it in my own, my thumb running over her thin, translucent skin. She was as old as Grandma had been when she passed.

"It's okay," I reassured her. "I mean, it's Maisie's life. I'm not going to let my daughter…" My throat tightened, and I closed my eyes while I got ahold of myself. This was why I didn't talk about it. Everything needed to be kept in its own neat little box, and when the time arose, I dealt with each one. But talking about it meant every box seemed to open at once and spill its contents all over me. I drew a stuttered breath. "I'm going to do whatever it takes to make sure she gets exactly the care she needs. No shortcuts. No opting for the cheaper treatment. I'm not risking her like that."

"I know. Maybe if we took up a town collection? You know, like they did when the Ellis boy wanted to go on the SeaWorld trip the year his mama died?"

My first instinct was to rebel, to outright refuse. This town had turned up its nose at me when I was pregnant and deserted at nineteen. I'd made myself what I was in the last six years, and asking for help felt like I was betraying all that I'd accomplished.

But Maisie's life was worth way more than my pride.

"Let's keep that as an option," I agreed. "There's nothing we can do about it tonight, so why don't you get some rest?"

"Okay," she said, patting my hand like I was five again. "I'll take myself off to bed." She rose with effort and then leaned over me, kissing my forehead. "You need to get some rest, too."

"I'm not tired," I lied, knowing I had hours of juggling things around for some financial magic.

"Well, if you're not tired, you should drop by Mr. Gentry's cabin. From what Hailey tells me, he's quite the night owl if you're seeking some company." She gave me an innocent smile, but I knew her too well to fall for that.

"Uh-uh. Not happening." I shifted the pile of bills to close the discussion. "Besides, I have two six-year-olds asleep upstairs. I can't exactly wander off and leave them, can I?"

"Ella Suzanne MacKenzie. I am well aware that Hailey sleeps in your spare room. In fact, she's out in your living room right now watching something god-awful on your television, and she's more than capable of listening for your kids. Who, I might add, are sound asleep."

"Honestly, you think we can count on Hailey as an adult?"

"She works out just fine when you have an emergency at the main house that you need to take care of, doesn't she? Your babies are perfectly safe, then, and it's not like

Maisie had chemo this week. So if you are hiding out from that utterly delicious man, that's on you. Don't you go blaming those precious babies or using them as an excuse. Understand me?"

My cheeks heated. "I'm not hiding out, and he's not…delicious."

"Lie." She pointed her finger at me like I was eight again and sneaking a cookie from the cooling rack.

"Whatever. I'm twenty-five years old, trying to run a growing business, raise twins on my own, and in the middle of…" My hands flailed, motioning to everything on my desk. "…cancer. I don't have time to go chasing romance. I don't care how good-looking he is." Or how massive his arms were. None of that mattered.

"Well, I didn't say a thing about a romance, did I? Hmmm?" She waltzed out, content with having the last word.

I slumped against my chair, letting my head roll back. It was all too much. The kids. Solitude. The bills. The threat to Maisie's life. Beckett's presence threw my carefully constructed system out of whack.

Sure, he was good-looking. And maybe Ryan had trusted him. But that didn't mean I did. It didn't mean that I had the capacity to even think about him. Except, well, when I obviously did. But it wasn't like I thought about him on purpose. He just snuck into my thoughts, invaded really, the same way he'd barged into my life.

I looked at the bulletin board next to my desk. It was bare except for the eight-by-eleven sheet of paper that had one message in big, block letters.

YOU ARE ENOUGH.

Chaos. I missed him with an ache that was almost irrational considering I'd never met him. I didn't even have a picture to mourn, just his letters, that written voice that had stretched across thousands of miles and somehow reached my soul.

And now he was gone just like everyone else.

And Ryan had sent Beckett. At least, that's what Beckett had said.

But I'd never actually seen the letter. I should have looked at the letter. That's what any rational woman would have done when a stranger showed up claiming to have been sent by her dead brother. She checked up on his claim.

I, however, had accepted it at face value. There had been something in his voice, his eyes, that simply felt like truth. But if there was one thing I couldn't handle, it was a lie. If he was lying in any way, I needed to know *now*.

Screw it.

I pushed back from the desk and was in the living room before I could give any clear thought to the matter, asking Hailey to listen for the kids. She agreed, her spoon halfway through a pint of ice cream that was consoling her from her most recent flavor-of-the-month breakup.

I grabbed my coat on the way out the back door and was halfway to Beckett's house before I had the urge to turn and run. What the hell was I doing? Showing up at his house in the middle of the night? Okay, maybe it wasn't quite the middle of the night, but it was dark, so it qualified.

Using my phone as a flashlight, I walked the shore of the lake, telling myself how stupid this was with each step until I looked up and saw the light on through his windows. Then I started up the path to his front door.

Why couldn't this wait? Why now? What was I hoping to gain, besides the truth of whether or not Ryan had sent him? Why did it matter now and not two weeks ago when he'd shown up and altered my sense of gravity? Why— Oh. Apparently I'd just knocked on his front door.

I guess that decision was made.

Run away, the immature nineteen-year-old inside me urged. Seemed the romantic part of my development had frozen at the age I'd shoved her into yet another box and slammed the lid home.

You're not a child, the mature part of me countered.

Before I could get into any more arguments with myself that might land me in the psych ward, the door swung open.

Holy. Shit. He was shirtless.

"Ella?"

And barefoot. Just workout pants.

"Ella, is everything okay?"

What the hell kind of body was that? How did a natural man have so many muscles, all hard and toned and cut in lines that seemed carved for a mouth? My mouth.

Two firm hands clasped my shoulders. "Ella?"

I shook my head, like I could shake the thoughts out, and dragged my eyes from the incredible shape of his torso past his whisker-stubbled neck, to those freaking eyes. I liked green. Green was an awesome color.

Green. Green. *Green.*

"Everything is fine. Sorry," I muttered, knowing I sounded like an idiot. "I didn't expect…" I motioned to his body.

"You thought someone else would be home?"

"No. I just thought maybe you'd have clothes on. Like a normal person." I forced a shrug, and he let go of my arms.

Then he grinned.

Ugh. He really was incredibly handsome. Annoyingly so.

"My apologies. I will remember to check with you

before I work out next time. Come on in. I'll grab a shirt." He held open the door so I could slide past him.

And he smelled good while working out? What kind of sorcery was this? Was this guy even a real person? No one looked that good, and smelled that good, and was kind to kids. There was a flaw.

He's special ops.

Yeah, that was a pretty big flaw. Not that I could even see this guy as a man, in the romantic sense. Like I had time for that crap right now, or even the energy. But I wasn't stupid, either, and something had flipped in me when I'd seen him with Colt.

Guys with puppies. Guys with kids. Either one was guaranteed to snag my attention, and this guy had both.

"I'll be right back," he told me as I stood in the entryway. "Feel free to make yourself at home, since... you know, you own it!" he called as he ran up the stairs.

My steps were tentative as I came farther into the cabin. Everything was just as we rented it; there was no personalization or anything that suggested he'd be here more than a few days, let alone seven months. No dirty dishes in the sink, no books left on end tables, no jackets thrown haphazardly on the backs of chairs.

Havoc came out of the living room, wagging her tail slowly, and I dropped down to see her.

"Hey, girl. Were you asleep? I'm so sorry to wake you up." I rubbed behind her ears, and she leaned into my touch.

A minute later he was in front of me, a black tee pulled over his chest. Yeah, that didn't lessen his sex appeal, unfortunately.

"So you do like my Havoc."

"I never said I didn't like her. I happen to think she's pretty great. Her handler, on the other hand..." I shrugged, glancing around the cabin. "You sure you're staying seven months? Looks like you're not even here for the weekend."

Just another sign that this guy wasn't sticking around.

He grinned, flashing white, even teeth and getting tiny crinkles around his eyes. "What, because I like my cabin neat? Clean? Uncomplicated?"

"Or sterile and impersonal, whatever you'd like to call it," I teased.

He scoffed. "So, what can I do for you, Ella?" He leaned back against the bar that divided the kitchen from the living room.

"I was hoping that you might show me Ryan's letter." The mood in the room changed instantly.

"Oh." He quickly schooled his expression, but I'd seen the initial surprise. "Yeah, of course. Just wait right here."

He sprinted up the steps again. I heard a drawer opening and shutting, and within a few heartbeats, Beckett was back.

"Here you go." He handed over an envelope that had probably once been white but was now smudged with dirt and softened by repeated handling. My fingers trembled as I flipped it over, seeing Beckett's name scrawled across the front in Ryan's handwriting.

My thumb brushed over the ink as my throat constricted, a familiar burn tickling my nose. Tears threatened for the first time since his funeral, and I quickly shoved the emotions as far away as possible. I kept them locked up tight, just like the boxes of his things that gathered dust in his old room. I'd eventually clean it out, sort through the things I knew Colt would want, but not yet.

That was on my after-we-get-through-cancer list, which at present was about fourteen miles long.

"You can take it with you," Beckett offered, his gruff voice softened to a level that drew my eyes to his. "In case you want some privacy to read it."

There was a deep sorrow in his gaze, a raw, unfathomable pain that sucked the air from my lungs. I knew that feeling; I *was* that feeling, and seeing it reflected in someone else somehow made my own feel validated and a little less lonely. There had been tears at Ryan's funeral. Larry, Ada…me, the kids, the few local girls he'd seen off and on for years, even the couple of guys who had come to represent his unit. But none of them had looked like I felt—like I'd been abandoned by the only person who really knew me…not until this moment with someone I considered a stranger.

A stranger I was connected to through the death of the person we'd both loved.

Given the state of the envelope, and how many times he'd obviously read the letter, I knew what he was offering, and what it cost him. That simple gesture meant more to me than every let-me-know-what-you-need from every well-meaning person who learned about Maisie, even more than the honest offers from Ada and Larry, whom I considered family.

Beckett was offering me the chance to walk out the door with a sacred piece of his history.

"No, that's okay. I'd honestly rather read it here. With you." Where maybe just once, I wouldn't feel so utterly alone in my grief for Ryan. "If that's okay?"

"Of course. Do you want to sit?" He rocked back on his heels and folded his arms over his chest. If I knew him better I'd say he looked nervous, but I wasn't familiar enough with any of his mannerisms to really make assumptions.

"No, that's okay." Sitting meant staying, which I definitely wasn't.

I opened the envelope and slid out the letter. It was lined notebook paper, the same he'd used to send me letters. The paper was even more worn than the envelope, the single page dirt-smudged at the folds.

Sucking in a breath to steady myself, I unfolded the letter and immediately recognized Ryan's handwriting.

"How many times did you read this?" I asked, my voice small.

"At least once a day since I..." Beckett cleared his throat. "Sometimes more, in the beginning. Now I keep it in my pocket to remind me why I'm here. That even though you won't let me help you, I'm trying my best to do as he asked."

I nodded and read through the letter in its entirety as slowly as I possibly could, savoring the last time I'd hear from my brother.

> *It's not fair to ask, I know that. It's against your nature to care, to not accomplish a mission and move on, but I need this. Maisie and Colt need it. Ella needs it—needs you, though she'll fight you tooth and nail before she ever admits it. Help her even when she swears she's fine.*
> *Don't make her go through it alone.*

There it was. The truth. Ryan sent Beckett, asked him to help, or rather—guilted him so well that Beckett had gotten out of a career he loved and moved to a strange place where the person he'd moved for blatantly ignored him at every possible moment.

Ryan's final request had been for me.

My eyes slid shut, and I counted as I took steady breaths, until the need to cry hysterically, to throw things at the lot fate had decided I was worthy of, had passed.

Then I looked at Beckett, realizing he'd retreated a few feet to lean against the wall, as if he'd sensed my need for space. But his eyes were locked on mine, the set of his mouth as stoic as I would imagine a special ops guy to be—as Ryan was.

"Thank you." I handed the letter back to him in the envelope.

"I'm sorry that I'm here, and he's not."

"Why don't you think you're worthy of love? Of family? Everyone's worthy of family." Even when I was at my lowest, I'd always known that. If it wasn't my parents, then it was Grandma, or Ryan, or Larry and Ada. Now it was my kids, too. What had happened to this guy that he didn't have that?

He pushed off the wall, walking past me toward the kitchen, leaving the letter on the closest counter. "He wanted to be here, you know. He was getting out at his ETS date, already told the commander he wasn't re-upping. He had every intention of being here for you from the moment he knew about Maisie." Beckett opened the refrigerator, taking out two bottles of water, and blatantly ignored what I'd asked.

I rounded the corner of the island to follow him.

"Yeah, well, he'd said that before, right after the twins were born. He came home on leave and with them both asleep on his chest, he promised me he was getting out. That he'd come home where he was needed. Funny thing, he didn't even last the month of leave before his phone rang, and he packed his bags and left. I stopped believing him after that. I don't put a lot of faith in pretty promises, even from men who say they love me. Now as for you, you quit a job you obviously loved and moved across the world simply to fulfill Ryan's request. That's loyalty. That's the very definition of family, and I can't figure out why you wouldn't think you deserve it when you have it."

He unscrewed the first lid and took a deep drink, then put the bottle on the counter and handed me the other. I took it out of habit, not because I was thirsty.

"You heading to Denver for Maisie's surgery in the morning?"

"You always dodge questions?"

A smile flashed across his face and was gone just as fast as it had appeared. "I'm not here for me. I'm here for you."

Every time he said that, I felt a tiny piece of the mortar in my emotional walls crack. Not enough to bring them down, or even weaken them. But it was there all the same, just waiting to expand and grow. No one had ever stuck around for me, let alone did what Beckett had done.

Not that this was permanent.

"You shouldn't be. You have a life. No matter what Ryan said in that letter, I'm not your responsibility. No matter how close you two were, you're very much a stranger. I appreciate every offer you've made, and what you've gone through to fulfill Ryan's wish, but this is too much." My words were harsh, but I kept my voice soft. I didn't want to hurt him.

"I'm not leaving." He echoed my tone.

Funny how the conversation was the same as the first time we met, but the connotation was so very different, and that made all the difference. I wasn't trying to shove Beckett out as much as I was trying to release him.

"You will." Just like Ryan had. Just like Jeff and Dad. Depending on Beckett would be the most foolish thing I could possibly do.

His jaw flexed, and he looked away for a moment. When his gaze returned, his eyes were a little harder. "I guess you're just going to have to wait and see."

Tension stretched the length of the kitchen between us, palpable enough to cut...or maybe to tie us together—the soldier and the woman he was honor bound to watch over.

"I'd better get going." I left my unopened bottle on the counter and walked past Beckett, through the hallway, and to the front door.

"I know this surgery is going to be tough. On her, on you. Please promise me that you'll call if you need anything."

I looked over my shoulder to see him standing in the hallway about five feet behind me. There was determination on his face, but that sorrow was back in his eyes. I owed this man nothing and knew even less about him, other than the fact that Ryan had trusted him.

I opened the door and stepped into the fresh air, wishing it could clear my muddled, overfull brain. But the thought pounded at me mercilessly, until I let it in—Beckett couldn't keep his promise to Ryan if I didn't let him. While I was many things, cruel wasn't one of them.

"I promise."

It wasn't a lie, because I had no intention of needing anything from Beckett. Pulling the door shut behind me, I left his cabin and headed back to mine. Now that I knew the truth, I could stop letting the guy invade my thoughts and get back to what I needed to focus on.

Maisie.

CHAPTER NINE

Beckett

Letter #11

Chaos,

    I missed Colt's Thanksgiving play yesterday. He was the Pilgrim with the line that invited the Native Americans to the feast. He practiced his lines for weeks. Talked about it constantly.

    And I missed it.

    Maisie wasn't strong enough to come home after her first session of chemo. Her cell counts dropped, and they wouldn't let us leave Denver until they rose to safe levels. It happens, at least that's what I've been told by one of the other moms here. Her name is Annie, and she's been a godsend these last two weeks. Her little boy is here, and I guess you could say she's taken me under her wing. The learning curve is unforgivably steep.

    We've been in Denver for almost two weeks now. It's the best Children's Hospital in Colorado, and it's where her oncologist is based, but I found out a few days after we got here that it's also not in our insurance network. How funny that I never thought about things like that before.

    Why can't I keep my thoughts straight? Even my letters are scattered now, but so is my brain.

    So yeah, two weeks, and I missed Colt's play. Ada went and taped it for me, but it's not the same. He put on such a brave face when we FaceTimed right after, but I know I let him *down. I swore when they were born I'd never let them down, and now no matter what I do, one of them suffers for it.*

How is that fair? I see the parents here who take shifts between the mom and dad, or the parents with only one child, and I feel this pang of horrid, selfish longing for what they have— the ability to balance.

I know, in the scheme of things, missing the play isn't a big deal. It's the first of many, right? There's loads coming for him that I can be there for, and Maisie needs me right now. But I can't help but feel like it's the first drop in the bucket, and I'm so scared it's going to eventually fill. I missed his first play when I swore I'd never miss anything, *and as the doctors are presenting me with treatment plans, I can see how much she'll miss. How much he will.*

Because I didn't just miss the first play, Maisie did, too. And instead of being on stage, she was in a hospital bed. The docs tell me her counts are on the rise, and they're hopeful we can go home tomorrow.

God, I hope they're right.

I hope you guys are getting some semblance of turkey over there, or at least a little downtime. Rest when you can.

~ Ella

I rubbed Havoc's head as I turned the truck through the Solitude gate, then drove along the curved road toward my cabin, passing Ella's. Her SUV was gone, which meant they must have left for Denver as planned. She'd been here this morning when I'd gone for a training session at my new job, and I'd had a flash of worry that something had changed their plans.

Not that she'd tell me.

Not that I even deserved to know.

She'd killed me last night, asking those questions, calling me a stranger. I'd nearly broken right there, but our circumstances hadn't changed, and if being only Beckett let me close enough to help, then I'd bury Chaos next to Ryan. God knew that was mostly the case already. I hadn't been far off when I'd implied that he'd died on that mission, too.

I didn't want to lie to Ella—even by omission—but if she knew who I really was, she'd kick me out of her life. Knowing would only lead her to asking questions I couldn't answer, and even if I did, the truth would exile me just as quickly as her discovery of the lie I'd been living. As long as she didn't find out, and I kept my feelings in check, I'd be the only one burdened by the ugly truth.

Once Maisie was healed, and Ella didn't need me anymore, I'd tell her.

I made the turn into my long driveway and then hit the brakes hard enough to bring Havoc to attention.

There was a strange Jeep parked in front of my cabin.

Who the hell could it be? I crept forward slowly, until a familiar figure walked around the side of the Jeep. Tall, broad-shouldered, with dark eyes, hair, and skin; I knew him at first glance.

Captain Donahue.

What could he possibly want?

"It's okay, girl," I told Havoc. "Just Donahue." I parked the truck and got out, Havoc jumping down after me.

"Loose Dog!" I called out the warning as she bounded toward him, knowing full well she wouldn't attack him.

"Ha, very funny," he said, dropping down to her

level.

She came to a halt directly in front of him and sat on her back haunches as I walked up to him.

"What are you doing here, Donahue?"

"Nice shirt," he said, nodding at my new Telluride Mountain Rescue shirt.

"What are you doing here?" I repeated.

He sighed and stood up. "Always one for words, aren't you?" He opened the Jeep door and leaned in, coming back out with a red Kong. "I brought you a present," he told Havoc. Her ears perked up as he showed it to her, but she didn't budge when he threw it into the woods. "Seek!" he called, but she still looked at him like he'd lost his mind. "What? You love those things."

I stood at her side and crossed my arms over my chest.

"She's really still that stubborn?" he asked, lifting his sunglasses to the top of his head.

"Yep."

She didn't even look at me, just kept her eyes trained on him.

"Fine. I was hoping with some time off, we wouldn't have to retire her...or you." He shook his head in exasperation.

"Seek."

With one word, Havoc sprung toward the woods to find her new toy. A smile spread across my face as Donahue rolled his eyes.

"Yeah, yeah. Point proven. She's yours and always has been. It's good to see you."

"Ditto, but you haven't answered my question. Why are you here?"

"Can we sit?"

I took him to the small patio behind the cabin where a full set of furniture sat in the shade of the three p.m. sun.

"You're about forty-five days out," he said as we sat in the red Adirondack chairs.

"Yep," I said, launching the Kong toward the lake. Havoc was overjoyed to run for it. She'd been put through her paces today in seeking work, keeping her skills honed for finding people, and she was tired but happy.

"I'm here to ask you to reconsider." He leaned forward a little.

"Nope."

"Gentry." He sighed, rubbing the area between his eyebrows. "We're a team."

"Not anymore." My voice dropped.

He looked across the lake to the small island. "Have you been out to see him yet?"

My silence answered.

"There was nothing you could have done for him," he told me for the hundredth time.

"Yeah, well, that's where we see things differently."

Havoc returned, and I pitched the toy again, the familiar motion comforting.

"Do you think this is what he'd really want? You to leave the team? Leave your family? You and Havoc are part of us."

"I'm doing exactly what he asked." I pulled the letter from my back pocket and handed it to him.

He read the letter and cursed as he returned it to the envelope. "I should have read the damn thing before I gave it to you."

"There's no chance I'm leaving. As much as I appreciate what you're doing here, I can't go back. I'm on terminal leave, and in forty-five days, I'll be out." I'd be permanently separated from the only life I knew.

"What if there was another option?"

"Unless that option is Mac coming back from the dead, I don't care. I can't care. What I want doesn't matter anymore."

"I get that. And I understand what you're doing here. Hell, I admire you for it. It's the ultimate sacrifice, and I have nothing but respect for you. But I know this…situation won't go on forever. I don't want you to turn around and regret this choice."

I shot him a look that clearly said I wasn't going to, but he kept going.

"What if I told you that due to the nature of our unit, I have the ability to place you on a kind of temporary disabled list?"

"I'm sorry?"

Havoc brought the Kong back, but I saw the exhaustion in her eyes and motioned for her to lie down. She'd fetch that thing until she dropped unless I gave her the signal, so I gave it.

"It's not what you think. You're not…disabled. But it was the only way the higher-ups and I could think to give you an out, here."

"And the fact that nothing is wrong with me?"

"I think we both know that's not true," he said, looking back across at the island. "Look, in the last ten years, you've never taken leave."

"And?"

"And you're exhausted. Mentally and physically exhausted. So on that basis, the paperwork's been done. You just have to sign it."

"I'm not coming back."

"Not now. But this gives you a year to think it over—longer if you need it. We can extend up to five. Pay, benefits, and easy reentry when you're ready."

"I already have a job." I motioned to my shirt.

"Not one where you make the kind of difference that you do with us. You're family, Gentry, and you'll always be welcome. Signing those papers to accept doesn't promise you'll come back, it simply gives you the option, which you're about to lose when your terminal leave ends. Or you sign the declination, and this offer dies immediately." He stood and took a few steps forward, his eyes on the island. "He really was one of the best, wasn't he?"

"He was the best of *us*."

Donahue turned and walked by me, pausing to put his hand on my shoulder. "The papers are at the special ops center outside of Denver. I emailed you the info for the exact office about an hour ago."

"What? Didn't want to leave them here?"

"I figured if I left them here, you'd burn them before you considered what I'm trying to offer."

I hated that he was right.

"It's good to see you, Gentry. Rest up. Do what you can for Mac's family, and when you're done with his mission, come home." He handed me Ryan's letter and left without another word.

There was a flicker in my soul—the restlessness that had lain dormant for a couple of weeks coming back to life. The need to focus on one mission at a time and move on. His offer was temptation, and I couldn't afford it, not when Ella needed me.

I threw together a bag for me and one for Havoc after checking my email to find the address. Best part of my current job was being on call only, not scheduled, and that didn't officially start for another week anyway. If I left within the hour, I could be in Denver by ten or so, if the six hours it had taken me to get here was the usual time. In seven hours I could sign the declination and put an end to any thought of taking Donahue up on his offer. Besides, maybe the trip would cure that little bite of restlessness that had her teeth in me.

Twenty minutes later I walked into the main house, Havoc at my side.

"Mr. Gentry!" Hailey said, perking up as I walked

toward her. She batted her lashes and leaned forward. "What can I do for you?"

She was exactly the kind of girl Mac would have gone for. Funny, gregarious, pretty, and interested.

But I was only Ella's—even if she didn't know it.

Be nice. Be civil. Use a softer tone. I repeated the reminders in my head, determined to make an effort with the people who mattered to Ella.

"I'm headed to Denver for a few days and just wanted to make sure you knew before I took off."

"Oh, of course—" The phone rang, and she answered, holding up her finger at me. "Solitude, this is Hailey. Oh, hey, Ella. What?"

Now it was me leaning on the counter.

"Well, do you have to have it? Of course, I realize that. I just meant I could overnight it..."

"What is it?" I asked.

"She left Maisie's big binder in the office," she whispered, covering the receiver.

"Her medical one?" That was one thing Ella had at every appointment. It kept every record of her treatments, every written lab result...everything.

Hailey nodded. "I know, Ella, just let me see what I can do..."

I snatched the phone out of Hailey's hand. "I'll bring it to you. Have Hailey text me your room number at the hospital." Before she could argue, I handed the phone back to Hailey. Turning toward the door, I saw Ada coming from the office with the binder in her outstretched hands.

"I heard. She'd just stopped in for a second this morning and left it behind."

"I'll take care of it," I told her.

"I know you will," she said. "Do you want us to keep Havoc for you?"

My first impulse was a hearty "hell no." But then

Colt's head popped out of the dining area.

"Havoc!" He raced forward and dropped to his knees to hug her, and she laid her head on his shoulder. "Please? Can we? She can sleep in my bed and everything. I'll throw her toy and feed her, I promise!"

"She goes where I go," I said to Ada.

"Not to the hospital. I know she's a working dog, but they'll let only service dogs in." Her eyes echoed her plea. "Mr. Gentry, Ella wouldn't let me go with her. Or Larry. And I know about...Ryan's letter and all." She glanced at Colt and back to me. "And I wouldn't want Havoc cooped up in a hotel if you were to...say, stay for the duration of the surgery tomorrow."

She was calling me out, no doubt. But she had no clue how badly I wanted to be there for Ella, or how hard it would be to leave Havoc.

A litany of swear words ran through my head, none of them adequate to express my conflicted feelings. Havoc would be safe here and cared for. It wasn't like we hadn't spent a weekend apart before. When we weren't deployed she was kenneled with all the other working dogs as per regulation, but she'd been with me every deployment and every moment since Mac had died.

But Ada was right, and Ella was going to be alone.

I took a deep breath and dropped down to look Colt in the eyes. "You have school tomorrow?"

He shook his head slowly. "Teacher day or something."

"Teacher work day," Ada corrected.

I nodded and rubbed my hand across his spiky hair growth. "Okay. Then you are in charge of her. Okay? Her bag is in the truck, and it has her food and favorite stuff." The more I explained how to care for her, the brighter his eyes became, until the kid was pretty much a Care Bear for all the joy he was emanating.

She'd be in good hands.

I got her bag and took it back to Colt, then dropped

to my knees in front of Havoc, took her face in my hands, and looked into her eyes. "Stay with Colt. Be nice." I added that little extra order so she knew I meant only *stay* and not *protect*. Teeth came out otherwise. But this was her choice, and if she showed any hesitation, she couldn't stay—she'd have to leave with me. It was the very reason we were retiring together.

Her head swiveled to look at Colt, indicating she understood not only the command but who he was.

"I'll be back in a few days. Stay. With. Colt. Be. Nice."

I let her head go, and she immediately trotted over to the boy.

"Good girl." Equal parts of relief and worry hit me right in the gut.

"It wouldn't be a good idea to separate them," I warned Ada.

"Will she bite?" she whispered.

"No. Not unless someone messes with him. If that happens, God help the person, because she'll only release a bite at my command. You still sure you want to keep her?"

"Absolutely." She wiped her hands across her crisp, spotless apron.

"Let's go, Havoc!" Colt said, racing out the side door of the house, her Kong in his little hands. She trotted with him, tail wagging.

Ada tilted her head. "It's funny…"

"What?"

"She looks like such a docile little thing. You'd never guess she'd be capable of ripping someone apart."

"She's like any other woman in that regard, ma'am."

Five minutes later I was driving toward Ella and Maisie, finally able to do the one thing I'd been sent here to do: help.

CHAPTER TEN

Beckett

Letter #2

Chaos,

I'm so glad you wrote back! First off, happy birthday, even though I know you're getting this weeks later. Looking at the dates on your envelopes, it's taking about four or five days for mail to reach me, which is crazy fast. I remember when it used to take six weeks.

Second, how about this? Let's always write in pen. Never erase, just say whatever's honest and comes to mind. It's not like we have a lot on the line, or need to put up a front.

It's okay that you're not good with people. In my experience, there are very few people worth making the effort for. I try to give everything I have to those closest to me, and keep that circle small. I'd rather be great for a few people than be mediocre for a bunch.

So let me ask you a question that won't get censored out—by the way, it's creepy to think that people read our letters, but I get it.

What's the scariest choice you've ever made? Why did you make it? Any regrets?

Most people would think that I would say it's having the twins, or raising them, but I've never been so sure about anything in my life as I am about my kids. It's not even Jeff—my ex-husband. I was too starry-eyed to be scared when he proposed, and I can't regret everything that happened, because of my kids. Besides, regret doesn't really get us anywhere, does it? There's no point rehashing things that have happened when we need to move forward.

My scariest choice was actually made just last year. I mortgaged Solitude, which isn't just a B&B, but a sprawling two-hundred-acre property. My grandma had kept it free and clear, and I wanted more than anything to keep that legacy, except we were run-down on every level. I couldn't bring myself to sell off any more land, so I made the terrifying choice to mortgage the property and throw everything into improvements, hoping to launch us as a luxury retreat of sorts. I've got my fingers crossed that it will work. Between the capital I took out for improvements to the cabins and properties and the construction loans on the new cabins to start in the summer, I'm this crazy mix of hopeful and scared. Not going to lie, it's kind of exhilarating. Nothing ventured, nothing gained, right?

Off to take on my next scary choice… volunteering with the judgy ladies on the PTA.

~ Ella

Wedging Maisie's binder under my arm, I checked my phone for the room number just as the elevator dinged on the pediatric oncology floor.

It was almost eleven p.m.; those moments with Colt had cost me some time, but I'd had a pretty smooth drive.

"May I help you?" a nurse wearing a kind smile and Donald Duck scrubs asked at the desk. She looked to be about midforties and really alert for how late it was.

"I'm headed to room seven fourteen for Maisie MacKenzie," I told her. One thing I'd learned in my decade serving in our unit was that if you acted like you belonged somewhere, most people believed you did.

"It's past visiting hours. Are you family?"

"Yes, ma'am." According to Colt, I was, so in a really convoluted way, I wasn't lying.

Her eyes lit up. "Oh! You must be her daddy. We've all been waiting to see what you'd look like!"

Okay, that one I wasn't going to lie about. It was one thing to throw the broad generalization out there, and another to claim the honor of being Maisie's dad. As I opened my mouth to speak, I felt a hand on my shoulder.

"You made it," Ella said with a soft smile.

"I made it," I echoed. "So did the binder." I handed it over, and she hugged it to her chest in an all-too-familiar gesture that made my chest ache. She should have someone to hold her during times like this, not some inanimate object.

"I'm going to take him back," Ella told the nurse.

"You go right on ahead."

I walked down the hallway with Ella, taking in the bear murals. "They weren't kidding about the bear floor label, huh?"

"Nope. It helps the kids remember," she answered. "Want to meet Maisie? She's still awake, despite my every effort otherwise."

"Yes," I answered without pause. "I would very much like that." Understatement of the century. Next to the pictures of mountains Colt had drawn for me, Maisie's pictures of animals were my favorites. But those belonged to Chaos. Just like with Ella and Colt, I was starting from scratch with Maisie.

Our steps were the only sounds as we walked down the long hallway.

"This wing is for inpatient," Ella told me, filling the silence. "The other two are for outpatient and transplants."

"Gotcha," I said, my eyes scanning the details out of habit. "Look, you need to know that nurse thinks—"

"That you're Maisie's dad," Ella finished. "I heard. Don't worry, she's not going to force adoption papers on you or anything. I left all the dad info blank because like hell were they going to call Jeff in case of emergency. He's never so much as seen her."

"I wish I could say that I don't understand how someone can do that, but it happens all too often where I'm from."

She paused just outside the room labeled with Maisie's name. "And where is that?"

"I grew up in foster care. My mom dropped me at a bus station in New York when I was four years old. Syracuse to be exact. The last time I saw her was when she had her rights terminated in court a year later. I've seen some horrible parents in my life, but also some great ones." I pointed to her. "And if your ex is so pathetic that he's never seen his daughter, then he didn't deserve her. Or you. Or Colt."

There were a million questions swimming in those eyes of hers, but I was saved by Maisie.

"Mom?" The tiny voice called from inside the room.

Ella opened the door, and I followed her in.

The room was a good size, with a couch, a single bed, a padded rocking chair, and the giant hospital bed that held a small Maisie.

"Hey, sugar. Not sleeping yet?" Ella asked, depositing the binder on a table behind the door and moving to sit on the edge of the bed.

"Not...tired," Maisie said, pausing in the middle for a giant yawn. She wiggled around her mom to peek at me. "Hello?"

Those crystal-blue Ella eyes took in every inch of me in cursory judgment. She was thin, but not too frail. Her head was perfectly shaped, and the lack of hair only made her eyes seem that much bigger.

"Hey, Maisie, I'm Beckett. I live in the cabin next to yours," I told her as I came to the foot of her bed, using the softest tone I had.

"You have Havoc." She tilted her head slightly, just like Ella.

"I do. But she's not with me. I actually left her with Colt to keep him company while I came to see you. I hope that's okay. It seemed like he could use a friend to talk to."

"Dogs don't talk."

"Funny, that's what your brother and I talked about, too. But sometimes you don't need someone to talk back to you. Sometimes we just need a friend to listen, and she's really good at that."

Her eyes narrowed for a moment before gifting me with a brilliant smile. "I like you, Mr. Beckett. You let my best friend borrow yours."

And just like that, I was a goner.

"I like you, too, Maisie," I said softly, scared my voice would break if I raised it any further than that.

Maisie was everything I knew she'd be and more. She had the same sweet, determined soul her mom did, but brighter and undimmed by time. And at the same moment that I felt overwhelming gratitude that she'd accepted me, I was swamped with the irrational anger that she had to go through this.

"We're going to watch *Aladdin*. Wanna watch, too?" she asked.

"We were *not* going to watch *Aladdin*. You were going to sleep," Ella said with a stern nod.

"I'm nervous," Maisie whispered to Ella.

If my heart wasn't hurting already, it was screaming now. She was so little to have a surgery like this tomorrow. To have cancer. What kind of God did this to little kids?

"Me, too," Ella admitted. "How about this. We'll start the movie, and I'll curl up with you? We'll see if we can't get you to sleep."

"Deal." Maisie nodded.

Ella cued up the movie, and I moved toward the door. "I'll leave you girls to your evening."

"No, you have to stay!" Maisie shouted, stopping me in my tracks.

I turned to see her eyes wide and panicked. Yeah, I wasn't going to be the cause of that look on her face ever again.

"Ella?"

She looked from Maisie back to me. "Maisie, it's really late, and I'm sure Mr. Gentry would rather have a nice big bed—"

"There's a bed here."

Ella sighed, shutting her eyes. I saw the battle she'd written about—the need to parent Maisie as if there wasn't an overwhelming chance that she was dying warring with the knowledge that she most likely was.

But that pleading in Maisie's eyes wasn't an issue of being spoiled; there was a stark need there. I crossed to her bed and sat on the edge. "Can you give me a reason?" I whispered so Ella couldn't hear us.

Maisie glanced back at Ella, and I looked over my shoulder to see her busying herself with inserting the DVD.

"You have to tell me, Maisie. Because I don't want to weird out your mom, but if it's a good reason, I'll go to bat for you."

She glanced up again and then at me. "I don't want her to be alone."

Her whisper ripped through me louder than an air raid siren. "Tomorrow?" I asked.

She nodded quickly. "If you leave, she'll be alone."

"Okay. Let's see what I can do."

Her little hand gripped the edge of my jacket. "Promise."

There was something solemn in the way she was asking that reminded me of Mac, of the letter. It was almost as if she knew things she shouldn't...couldn't.

"Promise me you won't leave her alone," she repeated, her whisper soft.

I covered her small hand with my own. "I promise."

She searched my eyes, passing judgment again. Then she nodded and lay back against the raised bed, relaxed.

I crossed the darkened room to Ella as she slipped off her shoes. "I'll absolutely leave if you want me to, but she's pretty adamant."

"What's her reasoning? I've never seen her demand something like that."

"That's between us. But trust me, it's pretty sound. What do you want me to do?"

"There's just the couch and that little bed." Ella bit her lower lip, but it wasn't intended to be a sexy gesture. Mac had the same tell when he was worried. "I wouldn't wish that on my worst enemy."

"I've slept in far worse conditions, trust me. It's not a problem. What do you want me to do, Ella?" I'd do whatever she wanted, but God, I hoped she wanted me, any part of me. Knowing how scared she was of this moment, of what was coming for Maisie tomorrow, and not being able to comfort her in the way she needed was killing me.

She released her lip with a sigh, her entire posture softening.

"Stay. I want you to stay."

My chest constricted in a way that made taking a deep breath impossible. So I sucked in a shallow one and ditched my jacket on the back of the rocking chair. "Then I'll stay."

The procession in front of me was solemn, almost reverent. The nurses pushed Maisie, in her bed, down the hallway toward the thick blue line that marked where the surgical wing became doctors-and-patients-only.

Ella walked by her side, Maisie's hand in her own, leaning over her daughter. Their steps were slow, like the nurses knew Ella needed every single second she had left. *They probably do know.* After all, this was just a normal day to them. Another surgery on another kid with another type of cancer. But to Ella, this was the day she feared and longed for with equal ferocity.

They paused just before the blue line, and I hung back, giving them the space she needed. With her hair pulled back, I could see the faint, forced smile on her face as she ran her fingers over Maisie's scalp, where her hair would have been. Ella's lips moved as she spoke to Maisie, the strain visible in the tense muscles of her face, the periodic flex of her neck.

She was holding it together, but the string was thin and fraying by the second. I'd watched her unravel since six a.m., when the first nurses came in to begin Maisie's prep. Watched her bite her lip and nod her head as she signed the papers acknowledging the risk of removing a tumor this size in a girl this small. Watched her put on a brave face and smile to keep Maisie comfortable, joking about how Colt would be so jealous of her new scar.

Then I watched the FaceTime conversation between Maisie and Colt, and my heart broke for them. Those two weren't just siblings, or friends. They were two halves of a whole, speaking in half sentences and interpreting one-word answers like they had their own language.

Though Ella was terrified, I knew it was Colt who had the most to lose when it came to Maisie, and there wasn't a damn thing I could do about it.

I pushed my hands into the pockets of my jeans to keep from going to her. That need pulsing through me was selfish, because holding Ella would help me but not her. There was nothing I could do for her besides stand and witness what I knew she feared would be her last moments with her daughter.

Powerless.

I was so damn powerless. Just like I'd been when we'd finally found Ryan's body, three days after the op had imploded. There was nothing I could do to bring back his heartbeat, to erase what had to have been the worst hours of his life, or miraculously heal the bullet wound that had entered at the base of his skull and exited...

Havoc. Sunset on the mountains. Ella's smile. I mentally repeated my three as I let out a shaky breath, blocking out the thoughts. The memories. They didn't belong here. I couldn't help Ella now if I was trapped then with Ryan.

One of the nurses spoke to Ella, and my throat squeezed shut momentarily when Ella leaned forward to kiss Maisie's forehead. Maisie's hand appeared over the rails of the bed, handing over a worn pink teddy bear. Ella nodded and took the bear. They wheeled Maisie down the hallway and through a set of swinging double doors.

Ella stumbled backward until her back landed against the wall. I lurched forward, thinking she might hit the floor, but I should have known better. She held herself against the wall, the bear clutched to her chest like a lifeline as she raised her head toward the ceiling, taking gulping breaths.

She didn't turn to me, or the nurses who walked past,

just drew inward as if she knew her only source of solace was going to come from somewhere deep within herself. My composure deserted me as I realized that she didn't look for comfort because she wasn't used to getting any, that this scene would be identical if I wasn't here.

But I *was* here.

Knowing it was an intrusion, and beyond caring, I walked forward until I stood in front of her. Her eyes were closed, her throat working as she battled for control. Everything in me ached to hold her, to carry as much of the burden as she'd let me.

"Ella."

Her eyes fluttered open, shining with unshed tears.

"Come on, it's going to be a long day. Let's get you some food and some coffee." If I couldn't care for her heart, I could at least sustain her body.

"I...I don't know if I can move." Her head rolled slightly as she looked toward the doors. "I've fought every day for the last five months. I've taken her to treatments, argued with the insurance companies, fought with her over capfuls of water when the chemo made her so sick she dehydrated. Everything we've fought for has been for this moment, and now that it's here, I don't know what to do."

I got a firm grip on my volatile emotions and reached for her face, only to stop myself and lightly grasp her shoulders.

"You've done everything you can. And what you've accomplished, how far you've brought her is astounding. You've done your job, Ella. Now you have to let the doctors do theirs."

Her eyes found their way back to mine, and I felt her torture like it was a physical pain through my stomach, the ceaseless cut from a dull knife tearing me in two. "I don't know how to give that control over to someone else. She's my little girl, Beckett."

"I know. But the hard part is already over. You signed the papers, no matter how difficult it was, and all we can do now is wait. Now, please. Let me feed you."

She pushed off the wall, and I retreated a step, putting a respectable amount of distance between us. "You don't have to stay. They said it's going to be hours, and not just a few."

"I know. Her tumor is on the left adrenal gland, and though it's shrunk, there's still some very real danger that she'll lose that kidney. A longer surgery means they're doing everything they can to save it, and that they're being thorough to get every scrap of that tumor out. I was listening when they prepped you this morning."

A sad half smile lifted the corners of her mouth. "You do that a lot. Listen. Pay attention."

"Is that a bad thing?"

"No. Just surprising."

"I don't care how many hours it takes. I'm here. I'm not leaving you."

An eternity passed as she made her choice, not just to get food but to believe me. To trust that I meant what I said. I knew the moment she'd decided, when her shoulders dipped, a tiny bit of the tension draining from her frame.

"Okay. Then we're most definitely going to need some coffee."

Relief was a sweet taste in my mouth, a gentle, full feeling in my heart. Unable to find the right words, I simply nodded.

"So the bear?" I asked two hours later as we sat in the waiting room, side by side on the couch, our feet propped up on the coffee table.

"Aah, this is Colt," Ella explained, lovingly stroking the face of the fuzzy, well-loved bear.

"Colt is...a girl."

"Maybe Colt just likes pink. You know, only real men can pull off wearing pink." She shot me a sideways glance.

"I'll keep that in mind."

After a light breakfast—her stomach was too queasy for more—we'd fallen into an easy rhythm of conversation. Effortless, even.

"The bears were a gift to the twins from my grandma. One pink, one blue, just like everything back then. But Colt fell in love with the pink one. Had to have it with him all the time, so the blue one became Maisie's. When they were three, Ryan came in and took Colt camping overnight. Maisie was always more of an indoor girl, and she begged to stay home, so I let her. But Colt almost refused to go. Maisie knew it was because they couldn't stand being separated. So she grabbed the blue bear, told him it was Maisie, and sent him on his way."

"So that's actually Colt's bear?"

Ella nodded. "He sends it with her every time she's hospitalized so they can be together, and he has the blue one at home."

Yeah, that gnawing pain had moved to my heart.

"You have incredible children."

Her smile was genuine, and I nearly lost my breath when she turned slightly, sharing it with me. "I'm blessed. I wasn't sure how I would do it when Jeff walked out, but they were always so...they were everything. I mean, sure, they were exhausting, and loud, and messy, but they brought out the color in life. I can't remember what the world looked like before I held them, but I know it wasn't half this vibrant."

"You're a great mother."

She made a motion to shrug off my compliment.

"No. You are," I repeated, needing her to hear me, to understand my awe of her.

"I just want to be enough." Her gaze darted to the clock, like it had every five minutes since Maisie had disappeared past those swinging doors.

"You are. You are enough." She blinked at me, and I cursed my tongue. I was going to give myself away if I wasn't careful.

"Thank you," she whispered, but I knew from the way she looked away that she wasn't sure.

"So what's next? Monopoly? Life?" I asked, trying to lighten the mood and distract her.

She pointed to the wooden box at the opposite end of the table. "Scrabble. And you'd better be careful. I have no qualms about kicking your butt, even if you are nice enough to sit with me all day."

I wasn't nice. I was a lying, manipulative asshole who didn't deserve to sit in the same room with her. But I couldn't say that. So instead I grabbed the box and prepared to get schooled.

"So you grew up in foster homes?" Ella asked me as we made our sixty-fourth loop of the floor.

Maisie had been in surgery for six hours, and we'd had an update from the surgical team about fifteen minutes ago that all was going well and they were trying their hardest to save her kidney.

"I did."

"How many?"

"I honestly can't remember. I got moved a lot. Probably because I was a horrible kid. I fought everyone who tried to help, pushed every rule, and did my best to get kicked out of my placement, hoping that would somehow make my mom come back."

I didn't expect her to understand. Most people who

grew up in normal houses with a quasi-normal family couldn't get it.

"Ah, the sweet, illogical logic of a child," Ella said.

Of course she got it. That was what drew me to her in the first place. Her simple acceptance of me through our letters. But from what I'd seen, she was like that—accepting.

"Pretty much."

"Which was the best home?" she asked, again surprising me. Most people wanted to know the worst, like my life was fodder for gossip to feed their salacious need for the tragedy of others.

"Uh, my last one. I was with Stella for almost two years, starting around my fifteenth birthday. She was the only person I'd ever wanted to stay with." Memories hit me, some painful, some sweet, but all glossed over with the kind of filter only time could give.

"Why didn't you?" We reached the end of another hallway and turned around, walking back.

"She died." Ella paused, and I had to turn around. "What?"

"I'm so sorry," she said, her hand squeezing my biceps. "To finally find someone just to lose them…"

My instinct was to rub my hands over my face, shake it off, and keep walking, but I wasn't going to move a muscle with her hand on me, no matter how innocent the touch was. "Yeah. There are really no words for it."

"Like someone picks up your life and shakes it like a snow globe," Ella offered. "It seems to take forever for the pieces to settle, and then they're never in the same place."

"Exactly."

She'd captured the feeling with the precision of someone who knew. How was it I'd never found anyone who understood what my life had been like, and yet this woman defined it without blinking an eye?

"Come on, we haven't quite worn a path through the linoleum yet," she said, and started our sixty-fifth lap.

I followed.

"This is taking too long. Why is it taking them so long? What's going wrong?" Ella paced back and forth in the surgical waiting room.

"They just haven't updated us in a little while. Maybe they're finishing up." I watched her from where I leaned against the windowsill. She'd been calm, collected even, until we reached the hour when they'd estimated the surgery would be done.

As soon as that hour passed, something flipped inside her.

"It's been eleven hours!" she shouted, pausing with her hands on her head. She'd long ago pulled so many strands of her hair loose that it floated around her, as disheveled as she was.

"It has."

"It was supposed to take ten!" Her eyes were wide and panicked, and I couldn't blame her. Hell, she was only giving voice to the same thoughts in my head.

"Is everything okay? Mr. and Mrs. MacKenzie?" A nurse popped her head in. "Anything I can do for you?"

"I'm not—"

"Yes, you can find out exactly what's going on with my daughter. She was supposed to be out of surgery over an hour ago, and there's been no word. None. Is she okay?"

The woman's face softened in sympathy. Ella wasn't the first mom to panic in the waiting room, and she wasn't going to be the last. "How about I go check for you? I'll come right back with an update."

"Please. Thank you." Some of the wild left Ella's eyes.

"Of course." She gave Ella a reassuring smile and left in search of information.

"God, I'm going insane." Ella's voice was barely a whisper.

She shook her head as she fought off a lower-lip tremble. I pushed away from the sill and was to her in four long strides, not halting to think about who I was or who she knew me to be. I simply wrapped my arms around her and pulled her to my chest like I'd wanted to since the first moment I saw her.

"You wouldn't be the mom you are if you weren't going a little out of your mind," I reassured her as she relaxed against me.

"I think I've blown right by little and straight to asylum-ville," she mumbled into my chest before turning her head and resting it just under my collarbone.

Damn, she fit against me exactly like I knew she would—perfectly. In another life, this is how we would have faced every challenge together. But in that life, Maisie was healthy and Mac was alive. In this world... well, she wasn't exactly hugging me back. Right. Because I had her arms pinned between us. Was she pushing me away? Was I that oblivious?

That realization hit me like a fire hose, and I loosened my arms immediately. What the hell had I been thinking? Just because she wanted me to stay with her didn't mean she wanted me to touch her. I was her default, and lucky to be that, but I sure as hell wasn't her choice or preference.

"Don't let go," she whispered. Her hands were still between us, but she wasn't pushing me away, they were simply resting on my pecs. If anything, she leaned in. "I'd forgotten what this felt like."

"Being hugged?" My voice was sandpaper-rough.

"Being held together."

Never before had a single phrase brought me to my

emotional knees.

"I've got you." I tightened my hold, splaying one hand wide just beneath her shoulder blades and cupping the back of her head with the other. Using my body the best I could, I surrounded her, imagining I was some kind of wall—that I could keep away whatever heartache was coming for her. My chin rested on the top of her head, and second by second, I felt her melt and give.

Although I couldn't tell her, I loved this woman. I would take on armies for her, kill for her, or die for her. There was no truth greater than that, and no other truth that I could give her. Because where she was honest and strong and kind, I was a liar who had already hurt her in the worst way possible. I had no right to hold her like this, but even worse—I wasn't going to move a muscle.

"Mrs. MacKenzie?" The nurse came back in, accompanied by Maisie's surgeon. "I just caught them as they were coming out of surgery."

"Yes?" Ella turned in my arms, and I let her free, but she took my hand, squeezing so hard I had a momentary concern for the blood flow to my fingers.

The surgeon smiled, and I felt a rush of relief more powerful than any time I'd escaped battle unscathed.

"We got it all. It was touch and go there for a while with her left kidney, but we managed to save it. You've got quite a stubborn little girl on your hands. She's in recovery right now, resting. As soon as she wakes up, we'll bring you back to see her, but don't expect her to stay awake for long, okay?"

"Thank you." Ella's voice broke, but those two words carried the kind of meaning that usually took hours to convey.

"You're welcome." The surgeon smiled again, exhaustion written on every line of her face, before leaving us alone in the waiting room.

"She's okay." Ella's eyes closed.

"She's okay."

"She's…she's really okay," she repeated. Then, as if someone peeled back whatever had been keeping her upright, she collapsed, her knees giving out under her. I caught her before she hit the ground and hauled her up against my side. "She's okay. She's okay." Ella said the phrase over and over again until the words came on heaving cries, the sobs rough and raw.

I hooked one arm under her knees and one behind her back, picking her up as she buried her face in my neck, hot tears streaking down my skin to soak my shirt. Then I settled onto the couch, holding her across my lap as her gut-wrenching cries shook her small frame.

She cried in a way that reminded me of the valve being released on a pressure cooker—the result of too much confined for way too long. And even though the relief was still sweet from the successful surgery, I knew there was so much more ahead for her—for them. This was simply a pause in the fight that allowed her a precious second to catch her breath.

"I've got you. She's okay," I told her, smoothing my hand over her hair. "You're both okay." I spoke in the present tense because that was all I could promise her.

And for right now, with Havoc safe with Colt, and Maisie tumor-free, and Ella curled in my arms, it was enough.

CHAPTER ELEVEN

Ella

Letter #21

Ella,

 Yes, I can believe the guy at the library asked you out. No, I don't think it's odd, or a prank. Why would you? It's not like I haven't seen your picture, which yes, I know, puts me at an advantage between us. Not sure if you noticed, but you're definitely not hurting in the looks department.

 Go ahead, give me your excuses. Yes, you have two kids, and yes, one of them is facing incredible odds. You own a very time-consuming business, and from what I know about you, you also tend to put yourself last when factoring anything into your life.

 But listen to me—scratch that…read me— none of that makes you "undatable," as you called it. Do you know what's undatable? Someone who's selfish, or consumed with the tiny things in life that don't mean anything. To me, the most attractive quality in a woman is her ability to give of herself, and Ella, you do that in spades.

 I get that you haven't gotten out there since Jeff walked out. I understand that for the last five years you've been consumed with raising your kids, building your business, and generally being everything to everyone. But that doesn't mean that you can't let someone in. Especially now.

I'm not going to say you need someone to lean on, because I know you've become the expert on standing on your own. But with what you're facing, I know it would help to have someone there to support you in the moments when you feel like it's impossible. Go out to dinner with the guy, Ella. Even if nothing comes of it, you'll know you gave the universe the shout-out. You can't turn away every good thing that comes to you because you're scared of what might happen, or not happen. That's the coward's way out, and you are no coward.

And honestly, who wouldn't fall for you? We're three months into this, and I'm half in love with you without ever having been in the same room. Just give the guy—give yourself—a shot at some happiness, because you deserve it.

Or you could wait until January, when I get to randomly show up at your door.

Just food for thought.

~ Chaos

"Need anything else?" I asked Maisie, handing her the iPad. She was all set up in the living room of the main house's residence, within shouting distance of Hailey and Ada.

"Nope," she replied, popping the *P* as she opened one of the apps her teacher had recommended.

"Your belly feel okay?" It had been two weeks since her surgery and, while the incision site looked to me like a monstrous, pink snake slithering across my daughter's belly, she swore the pain was nearly gone.

Maybe it was the way she'd slept the first few days after, or her sore throat from the twelve hours of intubation, or the feeding tube that had stayed with her for days, but I had a hard time believing her. Or perhaps it was that my pain tolerance on her behalf was so much lower than hers had grown to be.

"Mom, I'm fine. No puking or anything. It's okay. Go." She looked up at me. "Besides, as soon as you leave, Ada will give me the sugar-free ice cream."

"I don't think you were supposed to tell me that." I laughed and pressed a kiss to her scalp, still shiny and smooth. Overhauling her diet had been a challenge, that was for sure. "You know why it has to be sugar-free, right?"

"You said sugar feeds the monster inside me. And even though the big part of the monster is out, the rest of him is in my blood. So we can't feed the monster."

"Right. I'm so sorry, Maisie."

She looked up at me with eyes that felt decades older. "It's okay, the monster doesn't like this kind."

I kissed her again before I left, grabbing her binder on the way out the door after letting Ada know I was headed out.

Stopping at the entryway mirror for a moment, I tried to smooth back the frizz that had developed in the braid I'd put into my hair this morning.

"Stop. No matter what you do, you're still gorgeous," Hailey remarked as she came up behind me.

"Ha. I can't even remember the last time I went to the gym or put on some makeup. I'm batting for doesn't-look-psycho. Gorgeous is way out of my league."

She propped her head on my shoulder, and our eyes met in the mirror. "You have the kind of gorgeous that shines through no matter what."

"Looking for a raise?" I teased.

"Nope. Just telling the truth. Now get out of here before you miss that meeting. Ada and I have Maisie. Don't you worry."

"Worrying has become my default emotion."

She searched my face for a second before her eyes lit up, which meant she was about to suggest something ludicrous. "I know just the thing."

"Hailey…" I groaned. We were friends, but her idea of fun didn't exactly fit with my life.

"Let's double date. I'll grab Luke, and you bring Beckett. We can go out to a movie, or dinner, or try out that new karaoke bar in the Mountain Village."

"A bar?" I let my tone tell her exactly what I thought about that one. That was the life of carefree people who didn't have responsibilities like kids. Or cancer. Or a kid with cancer. You know, normal twenty-five-year-olds.

"Yes. A bar. Because if anyone could use a drink, it's you, Ella. And I know Beckett would be up for taking you out."

My spine stiffened. "We're not…it's not like that." Just the thought of Beckett had a blush rising to my cheeks.

"That man has his eyes on you whenever you're in the same room. Come on, how many times did he drive back to Denver after Maisie's surgery?"

I turned away from the mirror to face Hailey. "Three times."

"In two weeks."

And every time he'd shown up, my heart had done this stupid, crazy leaping move. Something had changed the day of Maisie's surgery. Not just because he'd been there, but because I'd wanted him to be. It had been the first time during Maisie's treatment that I'd allowed myself to not just lean on someone, but let them hold me up.

The morning he'd shown up with Colt as a surprise—about three days after the surgery—I'd just about melted into a puddle of goo. He seemed to know exactly what I needed—what Maisie needed—and provided it before I could even ask for it.

"Yes, in two weeks, but it's not romantic."

"Uh-huh."

"It's not! He's here because Ryan asked him to be. That's it. Nothing more." At least that's what I told myself whenever I found those green eyes watching me or me watching him.

"And you don't find him attractive or anything, right?"

"I…" Dark green eyes the color of pine, thick hair and thicker arms, washboard abs that trailed down to—*get a grip*. "Of course I do. I've seen the man." *And felt him.*

I'd felt the protective way he'd held me—tight, but not oppressive, as if he'd simply known that I needed to be held together in that moment. Felt the gentleness of his hands when he'd wiped away my tears after sobbing out everything I'd held in. Felt the joy he was capable of when Colt had climbed into bed next to Maisie and held his sister. Felt the overwhelming capacity for love that he had even if he didn't want to acknowledge it.

Yeah, I *felt* entirely too much when it came to Beckett.

"Well, yeah. You'd have to be dead not to notice. Because he's hot, Ella. And not in a passingly nice kind of way. He's hot in a take-me-on-the-kitchen-counter-and-let-me-bear-your-children kind of way. Plus, he's starting to speak in more than one-word answers, which shows definite potential in the moving-past-broody department."

A flash of something hot and ugly hit my stomach and was gone as quickly as it came. *Jealousy.* There was no reason to be jealous of Hailey. Sure, she was beautiful, and available, and didn't have so much baggage attached to her that there was a giant Samsonite tag on her forehead, but the minute we'd come home from Denver, she'd completely stopped seeking out Beckett. And it wasn't because she wouldn't be interested. I'd heard the gossip getting coffee yesterday—half of Telluride was interested in the newest Search and Rescue member.

It was because Hailey thought maybe I was interested.

"He has always spoken in more than one-word answers, and I already have children, remember? Besides, speaking of children, if I don't walk out right now, I'm going to be late for this meeting."

"Okay. Go. Run. But that man lives next door, and from what I've seen, you're going to have to deal with all that"—she motioned to my red face—"pent-up frustration somehow."

A guest walked in, the bell ringing with the light tinkling sound that had taken me hours to decide on.

"Saved by the bell," Hailey whispered before turning to our new guest. "Welcome to Solitude! You must be Mr. Henderson. Your cabin is all ready for you and your wife." Her smile was wide and mirrored by the hipster-looking twentysomething.

Summer hiking season was almost upon us.

I took my opportunity, and the binder, and escaped out the front door.

It was 10:31 when I pulled in, but I parked in the elementary school's designated spots like a good parent and took the extra minute hit to my already tardy arrival.

"Ella!" Jennifer smiled out at me through the glass. "They're all set up for you."

"Hey, Jennifer." I signed in on the clipboard and opened the door when the buzzer sounded.

"How is Maisie feeling?" she asked as she walked me into the offices that sat just behind the reception desk.

"She's good, thank you. Surgery went well, and she's ready to return to school on Monday."

"Really? Already? That's amazing!"

"You'd be shocked to see how quickly kids bounce back, and as long as her levels are good, she's safe here."

"I just can't believe she beat it that quickly!"

Oh, no. I saw that look in her eyes, and I hated to be the one to dash it. "No, Jen. She had the tumor removed, and they got it all, but she's Stage Four. Her bone marrow is still overwhelmingly cancerous. She just made it through the first step."

Her face fell. "Oh. I'm sorry. I guess I didn't understand."

I offered her a smile. "Don't worry. Not many people do, and I hope you never have to. She's fighting."

Her lips pressed together in a flat line before she nodded her head. "Of course." She opened the door to the conference room, and I squeezed her hand as I passed, reassuring her that she hadn't said anything worthy of embarrassment.

"Ah, Ms. MacKenzie, I'm so glad you could make it," Principal Halsen said from the head of the table. His tie was as straight as his face.

Apparently we were all business today.

"Ms. May." I smiled at Maisie and Colt's teacher. She was in her late twenties, and Colt had only the best things to say about her. A pang of guilt smacked me square in the chest at how absent I'd been from school activities this year.

Yeah, I definitely wasn't winning PTA Mom of the Year over here. Not even Okayest Mom. I was pretty much the Nonexistent Mom.

"And this is Mr. Jonas, who is our district superintendent and will be joining us today." Principal Halsen motioned toward the older gentleman at his left. The man nodded at me with pursed lips that morphed into a forced smile.

"Mr. Jonas."

I took the seat at the end of the conference table, leaving two empty seats between me and what felt like the army that had gathered against me, or rather Maisie. The loud sound of the binder's zipper opening was almost obscene in the silence.

"So, Ms. MacKenzie—"

"Ella," I reminded him.

"Ella," he agreed with a nod. "We needed to meet today because of Maisie's attendance record. As you know, she needs to be present for a minimum of nine hundred hours to complete kindergarten. Right now, between her absences and times she's needed to leave early, or come late, she's at about seven hundred and ten."

"Okay?" I flipped through the binder to her school section, where I kept record of her days, hours, and documentation.

"We feel at this point, we need to discuss her options," Principal Halsen said, pushing his glasses up his nose and opening the manila folder in front of him.

"Options," I repeated, trying to understand.

"She hasn't met the legal requirement," Mr. Jonas said, his voice soft, but his eyes telling me that the issue was cut and dried in his opinion.

"Right." I flipped to the letter I'd kept in a page protector and took it out of the binder. "I absolutely agree that she hasn't met the requirement, but the district assured us in this letter dated in November that you wouldn't hold her to it. That rule is waivable in the regulations by the district due to catastrophic illness, and that's what you agreed to."

I slid the letter down the table. Ms. May caught it and passed it along, sending me a sympathetic smile.

"We did. And we're not here to throw ultimatums at

you, Ella," Principal Halsen assured me. "We're here to discuss what's best for Maisie. We made this agreement without looking at her long-term future."

Because they hadn't thought she'd make it this long.

"What's best for Maisie…" I repeated softly. "You mean, like not having Stage Four neuroblastoma? Because I definitely agree—that's not in her best interest."

Mr. Jonas cleared his throat and leaned forward, resting his wrinkled, folded hands on the table. "We absolutely sympathize, Ms. MacKenzie. What your daughter has been through is tragic."

And there went my hackles, rising as my spine straightened. "It's not tragic, Mr. Jonas. She's not dead."

"Of course not, my dear. We're not saying that any of this is fair, but the truth is that Maisie might not be ready for first grade."

My dear. Like I was a little girl in bloomers asking for a pretty new doll. To hell with that.

"We've done everything you've asked. Ms. May has been quite accommodating, and I assure you that she's ready."

"She is." Ms. May nodded.

Principal Halsen sighed, taking off his glasses and cleaning an imaginary spot. "Let's look at this from a different angle. Can you tell us where she's at in her treatments? What we can expect in the coming months?"

I flipped back to the sheet where I kept the estimated treatment plan, realizing we'd gotten to a point where I wasn't sure. We were at a crossroads.

"She just completed a major surgery two weeks ago. She's healing wonderfully and is ready to come back to school on Monday. Then the week after, we'll be in for another round of chemo, which as you know means she's gone a solid school week. We're hoping her levels will remain stable enough to come back for the end of school, but there's no telling. Then we're into summer. I'll know more when we go in for chemo and I can meet with her oncologist."

The administrators shared a look that made me feel like I wasn't on the other side of the table but the other side of the battlefield. I felt that change come over me—the one that had appeared the moment they'd placed the twins in my arms—like pieces of armor clicking into place as I prepared to defend my child.

"Have you thought about having her repeat kindergarten? If she's in a better situation to be fully present next school year, then it wouldn't harm her. We wouldn't force it, of course, but it's worth a thought. In fact, a lot of our parents hold back their children at the kindergarten stage for various reasons. Certainly this procedure qualifies—"

I snapped.

"With all due respect, it wasn't a procedure. It was a twelve-hour, life-threatening surgery in which they removed a tumor the size of a softball from my daughter's adrenal gland. This isn't an inconvenience; this is cancer. And no, next year won't be better. She's fighting for her life, so excuse me if I don't share your worries that she may have missed the critical day of kindergarten when you covered the life cycle of the butterfly. Statistically she might not even…" My throat closed, my body rebelling against the words I hadn't spoken since the day they'd given me her odds. "Next year will not be better."

"And you don't wish for her to repeat her kindergarten year." Principal Halsen wrote down a note in the folder.

"It's kindergarten. Do you seriously feel like she needs to?" A repeat wouldn't just be hard for Maisie to swallow, but for Colt as well. They'd be a year apart in school, which would mean that even if—when—she beat the cancer, she'd have to look the consequences in the eye every day.

"She doesn't," Ms. May spoke up. "She's quite bright, and she'll do just fine in first grade," she told the administrators.

The two men conferred quietly for a moment before turning back to me. "We'd like to offer you a solution. Transfer her to an at-home program. Kindergarten isn't as academically challenging as first grade, and next year, she'll need the flexibility."

"Pull her out of school."

"School her at home," Mr. Jonas corrected. "We're not against you, Ms. MacKenzie, or Maisie. We're genuinely trying to figure out the best solution. She's not in school for the required hours, and next year her workload will increase exponentially. Couple that with the liability of having her here with her weakened immune system, the worry placed on the staff, and the other children, and we all might be more comfortable— including Maisie. She could keep the best schedule for her health if she were schooled at home."

Other cancer moms did that. I'd spoken with a few of them, but it always seemed like they pulled them out as a last resort...when they were dying. It wasn't so much the physical act of removing her from the school as it was the emotional acknowledgment that she couldn't go.

And that was equally devastating to us all—Maisie, Colt, and especially me.

But it would relieve stress on her, on her levels, on the days she couldn't get out of bed. On the mornings she spent lurched over the toilet, crying, only to look at me and swear she could make it.

"What would it entail?"

"I could teach her," Ms. May offered. "I'd come by in

the afternoons whenever she felt well enough. She'd stay on track, she'd be exempt from district hour requirements, and we'd be able to personally tailor the program."

"Can I think about it?"

"Of course," Mr. Jonas said, passing back the letter from early in her diagnosis.

We adjourned the meeting, and Ms. May walked out with me. I felt numb, or maybe it was simply that I'd been hit so hard and so often in the last six months that I no longer registered pain.

"Colt is just heading to lunch if you'd like to see him," she offered.

Colt. He was exactly what I needed right now.

"I'd very much like that," I told her.

She reached for my hand and squeezed it lightly. "He's a phenomenal kid. He is kind, and compassionate, and defensive of the smaller kids."

My smile was instant. "I lucked out with that guy."

"No. He's phenomenal because he has an exceptional mother. Please don't forget that in the midst of everything. You're a great mom, Ella."

I couldn't think of anything to say that wasn't a rebuttal of that statement, so I simply gave her hand a squeeze back.

Then I stood with a dozen other moms who were lined up outside the cafeteria, all waiting for their kids. Most were the normal PTA moms, the ones who had impeccable minivans, color-coded day planners, and stylish but sensible fashion. Some I knew, some I didn't.

I looked down at my Vans, worn jeans, and long-sleeved tee, and felt...unkempt. I'd never really understood the phrase "let yourself go," but this moment? Yeah, I got it. I couldn't remember the last time I'd cut my hair, or taken the time to actually put on more makeup than concealer for under my eyes and mascara. None of it mattered in the scheme of things—of saving Maisie—but right now, I felt the separation between me and these women as certainly as if they were in ball gowns.

"Oh, Ella! It's so nice to see you!" Maggie Cooper said with a hand over her heart, flashing a diamond bigger than her knuckle. She was a year older than Ryan and had married one of the corporate guys from up in the ski village. I'd half expected their engagement announcement to read "local girl makes good."

"You, too, Maggie. How is…" Crap. What was her kid's name? The obnoxious one who'd colored on Maisie's backpack with permanent marker and thought it was cute to force kisses on her? Doug? Deacon? "Drake?" *Phew*.

"He's great! Really soaring at piano right now and looking forward to soccer. It starts next week in case Colt wants to play. Look, I meant to ask, have you thought about treating Maisie holistically? I mean, those medicines are really poisonous. I was reading this blog that talked about eating just cassava root or something? It was really intriguing. I can absolutely send it to you."

Yeeeeeah. Thank God I'd gotten good at plastering a smile on my face and nodding. "Sure, Maggie. That would be great." I'd learned over the last six months that the easiest way to deal with the well-meaning advice-givers was just to say thank you and noncommittally agree to read whatever research they'd found about snake venom or whatever.

Lucky for me, the class rounded the corner, carrying lunch boxes or lunch cards.

"Great! And I found a bunch on organics! They're supposed to be great for kids with leukemia and everything."

"Neuroblastoma," I said over the kids' heads as they

came between us in the hall. "She has neuroblastoma."

"Oh, right. I get confused with all those cancers." She waved it off like there was no difference.

"Oh my God. Who is that?" the mom next to her asked, looking pointedly down the hall.

I turned to see Colt walking just behind the class with a million-watt grin and Havoc in between him and Beckett.

Beckett, who was sporting cargo pants like he wore to work, and a navy-blue Telluride Mountain Rescue T-shirt that stretched perfectly across his chest and around the swells of his biceps.

"I have no clue, but sign me up," Maggie said, her eyes locked on Beckett as her son found her.

Beckett nodded at something Colt said and took off his baseball hat, placing it backward on Colt's head. Ugh, my stupid freaking heart flipped right over and got that teenage, glowy feeling that I most definitely didn't have time for.

"Seriously." The other mom sighed. "Fresh blood?"

"Seasonal. Has to be," Maggie answered.

Beckett looked up and immediately saw me, a smile transforming him from gorgeous and broody to just flat sexy. When was the last time I'd even thought about a guy in that way? Jeff? As if acknowledging it gave it life, I felt a low hum in my belly, like my sex drive had just kicked on after almost seven years of lying dormant.

"Mom!" Colt saw me and ran, bypassing the line to jump at me.

I caught him easily, lifting him against my chest. For a split second, I worried that I'd just crossed the big-boy line, but as intuitive as he was, he put his head down and squeezed me tight.

"I'm so glad you're here," he said, and I let him down, having gotten my Colt fix.

"I am, too." Beckett's voice slid over me like raw

sugar, gravelly and sweet at the same time.

From the corner of my eye, I saw Maggie's jaw drop, and then she disappeared, hopefully to the lunchroom, even though I knew those few words would set the gossip tongues wagging.

"What are you three doing?" I leaned down and rubbed Havoc behind her soft ears. "Hiya, girl."

"Beckett was here for show-and-tell!" Colt exclaimed.

Oh God, I'd forgotten.

"Oh, buddy. I totally spaced that you needed something to share today. I'm so sorry." At what point was I going to stop screwing up and get my shit together?

"No, Mom, it's okay! Beckett told me last week he'd bring Havoc in, so I took it off your kitchen calendar. It was so cool! She chased her toy, and then Beckett hid me in a tree and told her to find me, and she did! Definitely the coolest show-and-tell of the year."

"I'm so glad!" And I actually was. My guilt slid away for a precious second, and I looked up at Beckett in gratitude. "Thank you," I said softly.

The slight tilt to his lips wasn't quite a smile. It was something softer, more intimate, and infinitely more dangerous. "I was happy to do it."

"I was here for a Maisie meeting and just needed a little Colt fix," I told him.

His brows lowered. "Everything okay?"

Before I could answer, Maggie was there with freshly applied lip gloss and a flyer, standing so close she was almost between us.

Beckett's posture stiffened.

"Ooh, Ella," she said, "before I forget, here's the information for the soccer team. I know Colt had wanted to play in the spring league, but we all understood with what Maisie's going through, well, you have a lot on your plate. But just in case you can fit in the time, we'd love to have him."

"Soccer? Really?" Colt lit up like a Christmas tree, and I wanted to smack Maggie and every other mom on the planet who had the ability to say yes without checking schedules for doctors' appointments and chemo sessions.

"Colt, we're really busy—"

Beckett gently cupped my elbow, turning away from Maggie. "Let me help."

"Beckett..." Letting him help meant depending on him, and letting Colt depend on him, too. And while I knew he had the best of intentions, I was also aware that his soul had the same restless demons Ryan's had.

"Please."

I was certainly glad he wasn't asking me to strip out of my clothes, because between that voice and the plea in his eyes, I was helpless. My head nodded before my brain got the better of it—and me.

"You want to play soccer, Colt?"

"Yes!"

"Okay, we'll make it happen."

Amid Colt's celebration, Maggie thrust the flyer in my face and turned her smile on Beckett. "And who might you be? One of Telluride's finest?"

His eyes lost their warmth, his expression turning distant, almost cold, and unlike any expression I'd seen from him. Was Maggie the exception, or was I?

"No, that's the sheriff's department."

His tone was curt, almost unrecognizable from the way he spoke to me and the kids.

"Private sector, huh?"

"Yes."

One-word answer. Maybe Hailey was right—she'd simply seen something I hadn't, because he hadn't shown it around me.

"Ooh, the special kind of search and rescue," she

said, taking the step that did put her between us. "The ones who get contracted out for the dangerous calls." Her voice lowered, and I stepped back to avoid asphyxiating on her perfume.

"I guess," Beckett answered.

"You know that company is actually funded by a conglomerate of the owners of the ski resort and the hotels in the village, right? They wanted something immediately available, knowing how busy the sheriff's office gets."

"Is that so?" Beckett stepped back, but Maggie followed. His jaw flexed and the save-me look he shot my way was anything but funny. He really was that uncomfortable.

It was definitely time to intervene.

"She's right," I said as Colt took my hand. "Her *husband* owns one of the hotels, right, Maggie?"

She openly glared at me, but her face turned sweet when she looked back at Beckett, well, appraised was a better word. Openly ogled was another way to say it. "He does, which I guess means, in a way, you work for me."

His eyes turned glacial. "I'm an independent contractor, which means I work for myself."

I moved to stand next to Beckett, and he relaxed just enough for the change to be visible. "It's always good to see you, Maggie, but I think these guys are getting hungry, right?" I asked Beckett.

He nodded. "It's always nice to meet other parents in Colt and Maisie's class."

The words were the right ones, but they were forced, like he'd practiced them in his head before saying them aloud.

Maggie's shoulders fell, but she quickly recovered. "Of course. I guess I'd better get back to Drake. Are you joining us?"

I looked down at Colt, who was luckily occupied with Havoc. He had to be getting hungry, and we were wasting lunch time out here.

"Actually, I was going to ask my Ella here if she wanted to grab some lunch with me." The words came out of him just like every other time we'd talked by ourselves. Easy. Natural.

Maggie noticed.

Point. Set. Match.

Whether or not it was true, I could have kissed him in gratitude. Not that I was going to kiss him, or touch him in any way that indicated anything more than friendship, if that's even what we had. What were we, anyway? Guilt-contracted neighbors?

Maggie nodded and spun on her heel, nearly taking me out. Beckett reached around, steadying my shoulder as she passed. Who cared about the truth? *Not me!*

After today's meeting and Maggie attack, I felt a sense of rebellion well in my stomach and spread outward. "Colton MacKenzie."

"Mom?"

"Wanna ditch the rest of the day with me? With us?" I glanced up at Beckett.

"Yes!"

"What do you want to do?" Beckett asked, crouching down.

Colt's mouth and nose wiggled back and forth as he thought. "I want to picnic with Maisie. If she feels well enough."

I'd so lucked out getting this kid.

"Picnic it is."

As we walked out to our cars, I brushed Beckett's arm, stopping him as Colt and Havoc walked ahead a few feet.

"You're not a big people person, are you?"

"That obvious?"

"Absolutely." But oddly endearing, too, realizing that he was different with me. "I just didn't see it until now."

"Yeah, well…I guess I'm just comfortable around you."

That simple admission felt like the best compliment, and I felt my cheeks warm.

"You realize what you did, right?" I needed him to understand the commitment he'd made, how precious the trust of a child was.

"With lunch?"

"Soccer, Beckett. That's three practices a week and games on the weekend. That means on the days I'm at the doctor with Maisie—"

"I'm at the field with Colt. I'm not going to let you down, Ella. Or him."

My teeth sank into my lower lip as I fought the urge to believe him, to trust that he'd be where he said he would be.

"Trust me, please."

"I know you have the best of intentions, but in my experience, guys…don't always show up." I spoke the last bit at the concrete between my feet. To be exact, they lied and said they would, then never did. Maybe their reasons varied, but the end result never did.

He tipped my chin up gently with his finger, and I found the courage bit by bit to meet his gaze.

"I will show up for you. For Colt. For Maisie. I will not walk away. I will not abandon you. I will not die." His words hit me smack in my heart with the force of a ton of bricks. "I will show up, and if you don't believe me now, that's okay. I'll earn it."

"I have no right to expect that of you." We weren't together, or anything else that would even imply he had any such obligation. I had to trust that his sense of duty to my brother was strong enough to hold him here, and trust wasn't one of my strong points.

"You have the right because I give it to you."

We stood like that, locked on each other, his hand beneath my chin, warring silently until I sighed and let my eyes close. "Okay. But don't let him down."

"I'm not going to. The sooner you believe that, the sooner I can pick up a little of that burden you're so hell-bent on carrying solo. Have a little faith in me."

I sucked in an unsteady breath and tried it out, the faith thing. "Soccer."

He grinned. "Soccer."

CHAPTER TWELVE

Beckett

Letter #18

Chaos,

I ran into Jeff's parents at the grocery store about an hour ago. It doesn't happen often, maybe once or twice a year when they're up to vacation, but it always slices me to the quick when it happens.

Why is that? After seven years, you'd think I'd be immune to seeing them, but I'm not.

There I was, standing in the drink aisle, staring at every flavor of Gatorade known to man, debating which flavor Maisie might not throw up. She's been so nauseated lately, but I know she has to stay hydrated because of these new meds and the potential for renal failure. Anyway, I'm thinking sour apple, right? Because at least it's green, so when she inevitably throws it up, at least I don't panic that it looks like blood. And when I was pregnant with the twins, sour stuff was the only thing that kept the nausea at bay. So I fill the cart, and when I get to the end of the aisle, there are Jeff's parents, picking out their turkey for Thanksgiving.

It's not like I don't know that it's Thanksgiving, or that people need turkeys. But I'm standing there, trying to figure out what to buy to keep my daughter alive, and they're debating the merits of a sixteen-pound over an eighteen-pound turkey.

Just like Jeff, they've never seen either of the

kids. I wrote them off the minute his dad showed up with a big check, divorce papers, and a request to terminate my pregnancy.

Then, two weeks ago, I swallowed my pride and asked his dad to add Maisie to Jeff's insurance—since Jeff works for him. He threw me out and told me that the kids were none of their concern. I guess Jeff's dating a senator's daughter, which makes my kids a liability. Maisie's dying, and they're more concerned with Jeff's image.

So, yeah. We don't speak.

But today, for some reason, it hit me harder than usual. Maybe it's because Maisie's so sick. Because when I think about Jeff, and the twins' questions about him that I can't avoid for much longer, I always think that the kids can seek him out when they're old enough. That's on him. And now, I realize Maisie might never get that chance. And though I don't want anything to do with him, I would never stop them from seeking those answers. But time might stop her.

And yet, I'm not asking her if she wants to meet him. I want all of the time she has. I don't want to share her with Jeff, and I honestly don't think he'd bring her anything but heartache.

The first thing I did after I got some of that Gatorade down Maisie was grab a pen and write to you. Because for the life of me, I can't figure out if that makes me a bad person, a selfish person. And worse, if it does, there's an overwhelming part of me that just doesn't care. Isn't that worse?

~ Ella

"Are you ready now?" I asked as Colt raced across the hallway of his mom's house, into the mudroom. The kid had been practicing for three weeks, and today was finally the Saturday of Memorial Day Weekend—game day.

The twins would graduate kindergarten—whatever the hell that meant—on Monday. Why they needed tiny caps and gowns was beyond me, but they'd sure looked cute for the little photo shoot Ella had done out by the lake.

"Cleats!" he shouted.

"In your bag." I lifted the small Adidas bag in the air as he skidded to a stop in his socks in front of me.

"You have them?"

"Yep, and your shin guards, and the sunscreen for your noggin. Now, are you ready to play, or what?" We had twenty minutes until we were expected at the field for warm-ups.

"Yes!" He jumped into the air, both hands stretched toward the ceiling.

"Okay, save a little of that energy for the game, okay? We're playing a team from Montrose, and they're going to be tough."

His forehead puckered. "They're six. Just like me."

"Yeah, well, you're tough, too. Now get your play shoes on, and let's go."

Colt scurried back to the mudroom, and I went in search of Ella, finding her in the office with Maisie stretched out on the love seat across from her desk, book in hand. "Hey, Maisie. Ella, you ready?"

She looked up from the eternal stack of paperwork on the mahogany expanse and quickly cloaked her panic, forcing a smile. "Yeah, just let me see if Hailey is back yet so she can keep an eye on Maisie."

"I want to go. Please, Mom? Please?" Maisie begged. She was looking flushed today, the color returning to her cheeks just in time to get hit with another round of chemo next week.

This was one of those moments I was so glad I wasn't a parent, because I'd give in every time. Every. Time.

Ella's brow puckered. "I just don't know, Maisie."

"I feel great today, and the weather is good, and I'll even sit in the car. But please? I don't want to miss his first game."

"You'd say you felt great even if you didn't."

"Please?"

Ella's eyes locked on mine. "It's your call," I said, well aware I didn't belong in that decision-making equation. "I can tell you that it's seventy-three degrees, light sun, and I have a shade tent in the car."

"But all the people…"

"Beckett can scare them off, right?" Maisie used those big blue eyes on me, and I threw up my hands immediately, backing away. Yup, I'd give in every time.

"So not getting involved, here. Ella, you decide, and I'll just be out there." Away from the women of the house who were currently glaring each other into submission.

"She can go," Ella relented.

We got to the field five minutes later than we should have, but I wasn't going to stress. It was little kid soccer, not the World Cup. I spun Colt on the seat, tying his cleats after I'd secured his shin guards. Then I held up the bottle of sunscreen.

"It's all goopy."

"It's spray. And really, you're the one who insists on shaving his head."

"It's for Maisie!"

"I'm not arguing with your reasoning, little man. But you know what I was told at your age? You're free to choose, but you're not free of the consequences of your choice. Shaving your head is awesome. Now, sunscreen."

It was almost four o'clock, but the afternoon sun was just as harsh for bald heads.

He folded his arms across the chest of his maroon uniform but didn't utter a word as I sprayed him down, careful to get his face with my hands.

"You're getting good at that," Ella said as she came around the front of my truck.

"He makes it easy," I said, and lifted Colt to the ground. "You're good to go."

He walked over to Ella, who dropped to her knees, which were bare in her khaki shorts. "Okay, what's the most important thing about today's game?"

Colt's expression turned fierce. "Play my position, show no fear, and tonight we dine on the souls of our enemies!"

Ella leaned sideways and raised an eyebrow at me.

"What?" I shrugged.

She stood and straightened his uniform. "Off you go."

"And keep your hands off the ball!" I shouted after him. He turned, throwing me a thumbs-up before racing toward his team.

"The souls of his enemies?" Ella questioned, holding back a laugh with her arms folded under her breasts. I didn't look at the way the move pushed them up toward the scoop neck of her maroon shirt. Nope. Didn't look.

"What? He's basically a man."

"He's six."

"Boys were trained as warriors at age seven in ancient Sparta."

She laughed, the sound utterly intoxicating. "I'll be sure to keep the Spartans off the invite list for his birthday party."

"Just to be safe," I agreed and was rewarded with another laugh.

This is exactly how her life should be, filled with

soccer games and sunshine and smiles from both her kids. This was exactly what she deserved. I just wasn't the person who deserved to give it to her.

Havoc jumped from the bed of the truck and kept me company while I set up the shade tent away from where the other parents were set up. The design let the fresh air in but kept the sun off Maisie while allowing her see the game. "Stay," I commanded Havoc, and her rump hit the ground at the opening of the tent.

When I got back to the truck, Ella already had her wagon loaded with the folding chairs. Maisie sat perched at the edge of the seat, and that's when I saw it—exhaustion. Man, she'd hid it well.

"Hey, why don't you head over and set up Maisie's seat, and I'll bring her down," I suggested to Ella. "That way she's not in the sun for too long."

Ella agreed and walked across the grassy expanse to the tent.

"You're exhausted," I said to Maisie, turning back to her.

She nodded, dropping her head a little. "I didn't want to miss it. I miss everything."

"I get that, but you also have to take care of yourself so you can do even more when you get better."

Her fingers skimmed over the place under her shirt where her PICC line ran in her arm, protected by a mesh armband. "I know."

It was the way she said it that made me take her hand. "I see a lot of soccer games in your future. Everything you're going through right now will one day be this crazy story you get to tell everyone, and it's going to look great on your college entrance essay, okay?"

"I'm six." A small smile tilted her lips.

"Why does everyone keep saying that to me today?" I asked. "Now, would you like a ride to the game?"

Her smile erupted in a flash of joy, and I scooped her up, adjusting her long, pink wind pants and matching long-sleeve shirt to cover all of her skin, and then her giant, hot-pink floppy sun hat. "Okay, I'll make you a deal," I offered as I strode toward the tent with Maisie in my arms.

"What's that?"

"I'll agree not to drop you if you agree to keep your hat from blowing off."

"Deal!" She giggled, a sound I decided was only outranked on my list of the best sounds ever by her mother's laugh.

Some of the other team moms and dads called out greetings, and I answered with a smile that I hoped didn't look forced, knowing I was damn lucky to have a place in Maisie's and Colt's lives, no matter how small. That role came with dealing with other parents, and I was working on it. Every practice the small talk got an ounce easier, the smiles a little less fake, and I started to see the other parents as individuals and not just... people.

I settled Maisie into the camping chair Ella had set up, and then propped her feet in a smaller one that served as a footrest. Seeing the small shiver that ran over her, I quickly pulled the blanket from the wagon and laid it over Maisie's legs.

"You sure you're okay?"

She nodded. "Just a little cold."

I tucked the blanket around her, and we settled in to watch the game. Ella started out as one of those quiet moms, more than a little camera happy but reserved in her commentary. By the second half of the game, she was full-on shouting for Colt as he scored a goal.

The transformation was hilarious and sexy as hell.

Or maybe that was the view of those mile-long legs in her shorts. Either way, it took a great deal of my concentration to keep my hands off the soft skin just above her knee. Damn, I wanted her. Wanted every aspect of her—her laughter, her tears, her kids, her body, her heart. I wanted everything.

Lucky for me, my craving for her physically was second only to my need to take care of her, which kept my libido in check.

For the most part.

Yeah, okay, that was a lie. The more time we spent together, the closer I came to kissing her just to see how she tasted. I wanted to kiss her until she forgot everything that weighed her down, until she'd forgive me for the lie I was living.

And the longer I kept my secret, the further away it felt. The more I dreamed of the possibility that she might let me stay in her life as just Beckett.

Not that I wasn't tempted to tell her who I really was. To tell her how her letters had saved me, that I'd fallen in love with her by her words alone. But then I realized how far I'd dug into her life—picking up groceries, taking Colt to soccer, hanging out with Maisie when she was too sick to go to the main house. The moment I told Ella who I really was, what I'd done, she'd kick me out and be on her own again, and I'd promised to show up for her and the kids. Keeping that promise meant not giving her a reason to throw me out. Telling her was selfish, anyway. It would only hurt her.

Chaos had no chance of helping Ella—of being there for her. Not after what had happened. I'd have to wait until Maisie was in the clear before coming clean to Ella. Then the choice would be hers.

"What is that kid doing? Isn't that illegal? He can't trip him like that!" Ella shouted.

"I think it was more of mutual clumsiness, there," I countered.

"Oh my God, he did it again! Get him, Colt! Don't

you let him do that to you!"

"You know, he's only six," I said, sweet as cherry pie.

She slowly turned to me with a glare and an openmouthed scoff. "Whatever."

I laughed and for the first time realized that I was utterly, completely content with my life. Even if I never got Ella, never tasted her mouth, never touched her skin, never kept her in bed on a rainy Sunday morning or heard her say the three little words I was starved for, this moment was enough.

Glancing back at Maisie in the shade, I saw her eyes closed, and the deep, rhythmic rise and fall of her chest. She was asleep with Havoc curled up under her outstretched legs. If she was already this exhausted, how the hell was she going to withstand another round of chemo next week?

"Oh no...no, no," Ella muttered, and I turned my attention back to the field.

The other team slipped past Colt, then the defense, and scored to win the game.

Well. Shit.

My heart ached when I saw Colt's face, the way his shoulders fell. But he shook hands with the opposing team like the sport he was, and then sat on the bench long after the coach finished the post-game pep talk. Seeing some of the other dads cross the field, I looked over at Ella, who looked almost as disappointed as Colt.

"Well, that sucks." She folded her arms across her chest, her long side braid brushing over her arm as she turned to look at me. "What do I say to him?"

"How about you give me a second with him?"

"Be my guest." She motioned toward the bench. "I'll pack everything up."

I crossed the field with his cleat bag in my hands, then dropped down in front of him to start untying the double knots he swore he couldn't play without.

"Man, I loved watching you play," I told him, slipping the first cleat free.

"I let him by. We lost because I messed up."

I untied the second cleat and then took it off, too. "Nah. You win as a team, and you lose as a team. There's no shame in that."

"I didn't want to lose," he whispered, like it was a dirty secret.

"No one does, Colt. But I can tell you sometimes the losses are just as important as the wins. The wins feel really good and let us celebrate what we did right. But the losses, they teach us more. They teach us to see where we can improve, and yeah, they feel pretty darn bad, and that's okay. As you get bigger, you'll see that it's not how you handle the wins that make you a good man, it's how you handle the losses."

I handed him the shoes he'd brought, and he put them on his feet as he thought, his little forehead puckered in the same lines Ella wore when she was working something out. Then he fastened the Velcro and hopped off the bench. "So it's okay to lose."

I nodded. "You have to lose sometimes. It keeps you humble, keeps you working harder. So yeah, it's okay to lose. Sometimes it's even good for you."

He heaved a giant, melodramatic sigh and then nodded. "Will you come with me for a second?"

"Sure," I answered without thought, following him past our bench to the away team's, where he found the kid who had scored the final goal.

The kid saw Colt and stood up.

Colt walked straight to him. "I just wanted to say that you're really fast. Good job today."

The kid smiled. "You, too. That was an awesome goal!"

They shook hands like tiny men, and Colt grinned as we walked away.

"I'm really proud of you," I said as we started to cross the field.

"Well, he's really fast. But you know what? We play them again at the end of the summer, and I'm going to be faster. I can wait that long to kick his butt."

I wanted to chastise him, but I was too busy trying my damnedest not to laugh. "Gotcha. Then we'll dine on the souls of our enemies?"

"Bingo."

He stopped midfield, and I had to backtrack a couple of steps. "Colt, what's wrong?"

He looked up at me, blocking the sun with a hand, and then glanced around to the other parents walking back to their cars. "Is this what it feels like?" he whispered so quietly that I leaned down.

"What it feels like?" I asked.

"Having a dad?" He tilted his head slightly.

Words fled at the same rate every emotion assaulted me. His question flayed me open, leaving me raw and exposed in a way I'd never felt before.

I crouched to his level and said the only thing that came to mind. "You know, I'm not sure. I never had a dad."

His eyes widened. "Me, either."

I'm here now. The words were there, in my head, at the tip of my tongue. But they weren't mine to say or to offer. Man, it was a slice of hell to fall in love with someone else's kid when you couldn't claim the love of his mother—or her mother. I looked across the field to see Ella sitting with Maisie under the shade, running their hands over the grass.

"What do you say we take the girls home?" I asked Colt as I removed my baseball hat and put it on his head to keep the sun off him.

"Good idea. Let's tend to the women." He strode toward the girls, and I didn't hold back the laughter this time. How the kid could have me near tears one second and laughing the next was beyond me.

"We lost," Colt told Ella as we walked back to the car. I had Maisie in my arms, her head against my chest, while Ella pulled the wagon behind us.

"Oh, man. Have to admit, I'm glad there aren't any enemy souls for dinner tonight," she joked, pulling him to her side. "I guess we'll just have to settle for ordering pizza."

"Pizza!" both of the kids shouted, then high-fived each other, Colt jumping to reach Maisie.

I got each kid locked into the booster seats I'd purchased for the truck and loaded the wagon and contents into the bed as Ella ordered pizza. Havoc jumped into the back between the kids. Ella had calmed down a ton since the oncologist told her Havoc was completely safe to Maisie as long as her levels weren't bottomed out.

I drove us back through Telluride as Colt and Maisie debated the merits of cheese versus pepperoni.

"Do they ever have a conversation where they finish a sentence?" I asked Ella.

"Nope. It's like they have their own language. They just know what the other is thinking before they finish, so they don't."

"Creepy, but cool."

"Exactly."

How natural it would be to reach over and take her hand, to brush a kiss across her palm. Everything about this felt effortless—right. The same as writing to her had been…not that she'd know about that anytime soon.

I pulled in front of the pizza shop and parked the truck. "A parking spot right up front? Looks like pizza was fated for tonight!" I declared.

The kids lifted their arms in victory, but Maisie's weren't quite as high. She was tuckering out again.

Both Ella and I got out of the truck, but I beat her to the sidewalk. "I've got it," I told her.

"You're not paying for pizza," she protested.

"But I am."

"Are not." She folded her arms across her chest.

"Am, too."

She stepped forward and stared up at me, all fire and stubbornness. My gaze dropped to her lips, parted and perfect. So kissable.

"I'm paying," she said, all soft and slow, like she knew I was struggling to keep my damn hands to myself.

"In your dreams."

Her expression went all soft, and I would have paid a million dollars to know what she'd just thought about. "Fine," she said. "But only if you agree to have dinner with us."

"Deal."

"Are not!"

"Are, too!"

We both turned to see the twins mocking us through their open door, giant grins on their faces.

"Yeah, yeah. Okay. Pipe down, you two, or I'll put anchovies on yours," I threatened without a straight face. "Should we grab another pizza?"

"I ordered three," Ella said with a shrug.

We stood there and smiled at each other like idiots, both knowing she'd planned on me staying for dinner long before our little deal.

Havoc jumped down as I walked toward the store, and I turned around, dropping to scratch her ears. "Protect Maisie and Colt."

She sprinted away, parking her rump just beneath their open door.

"Ella!" Hailey waved, and I walked into the shop as the two women started chatting near the bed of the truck.

Three pizzas and five minutes later, I walked out of the shop and nearly dropped the boxes.

An older, well-dressed couple, coming from the opposite end of where Hailey stood talking to Ella, had paused. It wasn't the pause that triggered me, it was the look on their faces. Utter, abject shock as they looked at the twins.

Havoc stood—she'd always been a good judge of character—and I started moving.

The woman stepped forward, as if she didn't have control over her own actions, and Havoc bared her teeth and began growling.

Ella turned at the growl, and when she sucked in her breath, I had all the info I needed. "No!" she snapped, not at Havoc, but at the couple. She marched straight up beside Havoc, bared teeth and all, and said it again. "No. Go. Now."

I came up behind the couple, then to the side, sliding the pizzas onto the passenger seat as I walked by to put myself between them and Havoc.

"Don't come any closer. She'll go for the jugular if you move one hand toward those kids." I kept my voice low and even. The minute I got agitated, Havoc got dangerous.

"That dog is a menace," the man said, sneering up at me.

"Only to people she sees as threats to the twins or Ella. Now, I believe Ella asked you to go." I walked forward, forcing the couple to retreat, knowing Havoc would follow and give Ella the room to shut the door so the twins wouldn't be exposed.

When I heard the door slam, I relaxed, and Havoc put her teeth away.

"Who, exactly, are you?" the woman demanded.

"That's none of your business."

"Those aren't your kids," the man seethed.

"They're not yours, either," I said. "But I'm theirs, and that's all that matters. And I can tell you that if you ever come close to them without Ella's permission, Havoc will be the least of your concerns."

When the man started to stare Ella down, I moved into his line of sight, blocking her from the disgust aimed at her.

"Beckett," Ella called softly, no doubt noticing the small crowd that was witnessing the exchange.

"Have a nice evening," I told the couple, then turned around and walked back to Ella, putting my hand on the small of her back and urging her into the truck, then shutting the door behind her.

The couple was gone.

I passed Hailey, Havoc at my side.

"Jeff's parents," she whispered.

"I figured."

"There's tequila in the freezer." She motioned toward the cab of the truck, where Ella sat in silence, stunned.

"Good to know."

"Who was that?" Colt asked.

"No one you need to worry about," Ella answered.

"Havoc was worried," Maisie countered.

"Havoc is a good judge of character," Ella muttered. "They were just some people I used to know."

"They weren't very nice," Colt noted.

"Nope. They never have been."

Ella was quiet as we drove back to Solitude and faked her smile through dinner. Then she got the kids to bed, and I sat on the couch, silently waiting as Havoc snoozed at my feet.

A half hour later, she came down the stairs, having changed into flannel pants and a tank top. Her mouth dropped into a surprised *O* when she saw me. "I thought you'd left."

"Nope. Sit." I patted the couch next to me and looked

away from the swells of her breasts that were lifted high along the neckline of her tank top.

She sank into the corner of the couch, bringing her knees up to her chest. "I bet you're pretty curious about what happened outside the pizza shop."

"Talk."

She rested her chin on her folded arms and took a deep breath. "Those were Jeff's parents."

"So I assumed."

Her eyes lifted to mine.

"You're just like Ryan when you do that, make conclusions about everything around you. People, too."

"Keeps us alive," I responded before I thought. My eyes slid shut momentarily at the blunder and the pain that followed. "You know what I mean."

She nodded. "They've never seen the kids before. Never even asked about them."

I knew most of that. Scratch that. Chaos knew. But I wanted Ella to tell me, Beckett. To trust me as much as she had that faceless pen pal. So instead of lying, or asking her to continue, I simply waited.

"Jeff walked out when I was eight weeks pregnant." She looked away, her face falling as she stepped into the memory. "He hadn't wanted to get married, not really. It was all very Meatloaf."

"What?" I rested my arm on the back of the couch and leaned in. "Like the food?"

"Like the artist. You know, 'Paradise by the Dashboard Light'?"

"Ah, gotcha. No ring, no sex."

"Bingo. We'd been together all senior year, and looking back, when I caught him lying about smoking—smoking of all things to lie about!—I should have walked away, but I was lost in that naive love-can-change-him mentality. Anyway, we were leaving for CU in the fall, and it all seemed really romantic. Run away and get married the day after graduation, have our wedding night in a hotel, and spring it on my grandma and his parents the next day."

"I'm guessing that went over real well." I hadn't seen an ounce of mercy in that guy, which never made for a good parent.

"Like a ton of bricks. Grandma cried." She swallowed and took a moment. "His parents disowned him, and we moved into one of the cabins for the summer, which were more camp-style than the ones you see now. Grandma was disappointed, but that never changed her love or her promise to pay for my college. Jeff was so sad after that first week. Honeymoon was over, I guess you'd say, and now he was stressed about how he was going to pay his tuition, and everything just spiraled. He'd gone from trust-fund baby to broke overnight. Four weeks after our little trip to the courthouse, I realized I was pregnant, and two weeks later, the doctor told me I was having twins."

I tried to put myself in her position at that age and couldn't. At eighteen, I'd enlisted in the military and was barely capable of caring for myself, let alone two other humans. "You're incredibly strong."

She shook her head. "No, because the minute the doc did that wand ultrasound after the blood tests, I had this moment where I regretted everything. Everything," she repeated in an instant.

"You were young; I can't imagine there's any young woman in your position who wouldn't panic."

"I was eighteen and married to a guy who didn't like to look at me anymore, well, unless I was naked. And even then…sex…" She shrugged. "Well, I guess it served its purpose. I told him the minute I got home, thinking he'd know what to do. He always had the plans, you know?"

"What did he do?"

"He sat there for a moment in shock, and I understood. After all, I felt the same way. Then he…he asked me to abort them."

My nails dug into the back of the couch, but I didn't say a word.

"And it was in that instant, when that choice was put on the table, that the shock faded, and I knew I wanted them. That there was nothing I wouldn't do to protect them. That's when I realized that I'd loved the person he pretended to be: strong, loyal, caring, protective…and it was all a giant lie. He put on a great act, but he wasn't some big, strong man who was going to carry me away to college and build this amazing life. He was a scared little boy who couldn't put anyone else first, and that included me. And there I was, realizing I'd die for the twins, and he wanted me to kill them because they were inconvenient, and so was I. I refused. He threatened. I refused. He was gone the next morning."

"I'm so sorry you had to go through that."

She shrugged. "It is what it is, and it taught me to never trust a liar. You lie once, chances are you'll do it again and again. Anyway, Jeff's dad showed up a week later with a big, fat check and divorce papers, telling me I could have the first when I proved I was no longer pregnant."

"Are you kidding me?" I growled. Now I wanted the asshole back in front of me, wanted that scrawny neck wrapped between my hands.

"Nope. So I signed the papers, snatched the check from his hand, and set it on fire right in front of him."

That's my girl.

"Nice. Very visual."

"Yeah, well, I was a little dramatic, and ended up burning that cabin to the ground. Literally. Everything was gone."

"So don't leave you alone with a lighter, that's what you're saying? No barbecue grill, no s'mores, no fireworks?"

She laughed, lightening the mood, but I still wanted

to strangle everyone in that damn family.

"And you stayed in Telluride and raised the kids," I assumed.

She nodded. "Yep. Jeff never came back. Not once. Patty and Rich bought a place in Denver, but they still come back at holidays, as you saw today. But they've never seen the kids. Never asked to, at least, when they'd run into me. Even when I asked them for help with the insurance for Maisie, Rich said that the kids weren't their problem. I won't make the mistake of asking for help again."

"I'm not sure they deserve to see the kids."

"Me either, but I worry that Maisie might not get the chance if she wants it, you know? I mean, one day, they'll grow up. They'll ask deeper questions and seek out their own answers. And Maisie..." She buried her face in her hands.

I slid forward, until the tips of her toes grazed the outside of my thigh. Then I gently took her hands away, almost hoping she was crying, that she'd learned to release that pressure valve at a steadier, easier rate than during Maisie's surgery.

But there were no tears, just a well of sorrow so deep it would drown an ordinary soul. But Ella was no ordinary soul.

"Maisie will have time to make her choice." I had no right, but the thought wouldn't leave, so I voiced it. "Do the kids ask about him? Jeff?"

"Sometimes. They're curious, of course, and Father's Day is always a touchy subject, but I've been really lucky to have Larry, and the kids have been pretty secluded from other kids out here. This was their first real year at school."

"What do you tell them?"

"That of course they have a father, because babies have to have a father and a mother. But they don't have a dad. Because while all men can be fathers, not all of them are qualified to be daddies, and theirs just wasn't."

Because your loser dad didn't want you. He wanted the next fix more than a screaming piece of shit like you. My mother's words banged around in my head like a ball set loose in a pinball machine.

"You are a terrific mother. I hope to God you've heard that often, because you really are." My thumbs grazed her wrist, just over her pulse.

"I didn't do anything anyone else wouldn't have done," she refuted with a shrug.

"No. Don't shrug it off. Because I am the product of someone who didn't do what you did—what you do every single day. Don't ever doubt that. Also, if I ever meet Jeff, I'm going to knock him out."

She gifted me with a small smile. "Don't do that. He's a lawyer in Denver now. He'd probably sue you for breaking his precious nose. You ever want to hurt Jeff, you have to hit something he cares about—his pocketbook. And honestly, we're better for him leaving. Life with him would have been miserable, and I wouldn't want the kids learning from that kind of father, especially Colt."

"I get that."

Her gaze flickered to my mouth and away.

She's not thinking about kissing you, I lied to myself. Because if I admitted the truth, I'd have her under me in three seconds flat. My hands would be in her hair, my tongue in her mouth, her gasps in my ear.

Silence stretched between us, screaming with the countless possibilities of what could happen next.

Slowly, I let go of her wrists and moved back to my side of the couch. "I should probably get going. It's late."

"It's nine."

"Help me out here, Ella." And now my voice sounded like sandpaper. *Awesome.*

"Help you out of what?" she asked, shifting her position so her legs were under her.

"You know what. Don't make me say it." The minute I said it, we were both screwed, and not in the physical sense. Well, okay, that, too.

"Maybe…maybe I want you to say it," she finished in a strangled whisper.

"I can't." *Not yet. Not while I'm a walking, talking lie.* If she looked at my lap, I definitely wouldn't need words. I'd gone rock hard the minute she'd looked at my mouth.

"Oh. I get it." She sat back on her butt, and alarm bells sounded in my head.

"Get what?"

"Like I'm going to say it?" She laughed in self-deprecation.

"Ella." It was a plea to speak, to not speak. Hell, I didn't know anymore.

"You don't see me like that. I totally get it." She reached for the TV remote.

"How exactly do I see you? Please, enlighten me." I leaned forward, stealing the remote. She'd opened this box and had better well dish it.

She huffed in annoyance. "You see me as a mom. As Colt and Maisie's mom. And of course you do, because that's what I am. A mom with two kids."

"Well, yeah," I said. Her motherhood—that selfless devotion she had to her kids—was one of her most attractive attributes.

She rolled her eyes with a little sigh, and the metaphorical light bulb went off in my head.

"You don't think I want you."

She shot me a look that confirmed my guess and blushed the same crimson of her couch. "You know, you're right. It's late." She faked a yawn. "Suuuuuuper late."

"I want you." Damn, it felt so good to say the words.

"Yeah, okay." She gave me a goofy look and a

thumbs-up. "Please don't make me feel any more idiotic than I do right now."

Yeah, enough of this bullshit.

I pounced in one smooth motion, taking her back to the couch, sliding over her as I gathered her wrists in one hand above her head and settled between her open thighs.

Home.

"Holy shit, you move fast." There was no fear or rejection in her eyes, just surprise.

"Not in every arena," I promised.

Her lips parted.

"Ella. I want you."

"Beckett...you don't have to."

Yeah, that soft little sigh she did was going to be my undoing.

I let go of her wrists, letting my fingers trail down her arm until I had one hand weaving my fingers into the hair at the base of her scalp and the other at the curve in her waist.

"Feel this?" Then I slid forward, letting my dick stroke along the seam in her pajama pants hard enough for her to gasp at the contact. I couldn't remember ever wanting to shred a piece of fabric so much in my life. "I've never wanted a woman as much as I want you."

I moved again, and her eyes slid shut as she let loose the sweetest moan.

My dick throbbed, knowing everything I'd fantasized about for the better part of the last eight months was one decision away.

"Beckett." Her hands found my biceps, her nails digging in.

"Don't ever think that I don't want you, because if things were different, I would have already been inside you. I would know exactly how you feel, and what you sound like, look like, when you come. I've thought about it at least a hundred different ways, and believe me, I've got a great imagination."

She rocked her hips against me, and I locked my jaw to keep from giving her exactly what her body was asking for. "Ella, you have to stop."

"Why?" she asked, her lips dangerously close to mine. "What do you mean if things were different?" Her eyes flew wide. "Is this because I have kids?"

"What? No. Of course not. It's because you're Ryan's little sister." Before I could do any more damage, I got the hell off her and sat back on my side of the couch.

"Because…I'm Ryan's little sister," she repeated, scooting so she sat upright, facing me. "And you think he'd, what? Haunt you?"

Three things: The letter. The cancer. The lie.

I repeated those in my head until I was certain I could look at her and not drag her back under me.

"Beckett?"

"When I was growing up, if I wanted something, I took it. Immediately. I had sex at fourteen with a girl in my foster home of the moment. I opened Christmas presents early if I was lucky enough to get one, and it was usually from my social worker or some charity."

"I don't understand." She wrapped her arms around her knees again.

"I took it immediately because I knew if I didn't, chances were I wouldn't get it. It was a now-or-never kind of thing—there weren't second chances."

"Okay."

"I can't touch you, can't talk about it, because I'm afraid I'll act on it."

"And why does that matter if I want you to?"

"Because I won't get a second chance. And I'm crap with people, with relationships. I've never had one that lasted more than a month. Never loved a woman I've slept with. And chances are I'd do something to screw this up, because it's not just my dick that wants you, Ella."

That *O* popped right back onto her face, and I closed my eyes to keep from lunging across the distance and kissing her. Knowing she'd let me—that she wanted it—sent my need from a bullet to a nuclear missile.

"And when I'd screw it up, because it would happen, trust me, it would hurt Colt and Maisie, too. You'd be on your own again, because there's no chance you'd let me hang around and help you out like Ryan asked."

"And there it is."

"There it is. You're Ryan's little sister."

"There were only five years between us. Not so little, you know." She reached for the remote.

"I'm well aware."

"So if Ryan were still alive…" She shot one last look at me.

I let everything slip for a millisecond, letting her see it all in my eyes, how badly I wanted her, and not just for her body. "Everything would be different."

"Everything?"

"Everything but the way I feel about you, which he probably would have killed me for. Where does that leave us?"

"You mean besides me being a dried-up spinster and you being honor bound to a ghost?"

"Something like that."

She rolled her head along the back of the couch, muttering something that sounded like a curse word under her breath. Then she sat up straight and powered on the TV with a click of her thumb. "That leaves us choosing a movie on demand. Because I'm not letting you walk out that door right now."

"You're not?"

"Nope. You walk out now, you might get all weird about this and not come back. Honor is a fabulous thing, but sometimes pride can be a lot stronger, especially when you convince yourself it's for the good of the other person."

Damn, the woman knew me.

"So movie it is," I agreed. "Just…stay on your side of the couch."

"I wasn't the one who crossed the center line," she teased with a smile that got me hard all over again.

Movie chosen, we sat and watched, both of us stealing sideways glances. There was that saying…the horse out of the barn. Yeah, the horse was out of the barn, and it wasn't going back in. Not no way. Not no how.

That horse was running amok and screwing with my carefully constructed control.

But I didn't complain when she moved over. Or when she pressed against my side. Nope. I lifted my arm and savored the feel of her curves, her trust. Still didn't complain when she lay down in my arms. Hell no, I held on and memorized every second.

I woke with a start at the door opening, reaching for a pistol that wasn't there. But Havoc was and, since her tail was wagging in a slow thump against the hardwood, I knew it had to be Hailey.

Yep. She tiptoed in, then saw us on the couch, stretched out in the spoon position, and gave me a grin before slipping into the guest room.

I put my head back down, breathing in the citrus scent of Ella's hair, and tightened my arm at her waist so she didn't fall off the couch. I would have slept balanced on a two-by-four if it meant I got to hold her.

Before I could fall asleep, I heard footsteps again, but this time they were coming from upstairs. Colt's face appeared right above me, and panic in his eyes told me he didn't care that I was wrapped around his mother.

"What's up, bud?"

"Something's wrong with Maisie. She's on fire."

CHAPTER THIRTEEN

Ella

Letter #13

Ella,

    I'm so sorry that you missed Colt's play, and no, it's not trivial. I get it, and I don't know what I could possibly say—or write—that would give you the peace of mind you deserve. You're being ripped in two different directions, and that has to feel impossible.

    But I can say that you're doing a great job. Yes, you missed the play, but Maisie needed you. There will be times as Colt grows up that he'll need you, and you'll miss something for Maisie. I think that's just part of having two kids. You do the best you can by both and hope it all equals out in the end. The guilt means you're a great mom, but you also have to let yourself off the hook sometimes. This is one of those times.

    What you're going through is a nightmare. You have to give yourself a little space to stumble, because you're right—you're not one of those two-parent households. So that means you have to take extra care of yourself because you're the only one they've got.

    Do me a favor and just hold on. Your brother is headed home as soon as he can. You won't be alone for long, I promise. He mentioned that Colt wanted a tree house, and while I'm visiting, I'll help him with it. Maybe it's not much, but it will give him a spot just his own, and give you the peace of mind that he's got something special.

I wish I had better advice, but I know you don't need it, just an ear, and you've got mine whenever you want it.

~ Chaos

"105.3." I read the numbers on the thermometer again, just in case I got it wrong the first time. Maisie was burning up. "I have to get her to the hospital."

"*We* have to get her to the hospital," Beckett corrected me from the doorway to the bathroom. "Get the Tylenol, wet rags, whatever you need, and let's go. Colt, do me a favor and wake Hailey?"

I heard the familiar scamper of Colt's feet down the stairs as I ripped apart the medicine cabinet looking for Tylenol. What could have caused this? The soccer game. It had to have been. But no one was near her, and her levels were great at her last appointment. What could she have caught in that short time?

I found the bubblegum pink bottle of fever reducer and poured the exact amount she needed into the tiny measuring cup.

"Ella," Beckett called my name from the hallway, and I stumbled out of the bathroom, medicine ready.

He had Maisie in his arms, against his chest, wrapped in her blanket. I placed my hand on her forehead and choked back every swear word that came to mind. This wasn't good. We'd been so lucky with her complications—the nausea, vomiting, hair loss, weight loss, it was all pretty standard, small stuff. But this was unknown.

"Maisie, love, I need you to open your eyes and take some medicine, okay?" I coaxed, running my free hand along her cheek.

Her eyes fluttered open, glassy from fever. "I'm hot."

"I know. Can you take this?" I showed her the cup.

She nodded, the movement small and weak. Beckett shifted his hold, helping her upright, and I put the small cup to her heart-shaped mouth. Such perfect little lips. She'd never had so much as a cavity or a broken bone before her diagnosis, and now she didn't bat an eye at medication.

She swallowed and jolted, her stomach muscles heaving.

"Baby, you have to keep it down, okay? Please?" I begged like it was her choice. Her jaw dropped, and she started to heave again.

"Outside," Beckett ordered, and went, leaving me to follow after him.

He carried her down the stairs and outside onto the porch, barely pausing when he had to open the door. The man didn't even give me a chance to get there first.

I stopped at the office, grabbing Maisie's binder from my desk and running out after them.

"That's better, right? Feel that air? Nice and cool. Take little breaths, Maisie. In through your nose, out through your mouth. That's right. Just like that." His voice was so soothing and calm, directly contrasting the rigid set of his jaw.

Maisie arched her neck, like she was seeking out the cool night air, and her breathing slowed as her belly calmed. She had to keep down the medicine, had to give us time to get to the ER.

"Better?" I asked, taking her little hand.

"A little."

"Good." I'd take a little. A little was better than throwing up the meds.

"Oh my God, Ella, what can I do?" Hailey ran out onto the porch as she tied her bathrobe, Colt just behind her in his bare feet.

"Can you keep Colt? Please? We have to get her to the ER."

"Absolutely. Where are you going to take her? The medical center is closed."

"Where's the nearest ER?" Beckett asked.

"Montrose is the only one open at this time of night"—I checked my phone—"or morning, rather. It's three a.m."

"That's an hour and a half," Hailey said quietly, like her tone mattered, or could change the distance.

"Not the way I drive," Beckett responded, already striding toward his truck.

"I'll be right back!" Hailey shouted, running into the house.

"Mom?" Colt appeared at my side, Havoc at his.

"Hey." I dropped down to his level. "You did great, Colt. You did exactly right."

"It should be me."

"What?"

"I should be sick, not Maisie. It's not fair. It should be me." His eyes were just as glassy as Maisie's, but because of unshed tears.

"Oh, Colt. No." My stomach lurched at the thought of going through this with him, too.

"But it's because she came to my game, right? It's my fault. I'm stronger than she is. It should be me. Why isn't it me?"

I yanked him forward into my arms, nearly crushing him against my chest as I hugged him. "This is not because of you. Anything that brought on a fever like this would have taken way longer. Do you understand? This is not your fault. You're the reason we can get her to the doctor. You're the hero in this, bud."

He nodded against my neck, and I felt tiny streams of wetness right before he sniffled. I rubbed his back until I heard the engine flare to life behind me, and then I pulled Colt back so I could look at him.

"Tell me you understand."

"I understand," he said, wiping away the traces of his tears. He straightened his little spine, looking so small and yet so old.

"I'm sorry that I have to leave you, but I gotta go, bud."

"I know," he said with a nod. "Please help her."

"I will." I kissed the promise against his forehead. "I love you, Colton."

"Love you, Mom."

"She's in the back seat," Beckett said from right behind me.

"Here," Hailey said, running back onto the porch with a box and thrusting it into my arms. "Ice, water bottles, washcloths, Motrin, your shoes, cell phone charger, purse, some other stuff."

"Thank you," I said, hugging her with one arm. "I'll keep you updated." I raced from the porch and climbed into the back of Beckett's truck, immediately surrounded by the smell of clean leather and Beckett. "Can you sit up?" I asked Maisie, who was in the process of unbuckling her seat belt.

"No."

"Okay, come here." I sat her in the middle seat, clicked the seat belt over her, and then had her lie across my lap.

Highway safety approved? No. But cancer was already doing its best to kill my kid, so I was just going to have some faith that we weren't going to add a car accident to my recent list of tragedies.

I glanced out the window to see Beckett hunched down to Colt's level. He pulled him in tight for a hug, engulfing Colt's tiny frame in his massive arms. A quick word to Havoc and he was headed in my direction.

He passed through the glow of the headlights and then opened the driver's door, climbing in and shutting it in one smooth move.

"You girls okay?" He adjusted the rearview mirror to see us instead of the road as he pulled through the circular driveway.

"We're steady," I told him, unable to think of another word to describe it. Was I okay? Was Maisie? No. But this was what it was, and I was solid.

"Okay." He turned onto Solitude's main drive. Everything was so quiet this time of morning. Where I was normally consumed with the noise of the kids, the radio, my own thoughts, all there was now was the sound of Beckett's tires on the blacktop. Smooth and steady.

With Maisie's head on my lap, I reached into the box at my feet, pulling out a washcloth and a cold bottle of water that had obviously just come from the fridge. "Think you can keep any of this down?" I asked her.

She shook her head.

Beckett's eyes met mine in the rearview mirror as we reached the Solitude gate. "Any objection to me breaking a few speed laws?" he asked as he turned onto the road.

"None." His foot hit the gas, and the truck took off. "Do you know the roads—?"

"Ella, do you trust me?" he interrupted.

Seeing as I was currently holding my sick daughter in the back of his truck as he drove us into the night, I would have thought the answer was obvious. *Duh*. That's exactly what he was getting at. "I trust you."

"Just take care of Maisie and let me get you there."

I nodded and got to work, pouring water on the washcloth and wiping her down.

Beckett had this, and I had Maisie.

"Margaret's PICC line is infected, and she's showing signs of sepsis," the doctor told us six hours later.

I immediately balked, coming to stand at the foot of my daughter's bed, where she was fast asleep. "No way. I keep that thing clean as…well, possible." My brain would have fired back a wittier response if I hadn't been going on about two hours of sleep. "I swab it, keep it wrapped, air it, everything that every doctor instructed."

The middle-aged ER doc gave me an understanding nod. "I'm sure you do. We didn't see any external sign of infection, which happens when it doesn't originate in the skin. Don't beat yourself up. This happens. But we need to treat her immediately. That means moving her to the ICU and starting antibiotics."

I wrapped my arms around my stomach and looked at Maisie. She was still flushed with fever, but they had it down to a little over a hundred, and she was hooked up to an IV for hydration. "Sepsis? Wouldn't I have known?"

The doctor reached over, grasping my shoulder lightly until I looked at him. "You wouldn't have. She's very lucky that she spiked that fever and you got her here so quickly."

I glanced over at Beckett, who stood next to Maisie's bed, leaned against the wall with one hand on her bed frame like he'd slay any dragons that dared to come close. I wasn't lucky to get her here; I'd been lucky that Beckett had been driving. That he'd been with me when the fever spiked.

I'd never have been able to shave a half hour off that drive time like he did.

"Sepsis. So, the infection is in her blood." I tried to recall everything I'd read over the last seven months, feeling like I'd just been thrown into the final exam for a class I hadn't been aware I was taking. Her blood pressure was low, I knew that from the monitors, and her breathing had been a little labored coming in. Second stage. "Her organs?"

He got that look on his face. The one doctors got when they didn't want to deliver bad news.

"Her organs?" I repeated, raising my voice. "She's six weeks post-op, and the doctors spent twelve hours saving her kidney, so could you please tell me if that was all in vain?"

"We need to see how she reacts to the antibiotics." His voice dropped into the soothe-the-mother-of-the-sick-patient tone.

Alarms as loud as church bells went off in my head, and my stomach dropped. "How worried do I need to be?"

"Very."

He didn't blink, didn't soften his expression or his tone.

And that terrified me even more.

The next hour was a blur.

We were transferred to ICU, where we were admitted. They wristbanded me with Maisie's information, and I nodded when they asked about Beckett, already digging through my binder for her history and insurance information.

Seeing as we were frequent-flyers at the affiliated cancer center, they had everything on file, so I could put the binder down. Until they started the IV antibiotics, then I picked it back up and started scrawling notes.

"Do we remove the line?" I asked the doctor, scanning his name tag. *Dr. Peterson.* Beckett moved to my side, quiet but solid.

The doctor scanned through his iPad before answering. "We need to weigh the pros and cons there. In the majority of cases, the line itself isn't the danger, and if we remove it, you're looking at the complications from inserting another one."

"It goes straight to her heart."

"Yes. But we've started aggressive antibiotics, and

we're monitoring her, especially her liquid input and output."

"Kidney function," I assumed.

He nodded. "We need to give the drugs a chance. If there's no improvement, we'll need to remove the line."

"So for now we wait."

"We wait."

I nodded, muttered thanks, or something, and took the chair next to Maisie's bed. *Wait.* Just wait. That was all I could do.

As usual, I was powerless, and my six-year-old daughter was fighting for her life. How was any of this fair? Why couldn't it be me in that bed? With the IVs and the lines and the monitors? Why her?

"How about I grab us some coffee?" Beckett offered, halting my downward spiral.

"That would be great. Thank you." I gave him a weak, forced smile, and he headed in search of caffeine.

The steady drip of her IV was my companion, the monitors letting out a comforting beep with each of her heartbeats. Her pressure was dangerously low, and I was quickly addicted to watching the screen as new measurements came in.

Wait. That was the course of action. Wait.

My phone rang, startling me, and I swiped it open to answer quickly when I saw Dr. Hughes's name pop up as the contact.

"Dr. Hughes?" I answered.

"Hey, Ella. I got a call that Maisie was admitted in Montrose; how are you doing?" Her voice was a welcome breath of familiarity.

"Did they fill you in?"

"They did. I'm actually on my way in right now."

"You're here in Montrose? I thought you were in Denver for another week or so." I flipped through the binder to find my calendar of when Dr. Hughes was scheduled.

"It's Memorial Day weekend, so I came to spend the weekend with my parents."

My relief at having her here was second only to my guilt. "I wouldn't want you to give up your weekend."

"Nonsense. I'll be there in about a half hour. Besides, it gives me an excuse to get out of listening to my mom's opinion on bridesmaid dresses. You're doing me a favor, I promise."

"You're getting married?" How did I not know that?

"Six months to go," she said, her smile shining through her voice. "I'll be there soon, just hang tight."

We hung up as Beckett walked in with a familiar white and green cup.

"You are a god among men," I said, taking the cup and holding it between my hands, hoping some of the heat would transfer to my skin, would wake up my nerves. Numb seemed to be my default state lately.

"I'll bring you coffee more often," he promised, pulling up a matching chair to sit next to me. "How's she doing?"

"No change. I'm not sure what I'm expecting. Instant results? Her to pop up and be magically healed from an infection I never saw? How did I not see it?"

"Because you're not a walking blood test? You've got to be a little easier on yourself, Ella. If the doc said there was no way to see this coming, then you need to believe him. Beat yourself up about your choice of baseball teams, or the fact that you're about two thousand miles overdue for an oil change, but not this."

"What's wrong with the Rockies?"

He shrugged. "Nothing if you like losing."

"Hey, they're the hometown team, and I'm not a fair-weather fan."

"That's what I love about you," he said with a smile as he watched Maisie. "Your unwavering loyalty, even to a team that clearly sucks."

"Just because you're a Mets fan…" I motioned to the baseball cap he had on.

"Guilty as charged." He looked at me and winked, and it became instantly clear: he'd distracted me from guilt-tripping myself.

I shook my head and sighed, grateful for the coffee and the split second I'd had to clear my head from going down the path of self-loathing that wouldn't do Maisie any good.

"I'm scared."

"I know." His hand covered mine where it rested on my lap.

"This is bad."

"Yes." His simple acknowledgment meant more than any well-meaning platitude. With Beckett, I didn't have to put on the brave face or smile when someone told me that they were sure Maisie would be okay when they really knew nothing of the sort. I could be horribly, bluntly honest with this man.

"I don't want to bury my daughter." I watched the rise and fall of her chest under the patterned hospital gown. "I don't know how to plan for something like that, or even consider it. I don't know how to look at Colt and tell him that his best friend…" My throat closed, denying the rest of my words the release they so desperately needed. I'd kept them inside for so long that they felt more powerful, like I'd fed the monster by keeping it hidden away.

Beckett squeezed my hand. Everything about him dwarfed me, including those long, strong fingers that held mine with such strength and care.

"From the moment they told me her odds, I refused to plan for that. Because planning for it felt like admitting defeat, like I'd already given up on her. So I didn't. I simply refused to believe that could even be an option.

And then…"

I closed my eyes as the memory slid over me, stabbing at me with a grief so sharp I should have visibly bled. Lowering his casket. The guns from the shore. The stern face of the soldier who had handed me a folded flag.

"Then I buried Ryan. What kind of God does that? Takes your only brother while toying with the thought of taking your daughter?"

Beckett's thumb stroked over my knuckle, but he stayed quiet. There wasn't anything he could say—we both knew it.

"Were you mad? When he died?" I asked, tearing my eyes away from Maisie to look at Beckett.

His focus shifted downward. "Furious."

"With God," I assumed.

"With myself. With every soldier in our unit who hadn't saved him, taken that bullet. With the government for sending us there. With the…" He swallowed. "… insurgents who pulled the trigger. With everyone who lived after he died."

"How did you get past it?" He was so calm, like the lake at five a.m. before a ripple of wind disturbed her surface.

"What makes you think I have?" His eyes met mine, and I saw it there, the pain he kept meticulously concealed. How deep was it? How much damage had been done to him through the years?

Beckett Gentry knew almost everything there was to know about me, and yet I knew nothing about him. Was it because I hadn't asked? Because I was so consumed with Maisie? With Colt? Because I secretly didn't want to know?

"Sometimes I think I don't really know you," I said softly.

A corner of his mouth lifted in a wry half smile.

"You might not know much about my past, but trust me, you know *me*, and that's more important."

Before I could question him any further, the door opened, and Dr. Hughes stepped in. She had on jeans and a blouse with her standard white coat.

"Hey, Ella."

"Dr. Hughes." Her name came out as the rush of relief it was.

"How's it going?" She picked up the chart at the end of the bed.

"We're waiting for the meds to work, or not work." *For Maisie's organs to shut down or not. For her to live or die.*

"Ah, and you wait so well," she said with raised eyebrows.

"Guilty," I answered.

She looked at Beckett and then our connected hands.

"Ah, this is Beckett Gentry," I said, slipping my hand free and patting his shoulder. *Lame.* "He's…" Holy shit, what was he? How did I introduce him? He wasn't my boyfriend. The guy wouldn't even kiss me, even though he was pretty much around twenty-four seven.

"I'm her late brother's best friend," he explained as he stood, offering his hand. "I understand you're Maisie's neuroblastoma specialist. She loves you."

Dr. Hughes shook his hand and smiled. "Well, I'm certainly glad to hear that. Maisie is a favorite of mine. And I'm pleased to meet you, Mr. Gentry. Ella has definitely needed some support. I'm glad to see she's getting it."

"I'll be here as long as she needs me." He answered the question she didn't ask, and her eyes went soft.

Another one bites the dust.

Then we got down to business. She asked a few questions and checked Maisie's chart for the latest labs, her brows knitting together at times as she read everything over. She listened to her breathing, checked out her IVs, and watched her pressure.

"How worried do I need to be?" I asked, knowing she wouldn't bullshit me.

Her sigh was deep, and she flipped through the chart again. "I don't know, and I can't say until we see how she reacts to the meds. I can tell you that she's way better off than she would have been in a few hours. You saved her life."

"Colt did," I said softly.

"Those two." She lightly chuckled. "One soul split between two bodies."

"He said he'd heard her crying in his dream," Beckett said. "He woke up and went into her room and found her burning up."

My head snapped toward his, wondering when Colt had— *While you were in the truck.* When he'd talked to Colt on the porch. The gratitude I felt toward Beckett for his connection with Colt was tempered a little with jealousy that he knew my son in a way I didn't.

Because Beckett was around more than I was.

"What's next?" I asked, needing to look past this.

"It will take a few hours, but once we're certain the meds work—"

"Not with this. With the treatments. Looking forward and all that." I didn't want to think about what I couldn't control. I wanted to focus on what I could. What to research next, to prepare her for. That, I could handle.

Dr. Hughes nodded, like she understood, and then sat in the last empty chair in the room, leaning forward on the small table. "We were supposed to meet next week," she said.

"Right."

"You sure you want to do this now?"

I glanced at my little girl fighting a battle I couldn't pick up a sword for, and instead chose another front. "I am."

"That last round of chemo didn't move her levels like we were hoping."

Having the tumor gone was all well and good, but if her bone marrow was still overwhelmingly cancerous, another one would grow. We'd cut off the top of the tree, but the roots were still alive and fighting.

"Is she developing a resistance to the chemo?"

Beckett's hand found mine again, and I gripped. Hard.

"It's a possibility. We'd discussed the MIBG treatment, and I think it's our best bet." She leaned down and pulled a pamphlet out of her purse, putting it on the table. "I got you some information on a trial." She looked over at Beckett, and I knew exactly why.

"You can talk about it in front of him. It's fine." Up until now, the only people who knew what my finances looked like were Ada and Dr. Hughes. And probably the cell phone company that had gotten used to me perpetually paying a month late.

"The trial will cover certain aspects, but not everything, and the only hospital in Colorado with the facilities to do this is Colorado Children's." She gave me a knowing look.

The cost was astronomical, and I had no way of covering it in cash. But I'd think about that later. "Submit the paperwork, and let's get her in."

"Okay. It needs to be soon."

"Doesn't everything?"

"Tell me about the MIBG," Beckett asked seven hours later as we ate dinner in the small cafeteria. Maisie slept upstairs, her pressure hovering, her temp fevered.

She'd woken up once and asked to use the bathroom, which just about made me cry in relief. Her kidneys were still functioning.

I pushed the bland excuse for fried chicken to the side of my plate. Why was all hospital food bland? Because they needed it to be gentle on stomachs? Or maybe I was wrong, and it wasn't, but I was too numb to really taste it.

Maybe all hospital food was really good, and we were just too preoccupied to ever notice.

"Ella," Beckett said gently, pulling me from my thoughts. "The MIBG?"

"Right. It's a relatively new treatment for neuroblastoma that attaches the chemo to the radiation that targets the tumor itself. It's pretty amazing stuff, and they can do it in only eighteen hospitals across the country, one of which happens to be in Denver."

"That's incredible. The same hospital where Maisie had her surgery?"

"The same." I poked at my mashed potatoes, dropping my jaw when Beckett shoved in forkful after forkful. "How do you eat that?"

"Spend a decade in the army. You'd be amazed at what sounds great for dinner."

And there was some perspective that had me reaching for my fork.

"Any drawbacks to the MIBG?"

"The trial isn't covered by my insurance." And there it was, the entrance to the nightmare that was my finances.

"You're kidding me." He blinked a couple times, like he expected me to change my answer. "Tell me you're kidding, Ella."

"I'm not." I took a bite of my chicken, knowing I needed the calories, no matter where they came from.

"So what do we do?" Two lines appeared right above

his nose as he leaned forward.

"The same thing I've been doing. Figure it out. Pay for it." I shrugged, pausing as I took another bite when I realized what he'd said. *What do we do?* We. Not *you.* We. I managed to swallow before I looked like an idiot with a chicken leg stuck in my face.

"What do you mean, the same thing you've been doing? How much haven't they covered?" His tone was calm and even but a little frightening for the intensity.

I shrugged and reached for a roll.

"I'm trying really hard not to lose it, so if you'd answer, that would really help me out."

I dragged my eyes from the roll, up his chest, to the vein bulging in his neck—yep, he was ticked—to his eyes. "A lot. They haven't covered a lot."

"Why haven't you said anything?"

"Because it's none of your business!"

He jerked back like I'd slapped him.

"Sorry, but it's not." I softened my tone as much as possible. "And what would I say? Hey, Beckett, did you know that I gambled my kids' health last year? That my insurance plan doesn't cover half of what Maisie needs? That I've blown through Ryan's life insurance keeping my kid alive?"

"Yeah, you could start by saying that." He raked his hand over his hair, clasping his hands at the top of his head. "Start by saying something. How much trouble are you in?"

"Some."

We waged a silent war, each trying to stare down the other. A few heartbeats later, I gave in. He was the one trying to help, and I was just being stubborn for the sake of privacy that I didn't really need.

"The hospital in Denver where she had her surgery is out of network. That means that anything done there, every time she sees Dr. Hughes there, or has surgery, or a treatment there, it's not covered by my plan."

"Is this? What's happening now?"

"Yeah, this is fine. But the MIBG wouldn't be. Or the stem cell transplant Dr. Hughes has already suggested."

"So what are the options?"

"Financially?"

He nodded.

"I don't qualify for government care, not with owning Solitude. I went through my savings the first month of her treatment, and her surgery wiped out the last of Ryan's life insurance. I mortgaged Solitude to the hilt last year for the renovations, so that's not an option, either. Even selling the property right now would barely cover paying off the mortgage. So that leaves me with becoming a super-stealthy bank robber or stripping online for singlecancermoms.com."

"That's not funny."

"I'm not laughing." A moment of silence passed between us as he digested what I'd said. He chewed slowly, like it was my words he was working over. "Look, I'm not the only one this happens to. Insurance companies deny treatments all the time. Or they tell you to go with the less expensive options they'll cover. Generic drugs, different hospitals, alternative treatments, that kind of thing. There are payment plans and grants for those who can qualify, and some trials will cover drug costs."

"Is there an alternative for the MIBG?"

"No."

"And if she doesn't get it?"

My fork hit the plate, and I slowly brought my eyes to his. "And if she doesn't respond to these drugs?"

The muscle in his jaw flexed as his eyes turned hard. This wasn't the guy who tenderly tied cleats or held my daughter—held *me*. This was the guy who killed people for a living. "You're telling me that Maisie's life isn't just in the hands of her doctors…but her insurance company? They decide if she lives or dies?"

"In not so many words. They don't decide if she can have the treatment, just if they'll pay for it. The rest, that's on me. I'm the one who has to look at her doctors and say whether I can afford the price tag on my daughter's life."

Horror flashed across his face, this guy who had seen and done things that would probably give me nightmares.

"Pretty screwed up, right?" I asked with a mocking smile.

"How much is it?"

"What part? The twenty-thousand-dollar chemo treatments that she gets once a month? The hundred-thousand-dollar surgery? The medication? The travel?"

He blew out a breath, dropping his hands to his lap. "The MIBG."

"Probably fifty K, give or take an arm and a leg. But it's Maisie's life. What am I supposed to say? No? Please don't save my kid?"

"Of course not."

"Exactly. So I'll figure something out. She'll probably need two rounds of the MIBG, and then the stem cell transplant averages about a half mil."

He paled. "A half million dollars?"

"Yep. Cancer is business, and business is good."

He pushed away his plate. "I think I've lost my appetite."

"And you wonder why I'm losing weight," I joked.

He didn't laugh. In fact, he didn't give me more than a one-word answer as we made our way back upstairs. I almost felt guilty for unloading on him, but it felt good in a weird way to share all of that, to acknowledge that so much of this wasn't fair.

He sat by me through the night, never once complaining about the chairs or the monitors. He watched every level like a hawk, flipped through the MIBG brochure, paced the hall outside. He FaceTimed Colt and Havoc, brought more coffee, and read through Maisie's binder, which at this point was more personal to me than a diary. He pulled his chair as close to mine as possible, and when I fell asleep around midnight, it was on his shoulder.

Beckett was everything I'd desperately needed these last seven months. What was I going to do when he inevitably left? Now that I knew what it was like to have someone like him in times like this, it would be a thousand times harder in his absence.

I woke with a start to find Beckett standing at Maisie's bedside. He looked at me with a huge grin as the doctor walked in.

Stumbling to my feet, I rubbed the sleep out of my eyes and gasped. Maisie was sitting up, her smile wide, her eyes clear.

"Hi, Mom!"

Blinking quickly, I looked at the monitors before responding. Her pressure was back up, her temp was down, her oxygen levels up. My hand flew to cover my mouth as my knees buckled, but Beckett caught me by the waist, pulling me to his side without missing a beat.

"Hiya, Maisie-girl. How are you feeling?"

"So much better," she answered.

My mouth trembled as I looked back at the doctor, who was flipping through the chart, listening to the report of another doctor. It was seven fifteen in the morning. The night shift had changed to day while I was asleep.

"Well?" I asked.

"Looks like the drugs are working. She's going to be just fine."

I turned my face into Beckett's chest before I lost it in front of Maisie. He wrapped his arms around me as I took deep, gulping breaths filled with his scent. I was literally expelling my fear and breathing him in.

"Did you hear that, Maisie? Looks like you're not getting out of tutoring next week," Beckett joked, his voice a gravelly, deep rumble against my ear.

He'd driven us here, taken care of me, of Maisie, of Colt. Uprooted his entire life to move in next door. He'd been steadfast every time I'd sworn I didn't need him and there the moment I did without any hint of I-told-you-so.

I took one last breath and turned back to the doctor, who gave me the satisfied nod of a job well done.

"We'll keep her here in the ICU another day, just to make sure, and then move her to pediatrics another few days for monitoring. Better safe than sorry."

"Thank you." There weren't any other words to say.

"You've got a little fighter there," the doctor said before heading out, leaving the three of us alone.

"I don't have Colt," Maisie said quietly, looking around her bed.

It took me a second to realize what she was saying. "I'm sorry, we left so fast that I didn't think to grab him." The bear was most likely sitting on Colt's bed, the lone pink spot in a sea of blue.

"Don't you worry, we'll have your mom grab him when she runs home tomorrow for a little bit. Sound good?" Beckett offered.

"What? Me run home?" Hell no, I wasn't leaving my daughter.

"Yep," he said with a nod. "If you leave by ten, you can get home, shower the hospital off you, and get to Colt's graduation by two."

Colt's kindergarten graduation. My mouth dropped, and my gaze flickered from Beckett to Maisie. How could I leave her here? How could I miss Colt's graduation? Sure it was a little silly, but I knew how important it was to him. How could I leave her here when she was supposed to be walking across the stage with him? How was any of this fair?

Beckett cupped my cheeks, stopping the ping-pong battle with my concentration. "Ella. She's stable. She'll be out of the ICU. I am more than capable of hanging out with her for a few hours. You need to be there for Colt. Let me do this. Stop splitting yourself in two, and let me help. Please."

"Yeah, Mom. You have to go. I don't want Colt to be sad," Maisie added.

"I don't have a way to get back."

"You take my truck."

Wait. What? Trucks were sacred to guys. He might as well be offering his soul on a platter. "Your truck."

"You do have a driver's license, right?" he joked.

"Well, yeah."

"Then it's settled. You'll grab Pink Colt when you go home tomorrow. In the meantime, Maisie and I will watch movies and hang out. What do you say, Maisie-girl?" He looked back at my daughter.

"Yes!"

"You're sure?" I asked.

"Absolutely." He took my hands and held them to his chest. "I swear."

The sweetest feeling unfurled in my chest, only to plant deep in my belly. It stretched through my body until I swore my fingertips tingled.

"Take lots of pictures, okay?"

"Okay," I replied, focused on the overwhelming emotion consuming me.

It had to be infatuation, right? Who wouldn't crush on this man a little? That's all it was, because there was no way in the world I was falling for Beckett.

Absolutely none.

He turned and high-fived Maisie, that little strip of white on his wrist screaming louder than my brain could deny. Because while my head had been panicked Saturday night, focused on forms and doctors and transfers, my heart had declared that this man was trusted. My heart had signed that paper while my head was consumed with other matters. This man was in my life, and in a way, mine. And Colt's. And most definitely Maisie's.

After all, that bracelet had her name written on it.

Oh God. I was in love with him.

CHAPTER FOURTEEN

Beckett

Letter #20

Chaos,

I feel like all I write to you about lately is Maisie's diagnosis. Honestly, sometimes I feel like that's all I think about. I've become one of those people with a one-track mind, and everything revolves around her.

So let's try to snap out of that for a few minutes. Christmas is coming. It's one of our busiest times of the year for guests, and as usual, we're booked solid through the first week in January, which is great for business and referrals.

I moved the kids to the last cabin we had available and took it off the books. It's the best way to keep Maisie safe when her levels bottom out, and so far it's working. And there I go again, back to the cancer.

We put up a tree in the cabin, and Hailey, my receptionist, moved in with us to help at night when I have to run out. I'm beginning to think the kids like the privacy better, too. Colt even asked for a tree house out back for Christmas, but I told him he'd have to wait for my brother to get home. I'm pretty handy, but a tree-house maker, I am not. It would probably bust apart before he stepped foot in it. I'm also wondering if it's a good idea to build him a tree house when we'll hopefully be back in the main house soon-ish. Soon. Whenever. Truth is, everything feels like soon lately.

*How are you guys holding up with the
holidays? Do you need anything? I had Maisie
and Colt send you a few pictures. They were
worried that you didn't have a Christmas tree, so
they drew a few for you and helped me bake this
weekend.*

*It's hard to believe it's already December and
that you guys are coming home soon. I can't
wait to finally see the person I've been talking to
all this time and show you around. Don't freak
out, but it's definitely what I'm looking forward
to most in the new year.*

~ Ella

Problem solving was a skill I was particularly proud of.
There wasn't an issue I couldn't fix, a puzzle I couldn't
piece together. I was good at making the impossible a
reality. But this felt like beating my head against a brick
wall just to see how it felt.

I flipped through the MIBG information for the
hundredth time and cross-referenced what I'd found on
my phone. *What I wouldn't give for my laptop.*

It was ridiculous that Ella's insurance didn't cover
the therapy, but mine would. Then again, if there was
one thing the military got right, it was health insurance,
which I still had since I'd gotten sidetracked and hadn't
signed Donahue's declination papers yet.

"I wouldn't have left the tower," Maisie said from
her bed, sitting up and bouncing slightly on the mattress.
We'd been out of the ICU since this morning, right
before Ella left for Telluride.

I glanced over at the movie—*Tangled*. Rapunzel.
Got it. "You would if your mom was an evil witch."

"But she's not, so I would have stayed." She tugged
her cap down farther over her forehead.

"But look at that big wide world. Are you saying you really don't want to see what's out there?" I set everything down on the table.

She shrugged, twisting her mouth to the side and scrunching her nose.

"There's a lot out there." I pushed off the floor, rolling in the chair over to the side of Maisie's bed.

"Maybe. Doesn't mean I get to see it."

There was no whine in her voice, just simple, accepted fact. It dawned on me how young she was, how much of her life she remembered, and how much of it had already been spent fighting. This had been a hellish seven months for Ella, but it must have seemed an eternity to Maisie.

"You will," I told her.

She glanced my way a few times before finally turning her head and meeting my eyes.

"You will," I repeated. "Not just the whole school part, either. That's just the beginning."

"I can't even graduate kindergarten," she whispered. "Please don't tell Mom I'm sad. She's already sad enough."

It was like talking to a mini-Ella, already concerned about everyone else but herself. Even their eyes were the same, except Maisie hadn't learned how to guard her thoughts yet.

"I have an idea," I said.

Forty minutes, another hospital gown, and a quick run to the nurses' station, and we were nearly ready.

"Ready?" she called from the bathroom.

"Almost," I tried to say, my mouth holding the tape dispenser as I wrapped the string around the frayed edge of a strip of my undershirt.

I ran the string up to the top of the hat and then taped it. Arts and crafts were not my strong suit, but this would do. I knocked on the bathroom door, and it opened far enough for Maisie to stick a hand out.

"Your highness," I said, handing her my creation. Thank you, God, for nurses and pediatric craft stations.

Maisie giggled and took it, shutting the door in my face. Man, she'd bounced back so quickly. The antibiotics were still pumping through her IV line, and she was still hospital-bound, but it was night and day from the day of the soccer game.

I kicked myself for the hundredth time for not noticing while I'd carried her to and from the car. There had been no fever then, no redness, nothing, but I'd known she was off, that she was overtired.

"Are you ready?" she asked.

I checked my watch. They would be walking across their little stage any minute now. "I am if you are."

"Give a speech," she ordered with the door between us.

"You know normally you wouldn't be in hiding, right?"

"You're not supposed to see me until you call my name."

"That's for a wedding," I told her, trying not to laugh. "The bride and groom aren't supposed to see each other until they meet at the altar. Not this."

The door opened, and I caught it so she could walk through, bringing her IV pole with her. She stepped around the door, and my smile flew so wide I thought it might split my face.

She wore a solid-colored hospital gown over her normal one, courtesy of the nursing staff, and on her head was my god-awful graduation cap. Those suckers were awkward to make. Her tassel, streaming from the side, was thick on the fringe, but I'd been under a little pressure. Not my finest work, but it would do.

"Please be seated," I ordered, moving to stand at the far side of the room at the foot of her bed.

Head held high, she walked over and took a seat at the table.

Motion from the door drew my eye, but when I saw it was just the two nurses who had helped me hunt for supplies, I threw them a quick smile and turned back to my one-girl audience.

"Speech," she reminded me with a serious nod.

"Right." I quickly grabbed the rolled-up paper that served as her makeshift diploma that I'd scribbled on. "Today is the start of your journey." What the hell was I supposed to say next? People weren't my strong suit, let alone kids.

She tilted her head, nearly losing the hat, and quickly righted it. "Go on."

"Okay." An idea popped into my head, and I ran with it. "I've heard it said that the greatest adventure is what lies ahead. Well, I read it, but we're going to use it."

Maisie stifled a giggle and then nodded in all seriousness. "Go on."

"And the story I read was about a fierce princess who wanted to fight for her kingdom. When all the men were called to war, she was told that as the princess, she had to stay behind and care for her people. She argued with the king that she could care for her people by fighting for them, but he ordered her to stay behind—to stay safe."

"He wanted her to stay in her tower," she said, leaning forward.

"Hey, at graduations, the graduates don't interact with the speakers," I teased her.

She grinned but sat back in her chair and made the motion like she was zipping her lips.

"Now where was I? Ah, the princess. Right. So the princess, being as smart as she was, knew she was needed. So she dressed like a man and snuck into the army camp, riding out to battle with the men."

Maisie's eyes lit up, and her mouth dropped open slightly. "What happened?"

"What do you think? She ran into battle in full armor, swinging her giant sword, and she struck down the Naz…uh…dragon, slaying it in one mighty swipe and defending her kingdom. She was the leader her people needed, because she was brave enough to fight."

Maisie nodded enthusiastically, and I almost forgot I was supposed to be giving a graduation speech…for a six-year-old.

"Right. So, as you embark on this journey of your education, you must remember to be brave like the princess."

"And tell all the kings they're wrong!" She jumped up.

Oh, this was not going the way I'd intended.

"Kind of. When you're…you know, big enough to swing a sword."

She seemed to ponder this for a second and then nodded with all seriousness.

"So," I continued. "You have to fight for what you know to be right. Stand up for the people who need your protection. Never let anyone tell you that you're anything less than a warrior because you're a girl. Because in my experience, girls are the strongest warriors. Maybe that's why all the boys try to keep them out of battle. They're scared they'll get shown up."

"Makes sense," Maisie agreed. "Is that it?"

"It is. Speech over." I tried to recall any graduation I'd ever had and failed, because I'd never had one. I'd shipped out for basic the moment I finished my senior year, the day before graduation. But I'd seen plenty in movies. I cleared my throat. "The time has come for you to leave the childish, carefree days of kindergarten and embark on your journey in elementary school. When I call your name, please rise and accept your diploma."

"Beckett, you know I'm the only one here, right?"

I shushed her. "I haven't said your name yet, graduate."

She gave me the same look Ella did when she was ready to call me on my crap, and I pressed my lips together to keep from laughing.

"Margaret Ruth MacKenzie."

She stood, regal as that princess, and walked toward me with her head held high, bringing her IV pole with her. When she arrived in front of me, I crouched down to her eye level. "Congratulations on your graduation." I handed her the diploma with one hand and shook her hand with the other.

"Now what?" she whispered.

"Now you flip your tassel to the other side."

She did the mouth and nose scrunch thing again and moved her tassel to the opposite side.

"I now pronounce you graduated," I said in the most official tone I could muster.

She grinned and laughed, pure joy radiating from her like sunshine. Then she launched herself into my arms as the nurses in the doorway began to clap.

I held her, careful not to squeeze too tight, but she didn't have that same issue, and hugged me to the point of near strangulation. Man, I loved this kid. Loved her strength, her tenacity, her kindness. She was one of a kind, and I hope she knew how precious she was, not just to her mom, but to the world.

As the clapping subsided, I glanced over to see no less than half a dozen nurses watching Maisie's graduation. The girl was magnetic—she drew people to her everywhere she went, and I was no different.

"How about a picture?" a nurse who looked to be about Ella's age asked.

"Yes! Absolutely!" I handed my cell phone to her, and she snapped a few of Maisie and me. "Thank you.

Now just the graduate," I said to Maisie, turning the camera on her as she struck a pose.

"It was Aowyn," the nurse said with a smile while the other nurses congratulated the graduate. "The princess who slayed the Nazgul. It was Aowyn."

Busted. "Tolkien fan?"

"Movie fan. Kind of comes with the territory when you work in pediatrics."

"Think she noticed?"

She shrugged. "It was a good speech. Little girls need more warrior queens."

"I like warrior queens," Maisie said, coming to stand next to me. "Is it time for *Moana*?" As quickly as her joy came on, she sagged a little against me, and I felt the tiredness take over.

"That sounds like a plan to me." Putting my forearm under her, I stood, lifting her slight weight, and carried her back to bed, her IV in my other hand.

She scooted back, sitting upright, and took off her cap as the nurses left. "Thank you," she said, playing with the tassel.

"I know it's not the same—"

"It's better." She met me with a look that left no room for argument.

I sat on the edge of her bed, adjusting her IV pole so it was closer to her.

"It's just the start, Maisie. You have so much ahead of you. The summers, the mountains, the sunrises. The choices you'll get to make when you decide which college you want to go to, the second you take off on a trip to backpack across Europe. Those are the moments when you find out who you'll be, and that's just a glimpse of what's waiting for you when you're past this."

"But what if this is all there is?" she whispered.

"It's not," I promised.

Her face twisted, her lips pursing, and tears welled in

her eyes. "Am I dying? Is that what's happening to me? Mom won't tell me. Please tell me, Beckett."

A vise gripped my heart, squeezing until I was sure it couldn't beat.

"Maisie…"

"Please. Am I going to die?"

I thought of the MIBG therapy she needed, the countless drugs, treatments, operations, transplants. Everything that was standing between her and a disease-free body.

"Not on my watch." I didn't care what I had to do. I'd find a way for her to get what she needed. I wasn't watching another kid die if I had the power to change her fate.

"Okay." She relaxed against the raised bed and took my word like it was gospel. Then she grinned as she played with the strands of her tassel. "I'm glad you're here."

Before I lost my shit in front of her, I leaned forward, pressing my lips to her forehead in a quick kiss. When I pulled away, I forced a smile and blinked back the awkward wetness in my eyes.

"Me, too, Maisie. Me, too."

"Gentry, I'm glad you're here." Mark Gutierrez met me as I parked the truck at the trailhead. He was in his early thirties, fit, with a full head of black hair and enough confidence to make him a good unit leader for our search and rescue operation, but he wasn't arrogant.

I was good with confidence, but arrogance was a deal breaker. Arrogance got men killed…kids, too.

Havoc jumped to the ground behind me, already wearing her work vest. That had always signaled her that play time was over, and I was relieved that our time in Telluride hadn't changed that. Between the trips to

Denver and the days I'd spent in Montrose with Maisie, I'd worried that she'd fall out of rhythm. I'd gone back to Montrose and brought Ella and Maisie home yesterday after being there for a week, and when the call came in this afternoon, Havoc had jumped right back into action.

"Hey, Havoc," Gutierrez said, moving toward her.

"Nope. She's in work mode." I cut off his access. She was on alert and sensitive at the moment, and I really didn't need to file an accident report that he'd lost a finger.

"Right. Sorry, we've never had a retired MWD."

"No problem. Bring me up to speed." Havoc stayed close to my side as we moved closer to the group of men. Half were in the Telluride uniform and others in the San Miguel County. "Why are we here if the county boys are, too?"

"They've been looking for hours, and the missing hiker is a VIP up at one of the resorts, so we got called in to add some manpower."

"Gotcha." The circle parted as Gutierrez and I joined in. Havoc was given a wide berth as she sat at my command.

The guy in the center, who was obviously in charge by the bullhorn hooked at his belt, shot us a glare as a greeting.

"As I was saying for you latecomers, Mrs. Dupreveny went out with her hiking guide this morning with her two daughters, ages seven and twelve."

Not a kid. Please don't be a kid. I refused to be responsible for the death of another child.

"When she fell, we believe breaking her leg, she sent the guide back with her daughters to call for help. Apparently they were surprised at the lack of service up on the Highline, so we can all assume the guide isn't a local."

A snort of exasperation went through the group. I sighed in relief that it was an adult out there alone.

"Guide returned at noon and called the county. We deployed search and rescue shortly thereafter with no luck. Rain was definitely not our friend."

I looked up at the sky. The clouds were still gray but no longer the water-heavy version known for the quick-tempered thunderstorms around here. We should be in the clear to work for a while.

"As you can tell, the rain has ceased, and we need to find her. Quickly. We've got about four hours left of good sunlight. According to the guide, he left her about an hour in and marked the trail with her bandana, which is pink. We found the bandana, and it's still there, but there's no Mrs. Dupreveny. Plan is to hike in as a group, then zone out search coordinates and get this woman back to her husband."

A hand went up from one of the Telluride guys. Capshaw, if I remembered correctly. I really needed to spend more time with the other guys when I went in, not just training Havoc.

"Capshaw?"

At least I got that one right.

"Who is taking point on this?"

A mumble went through the group, and I saw it for what it was, two rival organizations working together, and hoped it wouldn't get in the way. Egos usually blew an op. I scanned the group, seeing another dog and handler on the opposite side in a county uniform. A yellow Lab who was changing his position from sitting to standing every minute or so. Restless.

Not my business.

"County is taking point. Telluride is here as support."

Another mumble.

"If you guys are done determining pecking order, can we get started?" I asked, impatience getting to me.

The guy's eyes narrowed in my direction and then Havoc's. "You're the new guy, right? The soldier? And the dog?"

Heads swung in my direction. "That's us. Now if we're done wasting daylight?"

He made the be-my-guest gesture toward the trailhead, and we took off. I tightened my small pack on my back and zipped the lightweight fleece across my chest. It was already cool and only going to get colder.

"Damn, gotta step on toes on day one?" Gutierrez asked, walking next to me.

"No point talking when the mission is pretty clear."

"Point taken."

We handed out radio frequencies as a group and hiked along the trail, crossing a bridge and earning a view of Telluride. It really was spectacular here, with the mountains rising on both sides of us, reaching toward the sky.

Ahead about twenty yards, the other dog sprinted through the meadow that ran alongside of us. Havoc stayed right by my side, her footsteps and breathing steady.

"So I saw you downtown with Ella MacKenzie," Gutierrez said, breaking the silence I'd been enjoying.

"Probably." I liked Mark well enough while we were on duty and occasionally made an effort with him on the conversation front, but Ella wasn't on my list of approved topics.

"Something going on there?" he asked in a locker-room-talk kind of way.

"Be careful," I warned.

"Hey, I know Ella. She's a good girl—woman. I used to be friends with her brother. He died. You know that, right? About six months ago."

My heart stuttered in a beat that had nothing to do with the altitude. "Yeah, I know."

"She's got kids, too. Good kids."

"Yep." What was this guy getting at?

He sighed, curving the bill on his cap in a nervous tell. This guy would be easy pickings at a poker table.

"Look, I'm not trying to be nosy."

"Sure you are. Question is: Why?"

He looked behind us, seeing what I already knew. There were about twenty feet between us and the nearest crew members. Enough distance to talk in private. "I'm just trying to look out for her."

"Good to know." There wasn't a soul on the planet who cared more about Ella than I did, and while it was almost cute—his concern—it was absolutely unnecessary.

"I'm serious. She's got a shit-ton going on, and if there was a short end of the stick to be had, Ella was given it. Between losing her parents and Jeff walking out—"

"You know Jeff?" My footsteps would have faltered if my body hadn't been on autopilot, used to pushing on when my mind went elsewhere.

"Knew Jeff," he corrected. "I hung out with his older brother, Blake."

"One preppy name after another," I muttered.

Gutierrez laughed. "That's so true. They both are— preppy assholes, that is. Trust-fund babies who never had to struggle a day in their lives. Both had their fortunes handed to them, and now their jobs."

A stab of pure hatred coursed through me like an acidic poison burning in my veins. Of course he had everything easy while Ella worked her ass off.

"So you know where he is?"

"Sure. He's working for his daddy's company in Denver. Engaged to the daughter of a politician, if his Facebook is true."

I stored the information away, feeding the plan that had been forming since I'd promised Maisie that she wasn't going to die.

"Anyway, you and Ella serious?" He looked at me

sideways, and I glanced at his hand. Nice wide gold band. Good. I wasn't in the mood to fight off some guy for Ella. Not when I couldn't trust myself not to beat the shit out of him.

"We're friends," I said in that noncommittal way. "I'm just helping her out."

He seemed to ponder that for a minute and then nodded. "Good. That's good. She needs all the help she can get right now with her kids."

"No," I corrected, my eyes scanning the forest line just in case we found our hiker. "She doesn't need help; she's honestly got it handled all on her own. But I need to help her. I don't want her to have to handle it solo. There's a difference."

Gutierrez nodded again, like a bobblehead, but sincere. Maybe I'd spent too much time around soldiers. Maybe civilians chatted about their feelings on hikes in the mountains. Maybe I was the odd one for being so closed off, not him for being so inquisitive.

"Sorry, man. It's just…it's a small town, and you're new. And after losing Ryan, I know she's hurting. I mean, they wouldn't even tell her what happened."

Of course they didn't. Because when ops went wrong, when soldiers were knocked unconscious instead of killed, then hauled out by insurgents into the desert, stripped of their uniforms, bound, gagged, tortured, and shot in the back of their heads while wearing nothing but their boxers, the military tended to hide it from their families and call it classified.

No one wanted to think of that happening to their brother.

"I mean, they wouldn't even let her see his body. That's got to mess with her. For all she knows, he could still be alive somewhere, and the military is covering it up to turn him into Jason Bourne or something. It's messed up."

The muscles in my jaw flexed as I clenched my teeth to keep my mouth shut. This guy didn't know anything, not what happened to Ryan, not that he was my best friend. He was just trying to watch out for Ella, to make sure I had a good, clear picture of what she'd been through. At least that's what I kept telling myself as we approached the search location.

The path was lined with aspens, which cut our field of vision to a minimum, but there it was, tied to the stump—a pink bandana. We gathered in another circle as bullhorn guy took center stage.

It was time to go to work.

"That's quite a dog you have there," Gutierrez told me about an hour later, when our hiker had been airlifted out and we were headed back down the trail.

"She's one of a kind," I agreed.

He then let me walk the rest of the way in silence, for which I was grateful. It had taken me months to let Ryan in, and years to become his best friend. Ella was the only person I'd ever had an instant connection with, and I smiled when I realized Maisie and Colt were on that list now, too.

We made it down to the trail base, and I opened the truck door for Havoc to jump in. She settled in the passenger seat, happy and a little tired.

"You did great today," Gutierrez said as he stripped off his own pack, loading it into the car parked next to mine.

"Thanks. It felt good to be useful."

"Yeah, I get that." He took off his hat and rubbed his head. "Look, about the stuff I said about Ella—"

"Don't. It's okay." My grip tightened on my doorframe.

"Small town," he said with a weak shrug.

It really was. Maybe not the village with the ski

resorts, but the old town. Especially when the tourists weren't around and it was mostly locals. They were all connected here, and I might not understand it, but I could do my best to respect it.

"Ryan hasn't been dead six months."

Gutierrez's head snapped up.

"He's been dead for five months and seven days, give or take a few hours. A few very *long* hours. I know, because he was my best friend. I served with him for the better part of a decade."

"Oh man, I'm so sorry." His whole posture slumped.

"Don't be. Never be sorry for looking out for Ella. I told you only so you'd know that there's nothing I wouldn't do to keep her safe, to take care of her and the kids. Nothing. They're the whole reason I'm here."

He swallowed and finally looked at me, taking a deep breath. "Okay. Thank you for telling me. If you need anything, or if she does, just let me know, or ask for my wife, Tess. Ella won't ever ask."

"Yeah, she's pretty stubborn like that."

A ghost of a smile crossed his face. "Something tells me you are, too."

"Guilty."

I drove home with a tired body, a content dog, and a mind that wouldn't quit running circles. I'd meant what I'd said: there wasn't anything I wouldn't do to keep Ella and the kids safe.

Or was there?

I hit the brakes as I passed Ella's cabin.

Her insurance wouldn't pay for the treatments that could save Maisie's life.

But I'd read over every scrap of information online about that hospital, and my insurance *would*.

I threw the truck into reverse and then turned down Ella's drive. I was out of the truck before the engine died, taking her steps two at a time and pounding on her door before my brain kicked in with every reason she'd say no, knowing I'd have to convince her to say yes.

"Beckett?" Ella asked as she opened the front door. She was in jeans and a long-sleeve tee, her hair in a thick side braid that made me want to grab ahold of it while I kissed her. "Everything okay?"

"Yeah. Sorry for the drop-by. Do you have a second?"

"Sure, come on in."

"Not where the kids can hear," I said softly, tucking my thumbs into my pockets.

Her eyebrows raised in surprise, but she stepped out onto the porch, shutting the door behind her. "Okay, what's up?"

"Your insurance won't pay for the MIBG therapy, or the hospital she needs, or the stem cell transplant."

"That's right." She folded her arms under her breasts and looked up at me, those blue eyes inquisitive but trusting.

"She has to have it, right? Or she'll die?"

"Beckett, what is this about?"

"Will she die without it?" I repeated, my words a little sharper than I'd ever used with Ella.

"Yes," she whispered.

I nodded to myself, turning around and pacing the length of the porch while Ella followed.

"Beckett!" she snapped.

I turned around and took a deep breath to steady my nerves. "Your insurance won't pay for it—"

"Right, we already covered that."

"But mine *will*."

"Okay?" She blinked at me, her forehead puckering.

"Ella, marry me."

CHAPTER FIFTEEN

Ella

Letter #15

Ella,

We lost someone today.

You'd think I'd be used to it after all this time, even callous toward it. A few years ago I was. I have no idea what's changed lately, but now it feels like every loss is exponentially harder than the last.

Or maybe they're the same, but I'm different. More angry.

It's hard to describe, but I'm somehow more aware now of my disconnection, my inability to forge emotional bonds outside of a few close friends. That small list includes you.

How can I be so connected to someone I've never laid eyes on, yet not the majority of the guys around me? Is it that you're safer through paper because you're not standing in front of me? Less of a threat, maybe?

I wish I knew.

I wish I had the words for this guy's wife, his kids. I wish I could take it away for them, take his place. Why does the world take the people who are loved, ripping holes in the fabric of other people's souls, while I'm allowed to skate by unscathed? Where is the justice in such a random system, and if there's no justice, then why are we here?

I feel that same restless urge taking over again, to accomplish the mission and move on.

Check the box, pull up the stakes, and know we made a difference.

I'm just not sure what that difference is anymore.

Tell me something real. Tell me what it feels like to live in the same place your whole life. Is it stifling to have such deep roots? Or does it let you sway instead of break when the winds come? I've gone with the wind for so long that I honestly can't imagine it.

Thank you for letting me unload on you. I promise I won't be such a downer next time.

~ Chaos

"I'm sorry?" I asked, staring at Beckett like he had two heads.

"What did you just say?" There was no way he'd said what I heard.

"Marry me."

Or maybe he did say it.

"Have you lost your mind?"

"Maybe." He leaned back against the porch railing but didn't cross his arms in front of his chest like he did when his stubborn switch was triggered. Instead he grasped either side of the railing, leaving his torso unprotected. Vulnerable. "But it would work. On paper, at least."

"I don't... I can't... I'm speechless."

"Good, that will give me a chance to convince you."

Oh my God, he was serious.

"If you marry me, the kids are my dependents. I can take care of them."

"You want to marry me to take care of my kids." I said it slowly, certain I had somehow heard it wrong.

"Yes."

My mouth opened and closed a few times as I tried to get a word—any word—past my lips. I just couldn't think of any.

"What do you think?"

"We're not even dating! And you...you want to get married?"

Havoc came trotting up to the porch, but she didn't go to Beckett. She sat next to me, like she'd sensed her handler had lost his fool mind.

"Not in the romantic sense!" He raked a hand over his face. "I suck at explaining this."

"Try. Harder."

"Okay. I was reading the MIBG papers in the hospital with Maisie, and I remembered what you'd said about your insurance not covering it. So I looked through the hospital website, and they take my insurance, and not at your coinsurance rate. The whole thing is covered."

"Good for you. Now you can get treated for cancer." How the hell could he just suggest that we get married?

"I'm not done explaining."

I wanted to throw him back in his truck and off my property, but there was the tiniest spark in me that lit up at the thought that Maisie could get the treatment she needed. And that little spark was hope. Man, I hated hope.

Hope fooled you, gave you the warm fuzzy feelings just to yank them away again.

And right now, Beckett was a big slice of warm, fuzzy hope, and I hated him for it.

Taking my silence for acquiescence, Beckett continued.

"If you marry me, the kids are covered. All of Maisie's treatments are paid for. No more fighting with the insurance people. No more generics. She will get the best possible treatments."

"You want me to marry you, to become your *wife*,

sleep in your bed—when you won't so much as kiss me—all for insurance? Like I'm some kind of pros—"

"Whoa!" He interrupted me, waving his hands. "We wouldn't have to actually…you know." His eyebrows rose at least an inch.

"No, I don't *know.*" I crossed my arms over my chest, knowing damn well what he meant. If he had the balls to suggest marriage, he could certainly lay out the terms.

He sighed in exasperation. "We'd only have to be married in the legal sense. On paper. We could live separately and everything. Keep your name, whatever. It would just be to cover the kids."

Oh my God, the man I loved was really standing in front of me, proposing marriage, not because he loved me back but because he thought it would save my daughter. Now I loved him even more, and hated both of us for it.

"Only in the legal sense? So you don't actually want me? You only want to protect my kids?" Great, now I sounded pissed that he didn't want me in his bed. *If my emotions could just pick a side, that would be great.*

"I thought we covered this already. I want you. That just doesn't play into me asking you to marry me."

"Can you actually hear yourself? You want me, but you don't want to marry me. But you're *willing* to marry me to cover the kids for insurance, as long as we don't actually live like we're married." All of the legal entanglement, none of the love, or the commitment, or the sex.

Which left us with the only aspect of marriage I was really familiar with: the part where the husband walked away.

"Exactly."

"Okay, this conversation is over." I turned, and then spun right back around to face him. "You know what? It's not. Marriage means something to me, Beckett! Or at least it used to. Maybe it's not the same for you, or you think because of the way I let Jeff divorce me that I think it's just a piece of paper, but it's not. It's supposed to be a lifetime of love, and commitment, and loyalty. It's supposed to be all those vows about sickness and health, and better and worse, and loving someone even on the days you don't like them. It's not, hey, let's sign this piece of paper and join up while it's convenient. It's supposed to be about building a life with the one person on earth who is meant to be yours. It's…it's not meant to be temporary. It's supposed to be *forever.*"

He stepped toward me and then stopped himself, tucking his thumbs in his pockets.

"It's about love, Beckett."

"And I love your kids. No *supposed to be* about it."

The intensity in his voice, his eyes, hit me smack in the heart. "They love you, too," I admitted. *So do I.* Which was why I couldn't agree to this. It would destroy them when it ended. Signing myself up for the hurt was one thing, but my kids? That was where I drew the line.

His whole posture softened, like my words had taken some of the fight out of him.

"I don't want to do anything that would jeopardize them, or you. I'm just saying that if they were mine, legally, or half mine, Maisie could get the treatment she needs. This could save her life."

That spark of hope flared, shining too much light on everything the kids and I had been through. All the sleepless nights. All the medical bills that piled up on my desk, threatening to bankrupt us. The overwhelming knowledge that if she didn't have the MIBG treatment, she most likely wouldn't live.

But what happened to her once Beckett was done playing house?

"I don't know you nearly well enough for this—not in the ways that matter."

His eyes flared with pain, and those defenses went back up. "You know me well enough to have given me decision-making rights for Maisie, right?"

"That was for a few hours so I could go to Colt's graduation, and only for the worst-case scenario!"

"Reality check, Ella. Your entire life right now is a worst-case scenario."

Ouch.

"Yeah, well you said it yourself: you've never been in a relationship that lasted more than a month. You weren't even willing to kiss me because you said you'd screw it up and that would hurt Colt and Maisie."

The anger vanished from his face instantly and was replaced with an overwhelming sadness. "You don't trust me."

My heart wanted to. My heart screamed that he would do anything for the kids. My head, on the other hand, wasn't backing down from his own declaration that it wouldn't last.

"I thought I knew Jeff. I loved him. I gave him everything, and the minute that everything turned into the twins, he walked. I never dated again. Not once. I swore that I'd never put my kids in a position to let someone walk out on them again."

"I would never walk away from them, or you. I will always show up, Ella."

"Don't you dare lie to me. The men in my life have a habit of promising with one hand and packing with the other."

"It wasn't a lie the first time I said it, and nothing's changed. It's a vow."

"That was for soccer! Not marriage! You can't stand there and promise me always when two weeks ago you weren't even open to the possibility of a relationship."

"It's just on paper, Ella!"

"It's not! The way you're proposing that I depend on

you—that my kids depend on you—is not on paper. That's very real. What if you walk away while she's mid-treatment? They'd stop it! How is that any better than me struggling right now to find the money? If anything it would be more damaging, because at least I know what I'm up against right now. Do you know what a long haul this is? Even if she beats it, the relapse rate… You don't understand the long-term implications of what you're offering, as well-intentioned as it may be." And it was; it was the most heartfelt, genuine offer I'd ever received. But life had taught me long ago that intentions were worth nothing.

"All I can give you is my word, and the promise that no matter what happens to me, they'd be covered. Maisie would live."

"You don't know that, either." My biggest fear slipped out as if it were nothing, but I should be used to it by now with this man. He had a way of stripping away my defenses, leaving me open to the elements. But I didn't know how to trust the appearance of sunshine after living in a perpetual hurricane. Not when there was the overwhelming possibility that he was simply the eye of the storm.

"I don't," he admitted. "But when she asked if she was going to die, I promised her that it wasn't going to happen on my watch, and this is the only way I can think of to keep that promise."

Ice ran through my veins, chilling me from the heart outward.

"My daughter asked you if she's going to die?"

"Yeah, when we were in Montrose—"

"And you're just now telling me this?" I stalked forward until I was only a breath away from him, glaring up at his stupid, perfect face.

"Yeah, I guess."

"And you promised her that she wasn't going to die?"

"What else would you have wanted me to say, Ella? That she has a 10 percent chance of living until November? That's only five months from now!" He had the nerve to look like I was the one who was nuts.

"I'm well aware!" My voice pitched breakingly high. "You don't think I keep a mental countdown in my head? That I'm not excruciatingly aware of every day with her? How dare you tell her that she won't die. You have no right to make that kind of promise to her."

"To her, or to you?" he asked softly. "She's a child who needs to be reassured, told how strong she is, that this fight is far from over, and yes, I realize how long this will take. I'm not about to tell her she's a few months away from defeat."

"You shouldn't have made that promise," I reiterated. "I don't lie to my kids, and you can't, either. This war she's fighting is overwhelming. It's David versus Goliath."

"Right, and you've armed her with a slingshot and sent her against the giant. I'm telling you that I have a damn tank, and you won't use it! Are you really going to watch her die because you won't gamble that I'm a decent guy? What do you want? Character references? A lie detector? Put me through anything you want, just let me save her!"

He swore, and that alone pulled me out of my anger enough to listen to the rest of what he was saying.

"You swore. I don't think I've ever heard you swear before."

He walked past me, running his hands over his hair until they clasped behind his neck. Once half the porch was between us, he turned around. "You have my most sincere apology for that. I haven't said a word like that aloud for over ten years. But the rest? I won't apologize for that. You can think I'm crazy all you want. I get it. You're scared of her dying and scared of what kind of guy she's chained to as a dad if she lives, even if it's only on paper."

"Yes and no."

"Which one?"

"I'm not scared of her being chained to you," I admitted softly. "I know you'd do anything for them. I see it in the way you take care of them, the way they trust you."

"But you won't trust me to stay."

How long could Ryan's letter possibly keep him here? Was he so honor-driven by that letter that he would sacrifice himself with a marriage? Could I trust that honor to keep him around long enough to save Maisie? This was all such a screwed-up tangle of a mess.

"I don't trust *anyone* to stay, and you've already warned me that I shouldn't. That you'll eventually walk out."

"Oh no. You don't get to use my words against me unless you get them right. I said you wouldn't *let* me stay—that you'd push me out. But it looks like you don't even need me to mess things up before you start shoving. Do you do that to everyone who gets close to you? Or am I just lucky?"

I ignored the truth of his jab, refusing to look in the metaphorical mirror he'd held up to my face.

"You know what? None of this matters. Not when it's a giant lie. We'd be committing fraud, Beckett. A fake piece of paper about a nonexistent relationship, and if we were caught... I'm not putting the kids through that."

His jaw set in a tense line, and he gave me a singular nod before turning and walking down the steps.

Havoc immediately abandoned me to follow him, tiny traitor that she was.

He turned at the bottom of the steps. "Are you really saying that you're not willing to bend your morals in order to save your daughter's life? To give me some of that precious trust that you keep locked up tighter than Fort Knox?"

I felt the verbal blow all the way to my toes. Was that really what I was doing? Choosing my own morals, my own trust issues over Maisie's life? Was I so jaded that I couldn't believe? Couldn't hope when my own brother had vouched for him?

Ryan.

"You want me to trust you?" My voice softened.

"I do."

"Okay. Tell me how Ryan died."

The color drained from his face. "That's not fair."

A piece of that warm, fuzzy hope burned up in my chest.

"Don't make me lie to you," he begged...or threatened. I couldn't tell.

I stood silently, waiting for him to say something different—to give me some of the trust he was asking for. To put himself in a position of vulnerability. But the longer we stared at each other, the more rigid his posture became, until he was once again the hardened soldier I met on his first day at Solitude.

I felt a sorrowful sense of loss, as if something rare and precious had disappeared before its value could even be realized.

"Have a nice night, Ella. I'll pick up Colt tomorrow for practice at ten."

"What? Soccer practice?" Like the fight we'd had was something normal and could be glossed over. Like we hadn't just shoved a stick of dynamite between us and lit the fuse.

"Yep. Soccer. Because I show up. That's what I do. When I make someone a promise I follow through, and that goes double for your kids. And, since you apparently won't take my word for it, I'm just going to have to show you over and over again."

He opened the door, and Havoc jumped into the truck. Then he climbed in and left me standing on the front porch with my mouth hanging open, trying to figure out what the hell had just happened.

"Well?" I asked Ada as I crammed another peanut butter cookie in my mouth. Colt and Maisie were asleep in our cabin, and Hailey was keeping watch while I reverted back to my childhood and spilled my guts to Ada.

"What do you want me to say?" she asked, taking another tray out of the commercial oven and setting it to cool.

"Your thoughts? Opinions, anything." Because I needed someone else to tell me that I wasn't psycho.

"I think an extremely handsome man offered you a way to save your daughter." She leaned back against the opposite counter, wiping her hands clean on her apron.

"What? So I'm the one who's wrong here? He asked me to marry him, Ada. That gives a veritable stranger rights over my kids for the sake of insurance. Insurance that he can revoke anytime he feels like filing for divorce. Hell, rights over Solitude."

"Only if you let it. You're telling me you couldn't draft a prenup or something that limits his rights? The same as you'd do with Jeff if he walked back through those doors?"

"Jeff isn't coming back."

"Exactly."

"What if he's a serial killer?" I asked, reaching for another cookie.

"He was Ryan's best friend."

"So he says," I muttered with my mouth full. Well, so the letter said. Ryan had never shared personal details about the guys he served with. He barely told me anything about Chaos when he asked me to be his pen pal, just that a guy in his unit needed mail. I missed my brother. I wanted my brother. I needed to hear his opinion, why he'd never talked about Beckett if they'd been best friends.

I missed Chaos, too.

Chaos. If he'd shown up at my door in January, everything would be different. I knew it in my soul. Maybe I was the psycho one. After all, I'd fallen for two different men in the span of what? Eight months? Pregnancy lasted longer than that.

But Chaos was dead. Ryan was dead. Mom and Dad were dead. Grandma? Dead, too.

Was I really going to add my daughter to that list?

"Didn't he have Ryan's letter?"

"Yeah," I begrudgingly admitted. "Maybe if there was a picture of them, or something. Anything."

"Did you ask?" She tilted her head and stared at me like I was ten all over again.

"Well. No."

"Huh. Seems like you already believed him, then, doesn't it?"

"Ugh." I let my head roll back and sighed my exasperation to whoever wanted to take my side. "You're on his side."

"I'm on Maisie's side. And that side looks a lot better when she's living."

Well, when you put it like that…

"I don't know what to do. I can't marry him, Ada. It's only a matter of time before he gets bored. Guys like Beckett don't play house."

"He's not your father. He's not Ryan. He's not Jeff. You have got to stop convicting him of their crimes."

She was right, and yet my heart still wouldn't accept it, my head wouldn't surrender. "Even if he sticks around long enough to get Maisie through treatment, eventually he's going to check the 'saved Ryan's sister' box and move on."

"And that's bad because…"

"Because it will break the kids' hearts."

"Funny thing about broken hearts—only the living have them."

I shot her a glare. "Yeah, I get it. At least she'd be alive to have a broken heart, right? But what if he walks out midtreatment? What if the insurance cancels and the hospital ceases her therapy?"

"Then she will have had more treatments than she's getting now, and we'll cross that bridge if we ever get there. Sometimes you just have to show a little faith, even if he is a veritable stranger."

"I don't know how to trust him with my kids." I reached for another cookie and broke it in half.

"That's a load of crap." She wagged her finger in my direction. "You already trust him with the twins. He takes Colt to soccer, and he's stayed with Maisie in the hospital with the privileges *you* gave him over her care."

I shoved another piece of cookie in my mouth and chewed slowly. Ugh, she was right. Hadn't I already admitted to Beckett that I knew he'd do anything for the kids?

"You know what I think?" Ada asked, taking advantage of my full mouth. "You're not scared to trust him with the kids. You're scared to trust him with *you*."

The cookie scraped my throat as I forced a quick swallow.

"What? I don't even factor into this. He said the marriage would just be on paper." Which—okay, I could admit—had actually hurt a little.

"But you care about him."

Too much.

"Any feelings I might or might not have don't

matter. This isn't one of your Christmas romance movies where they fake-marriage themselves out of a conundrum, break into snowball fights, and fall in love. There's no happy-ever-after here."

Of course that knowledge hadn't stopped me from falling for him, anyway.

"Ella, it's June, there is no snow."

"You know what I'm talking about."

"Are you honestly going to sit there and tell me that you're going to draw a line on what you're willing to do to keep Maisie alive?"

And there was the kicker.

Shit. What wouldn't I do for Maisie? With a cool enough head to get some perspective, I knew there wasn't a line. I'd risk hell and damnation for her. I'd sell my very soul.

Beckett could potentially save Maisie. The only obstacle was my own stubbornness and fear.

But what if there was a way to leave my fear out of the equation? To directly link Beckett to the kids without my baggage getting in the way?

"I guess I have to talk to Beckett."

Colt flew through the front door after practice, flushed and happy. "Hi, Mom!" He was a blur, kissing me on the cheek and then racing up the stairs to his room.

Beckett stood in the doorway, his baseball hat in his hand. His shorts rode low on his hips, and that incredible expanse of abs and chest was covered up with a Pearl Jam concert tee. His eyes widened when he took in my sundress and the bare expanse of my legs, but he quickly looked elsewhere. "He has a game tomorrow, but I know Maisie is supposed to go in for chemo."

"We'll leave after the game. She doesn't start until

Monday, and they'll need to see if her platelet levels are high enough to even do it. The infection screwed up a lot of stuff."

"Okay, just let me know. I can take him, of course." He started backing out of the house, and I nearly cursed.

"Thank you. Look, Beckett, about yesterday?"

He stopped, slowly dragging his eyes to mine and keeping them there instead of on my bare shoulders or the sweetheart, strapless neckline I'd chosen just to get his attention. Sure, the dress was old, but at least it still fit.

When it became apparent that he wasn't going to speak, I forged ahead.

"I trust you with my kids."

His eyes widened slightly.

"I needed to say that first, for you to know that everything we fought about last night…most of that isn't about the kids. It's about me. You've done nothing but prove yourself since you got here, and it was wrong of me to ask you to tell me about Ryan when I know it would cost your integrity. Ironic really, right? I was asking you to prove your trustworthiness by breaking your word. I'm sorry."

"Thank you," he answered quietly.

"There's someone I'd like to have dinner with tonight."

His eyes narrowed.

"With you," I quickly corrected. "Dinner with you and the someone."

"You want me to chaperone a date?" His voice dropped to that low, sandpaper-rough tone that woke up my body in parts that had been asleep since Jeff.

"No. I want to meet with my lawyer, and I'm hoping you'll go with me. About"—I glanced over to where Maisie was napping on the couch—"what you offered yesterday. Kind of."

Surprise widened his eyes for a second, and I savored the reaction. I didn't have many opportunities to shock Beckett.

"Kind of?"

Hope flashed in his eyes, catapulting my heart into my throat. "I want to ask some questions first before I say anything. I don't even know if what I'm thinking about is possible, but I'd be really grateful if you went with me to figure it out."

"Of course. What time?"

I looked at the clock and then forced a smile. "In about forty-five minutes?"

Instead of scoffing, or snipping that it was too short notice, he simply nodded, saying, "Okay," and walked out.

I used the time to pack a little for our trip, force Colt into the bathtub, and throw dinner for the kids into the oven. I took Maisie's temp when she woke up and sighed in relief at the beautiful 98.5 reading as Ada arrived. Then I generally puttered in nervousness before putting on what little makeup I had, which meant a swipe of mascara and a little lip gloss.

Not that this was a date or anything.

Beckett arrived exactly a half hour after he'd departed, his scruff shaved off, smelling like soap and leather, and him. *Unh.*

"Ready?" he asked after hugging both the kids.

"Yep," I said, grabbing my purse and a white cardigan.

We walked down the steps, and he opened my door for me. At the moment, in his dress pants, open-collared shirt, and dark blue blazer, he looked more gentleman than special ops soldier, but I knew it was just icing. He might look all fluffy and frosted, but under the clothes he was devil's food, period.

And I really, really, *really* liked chocolate.

I climbed up into the truck, and he shut the door, but not before he let his eyes linger on my legs for a moment longer than necessary. *Good choice on the heels.*

Our drive into Telluride was quiet, accompanied by only a little classic rock streaming through the speakers.

"This was Ryan's favorite," he said quietly, catching me off guard. "Used to drive me nuts with it."

Thunderstruck.

"Yeah, it was," I agreed. "Did he still play—"

"A wicked air guitar?" Beckett asked with a smile. "Oh yeah. Every chance he got. Between this and Poison, I've had my fill of watching him fingerpick at nothing. Did he ever tell you we got to meet Bret Michaels?"

"What? No way!"

"Check the glove box." He motioned with his head, and I eagerly fumbled with the latch until it opened. "Under the manual."

I pulled out a white envelope thick and distorted with pictures.

"I think it's about halfway through."

I flipped through the pictures, seeing Beckett all over the world, with other soldiers like him, like Ryan. Until I looked closer and saw that it *was* Ryan in a group photo. My breath caught, and I ran my thumb over his familiar face, an all too familiar ache settling in my chest.

"I miss him," I said quietly.

"Me, too." His knuckles whitened on the steering wheel. "It's a good thing, though. Missing him. Grief means you had someone worth grieving."

I found a picture where the soldiers were three rows deep, all camo'd and bearded. For just that second, I let myself wonder, and before I knew it, my mouth opened. "Which one is Chaos?"

Beckett's head snapped toward mine as we reached a red light, and I felt a split-second of guilt. Did Beckett know how Chaos had felt about me? Or the way I'd felt about him?

His gaze dropped to the photo. "He's third from the left."

I searched the picture, hungry for my first sight of Chaos as we pulled into a parking spot in front of the restaurant. There was Beckett, serious as always... "There are two other soldiers three rows in." Both had thick, short beards and sunglasses on.

The driver's side door shut. Beckett had already killed the ignition and gotten out of the truck.

"I guess that subject's closed," I muttered, examining the faces one last time before sliding them back in the envelope with a heavy heart. Would I ever get to look again? Ever get the chance to ask questions?

I put the pictures back into the glove box just before Beckett opened my door and helped me down. Heels and running boards weren't always the easiest combo. Then we walked into the restaurant, a little family-owned Italian place I loved.

When we reached our table, Mark was already waiting, and stood.

"Whoa. Gutierrez?" Beckett asked as Mark came around the table and kissed my cheek.

"Nice to see you, Gentry. Shall we sit?"

Beckett held out my chair, and I took it, scooting in. It was an almost archaic gesture, but it made me feel protected, cared for, and a little off-balance.

"So you don't just run the rescue crew," Beckett said as the men took their seats.

"Nope, I'm just a volunteer. Keeps me on my toes, and it's not like there's a ton of family law business here in Telluride." He shrugged. "Kind of like you, just doing it for fun, now."

Beckett nodded slowly.

"So I guess you two know each other," I said lightly, even though the moment felt anything but. "Thank you, Mark, for meeting us on a Saturday night. I know you and Tess have date night."

"No problem. She's actually in Durango for the weekend with the kids. Trust me, I'd much rather be here with you than having dinner with my mother-in-law. Now what's up?"

"Want to fill him in on your proposal?" I asked Beckett, and he took the reins.

It took a glass of wine and all of dinner, but he explained everything as thoroughly as possible, from the treatments, the bills, the insurance, to his idea of marriage.

Ella Gentry.

I mentally smacked that picture out of my mind. I'd gotten married on a whim once, and a second time was definitely not in the cards. I didn't care how good his name sounded attached to mine.

"Do you want to marry Ella?" he asked Beckett as the waitress cleared our plates.

"Would you want to marry a woman who had no interest in marrying you?" Beckett answered.

My head snapped to look at him. No interest? It wasn't lack of interest in Beckett, it was an overwhelming interest in my sanity and…logic.

"But I would, if that's what she wan—needed," Beckett finished.

Great. Now I was the damsel. All I needed was a giant light-up sign above my head that flashed with the words "in distress," and my life would be complete.

"Okay, then let's not push that option," Mark said, his gaze flickering between the two of us. "No one wants an arranged marriage here. So, Ella. Now that I have a good idea of what's going on, it's your turn. On the phone you mentioned an idea?"

"Right." I pivoted in my chair to look at Beckett. "What you're offering is to basically make Maisie your daughter? Right? Even if it's only on paper?"

"Yes. Colt, too...as my son, obviously. Legally."

Just the words sent a spiraling warmth through my belly, or maybe that was the wine. Either way, it gave me the courage to continue.

"I'm a little damaged."

He quirked an eyebrow as if to say *tell me something I don't know*.

"And sometimes that damage blinds me. It gets in my way and holds me back. And I'm okay with that. But I'm not okay with it hurting Maisie or Colt. So, if there was a way for you to be their legal father, giving them all the same protections that being my husband would...without me being your wife, would you want that?"

"Not marrying you?" His brows drew inward.

"Removing me, and my damage, from the equation," I clarified before dropping my volume to a whisper only Beckett could hear. "As someone wise once told me, it's not about not wanting you."

"I don't understand."

"Would you want the kids if I wasn't part of the deal?"

"Yes." He answered without hesitation.

"Forever?"

"Always."

That warmth in my stomach spread, combining with the love that burned so brightly in my chest. I half expected to light up like a Care Bear.

I forced my eyes away from Beckett's to where Mark sat, his gaze darting between us, his mind already at work.

"Can he adopt them? Without marrying me?"

Beckett drew in a sharp breath.

"Is that something you'd be willing to do?" Mark asked Beckett.

"Yes." Again, the answer came instantly.

"Have you thought about what that would really mean?" Mark asked me.

"Yes. I know it puts the kids at some risk."

I felt Beckett tense next to me, like a crackle of energy in the air.

"It could," Mark agreed. "It would be like having another parent—there would be support to consider, visitation, custody rights, both physical and decision-making. It's basically sharing your kids with him. But it protects them more, too. The moment he adopts them, they'll be covered by his insurance no matter the status of your…relationship. The military will always see them as his."

"Even if he's out?"

Beckett's jaw tensed. "Yep. You could even sue me for support if you wanted."

"I would never sue you for support."

"I wouldn't care if you did."

"Right, but you're still giving up a portion of your rights, Ella."

My hackles bristled. The twins had always been mine, and only mine.

"Can we lessen the risk?"

He leaned back, continuing his appraisal of us both. "Sure. You'd just have to draw up a custody agreement to be signed immediately after. You could say that you have sole physical custody, he has zero rights to visitation, but you should share decision-making, or it looks pretty darn fraudulent. You wouldn't even have to file it unless there's an issue. Just in case someone comes looking."

"Is it fraud?" I needed to know. I'd probably still go

through with it—Maisie's life was worth some jail time—but I had to know. "I mean, the marriage would seem way more fraudulent to me. If neither of us want to marry the other, and we're living in separate houses with separate names, then that's more fraud than Beckett wanting to be there for the kids, right?"

"Do you want to parent the kids?" Mark looked straight at Beckett.

"Yes," he answered without a second thought. "I love them. Nothing would make me happier than to protect them like this, to give them whatever I can."

"You're going to have to do a little better than that with Judge Iverson. He's a softy for Ella, always has been, but you're not a local. He's not going to trust you just because you showed up for some soccer practices."

Beckett took a deep breath and toyed with his glass. "I didn't have a father growing up. A lot of guys who hit first, or just generally ignored me, but no one I considered a dad. When Colt and I were walking back across the field after a soccer game, he asked if that was what having a dad felt like, and I couldn't tell him yes, because I didn't know—and he didn't know, either. I want Colt and Maisie to know what it feels like to have a dad—in whatever capacity Ella would let me be there for them. I just want to be the guy they can depend on."

"That's pretty much the definition of fatherhood, and I think you'd hold up just fine in court. It's not fraud if you are adopting so that you can help raise them. The insurance is definitely a perk, though—one that Judge Iverson would see. But he lost his wife to cancer about ten years back, so I honestly think you've got a good shot that he'd choose to see it as just that: a perk and not the reason. Would the lack of rights bother you?"

He shook his head. "Maisie dying bothers me. I would never take anything from Ella that she didn't want to give, and I'd never do anything that would hurt the kids."

I thought of the pictures the nurses had shown me of the little graduation ceremony that Beckett had given Maisie. She loved him. Colt loved him just as much, and I was right there with him. They already had so much to lose when it came to Beckett.

"Would they have to know? Right away, at least?" I blurted out. He could absolutely hurt the kids the minute he walked away. To give them a dad just to take him away was cruel. Once Maisie was in the clear—hoping Beckett was still content in Telluride that far in the future—we could tell them...once her heart was strong enough to withstand the potential fallout of the opposite being true.

Beckett went stiff, but his gaze stayed steady and unwavering in Mark's direction.

"Uh..." Mark's eyes shifted between us. "I guess not? Kids don't have to be informed or give consent until they're twelve. We'd just have to talk to Judge Iverson. Seeing how he's always favored you, and his hatred of the Danburys, well, I think we could sway him to agree."

"So we could really do it?" I asked, that tiny flame of hope flaring up again. "Even though we're not married?"

"Marriage might be the easier route," Mark said with a shrug.

"I just can't. Not after what happened last time. I'm in no rush to get a ring on it."

"Which is exactly what you should tell Judge Iverson if he asks. Our definition of family has changed a ton in the last couple of decades, and marriage isn't the determining factor anymore. And, since you're the children's mother, and they're not wards of the state or anything, the only complication would really be Judge Iverson's opinion. A single man can absolutely adopt his partner's children without them being married. You guys just might have to play up the partner part a little."

My cheeks warmed. I hadn't had a "partner" since Jeff, and he wasn't really ever that, anyway.

"So basically I'd be trading my sole decision-making rights, and that's it?"

"Basically." He fiddled with his wineglass as he watched us, his eyes seeing way too much.

"But you'd be gaining Maisie's life," Beckett answered. "And you know I'd never do anything that would cross you when it came to the kids. I'm not some villain. I'm just trying to help."

"I know," I said softly, and I did, but trust wasn't something I handed out like candy.

"There's one catch. You're going to have to get Jeff to sign over his parental rights."

Pretty sure a nuclear bomb going off would have had less impact on my heart.

"Why? He's not on the birth certificate, and the kids are MacKenzies, not Danburys."

"Ella, everyone knows Jeff is the father. Whether or not you admit it on the birth certificate doesn't eliminate his rights. One paternity test and the adoption would be voided. I'm not saying he'd ever exercise his rights, but the judge is going to require the release. No release. No adoption."

"Right," I replied, my voice almost mouselike. I didn't want to see Jeff. Ever. That was like ripping open a fully healed scar just for fun.

We thanked Mark, Beckett paid for dinner, and we left, riding back to the house in a tense silence.

"What way are you leaning?" Beckett asked as we pulled through Solitude's gate.

"The way that doesn't require me seeing Jeff." I slammed my eyes shut. "That's a lie. I know what you're offering is a godsend, not just for Maisie, but for Colt.

For me. I just can't bear the idea of having to ask him for *anything*."

"I'll handle Jeff," Beckett promised. "Besides, he'd probably run screaming if you showed up. At least I can blindside him."

"You'd do that for me?" I asked as we reached my cabin, the truck coming to a soft stop.

"I would do anything for you." His eyes locked onto mine in the dashboard lights, intense and a little hurt. "What is it going to take for you to believe me? To trust me? You want my background checked? Do it. You want my credit score? Awesome. My bank accounts? I'll add you on. You have my word, my body, my time, and I'm standing here offering my last name. What else can I give you?"

"Beckett," I leaned toward him, but he backed away.

"Not that you'd ever give them my last name, not when they don't even get to know what we're doing. Right? I can be their legal father, but I'm not good enough to be their dad."

"That's...that's not what this is about."

"Oh, I know. It's that you don't trust me to stay. You think I'll walk out just like Jeff did. You think it will hurt the kids even more."

"I figured we could tell them once Maisie was healthy."

"If I'm still around by then, right?"

I hated and loved that he knew me so well. I didn't even have to answer. He saw it in my eyes.

"Yeah. Okay." He killed the engine and removed the keys. "I don't even have the right to be upset. I know what I'm offering, and the being dad part isn't in there, right? Just the legal protection. You need something, I'm giving it to you, just like I promised I would. Simple as that."

He opened the door and got out of the truck. I followed quickly after, watching his back retreat down my driveway, toward the lake.

"What are you doing?"

"Leaving my truck here. I'll get it tomorrow before the game. The walk will do me good."

"Beckett!" I called after him.

"Don't worry, Ella," he called back. "I know my role. I've got it. And I'll still show up. That's how badly I want…"

He didn't finish, just threw up his hands and kept walking.

But I finished that sentence for him in my head about a dozen different ways.

How badly I want you.

How badly I want your kids.

How badly I want to be in your life.

How badly I want to show up for you.

How badly I want Maisie to live.

Every single one I came up with made me feel worse for not trusting him. But the guy was up against a lifetime of people making promises and leaving me.

And I was up against a lifetime of no one trusting him.

Weren't we just a pair?

CHAPTER SIXTEEN

Beckett

Letter #15

Chaos,

    I'm so sorry you lost someone. I can't imagine how hard that must be, to grieve and still carry on with what you're doing. Every time I lost someone, my parents or my grandmother, it always shut me down, like my body couldn't process the enormity of my feelings. It says a lot about the kind of man you are that you can continue to show up, and I mean that in the best of ways.

    You say you're bad with people, that you don't connect, but that's not who I see when I open these letters. Or rather, who I hear. Someone who can't connect wouldn't be so open. Heck, they wouldn't have written back in the first place. But you did, and I'm grateful.

    Maybe you simply choose who you connect with, and that's okay. I don't think anyone wakes up and decides to be the social butterfly like my brother. That's probably why you two are good friends. You balance each other out.

    You know who else I bet you'd connect with? Kids. Maybe not everyone's kids, but definitely your own. Have you ever thought about kids? It's a random question, but I'm curious. Probably because I had mine so young, and I can't imagine not having them, I kind of picture everyone I meet with kids.

    Except Hailey. She's one of my closest friends,

*and I'm sure one day she'll make a great mom…
after she successfully adults on her own for a
while. Successful being the key word there. I bet
you'll love her when you get here. She's gorgeous,
and fun, and doesn't picture everyone she meets
with kids.*

*Anyway, I bet you'd be a great dad. Brooding
and tough, but also sneaking in Star Wars
marathons on lazy weekends. I could absolutely
picture it…if I could picture you. Yep, I'm still
hankering for a picture.*

*I hope I managed to distract you for a few
minutes. I hope you know how very sorry I am
for your loss.*

~ Ella

I stood at the window of the downtown Denver high-
rise, looking out over the city. This definitely wasn't a
place I could set down roots. Two months in Telluride
had taught me that concrete and I weren't compatible in
the long-term sense.

Plus, Denver didn't have Ella.

It had been a week since our fight in the truck, and
we'd been polite…even friendly. But that easygoing
rhythm we'd always had was nowhere to be found. Not
with everything hanging between us.

If I wasn't careful, she'd realize I was in love with
her, and then we'd be in even deeper shit.

I'd never had a woman prick my temper the way
Ella did. Hell, I'd sworn at her. I'd also never had a
woman I cared to see more than once or twice, or one
who owned my soul the way she did. Of course I'd agree
to whatever terms she had when it came to the
adoption. Not just because I was desperate to save
Maisie and protect Colt, but because I'd give Ella

whatever she wanted if it simply made her smile.

And in return, she was giving me a family, as screwed up as the justification was. The kids would be mine, in every way that mattered to me. I could love them, protect them, make sure they had everything they needed. I'd get Maisie approved for every treatment and make sure Colt knew I had his back every day of his life. I'd prove myself to Ella, show up until she couldn't doubt me ever again, and then I'd win her heart.

Until she finds out what you did.

Yeah. That. It didn't matter how hard I tried to ignore it, my secret hung over my head like a guillotine.

At least the kids would be protected when Ella kicked me out. It wasn't like she'd unadopt the kids or risk Maisie. This was the one way I could fulfill my promise to Ryan and placate my aching heart, knowing one day the past was going to catch up to me.

My cell phone dinged, and I swiped to open the message app.

DONAHUE: Updated papers are ready with new dates. You sure about this?

My fingers paused over the keys. I was sure that I wanted Maisie to live, and this was the only means to that end.

GENTRY: Yep. But it doesn't mean I'm coming back.

DONAHUE: You keep telling yourself that.

I slid my phone into my pocket, not bothering to reply.

"Mr. Gentry," a voice called out from behind me, and I turned around.

"Mr. Danbury," I answered. So this was Jeff. He basically looked like an overgrown frat boy who'd been poured into his father's suit. His hair was blond and slicked back, his eyes gray and calculating.

We shook hands, and I quickly took my seat across from him at the conference table, scared that I'd lose it and crush him for having touched Ella, let alone abandoning her and the kids.

The hell with him. He didn't deserve her, and he sure as hell didn't deserve them.

He adjusted his suit coat, and I did the same, unbuttoning the bottom button. At least Denver had good, fast tailors.

"So what can I do for you, Mr. Gentry?" he asked.

"I understand you're the youngest junior partner at your firm."

"I am. Just graduated law school as a matter of fact."

"Perks of having a dad with his name on the wall?" I asked, motioning to the firm's name.

His smile fell. Jeffy-boy didn't like having his silver spoon brought up. Guys like him were all the same—they'd had their cushy lives handed to them, and they despised any speed bump that kept them from the prize. God knew he'd run right over Ella.

"I consider it part-ownership in the family business," he said with a shrug.

"Ah, family. I'm so glad you brought that up." I pushed the manila envelope across the table, and he caught it.

"What the hell is this?" he asked, scanning the paper.

"You know what it is, unless that fancy law degree didn't teach you how to read. Sign it."

He read it again and then put it down slowly. Then I saw it, the look that said he thought he had one up on me now that he knew what I wanted.

"What did Ella pay you to do this?"

"I'm sorry?"

"There has to be a reason. It's been years."

"There is. I'm adopting the twins."

His smirk fell off his preppy face, and his gaze dropped to my hand, looking for a ring. "You marrying her?"

"I can't see how that's any of your business."

"Well, seeing as you'd like to adopt my kids—"

All emotion drained from my body in a familiar retreat. The sensation the same as every time I stepped into combat, preparing me to commit unforgivable atrocities.

"They're not your kids," I said.

"Yeah, I'd beg to differ on that, considering how many times I screwed her in the two months we were married. Small-town girl with a small-town mind just wanted a ring first."

If Havoc had been here, she would have gone for his throat based on my tension level alone.

"You might be their biological father, but you're sure as hell not their dad. You've never so much as seen them, spoken to them, or had any interaction. They. Are. Not. Your. Kids. They're mine."

As soon as the words left my mouth, that sweet pressure was back in my chest, the love I had for them overpowering my instinct to void my emotions.

"So what exactly is in this for me?"

"Are you serious?"

He shrugged. "Consider it a business transaction. You want something I have. What are you going to give me for it?"

"How about I tell you what I'm *not* going to give you?"

He sat there expectantly while I did my best to keep a level head.

Three things: Maisie. Colt. Ella. They were the reason and the only things that mattered.

"I'm not going to give you the over-two-million-dollar bill for Maisie's cancer treatments that's going to come due in the next year."

He swallowed but showed no other outward sign of hearing me.

"Reason enough? Or we can just add her to your insurance, since you're so keen on calling them *yours.*

I'm sure that would go over really well with your dad, considering he told Ella about six months ago that he really didn't care if Maisie lived or died as long as she left him and you the hell alone. I'm sure that would be great for business if it got out."

"Is that a threat?"

"Not in the least. Why would I do that when you're going to sign that release, and your little secretary outside is going to notarize it all nice and pretty?" I leaned back in the chair.

"Fine. I'll sign it." He ripped a pen out of the cup in the center of the table and scrawled his name across the paper. I didn't relax. Not yet.

"Have it notarized."

He cursed under his breath but pushed back from the table and barked for his secretary from the doorway. A twentysomething woman in a tight pencil skirt hustled over, signing the bottom of the document and stamping it before running back to her desk.

Jeff shoved the folder at me, and I looked over the document, making sure it had been signed and notarized correctly. I wasn't doing this a second time.

"Now if there's anything else?"

I let my smile loose. "Yeah. Get your checkbook."

"Excuse me?" His eyes popped wide in indignation.

"Get. Your. Checkbook. You're going to write Ella a check for six years of back support on the kids. Now."

"The hell I am. Besides, I just started working last month. What do you want? Thirty percent of nothing?"

"Yeah, but your million-dollar trust fund kicked in the minute you attended your first class freshman year of college. So you're going to write a lovely, fat check to Ella."

"How did you know that?"

"Not important. You're going to write what you owe her, or I'm going to take this document to your fiancée's dad. What is he? A senator? And then I'm going to leak it to the press that you not only abandoned those kids, but you left their mother destitute while she struggled to afford the cancer treatments Maisie needs. How do you think that's going to play out in the press?"

"You'd ruin me."

I took a deep, steadying breath. Even knowing that Maisie had cancer didn't affect this selfish prick. "Yeah, that's the idea."

"Why? Because I ruined Ella? Like she had a future anyway."

"You think you ruined Ella? There's no man on the planet who could do that. Don't flatter yourself. The only reason she's not here is because you're not worth her time. Now get your checkbook."

He left the conference room, returning quickly with his pen poised over an open checkbook. "How much?"

"Whatever you think it's worth to keep your future father-in-law happy and your father's name on the wall."

He scrawled his pen across the check and then flung the paper at me.

The check rustled to a gentle stop right in front of me, and I took it, folding it in half and slipping it into my breast pocket.

"You're not even going to look at it?" he squawked.

"Nope. It's either enough, or it's not." I stood, buttoning my suit coat, and headed for the door, file in hand.

"How did you know about the trust fund?" he asked again, still seated.

I paused, my hand on the door, debating.

What the hell. Why not?

"Oh, you know. Small-town people with small-town minds, they have big hearts and bigger mouths. And just for the record, the best thing you've ever done in your life is walk away from Ella. You never came back to mess with the kids. I'd keep to that tradition if I were you. I protect what's mine."

I walked away without a second thought, heading for a little army base just outside of Denver. There was another set of papers that needed signing today.

"Beckett!" Colt flew through the door and launched himself into my arms, like I'd been gone two weeks instead of two days.

"What's up, little man?" I lifted him into the air, savoring the smell of cinnamon and sunshine as I shuffled the folder in my hands.

"We're baking!"

I carried him into the house and was greeted by the same scent. "Apple pie?" I asked.

"How did you know?"

"Well, the only thing that smells that good while it's baking is apple pie or Little Boy Pie and, since you're still here, I went with the apples."

Havoc swirled around my legs in greeting, and I set Colt down to give my girl a little behind-the-ear rub. "Good job," I told her, knowing she'd stuck by Colt's side.

"Beckett!" Maisie called out from the couch.

"How's my best girl?" I asked, coming around to crouch next to where she lay. She was pale, her skin nearly translucent. "Feeling okay?"

She shook her head.

"If you could get her to drink something, I'd pretty much fork over my soul," Ella said, coming from the kitchen, a smattering of flour on her forehead.

A pang of yearning blended with pure lust. I wanted this life and this woman. Wanted the freedom to steal her away from the kids for a second and get my hands on her. Kiss her. Touch her. Watch her eyes flutter shut in pleasure. Watch the worry lines fade from her brow.

"Apple pie, huh?"

"It's her favorite, so I thought maybe…" She shrugged.

"What do I have to bribe you with to get a few capfuls of Gatorade down you?" I asked Maisie.

She looked up at me, those blue eyes turning deadly serious. "No more *Moana*. Get me *Star Wars*. It's *not* scary." She shot a little glare in Ella's direction.

Ella scoffed, but nodded to okay the transaction.

"Deal. I have the green apple flavor you like at my house. Give me a couple minutes with your mom and I'll get it, okay?"

"Deal."

I pulled her blanket up a little farther and followed Ella into her office.

YOU ARE ENOUGH.

The handwritten sign I'd sent her hung on the bulletin board. Hell yes, she was enough. I was the one who lacked in just about every department. Including the honesty one.

How weird was it to be jealous of yourself? To know another version of you had a piece of the woman you loved?

"How are her platelet levels?"

"We're going into the medical center tomorrow morning for another transfusion. They can do it in Telluride, so at least it's close."

I nodded and handed Ella the folder.

Her fingers trembled a little, but she opened it. Then her mouth dropped open. "You did it."

"I did. You're free. The kids are free."

"How?" She read it again.

"I'm very convincing."

She grinned up at me. "That, I believe."

I slipped the check into the folder, letting it fall on

top of the document. Her mouth fell open.

"What is this?"

"What you're owed."

She sat back, her butt perched on the edge of her desk. "It's half a million dollars. Why would he... What did you do?"

"Got you a little of the money he should have given you all along."

She looked up at me, her face a myriad of expressions I couldn't keep up with. "I don't want it."

"I figured."

"You did?"

I nodded. "You raised them on your own. I figured the last thing you'd do is take the money now. That would give him a feeling of ownership you'd never allow."

"Then why did you bring it?"

"You said once that to hurt him I had to hit the money. So I hurt him. I brought you the check because I won't ever take a choice like that from you. That money could pay off all the debt on Solitude, or pay for treatments for Maisie. Or for their college in the future. I wasn't taking that choice."

"I don't need it for Maisie, now."

"Not if you want me to adopt her, you don't. That's another choice I won't force on you. I'm not Jeff. And this gives you options. That check means you're not cornered. You don't have to choose me."

We stood there, our eyes locked in a silent conversation as she considered. Mine begged her to trust me. To lean on me. To need me even a small percentage of the way I needed her. Hers pondered, weighed, and decided, staying locked with mine as she ripped the check to shreds.

"I choose you. And now I'm free. We're free."

I grinned because I knew I wasn't free anymore—I was hers...theirs.

CHAPTER SEVENTEEN

Beckett

Letter #3

Chaos,

Parenthood sucks. Sorry, I know we don't know each other well enough for me to say something like that, but it does. At least today it does.

I just spent the better part of my afternoon in the principal's office. Not only that, but it was the same principal from when I was a kid. I swear, I sat down in that squeaky pleather chair across from his desk and I was seven all over again.

Except now I'm the adult, and my kids are the ones putting me in the hot seat.

Colt and Maisie are in the same kindergarten class. I know, I got a ton of crap about putting twins in the same class, and how it doesn't let them cultivate their own identity, but those so-called experts never had to look at my blue-eyed heathens and listen to them refuse to be separated. And by refuse, I mean we tried. For the first week of school, I had to pick them up every day by nine a.m. because they kept leaving to go to the other's classroom. Finally, we relented. You know the phrase "pick your battles"? It was more like "concede the war, you're losing." But fine.

Anyway, there's a little boy with a huge crush on Maisie. Cute, right? Not so much. Today at recess, he decided the whole class would play "kiss tag," where I guess instead of tagging *someone with your hand, you plant one on them. Nice, right? Maisie didn't want to play, so the boy started chasing her anyway, eventually tripping her and kissing her despite her objections. Naturally, she shoved him off and decked him. My brother would be proud; she landed that punch just like he taught her.*

Colt heard the commotion and went running. When Maisie told him what happened, he kept cool, but the other little boy called her a not-nice name that rhymes with witch (according to Colt), and well...Colt went ballistic.

The other boy has a black eye and a mouthful of playground sand. Did I mention I went to school with his mom? Super awkward small-town life.

Colt has a week of detention, which Maisie is demanding she serve with him. They're five years old. FIVE YEARS OLD, Chaos. This is kindergarten. How the hell am I going to survive the teen years?

Ugh. That's all for today. Parenting sucks.

~ Ella

My alarm went off, and I was up and running. Literally. I hit the six-mile mark along the Solitude grounds, showered, and went into work, which was now completely volunteer-based since I signed Donahue's papers. There I ran Havoc through some drills and worked her on the rappelling harness.

It was a pretty typical Friday.

Except today was adoption day, and that changed everything.

Jeff had signed the papers a little over a month ago, and we'd found out a few days ago that today was the day.

Every day had been a grueling wait, but my insurance had let me enroll the kids based on the pending adoption paperwork, which meant in two weeks, they would be covered. And in a month, Maisie could get her first MIBG therapy.

I parked the truck in front of the main house, and Havoc and I nodded to the new guests as we walked inside. The summer was bustling with business, and Ella was busy tending to customers and placating the picky ones. I guess the words "luxury accommodations" was the signal for assholes to emerge from the general population.

Oh, look, she was dealing with another one.

Havoc and I waited just inside the double doors as a woman in her midfifties was shaking her head at Ella.

"And that's just not what we were looking for. I specifically asked for lakeside, and we're facing a very lovely view, but it's certainly not water!"

Ella looked over the woman's shoulder at me midlecture, and I sent her a consoling look. At least I hope it was consoling, because she almost giggled.

She motioned with her head toward the back, and I took the cue. I walked Havoc through the main house, spotting Hailey at the desk and Ada in her glory, putting fresh-baked cookies on the table. We made our way to the back and opened the door to the residence.

"Beckett!" Maisie came running around the corner, and I caught her before she skidded into the wall. "You have to help me! Colt has the best hiding place, and I can't find him! It's not fair! He can run faster, and he knows it!"

It was amazing what a month off chemo had done for her energy level.

"How long have you been looking?"

"Forever!" She dragged out the word to make sure I understood exactly how long forever was.

I gave her a look, and she relented.

"Twenty minutes."

"Man, that *is* forever," I agreed. "Want to find him super quick?"

"Yes!" She jumped up and down.

"Ready?" I asked her as I stood.

"Yes!" she repeated, still jumping. *Man, if I could bottle that energy, I would be a very rich man.*

"Havoc, sit."

Havoc sat, looking up at me for my next command. She'd heard the tone and knew it was time to work. Plus, I wanted to experiment a little.

"Seek Colt."

She was off like a shot, sniffing the ground around the living room, the dining room, and then bolting up the stairs.

"You'd better follow her, Maisie."

Maisie took off at a dead run just as Ella opened the door, quickly stepped inside, and shut it. Then she leaned back against the wood, letting her shoulders sag.

"Was that my daughter impersonating a track star?" she asked, her tone more than tired.

"It was. She's with Havoc. Apparently she feels that Colt used his health as an unfair advantage in the hide-and-seek game, so I'm leveling the playing field."

Right on time, Havoc barked, and there was a small thud and a series of loud laughs.

"Not fair! That's cheating!" Colt yelled.

There was an avalanche of footfalls down the stairs, and the three of them appeared in the hallway.

"Good girl," I told Havoc, who trotted over to accept the last treat I had in my pocket from our earlier session.

"Can we go outside? Please?" Maisie asked.

Ella bit her lip.

"Please?" Colt begged, making it the longest word

on earth.

"Okay. Just stay away from the guests, and be safe," Ella relented. "And take a hat!"

"Havoc, stay with Colt and Maisie." The trio ran out the back door before Ella could change her mind.

"It's like having her back," Ella said with a sigh. "Off the chemo, she's so energetic and happy and has a great appetite. With her levels up, she can just be a kid for a second. I'm glad we have this month before the MIBG treatment."

"Me, too."

Ella pushed off the door and walked to the window, pulling the curtain aside to watch the kids play in the field just behind the house. "I never worry about Havoc with them. Is that weird? I saw her go all growly on Jeff's parents, and I still don't worry."

I came up next to her, our shoulders touching, watching Havoc leap and chase the toy Colt had thrown. "I'd told her to protect them. Usually I say to stay with them, but we were on the street, and I said protect. She'd still kill anyone who messed with them right now, but not a kid or a guest or someone who didn't have that tension she picks up on. When I say 'protect,' that puts her on alert. Right now, she's just playing with them."

"She's amazing."

"She's changed a lot since we left the unit. While she was working, she was kenneled, trained, handled by me, but she didn't really get dog time. Even on deployments, she slept with me, worked with me, and never left my side, but still, no real dog time. Here, she works, but she's learned to be safe with the kids and the guests."

"She's domesticating," Ella said with a smile, then nudged my shoulder. "Like someone else I know."

I laughed. "You ready for this afternoon?"

"Yeah," she said with an enthusiastic nod. "How about you?"

"Nervous, humbled, happy, in sheer awe of the level of responsibility that comes with tiny humans."

She looked up at me with tired but happy eyes. "Says every new father ever."

"I wouldn't know."

"Me, either. Guess we'll figure it out together. Hard to believe this was our home, I'm so used to living in the cabin now."

"Think you'll return once it's safe for Maisie?"

"I honestly don't know. I really like living at the cabin and having that privacy, that line between home and work. Living here, I was always at work." She rubbed her forehead with her fingers and then tightened her ponytail.

"You okay? I mean, don't smack me for male stupidity, but you look a little tired."

She turned around, sitting on the window seat. "That's because I am tired. Maybe it's because Maisie only has scans this month, so my brain can take a little break from the normal insanity, and everything else just catches up."

"What can I do?"

"You're adopting my kids today so my daughter doesn't die. I think that fulfills every requirement you could ever dream up."

"I'm not just doing it for Ryan," I started, but stopped when the door to the residence opened and Hailey raced in, her cheeks flushed and her eyes bright.

"Conner Williamson just asked me out!" she exclaimed.

"No way!" Ella jumped up.

"Right? I've only been crushing on him since when? The ninth grade?" She spun in the middle of the floor, her arms outstretched. "Conner Williamson asked me out!"

Ella laughed. "I'm so happy for you!"

Hailey ran over and hugged her. "This is it! I just

know it! He's going to fall madly in love with me, and we're going to get married and have babies and it's going to be perfect!"

"Yeah, it is!" Ella agreed.

I saw something twist in her face, like her joy had somehow morphed into a panic-laced sorrow.

"Is it okay if I take off an hour early tomorrow?" she asked, pulling back with her hands on Ella's shoulders.

"Totally!" Ella forced a smile, and I might have believed it if I hadn't seen her slip.

"Thanks!" Hailey squeezed Ella again and danced away, spinning for good measure near the door and leaving.

"Ella," I said softly, stepping in front of her so she couldn't run away.

"What?" She shrugged and tried her damnedest to fake a smile, but her bottom lip trembled.

"What's going on? And don't say nothing." I gently took her shoulders in my hands.

She shrugged. "I'm fine."

"Ella, in five hours we're about to share children. And yeah, I get it. I'm not really their dad, just the insurance provider, but don't you think we have to be able to be honest with each other? The good, the bad, the exhausted."

"She's so excited." Her voice was a whisper.

"Yes."

"And I can't remember what that feels like anymore. To get that excited. To be asked out on a date. I mean, it's been seven years. Seven, Beckett." She clasped my biceps, her nails no doubt leaving half-moons in my skin. "I'm pretty sure my virginity has regrown, that's how long it's been."

"Yeah, I don't think that's how that works…"

"And I love my life. I love Colt and Maisie and this business. I'm proud of my choices, you know? I'm proud of them!" Her voice pitched upward.

"As you should be."

"And everything with Maisie. That's all I think about lately. I mean, it's July, right? So it's been nine months since she was diagnosed. Nine months. And I will do anything to make sure she lives—"

"Like let me adopt her," I interjected, thinking it would help.

"Exactly! Like find the sexiest, most infuriating, addictive man I've ever set eyes on and then shove him not into the friend zone, but the brother's friend zone, and then catapult him into the daddy zone, where, get this—he's still untouchable."

A rush of heat slammed through my body. I'd done so well keeping my hands to myself since our almost-disaster on the couch. I'd run six miles a day, taken cold showers, swam in the lake, you name it, all with the intention of keeping my hands off Ella, and with one tirade, she had me teetering on the edge of self-control. It had been almost a year since I'd had sex, and my body was reminding me in a very hard, very painful way that the only woman I wanted was standing in front of me, complaining that I was in the friend zone.

"Okay, stop. You didn't shove me into the friend zone; I put myself there. And the daddy zone, too. That's on me. Not on you."

"Then you're stupid!" she yelled, her eyes alight with the cutest indignation. "I mean, the friend zone, not the dad stuff."

"You're so cute."

Her eyes narrowed.

Oh damn, wrong choice of words.

"Cute? I'm cute? No, that's the issue. I haven't had my hair cut in a year, do you know how that feels? It's not the hair—I'm not that vain—it's the time, Beckett. The time it takes to invest in yourself as a woman, and

I'm not a woman anymore. I abandoned my makeup, my Sunday-night candle baths, I haven't slept a full night since Maisie's diagnosis, and I've been stuck wearing pants for a month because I haven't shaved my legs."

"I like you in pants."

"That's not the point! It's July, Beckett! July is for shorts and hikes and suntans, and being kissed under the moonlight. And I'm in jeans with no kisses, and my legs look like a Yeti somewhere in the Himalayas lent me his coat!"

"Wow, that's…really visual." *Don't laugh. Do. Not. Laugh.*

Oh yeah, those nails were leaving marks.

"I'm not a woman anymore. I'm a mom. A mom who can't be anything other than a mom because her kid might not live through the year." She deflated like a popped balloon, her hands leaving my biceps and her head landing with a small thud against my chest. "God, I'm selfish."

I wrapped my arms around her and pulled her in tight. "You're not selfish. You're human."

"Hair doesn't matter. Not on my legs or on my head. Not when Maisie doesn't even have any. I told you, we get a month of downtime, and my brain just runs amok on crap that doesn't matter." She mumbled the words into my chest.

"It matters because you matter. You know when you're on an airplane, and they tell you to put the oxygen mask on you first before your kids? This is that. If you only put the oxygen on your kid, then you pass out and can't help them. Every once in a while, you have to take a breath, Ella, or you're going to suffocate."

"I'm okay. I just needed to get that out."

"I know you are, and I can take it."

She pulled back an inch and gave me a sexy-as-hell

smirk.

"What?" I was almost afraid of her answer.

"Oh, nothing. It just doesn't *feel* like I'm in the friend zone." She shrugged.

Oh shit, I was hard, and I'd yanked her right against me.

"I never said I didn't want you, Ella. As a matter of fact, I'm pretty sure I said the opposite. Nothing's changed."

She blew a long breath out through her lips, moving a strand of blond hair that had slipped free of her ponytail. "Yeah, and it doesn't matter anyway. Hairy legs and all."

"You're killing me." I took her hand and turned around, then left the residence with her in tow, winding our way to the front desk where Hailey was handling paperwork of some kind. "Hailey."

"Beckett," she said in a mock-serious voice.

"Take Ella right now to get her hair cut. Get her a massage, a seaweed bath, or whatever it is you girls like to do. Paint toenails, get new clothes, all of it. You have five hours, and then I need her at the courthouse. Can you do that?"

"Beckett—" Ella objected.

"Stop," I pleaded. "You're giving me the gift of your kids. Let me give you a few hours. And afterward, we'll go out. To an actual restaurant with actual menus and no crayons on the table. No lawyers. No kids. Just us. And you'll feel as pretty as you always are to me."

"Ella, if you don't jump this guy, I will," Hailey stated.

Ella silenced her with a glare. "Hailey has to work."

"I'll handle the phones and guests," I offered.

"You will?" Ella scrunched her mouth to the side just like Maisie. "And you won't kill anyone who annoys you?"

"I will do my best to leave your business intact." I

pulled out my wallet and then handed Hailey my credit card. "Don't give this to Ella, she won't use it. Please go make her feel like a woman."

"This is going to be so much fun!" Hailey skipped out from behind the front desk. "I'll grab my purse, and then we'll go!"

"And I'll keep an eye on the littles," Ada chimed in, having caught the end of the exchange. "I'll put them to bed, too. You kids stay out as long as you like." She shouted the last part as she walked back toward the kitchen.

"Are you sure?" Ella asked me.

God, she was so beautiful. I took her hand and pulled her into an alcove just off the front hall. "You're stunning. You don't need makeup. There has never been a moment since I met you that I saw you as anything less than an incredible, exquisitely beautiful woman. But I understand that you don't feel the way I see you. So yes, I'm sure."

"You're always taking care of me," she whispered.

I gave in to impulse, letting my thumb slide across the soft, flawless skin of her cheek. "That's the idea." We were too close, the air too charged, and I loved this woman too much to keep a cool head. Before I inevitably pinned her to the wall and proved to her that virginity didn't just regrow, I needed to let her go. "I'll see you at the courthouse at four thirty," I promised. Then I lifted her hand, flipped it over, and pressed a long, soft kiss directly to the center of her palm, wishing more than anything that it was her mouth.

Her breath caught as I closed her grip, like she could hold on to the kiss.

"What was that for?"

"To prove that I don't give a crap about hairy legs. Plus, now it hasn't been seven years since you've been kissed."

Her lips parted, and her gaze dropped to my mouth. *Shit. Shit. Shit.*

I wasn't sure *need* was even the appropriate word for how badly I wanted Ella anymore. It was a constant ache that simply existed as my normal. Before I could do anything else I might regret later, I stepped out into the entry hall.

"You're positive you can handle the desk?"

I gave her a grin and winked. "I've got this." And I did. Maybe Ella and the kids were the only ones I really connected with, but I'd come a long way with the general public in the last four months.

Hailey grabbed Ella's hand and pulled her out of the house, sputtering, stunned face and all.

I made a mental note to wink at the woman more often.

CHAPTER EIGHTEEN

Ella

Letter #4

Ella,

Your kids are awesome. Seriously. I guess laughing probably isn't the right reaction to that story, but come on. That kid got his butt kicked by not just one but both of your kids. You're raising a couple badasses. Sorry, but that's actually the best word to describe them after that story.

As for kids of my own? Not sure that's in the cards for me. Not because I don't like kids. I honestly do. They're brutally honest, which is a trait usually lost by adulthood. But, I wouldn't know the first thing about being a dad, since I didn't have one. Maybe that's a good thing, since I don't have a bad example of fatherhood, either, but really, the only examples of dads I have in my life came from television.

I'd be too scared I'd screw up a kid.

But if I knew what I was doing? Yeah, kids would be great. I've never been the guy with the toss-the-football fantasy, but I could definitely picture something like that. I honestly don't think about it, or anything in the future, really. When you want something, or have a dream, you have something to lose. I'm not a fan of being put in the position to lose anything. Not to say that I'm not a little reckless, but only with myself and the things I can control.

It's wanting something that gets you into

trouble. Wanting makes you discontent, when I need to be grateful for what I do have. I learned that lesson young. I like to think it makes me a better person—being content with what I have— but I hear your brother talk about you, and your family, and I wonder sometimes if maybe that lack of want is really a small form of cowardice. In that way, you're much braver than I am. You have the ability to love beyond yourself, to risk your heart every day through your kids.

I respect that as much as I envy it.

Also, tell Maisie the next time a guy comes after her, she needs to go for the nuts. Little bullies grow up to be big bullies.

~ Chaos

"He winked at me," I told Hailey as I tried on the lavender dress. "Winked."

I loved the man, was seconds away from sharing my kids with him, and he'd *winked* at me. Pretty sure I'd hovered on the edge of an orgasm from that alone. Since when did he turn on the charm? And where had that charm been the last four months?

Broody Beckett, I adored.

Protective, playful Beckett, I loved.

But that Beckett who winked and kissed my palm? Yeah, I was lucky I hadn't spontaneously combusted and burned down my business.

"So you've told me about a dozen times since we left the house. A few times at the salon, at least once during pedicures, and six or seven times while we were getting waxed. Did you see the 'these rooms are for the quiet relaxation of others' sign? Pretty sure we're never going to be allowed back at that spa." She flipped through her phone.

"Whatever. I've just never seen that side of him. He was all…"

"Flirtatious?" she asked, looking up. "Ooh, I like that one. Your boobs look great."

I ran my finger along the neckline. "It's not too much?"

"Nope. It's retro hot. You look like a fifties housewife who gets her kink on in the bedroom."

I rolled my eyes but moved my hips so the bell of the knee-length dress swished lightly. I loved the halter neck, the sparkly belt that defined my waist, and even the slight plunge of the neckline. Mostly, I relished the feeling I had being in the dress, that I was a woman, curved and soft and freshly pampered.

"I think I'm going to get it."

"Beckett is going to lose his fool mind." She hopped up and walked around the dressing room pedestal, appraising the lines of the dress. "Yep. This is going to end up on the bedroom floor."

"Sure it will. Mine."

"Seriously?" Hailey popped a hip and shot me a more than exasperated look.

"He's afraid that being more than…whatever we are, would potentially screw us in the long term, and with the kids involved, and the Ryan stuff…" I shrugged.

"So walk into his room naked. That'll change his mind."

"Are you out of your mind? Why would I do that? I've had sex with one guy, Hailey. One. And that was seven years ago. To tell you the truth, it didn't exactly ring my bell."

"Because he probably didn't know where to find your *bell*."

I shook my head and smoothed the soft purple fabric beneath my newly manicured fingers. "It doesn't matter. Beckett isn't interested in me like that, and quite frankly, I shouldn't even be having this discussion. I have bigger issues to worry about."

I stepped off the podium and headed for the dressing room, leaving Hailey outside.

"He hasn't slept with anyone since he's been here, did you know that?" she asked through the slats in the door.

"What? How would you even know something like that?" I slipped off the dress and draped it on the hanger carefully.

"Because it's a small town, nitwit. Everyone talks, and Beckett is very gossip-worthy. Speculation is he's either gay or interested elsewhere…"

"I can tell you for certain he's not gay." I'd felt every delicious inch of him against me earlier, saw the way his muscles tensed when he pulled away.

"Duh. He's not sleeping around because he wants *you*. Trust me, if I saw an opening there, I'd be all over that. I honestly don't know how you haven't just climbed on top of him and—"

"Because he told me no!" I flushed, thinking of our little failed moment on the couch. "Honestly. He told me no. His loyalty to Ryan trumps everything else."

"Ella?"

"What?" I said, grabbing my shirt.

"You didn't take the dress off, right? Because you're supposed to meet him at the courthouse in like ten minutes."

I grabbed my phone, swiping the screen to see the time. "Shit," I muttered.

"Put these on, too." She dropped a pair of black heels and a silver shrug over the door. "Come on, unless you want to be naked at the courthouse. And while, yes, I do think that would accomplish the sex mission, I do think it might interfere with the adoption mission."

I dressed quickly and walked out of the dressing room.

"Turn," Hailey ordered, and when I did so, she snapped the tag off the back, already holding a shoebox and another set of tags. "Come on!"

With an armful of my own clothes, we walked up to the register.

"She's wearing all this." Hailey dropped the tags and box on the counter.

The teenage boy looked me over and smiled. "I can see that."

"But not for long," Hailey added with a little wink.

Seriously, what's with the winking today?

Hailey paid using Beckett's credit card, and I felt that same flash of guilt I had at the salon. But I didn't have time to focus on it as we raced for the courthouse.

Beckett stood outside in a perfectly tailored suit, his hair styled in sexy disarray. When he saw me, he smiled slow and wide, taking the time to drag his eyes from my polished toes to the soft waves of blond that fell to just beneath my breasts. He finally met my eyes and visibly swallowed.

"Wow."

"Four thirty-one, and she's all yours!" Hailey declared, handing Beckett his credit card.

"Thanks, Hailey." He tucked the card inside his breast pocket.

"What do you say, Ella MacKenzie? Want to make me a dad?" He offered his arm, and my heart fluttered like the thousand butterflies that had taken up residence in my stomach.

"You could definitely go for that later," Hailey whispered as I walked by, but I just shot her a little glare and turned my attention to Beckett.

Then I forgot all about Hailey and took his arm.

He smelled incredible and, as he opened the door for me, I leaned in to take a deeper breath. It was like the guy rubbed himself in new leather and wind and really yummy things. Whatever it was, it absolutely worked for him.

We walked through the foyer, and I paused at the sweeping staircase.

"What's wrong?" he asked, his tone gentle.

"The last time I was in this courthouse, I walked out married to Jeff. And as wrong as that decision was, I can't regret it, because it gave me the twins. It led me to this moment. To you."

His grip tightened on my hand, and his attention flickered to my lips.

Kiss me.

"There you two are!" Mark called from the head of the stairs. "Let's get this show started, shall we?"

"Shall we?" Beckett asked, his voice low and rough.

"Yes. Let's."

A half hour later, we walked out of the courthouse with a piece of paper that said Beckett was now Maisie and Colt's father.

I knew it was only to protect Maisie, to give her the very best shot she had at beating the disease, but the moment we'd both signed, it felt more significant than a business transaction.

A tiny but undeniable flame of hope had flared in my heart that it wasn't just on paper—it was real.

My kids were now Beckett's, too.

And I was head over heels in love with him.

"I hate him!" I swore as I slammed my front door four hours later. Beckett's headlights faded as he headed back to his cabin.

"Hate who?" Ada asked, coming out of the kitchen.

"Beckett is my guess," Larry said from the mudroom floor, where he was repairing Maisie's dollhouse.

"Yes, Beckett!" I snapped. "Oh, thanks, Larry. I re-

REBECCA YARROS   271

ally appreciate that."

"Did the adoption not go well?" Ada asked quietly, pulling me into the office.

"No, it was great. The whole night was perfect! He took me to dinner and ordered wine, and then took me up the gondola to the Village for one of those little open-air concerts and danced with me. The man danced with me! And then he brought me home, walked me to the door, and hugged me. He *hugged* me good night."

The worry fell right off her face, and she sighed with a soft smile. "Oh, Ella. You've gone and fallen in love with him, haven't you?"

"He hugged me!"

"Not that I blame you. He's a good man; he really is. He's spectacular with the kids, and kind, and dependable, and really easy to look at. Add in his knight-in-shining-armor complex, and you were bound to fall for him." She took my hands.

"He hugged me," I whispered.

"What are you going to do about it?"

"Nothing. He's already made it clear that's off the table, and I can't blame him. I'm not exactly baggage free, you know. Two kids, one who is sick, a business to run, huge trust issues. I'm not really what someone like him would look for."

"And what exactly is he like?"

"Pretty perfect."

Ada sighed and dropped my hands. "Okay, well, you feel free to stay in here and pout. But just in case you feel like acting your age and doing something spontaneous, Larry and I are taking the guest room for the night. So we'll be here. All night. And into the morning. You know…just in case."

"I do act my age."

"Oh, honey, you don't, and you never have. You're not old, not damaged, not a dried-up spinster. You're twenty-five. So yeah. I'm going to bed."

I stood in my office, unwilling to move but also unready to take off my heels. That felt a little too much like defeat.

YOU ARE ENOUGH.

I stared at Chaos's words, chanting them in my head. He was right. I was enough, and I was done being a passive participant in whatever my relationship was with Beckett.

Glancing at Maisie's handmade diploma, my eyes lingered on Beckett's choppy handwriting. What was it with military guys and their worse-than-doctor handwriting? His was just as bad as Chaos's, and that was saying something.

I'd lost Chaos before I could act on my feelings, and I wasn't going to make the same mistake with Beckett.

I left my office, snatched my keys off the entry table, and walked out. I could have sworn I heard an "attagirl," coming from the guest room window as I climbed into my car, but when I looked back, the room was dark.

"You are enough," I mumbled to myself the entire time I drove to Beckett's cabin. His lights were on, so at least I wasn't waking the man up. I parked the car, and then I swallowed back the slight taste of panic that flooded my mouth, straightening my back as I walked up his steps.

Knock. Knock. Knock.

I set my knuckles to the door before I could chicken out, but in the precious seconds it took for Beckett to answer, I started to grow some very chicken-like feathers around my heart.

"Ella?" he answered, flinging the door open wide. He was still in his suit, but he'd loosened his tie and unbuttoned the top button at his throat, revealing a small section of skin that I was suddenly desperate to kiss. "Is everything okay? Is it Maisie?"

"Maisie's fine," I told him, both annoyed and loving him more because he thought of her first.

"Oh good. What's going on? Come on in." He stepped aside, and I walked into the cabin, heading down the hallway. Where before it had been cold and impersonal, now it had pictures that Colt and Maisie had drawn hanging in various places, like those I found myself staring at on his fridge as I wandered into the kitchen. He'd adapted his "neat and orderly" and let us "complicate" the very space he lived in. Silly, but the pictures calmed a tiny bit of my rampant fear that Beckett would disappear one day.

"Do you want a drink?" he asked slowly.

"No." I spun around to find him leaned back against the counter. He'd ditched the suit coat on our walk in. "You took me on a date."

"Yes." He gave me a sexy little smile as he unbuttoned the cuffs of his shirt, and I wanted to kick him.

"You took me on a date. Dinner, dancing, romantic little walk. Then you took me to my door and hugged me. Like I'm your sister." I stalked forward, and his expression changed, a look of hunger flashing before he got it under control.

"I did. Guilty on all counts."

"I'm not your sister, Beckett."

"I've noticed." He sucked in a deep breath and put his hands on the counter, his knuckles turning instantly white.

I brought myself flush against him, nearly groaning at the press of his hard muscles under my fingers as I rested my hands on his chest.

"Well, maybe dates have changed in the last seven or so years, but in my limited experience, they end with a kiss." I rose up on my tiptoes until my mouth hovered just under his.

"Ella." He said my name like a plea, but for what? To give us what we both wanted? For me to back away and leave him to sleep with his honor?

"Tell me what you want. Because I want to kiss you. Even if it's just this once." I closed the tiny gap between our mouths and brushed my lips over his. How could a man that hard have such soft lips?

His body turned to stone against mine, every muscle locked. Under my fingertips, his heart started to pound.

Growing bolder, I kissed him softly, lingering on his bottom lip. Then I retreated just enough to look into his eyes. The rest of him might be a statue, but those eyes said everything he wouldn't, and he was a second away from—

His mouth slammed against mine, and the rest of him came alive. One of his hands tunneled through the back of my hair while the other wrapped around my waist and tugged me even closer.

I opened under him, and his tongue swept inside, taking, consuming, learning every line of my mouth. A moan slipped from my lips, and I buried my hands in his hair, tugging gently at the short strands.

Then I kissed him back like I'd been dreaming about for months.

Our mouths tangled, the kiss tasting sweet, like the wine we'd finished after our dance, and just as intoxicating. He sucked my tongue into his mouth, and I eagerly rubbed against his, stroking and caressing. Good God, the man knew what he was doing.

My entire world existed in this kiss, in the feel of Beckett's arms around me.

He switched the tempo, gently sucking at my bottom lip before tilting his head and kissing me deeper until I became nothing but need. Heat rushed through my veins, bringing me to life, a euphoric variation of the tingles in my limbs after they'd fallen asleep and were brought back to feeling.

"God, Ella," he groaned, his fingers tight in my hair.

"Yes," I urged, loving everything about this. He curved his body over mine, then lifted me by my ass and spun, setting me on the counter. Then he used both hands to hold my head and kissed me until I couldn't remember my own name—only that I belonged to him.

My fingers ran along his neck, until I had ahold of his tie from underneath, curling my fingers through the space where he'd loosened the knot.

"I could kiss you forever," he said against my mouth.

"I'm okay with that."

He smiled, and I couldn't help but mirror it. Everything about this felt so incredibly right. He brushed back a strand of my hair from my face with a tenderness that made my heart lurch, like it was reaching for him. *I love this man.* That thought alone sent my need up a notch, until I was aching and restless.

My sex drive the last seven years had been a broken circuit, and suddenly the lights were coming back on, as Beckett flipped switch after switch.

Kissing me again, he slid his arms around me, and when he pulled me to the edge of the counter, I parted my thighs, bringing us together from lips, to chest, to hips. There was an edge to the kiss now, a rough desperation that could only be the result of the desire we'd both kept tightly leashed the last few months.

I cursed the layers of fabric between us, wishing I'd chosen a shorter, less fluffy skirt. He broke our kiss, and I gasped, sucking in some much-needed air when he put his mouth to my neck. *Holy shit.*

"Beckett," I whimpered, letting my head roll back and giving him unfettered access to whatever parts of me he wanted. They were all his.

He supported my arched back with one hand and

flicked open the lone button of my shrug with the other, never pausing in his assault on my neck. He rained long, openmouthed kisses down my neck, over my collarbone, and down to my neckline.

My heels hit the hardwood floor as I kicked them off, locking my ankles around his waist to bring him harder against me.

That earned me another groan from his lips. Leaning back, I braced my hands on the cool granite, so at odds with the heat of my skin. He ran his hands over the sides of my breasts, to my waist, down over my dress-covered thighs, until he reached the bare skin of my knees.

I'd never been so glad I refused panty hose in my entire life.

Strong hands slid beneath my dress, running up the sides of my legs. His skin was rough and calloused, yet his touch gentle but for the press of his fingers when he squeezed at the top of my thighs. I had the insane urge to ask him to tighten his grip, to leave some kind of mark that would tell me tomorrow that this had really happened—it wasn't all a dream.

He kissed me, taking my mouth in a rhythm that made my hips arch into him, wishing his hands would move. I'd never been kissed with such expertise or care, never felt my blood rise to a fever pitch like this. It was utter, complete, delicious madness.

His thumbs stroked down the line of my inner thighs, brushing the edge of my panties, and I felt the sensation *everywhere*. In my core, my belly, the tips of my breasts. That simple motion caressed my heartbeat and sent it skyrocketing.

"More," I begged, squeezing my thighs around him, needing the pressure to ease the ache, even if just a little.

Like I'd bitten him, he released my thighs and

stepped back, my shock loosening my grip enough that he broke the lock on my ankles.

"Okay, that's the opposite of more," I said, my words as choppy as my breath.

He leaned back against the other counter, his chest rising and falling just as rapidly as mine. At least I wasn't the only one affected by that kiss. He looked flat-out tortured and a little angry as he ripped his tie loose.

Damn, that was sexy.

He closed his eyes as his hands tugged at his hair. He was the very picture of an intensely aroused man who couldn't get a grip on his control, and maybe I was mean, but I loved knowing I'd put him there.

"Beckett."

"No." He shook his head as he opened his eyes. The way his gaze raked over me, my dress barely covering my still-spread thighs, was intense enough to send another wave of pure lust through my system. "Not like this."

A quick cut of fear slid down my sternum. Had the kiss not been the same gravity-bending event for him that it had been for me?

"You'd prefer to wait another four months to make out? Because this is us, Beckett. I'm always going to be Ryan's sister. I'm always going to want you, and if the way you just kissed me is any indication, you want me just as badly."

"I always knew it would be like this between us. From the moment I set eyes on you, I knew the minute my hands…" He caught the side of his bottom lip between his teeth for a second, then gripped the counter.

"Your hands what?" I taunted, sitting up straight and giving my arms a rest.

"I knew the minute I got my hands on you, it would take a miracle for me to stop long enough to get a rational thought in my head. Touching you… God, Ella, if you had any idea how badly I want you, you would not still be sitting on my counter looking at me like that."

"Maybe I do know." I ran my tongue over my lower lip. "Maybe I feel the same exact way. And rational thoughts are overrated."

"Think this through."

"Why? Maybe I want to be reckless for once. Maybe I like the way you take every rational thought out of my head. Maybe that's exactly why I need this—need you." The ache centered between my thighs had me shifting my hips. Sex had never been something I sought out, or a big fireworks show, but I never remembered it starting with this torturous, clawing need, either.

"I'm really trying here."

Trying my patience.

The sting of rejection was sharp. I brought my knees together and buttoned my shrug with trembling hands. "I don't get you. I tell you I want you to kiss me, and you jump across the couch. I shave my legs and put on a dress, and you hug me good night. I throw myself at you, and you kiss me like I'm the only woman in the world, and now you're over there. Beckett, I can't make my wants any clearer, and I can't be the one who always has to chase you. If you want me physically, but don't want *me*, then say it. Because I'm done listening to you tell me no like there's something wrong with me."

He had the nerve to look wounded, like his constant arm's-length approach to our physical nearness was more painful to him than it was to me. Like I wasn't the one constantly trying to push our relationship out of the friend zone.

"Do you see me as a sister? Is that it?"

"Hell no!" He sighed. "And now I've sworn at you twice."

"I really don't mind. You could throw in an F-bomb

if it meant you were interested in using it as a verb." I put my hands on the counter and prepared to jump down, find my shoes and my dignity, and take my sexually frustrated butt home.

"Look at me." His voice had taken on that gravelly tone that I loved.

I brought my eyes to his, wishing I could understand what the hell the man was thinking about. What kept him from taking what I knew—or at least really hoped—he wanted. "What are you thinking?" I broke down and asked.

"I'm counting how many glasses of wine you had. Two at dinner. One after the concert, and it's been what? Five hours?" His eyes narrowed in thought.

"I'm not drunk, if that's what you're implying! Like I need alcohol as an excuse—"

"Oh no," he cut me off, dropping his voice even lower. "I'm not asking for you. I'm asking for *me,* so that I know when I ask this next question, you're not too drunk to answer it."

My tongue wet my suddenly dry lips. "Okay."

"Do you want me, Ella?"

"I think I've been pretty clear that I do."

He shook his head. "No. I didn't say 'do you want to make out with me?' Do you want *me*? Because I'm standing here, trying to keep my hands on the counter so I don't send them up your dress to the insides of your thighs."

My lips parted, too heavy to stay closed.

"Because I know once they're stroking over that soft skin, there's no way I'm going to be able to breathe without taking you, sliding inside you like I've fantasized about for entirely too long." He enunciated that last bit, driving home exactly what he wanted to happen in case I hadn't gotten the picture.

That was exactly what I wanted, craved...needed

more than the very breath he was talking about.

"And once that happens, everything changes between us, Ella. So I need you to tell me that you want me, or walk out that door before something happens that you're not ready for."

I couldn't remember being more ready for anything in my life.

"I." I opened the button of my shrug. "Want." I took it off. "You." I dropped it to the floor.

"Ella." He pushed off the counter.

"Here and now," I added, unfastening the button of the halter behind my neck, just in case the man needed my consent—hell, my plea—on record. The straps fluttered to my sides, the curves of my breasts holding the neckline in place.

"Thank you, God." He didn't bother with the buttons on his shirt, just reached over the back of his head and pulled it off in that incredibly sexy way guys had. But Beckett made it about a hundred times sexier as his torso was revealed.

All rippling muscles and kissable skin. *Pretty sure I could orgasm just looking at him.* Not that I'd ever had that happen without a little battery-powered assistance, but if there ever was a moment, this was it.

"You are so…" I waved my hands in his direction. "All that is just… I don't have words."

"Good," he said, dropping his shirt to the floor. "Because I'm going to need to use that mouth for other things besides talking." He closed the distance between us in two strides, took my knees in his hands, and parted my thighs. Then he made good on his promise, sending his hands up my dress until they reached the tops of my thighs, only to grip, then pull us flush.

I locked my arms around his neck when he kissed me. It was deep, powerful, and primal, his mouth taking mine like he was staking a claim. Unleashed, Beckett kissed with a little less finesse and a lot more urgency. My body responded, tightening my breasts and rushing heat over my skin.

I gasped against his mouth as his thumb slid beneath the edge of my panties, and my nails bit into his scalp lightly when he parted me and grazed my clit.

"Beckett," I pleaded, pushing my hips toward him in reflex.

"I've got you," he promised. Then he kissed me slowly, his tongue sliding with mine as his thumb worked me over, swirling, stroking, and pressing, turning that warmth in my belly into a knot of tension that he wound tighter and tighter.

I moved restlessly, my need to feel his skin against mine warring with my equal need to keep his hands exactly where they were. As if he sensed my thoughts, his unoccupied hand skimmed up over my waist to my back, where he unzipped my dress.

The fabric gave way easily, baring my strapless bra. I arched, pressing my breasts against his chest, and he pressed his thumb against my clit, sending bolts of pleasure through me, sweet and sharp at the same time.

Stilling his thumb, he did some form of witchcraft behind my back that unsnapped my bra, freeing my breasts as it fell to my lap. He broke our kiss to look down at me, reverently cupping a breast and running his fingers over my hardened nipple.

"Perfect," he said before dipping his head to take it into his mouth. Moving his thumb at the same time, I arched my back and cried out.

It felt so damn good.

I threw my hands behind me to catch my weight and gave myself over to his mouth and fingers. That tension in me spiraled tighter until I was wound impossibly tight, my muscles locking in what I hoped might be my first—

"Beckett!" I screamed his name when he pressed my clit in a deep stroke, sending my body into full meltdown as my orgasm took me over the edge, the release coming in powerful waves that tilted the earth's axis.

He kissed me down with light, sipping caresses of his lips against mine. Until I summoned the strength to open my eyes and found him watching me, a look of utter adoration on his face.

"I could watch you do that a million times and still want more."

"That was…" What was it about this man that stole all my words and turned me into a half-sentence-producing moron? "Good job."

He grinned. "Good job?"

Oh God, I'd just verbally high-fived the guy.

"Well, yeah. I've never…without…well, with someone."

His eyes widened in understanding. "There's so much more."

"Yeah, I like that plan." Before I could say something else ridiculous, I kissed him, running my hands down his back. His skin was firm, warm, and so very soft. When I reached his belt, I skimmed my fingers along his waistline, savoring the way his abs flexed, and he sucked in a breath between kisses.

When I got to his zipper, I grew bold and took his erection in my hand and lightly gripped him. He was as hard as the granite beneath me, long, thick, and—if it was anything like the rest of his body—no doubt perfect.

His indrawn breath turned into a full-on hiss of air between his gritted teeth.

"Ella…"

I simply looked at him, letting him see how badly I wanted him, this, us. All of it.

Instead of stopping me, he simply nodded and shut

his eyes for the few seconds I had of stroking up and down his length.

"God, baby," he whispered.

He gave me one more chance to stroke, and then took my hand away, putting it on the counter. Before I could complain, he took his wallet out of his back pocket, slapping it on the counter next to me.

Then—thank you, all that is good and right in the world—he unsnapped his pants, kicking off his shoes and stripping down to nothing so quickly that all I could do was watch in appreciation.

The man was straight-up perfection, and all mine for the touching.

My mouth watering, I ran my fingers from his pecs down the lines of his abs, taking the time to fall from one ridge to the next. He wasn't just defined, he was built, his muscles bulging down his stomach.

He stepped forward, between my thighs, and kissed me until I couldn't think of anything except the feel of his mouth, the warmth of his skin, the rhythm of his breath. He lifted me slightly, adjusting my dress so my butt hit the granite, then slid the fabric over my head, leaving me in nothing but my blue silk panties.

Then he locked eyes with me, hooked his thumbs in the straps, and dragged them down my legs and off. There was no time to be embarrassed, not when he was kissing me, skin to skin. The contact heightened everything, and our hands were quickly everywhere—touching, seeking, discovering each other.

When he slipped his hands between my thighs, that familiar pressure built again, the ache within me beginning to pulse.

"So beautifully wet," he said between kisses.

Then he slid a finger inside me, and I almost came off the counter. "That feels incredible." I rocked against his finger, and he added another, the stretch making that ache throb.

He flipped open his wallet with his free hand, sliding a foil packet free.

"Upstairs?" he asked.

"Here. Now. No more waiting." Nearly mindless over the steady, deep strokes of his fingers, I grabbed the condom and ripped it open. My hands shook as I brought it to the head of his erection. I'd been right, even that was perfect.

"I don't know— Oh God, Beckett!" He'd added a third finger while his thumb gently grazed my hypersensitive clit.

"Need help?"

"Yes. No experience with…" I groaned when he curled his fingers, finding that elusive spot inside me that had my hips moving to ride his hand. "These. Pregnant at eighteen, remember?"

He covered my hand with his, pushing us down his length slowly until he was covered. "That may have been the most erotic thing I've done in my life," I whispered.

"Me, too. You take everything in my life up a notch."

His mouth met mine in a long, carnal kiss that ended with him gently tugging at my bottom lip. His fingers slid free of me, and I tensed as he leveled his hips with mine.

"Nervous?" he asked, kissing the spot just beneath my ear.

"A little. It's been seven years since I've done this."

He took my face in his hands and kissed me softly. "Pretty sure it still works the same way."

I smiled and instantly relaxed with another kiss.

"Don't worry, I've got you," he said again, and the words took my nervousness like it never existed.

As if he wasn't positioned between my thighs, he took my mouth with care and, within a few moments, I had my ankles locked around his waist, savoring the contrast of his hard frame with my curves. He stroked down my body, bringing that fire back even hotter than it had been.

When my hips started rocking against his fingers he leaned his forehead against mine. And when that ache roared, and I reached for his hips, he gripped mine, nudging his erection at my entrance.

"Please," I said, arching against him.

Keeping one hand on my hip, he gripped the back of my head with the other and brought us so close our breaths mingled, but he didn't kiss me, simply watched my eyes as he pushed inside me inch by slow inch.

I let out a soft moan as he seated himself, so deep that I could feel him throughout my body, as if he'd pierced my soul.

"Ella," he groaned. "God, you're everything."

He shifted the hand on my hip to under my ass, lifting me slightly and pulling me to the barest edge of the counter before he began to thrust in a deep, sure rhythm. Our bodies moved like we'd been making love together for years instead of moments, like he was the only man I'd been created for.

I wrapped my arms around him, holding the back of his head as he took me higher and higher, each stroke bringing that tension to the breaking point, until our bodies were slick with sweat.

He didn't change his pace, just took me over and over like it would last forever, like there was no goal other than feeling that moment. There were no alarm clocks, no schedules, nowhere more pressing to be than right here in the arms of the man I loved.

My muscles locked, straining for release, and Beckett kissed me, at the same time sliding his thumb between us to stroke my clit. I came apart, crying out as the orgasm washed over me, deeper and harder than I'd ever felt in my life. He took my cries into his mouth, like he was feeding off my pleasure, like it was more than sex to him, too.

I held him close, emotion taking me beyond reason.

"I love you." The words tumbled from my mouth without preamble or thought.

He paused, his eyes flying wide. Then he kissed me deep and hard as he thrust wildly, without rhythm, tensing in my arms and letting go, burying his face in my neck as he found his release, my name on his lips.

Before I could feel awkward, he pulled back, taking my face in his hands. Our breathing was erratic, and his slowed before mine did. "I love you," he said, keeping his eyes locked with mine.

"Really?" It was almost too much to hope, to have that kind of happiness.

"I've loved you since the beginning. Nice to know you caught up."

My smile was instant and matched his.

"Now, how long do we have? Because I'd like to take you upstairs and do this again properly."

If that wasn't proper, I couldn't wait to see what was.

"All night. We have all night."

"I can work with that."

And he did.

Another three times before breakfast.

CHAPTER NINETEEN

Beckett

Letter #4

Chaos,

David Robins asked me out today. Who is David Robins, you're probably asking? He's actually quite the catch around here. Twenty-eight, good-looking, firefighter, all the romance novel stuff. Any girl in her right mind would have said yes.

Of course, I said no. I told you once, I don't have time for men, and nothing's changed in the last six weeks that we've been writing each other. I've finally got Solitude ready to take the world by storm, and I just can't afford the distraction.

But then, sometimes when I'm lying in bed at night, I wonder if that's all it is. Of course I didn't date while I was pregnant. Sure the divorce went through, but I had bigger matters on my mind. When Colt and Maisie were born, that first year was a blur between feedings and teething and two babies on two schedules. Sure, they're cute now, but they weren't so cute at two a.m., I promise. Then they were toddlers, and I was still running around like a chicken with my head cut off, or a single mom with twins—whatever. Now they're in kindergarten, and I feel like I'm finally getting my feet under me.

But I still said no when David asked me.

What the heck am I waiting for? It's not like I need a lightning bolt. I'm not a silly romantic girl anymore. I know there's more to a great *relationship than chemistry.*

    But I also don't want to end up the crazy cat lady down the street. I've honestly never been a cat person, so that would probably be an issue at some point.

    What about you? Is it difficult dating when you're gone so often? Is it something you think about? Happy single? It's got to be hard trying to start something when you're usually halfway around the world, huh?

    ~ Ella

She looked so peaceful while she slept. Usually Ella was going a mile a minute—always somewhere she needed to be or something she needed to do, but while she slept, everything about her relaxed.

She deserved to look like this all the time.

I looked past her sleeping face to the clock. Seven thirty a.m. I hadn't slept this late, or this well since…I couldn't even remember when. No nightmares and no runaway thoughts, just Ella and sweet, blissful sleep.

Havoc woke, shaking off her sleep, and laid her head on the bed.

As quietly as possible, I got up, grabbing a pair of sweat pants and putting them on. We might have been secluded out here, but I really didn't want to shock the hell out of any guests who might be taking a morning stroll around the lake.

We made our way through the house, and I opened the door on the back deck. Havoc ran out and was already to the woods by the time I made it down the steps to the patio beneath.

The stones were cold on my bare feet, but I stood there anyway, letting the chill take the warmth of my bed. Cold meant it was real. Ella was upstairs in my bed.

I'd spent last night showing her exactly how I felt about her, and if Havoc hurried up, I might be able to sneak back into bed and show her again.

She loved me.

The joy that I felt at that knowledge was tempered by my guilt from knowing that I didn't deserve it. I'd won her love by default, because she only knew this side of me — I'd kept the other carefully tucked away. Hidden like the dirty little secret it was.

"What do I do now?" I asked Ryan, looking out toward the island.

I'd pushed her away until I'd broken, my self-control next to nothing when it came to that woman. If I'd been a better man, I would have sent her away last night. Would have stopped after that kiss. I definitely wouldn't have taken her on the kitchen counter, and then in my bed, and in my shower. A better man would have told her the secret then, now that the adoption was done and Colt and Maisie were protected financially.

A better man would have come clean and taken the consequences.

Clearly, I was not the better man.

I hadn't told her because I didn't want to lose the look from her face. Didn't want to lose the warmth of her love, her body, her heart. I wasn't ready for my dream to be over yet. Hell, I didn't tell her because I was selfish and in so deep now that there was no getting out.

Havoc ran back to me, and I rubbed her behind the ears. "Shall we grab some breakfast?"

We walked up the deck stairs and through the sliding glass door.

"Oh!" Ella paused with her butt in the air, trying to get her shoe on. "Good morning?" She was already dressed in what she'd worn on our date, her hair pulled up in a knot, and her cheeks rosy from sleep and sex.

"Was that a question? Because I happen to think it's a pretty great morning." I walked through the living room to where she stood at the edge of the kitchen.

"Well, yeah. I mean, I think so?" She gave me an awkward smile that would have made any rom-com director proud.

"But you're not sure?"

Her eyes ran down my chest and back up, her cheeks turning an even deeper shade of pink. "No, I'm sure. It's a good morning."

Holy crap, she was embarrassed. My Ella, who didn't care what anyone thought of her, was all sorts of discombobulated in my kitchen at seven in the morning.

"Coffee?" I asked, letting my hand slide around her waist to her back as I passed by her.

"Oh. I have to get home. I'm sure the kids are up and…all that." She started looking around the counter, moving the coffee maker to the side.

"Ella, what are you looking for?" I asked.

"My keys? I know I had them, right? Because I drove over, but I don't remember what happened to them once I walked in. I got distracted, I guess."

I reached for her hand, taking hold of it and turning her to face me. "You didn't have them when you walked in. My guess would be that they're in your car."

"Oh no! What if someone stole it!" She started to move, but I blocked her path with a side step.

"Honey, we're in the middle of nowhere. No one stole your car."

Her eyes closed. "Why would I leave them in the car? Because that's what mature adults do, right? They leave their keys in the car while they run off and do whatever it is they want."

She was so flustered and cute, but I knew what was triggering the minor meltdown, and we had to sort it out. Now.

"Open your eyes. Ella. Please."

Slowly her lashes fluttered, and those baby blues looked up at me. "What?"

"I'm in love with you. I was in love with you before we slept together, and I'll be in love with you for the rest of my life if my heart is any indication. Nothing about last night changed that. I'm me. You're you. We're…whatever you want us to be."

"What are we?"

"What do you want us to be?" My chest tightened, waiting for her to answer. Whatever she wanted, I'd give her.

"What do *you* want us to be?" She turned the tables.

Suddenly I saw every discussion over what we'd be having for dinner for the next fifty years. "I want you. I told you that last night."

"You wanted sex. It's daylight now, and I'm not holding you to whatever you said last night. And I know this has got to be the most awkward morning-after ever, so I'm sorry, but I don't have a lot of experience in this department." She pulled her trembling lip between her teeth.

"I want you. All of you. Trust me, getting to put my hands on you is a pretty big perk, because I'm not sure if anyone told you or not, but you're incredibly gorgeous. But I want more than a night of you in my bed. Or on the kitchen counter."

I guess she really could turn a deeper shade of pink. I hadn't thought it possible.

"So where does that leave us?"

"Well, my day is clear. So I figured we'd pound on the clerk and recorder's office until they opened on Monday, and then we'd immediately marry." Her jaw dropped, and I couldn't help but continue. "Unless you're more of a hop-a-flight-to-Vegas girl, in which case, I'm down. Then we're moving to my small yet loyal cult of doomsday followers. I've already made preparations for you and the kids in the fallout shelter, where you'll tend grapes."

She blinked, her mouth still agape.

"Unless you'd rather be assigned to the goats." Thank God for all the nights Ryan had made me play poker; I was able to keep a straight face.

"You're kidding."

"Yes." I took her face in my hands.

"Oh, thank God." Her entire frame relaxed.

"I figured we'd date. Like normal people. Look, you waited for marriage to sleep with your first, so I know what it means to you. And if you wanted to go get married today, I would absolutely—"

"Don't finish that!" She put her hand over my mouth. "Dating is good. I like dating."

I kissed her hand, and she let it fall away.

"Okay. Then we're dating." My smile was so wide it hurt my cheeks.

"Exclusively," she said with a nod.

"Twist my arm, why don't you?" I bent for a kiss, and she stepped back with that don't-mess-with-me look she was so fond of. "Exclusively," I agreed. "Ella, there's a reason I haven't been with anyone since I came here."

"Oh, because you're out of shape and wanted to tone up a little first?" She gave me a mocking head tilt.

"Ha. Because from the moment I saw your face and heard you speak, you were the only one I wanted. You ruined me for anyone else before you ever knew my name." She'd ruined me from the second she'd said she regretted writing in pen. She'd had every ounce of my soul when I finished that first letter. "Now that I've had a night with you, I don't want only one. I want them all, and I'm willing to take whatever you want to give me."

She looked torn for a second and then sighed in frustration. "That was *really* good. I don't have anything that awesome to say. I just love you."

I kissed her softly, a simple caress of our lips, because I couldn't help myself. "That's the most awesome thing you could have said. Trust me. It's not something I'm used to hearing." Or anything I deserved, but I was the asshole who was going to take it.

"What do we tell the kids about us? I know that's not usual first-date conversation, but we're not exactly usual."

"I'll take my lead from you. Whatever you want to tell them, we'll tell them."

She brought her arms around my neck. "Well, I mean, you are their father."

"Have to say that I love hearing that, too." *Even if it's just between us*. I knew this wouldn't change the way she felt about keeping the adoption secret, and that was okay. For the first time since I arrived in Telluride, I felt like I had time. Time to win her over, time to earn her trust.

"Okay, we'll tell them we're dating. It's not like we'd be able to hide it around them for long anyway." She pressed against me.

"And why is that?"

"Because I have no idea how to not kiss you all the time now that I know how incredibly good at it you are." Her fingers curled in my hair.

"Now look at who's saying all the awesome things."

Then I reminded her exactly how good at it I was. Until she stole every thought from my head, and I was once again at her mercy.

Were people allowed to be this happy? It seemed almost unnatural to have this as my new normal. I woke up, went to work, had dinner with Ella and the kids, and stole kisses when they weren't looking.

I hadn't been lying when I said I could kiss her forever.

She was a thousand different kisses in one woman, the soft and tender, the deep and passionate, the hard and desperate. I never knew who I was taking in my arms, and yet they were all Ella.

Everything was Ella.

I'd taken a leap of faith and reserved my cabin indefinitely. Ella had protested the cost, but I'd handed Hailey my credit card with a smile. Indefinitely wasn't forever, and I'd already found the perfect place to start on something more permanent.

Turned out I'd gotten some sound investment advice from a friend, and the location was perfect.

"What do think about a zip line?" Colt asked from the back of Ella's cabin, staring up at the tree house we'd spent the last ten days building.

"I think that's something you'd need to ask your mom about, because I'm so not getting into that fight." I ruffled the short, buzzed locks of his hair. He'd stopped shaving it the month Maisie had gotten to skip chemo, and it was growing back quickly.

It had been a month since I'd adopted the kids, and eleven days since Ella had taken Maisie to Denver for her first MIBG treatment.

"I'd wear a helmet!" he argued.

Stay strong, I reminded myself. It had been just Colt and me for the last eleven days, with some help from Ada and Hailey, of course, and I was surprised he wasn't ruling the roost yet. Probably because he'd spent more than half of those days in school.

"Oh, I don't think that would even be a debate. Stop pushing your luck, kid."

He sighed. "Fine. But what about a dirt ramp for my quad?"

Huh. Now that idea had some merit. "Hmmm."

He saw my weakness and pounced, revealing that grin. "You know what?"

"What?" I asked with my hand on his shoulder.

"I think I was right. You know, back at the soccer game."

I tried to think of which game he was referring to out of the dozens he'd had so far. "About what?"

"This *is* what it feels like to have a dad."

Oh shit, I was going to cry.

"Well, maybe not *every* dad. I know Bobby's dad couldn't build this. And Laura's dad is really cool, too; he flies planes. Maybe all dads are just cool in different ways, you know? Like some dads aren't even, you know…dads."

"Yeah," I said softly, because I couldn't think of another word. My brain was mush, right along with my heart.

"I've put a lot of thought into this." He gave me a serious nod.

"I can tell. I love you, little man."

"Yeah, I love you, too. And I'd really like a dirt ramp."

I laughed as Ella pulled into the driveway.

"Mom's home!" Colt ran up the hill, Havoc happily chasing him, and me at their heels. Funny how I'd been deployed for a year, sometimes more, and yet the last eleven days seemed longer than any of that.

Time moved slower when you missed the person you love.

I got to the driveway in time to see Ella hop out of her car and hug Colt. Then she rubbed Havoc's ears and cooed something at her before standing back up and pushing her sunglasses to the top of her head.

"Hey, you." She smiled, and my chest threatened to explode. I loved her more now than I had a month ago, or even four months ago. I didn't know how my heart was going to contain all of this emotion if it kept growing at this rate.

I picked her up and kissed her, feeling the rush of

home like I always did when our lips touched. "I missed you."

She held my beard-rough cheeks and kissed me again. "I missed you."

"Yeah, we get it. You missed each other." Colt laughed, already throwing open the back door. "Do you glow? Do you have superpowers?"

"I don't think so," Maisie answered, her voice quieter than usual.

"How do you know? Did you check? You might have spidey senses."

I set Ella down and headed toward the open door, where Maisie was swinging her feet out. She landed and was instantly enveloped by Colt, who was now a good two inches taller than her.

"I missed you!"

"Me, too," she said softly, laying her head on his shoulder.

I looked over at Ella, who gave me a tight-lipped, sad smile.

"I have so much to show you!" He tugged her hand, and she nodded, starting to walk after him down to the tree house, no doubt.

"She's tired," I said to Ella, taking her hand as we followed the kids.

"Exhausted. She had a transfusion while we were there, but her appetite is still off, her red counts are low, and she's just… Is that a tree house?" Ella stopped, gawking up at the tree house we'd built between two pines.

"Like it?"

She laughed. "You built him a tree house. He always wanted one." That laugh turned to a small indrawn breath as her face contorted with sadness for a moment. Then she squeezed my hand and forced a smile. "Thank you. Ryan…he and…well, you built it, and it's amazing."

Ryan and Chaos. I knew exactly where she'd been going with that one.

I'm right here. I never left you. But I did destroy you.

I didn't say any of those things, simply kissed her wrist. "Want to see?"

"Yes!"

I led her to the ladder, where Colt and Maisie stood. "Okay, Colt, why don't you take your mom up?"

"Okay!"

"You sure this thing can support our weight?" Ella asked as she watched Colt climb. The kid scurried up the ladder with a freakish quickness. He was going to be one hell of a climber when he grew up.

"It had half the search and rescue team on it last week," I told her. "Unless you're going up there with ten of you, we're good."

"Called in the big guns, huh?" she teased.

Colt screamed, and I looked up to see him fall from the top of the ladder.

Shit!

I stepped forward, arms outstretched and ready as Ella gasped.

Just before he would have reached me, he caught himself, his little hands grasping the thick center of the wooden rung.

"Colt!" Ella shrieked.

He found his footing on the rung above my hands and looked down on us with a huge grin. "That was cool."

I sucked in a lungful of air and blew it out slowly, willing my heart to get out of my stomach. That kid was going to be the death of me.

"That was *not* cool!" Ella yelled, her voice pitched high and borderline panicked.

"I'm fine. See?" He let go of the ladder in a quick release and grabbed it again before falling back.

"Knock it off! I've spent weeks in the hospital with your sister, and I'm not prepared to go back!"

"Okay, okay," he muttered and climbed back up, making it to the top of the ladder and disappearing through the hatch.

"You okay?" I asked Ella.

She took two steps and buried her face in my chest with a huge sigh.

"He's fine. It was just a slip." My arms closed around her, and I kissed the top of her head. "Accidents happen."

"I don't have enough energy for accidents. Can't we just put them both in a bubble?"

"I'll work on building one of those next." I glanced over at Maisie, who was studying the tree house supports. "What do you think?"

"It's awesome!" She grinned.

"Today, you're my favorite."

"I heard that!" Colt yelled down, directly above us. "Send her up or walk the plank!"

"No one is walking a plank," Ella warned me as she left my arms and started up the ladder.

"There's no plank," I promised her.

"I think you have that backward," Maisie called up to Colt. "We're already down here."

"Whatever! Get up here!"

"Watch this," I told Maisie, pulling the net harness down from where it was stored on the tree. I spread it out with one hand and sat her in it with the other. "Now hold on to the sides."

Her eyes lit up as the net rose around her, and she grasped the edges, hooking her fingers through the white loops. "Really?"

"Ella, prepare to receive!" I called up. I looked through the secondary hatch and saw Ella nod, confused but ready. Then I went to the pulley and started to heft Maisie upward.

"Ahhh! This is so cool!" she squealed.

She made it through the hatch, and Ella got her out of the seat. Then I took the ladder and met my little family on the porch. We were about fifteen feet in the air, and we'd chosen a spot where the kids could see the lake. The kids, who were currently checking out the cool things Colt had asked for in the tree house, like a table and chairs, a play kitchen, and a giant cardboard tube we'd painted red because he wanted to call the tree house "the Death Star."

"This is amazing," Ella said, wrapping her arms around my waist. "Ryan would have loved it."

"Yeah, but he'd wanted a giant trampoline for Colt to jump on from up here."

Her eyes flew wide.

"Well, Colt asked for a zip line."

"From up here?"

"Hey, he's your kid," I said with a shrug and hugged her closer to me.

"I like this," she whispered. "Coming home to you, knowing Colt wasn't lonely."

"Me, too." I kissed her forehead. "It's all really normal, and I know it sounds crazy, but I'm really loving normal. Spending time with you and the kids, getting you alone whenever I can, it's really…"

"Perfect," she supplied.

"Perfect," I agreed, looking over my shoulder to make sure the kids were occupied before I kissed her.

Our lips met, and then Ella deepened it. I was more than happy to oblige. Our tongues touched briefly, and then we broke apart, hearing the kids coming.

"Isn't it so cool? It's like you're all alone up here!" Colt said.

"Almost alone," Ella answered, shooting me a knowing smirk.

"Almost, but not quite," I agreed over the kids' heads

as they looked out at the lake.

"I love it," Maisie told me with a grin.

"Then it was all worth it."

They ran to the other side of the house, and Ella leaned against my back, wrapping her arms around me.

"Can I get you alone later?" she asked, her hands skimming under my shirt to run the lines of my abs.

"Yes, as many times as you can handle." God, I wanted her. Needed to get her under me, over me, around me. Needed to feel connected to her in the way that only sex gave us, the moments when there were no worries, no cancer, no kids underfoot, just us and the love we had for each other.

Before she could answer, my phone rang. I reached between us to my back pocket and pulled it out, swiping to answer. "Gentry."

"Hey, I know you're not on call this weekend, but we've got some lost hikers," Mark's voice came through the line.

I sighed. All I wanted to do was have dinner with the kids, tuck their smiling faces into bed, and then get very *alone* with their mother.

"How lost?"

"They missed their check-in four hours ago."

"Go," Ella urged, kissing my arm where skin met shirt. "I know you're needed. Go."

"I'll be there in twenty." I hung up the phone and pulled Ella into my arms. "I'm so sorry. This is the last thing I want to do right now."

"Oh, trust me, you're the only thing I want to do right now," she said with a kiss on my chin before releasing me. "Stay with me tonight after you're done?"

I nodded. We limited sleepovers, but I wasn't arguing. Not tonight. "I'll be back as soon as possible. I promise," I told her before kissing the kids on the forehead as they ran by again. "Can you get Maisie down?"

"I've got this. Go," Ella ordered.

I let my eyes roam her body and sighed in a pout. "Tourists."

She flat-out laughed. "Hey, this is normal life. You were the one championing normal, right?"

"As long as normal means I come home to you tonight, I'm good with it."

And I was. Me, the guy who never wanted roots, was all about laying them deep here. This was what I wanted. This life. Ella. Colt. Maisie.

Normal. Everyday, ordinary normal.

I just needed Maisie to live, because there was no normal without her in it.

SIX MONTHS LATER

CHAPTER TWENTY

Ella

Letter #5

Ella,

Ah, the dating question. I honestly don't really date. Why? Because my life isn't fair to any woman. We head out at the drop of a hat. And not like, "Hey, I'm leaving next week." More like, "Sorry, I won't be home for dinner... for the next couple of months." Seems like a crap way to start a relationship when I never know when we'll get home. Take this trip for example. We figured it would be a couple of months. Definitely not the multiple-stop journey it has been. I couldn't imagine leaving a girl at home to wait through that.

So, without sounding...like a douche, I just prefer to not have long-term relationships. On some level, I'm also not sure I'm capable. When you grow up knowing nothing of a working, good relationship, it's pretty hard to see yourself in one.

As for Robins, if you want to go, go. Don't hide behind your life, or your kids. If you're scared to get out there and risk yourself, then say that. Own it. What you went through would make any normal person a little gun-shy, no doubt. No one is going to think less of you. Just don't hide behind excuses. You'll be stronger when you identify what sets you on edge. And honestly, I've seen pictures of you. You're not going to end up as the crazy cat lady, I promise.

Am I happy single? I think happiness is a relative term, no matter what the subject. I quit striving for happy when I was about five. Now I go for content. It's easier to attain and doesn't leave me feeling like there's something missing. Eventually I'll get out of the military, and then maybe we'll see, but that's a decade or more away. For now, this is the life I love, and I'm content. Goal attained.

Tell me a little bit about Telluride. If I came into town as a tourist, what absolutely has to be seen? Done? Eaten?

~ Chaos

Content. I'd been looking for the right word to describe my feelings about my blur of a life lately, and that was it: I was content.

I loved Beckett with an intensity that was almost frightening. That hadn't changed—and something told me it wouldn't. But I also knew there were things about him I'd never know. Even seven months as a couple hadn't filled in all the holes of who he had been before he'd shown up at Solitude.

Most of the time, he was the Beckett I knew, but there were moments when I caught him staring out at Ryan's island, or when he woke up from a nightmare, that I couldn't help but wonder if I'd ever know him as well as he knew me.

Maybe that was simply what came with the territory when you loved a man like him. I'd learned a few months into our relationship that love was mostly about compromise, but it was always about acceptance. There were dozens of little things about him that could annoy the socks off me, and the same went for him, but for the most part, we were who we were, and we loved each other. There was no point trying to change each other, we either wanted to grow or change ourselves, or we didn't. After you accepted that about someone and still loved them, you were pretty much indestructible.

Beckett had accepted that I was always going to be overprotective of the twins and that I wasn't anywhere near ready to tell them that he'd adopted them. I'd accepted that there were simply parts of him that would always remain shadowed and secretive.

But there was no denying that my choice to keep the adoption under wraps was directly impacted by the moments Beckett distanced himself when I asked about his past.

It wasn't that I didn't trust him. He would die for me. For the kids. But until I knew with 100 percent certainty that he'd stay—that those shadows in his eyes wouldn't lead to me finding his bags packed—the twins couldn't know. God, they loved him, and even the chance that Beckett could destroy their hearts by being the second father to abandon them was too big of a risk to take. Not while Maisie was still fighting for her life.

The thought of losing Beckett stuttered my heart, and I reached across the console of the truck to take his hand as he drove us along the familiar roads to Montrose. He lifted my hand and kissed the inside of my wrist, a habit I happened to love, without taking his eyes off the road. Snow rose on either side of us, but at least the roads were clear. February was always an unpredictable month.

"You good back there?" I asked Maisie as she played on the iPad Beckett had gotten her for Christmas. It matched Colt's almost identically except for the case.

"Yep, just working on a spelling game Ms. Steen gave me for homework." She didn't look up, just kept swiping away.

"Did you bring Colt?" I asked, spotting the pink bear wedged into the seat next to her.

"Yeah. He was mad that he couldn't come, so I promised him Colt would come." She met my eyes in the mirror and forced a little smile.

"You're nervous."

"I'm okay."

Beckett and I shared a sideways glance, and we both let it go. She'd been through thirty-three days of hell a month ago. The mega-chemo had been the most vicious part of her treatment.

She'd thrown up. Her skin had peeled. She'd had sores down her GI tract and had a feeding tube placed because she couldn't keep anything down. But as soon as she'd finished that course of treatment and the stem cells had been transplanted, she bounced right back. She was astonishing on every level that a little girl could be.

I couldn't say I was happy, not with Maisie still fighting for her life, but we'd passed the year mark in November, and she was still here. She'd had another birthday, another Christmas. Colt was taking snowboarding lessons. Solitude was booked solid through the ski season and summer, and Hailey had moved out a few months ago, knowing I could depend on Beckett, who had taken shifts between Telluride and Denver, to be wherever he was needed most.

Everything came back to Beckett. He took the worst days and made them bearable. Took the good days and made them exquisite. He picked up the kids, took Colt to school, took Maisie to local appointments, made dinner on nights I couldn't get away from the main house—there was nothing he wouldn't do.

So maybe I couldn't say that I was happy, but I was content, and that was more than enough.

Chaos would have been proud.

It had been almost fourteen months since I'd lost him and Ryan, and I still had no clue why. That was part of Beckett's past I had a nearly impossible time accepting. Only nearly, because I heard him scream Ryan's name in the middle of a nightmare a few months ago. That scream told me he wasn't anywhere near ready to talk.

Ryan and Chaos were gone.

Beckett was alive and in my arms, and that meant I had all the time in the world to wait until he was ready.

We pulled into the hospital parking lot, and Beckett carried Maisie through the slush-filled lot as I followed in his footsteps, thankful I'd worn boots.

Maisie was quiet through check-in and vitals, and dead silent as she had her blood drawn and went through the CT scan.

By the time we were put into an exam room to wait for Dr. Hughes, she was almost a statue.

"What are you thinking about?" Beckett asked her as he sat on the exam table.

She shrugged, kicking her feet under the chair. They'd made a deal after the second MIBG treatment—she wasn't sitting on exam tables any more than necessary. She said they made her feel like she was a sick kid, and she wanted to believe that she was getting better. So Beckett would sit on the table until the doc came in, and then they would trade places.

"Me, too," he said, mirroring her shrug.

"Me, three," I added.

That earned us a little smile.

Dr. Hughes knocked and opened the door. "Hi there, Maisie!" she said to Beckett.

"Busted," he stage-whispered.

Maisie grinned and jumped up to take his spot as he took her chair and then my hand.

"How are you feeling?" Dr. Hughes asked, doing the

usual physical checks.

"Good. Strong." She nodded to emphasize her point.

"I believe you. You know why?"

My hand tightened on Beckett's. As steady as I tried to appear to Maisie, I was terrified of what she was going to say. It seemed so unfair to put a little girl through so much and not have it work.

"Why?" Maisie whispered, her arms crushing Colt's teddy bear.

"Because your tests look great, just like you. Good and strong." She tapped Maisie on the nose with her finger. "You are a rock star, Maisie."

Maisie looked back over her shoulder at us, a smile as wide as the state of Colorado.

"What exactly does that mean?" I asked.

"We're looking at less than 5 percent on her bone marrow. No change since you left the hospital last month. And no new tumors. Your girl is stable, and in partial remission."

That word tripped something in my brain, and it short-circuited just like it had the first time they'd said cancer, except this time it was in the joy end of disbelief.

"Say it again," I begged.

Dr. Hughes smiled. "She's in partial remission. It means no new treatments for the time being. I'll probably want to do a session of radiation in a couple months to mop up any of the microscopic cells, but as long as her scans are coming back clean, I think we can give her a little break."

Everything went blurry, and Beckett's hands wiped at my cheeks.

I laughed when I realized I was crying.

We listened to Dr. Hughes explain that it wasn't a full remission. She had made significant progress but hadn't been cured. She was hopeful that the radiation treatment would wipe out the rest, and then we could schedule immunotherapy.

Then she reiterated that over half of all kids with aggressive neuroblastoma relapsed after they'd been declared in full remission, that this wasn't a guarantee but a much-needed break. Her weekly scans could even be done locally in Telluride, and she'd review them in Denver, no need to drive to Montrose.

I wrote down everything I could process in her binder, hoping I could make sense of it all later. Then Maisie hopped down from the table, and we walked to the car. Maisie and Beckett chattered and laughed, joking about how much ice cream she was going to eat while she had a couple of months off treatment. She declared she was going to eat an entire Easter basket full of chocolate and peanut butter cups.

Beckett hoisted Maisie into the truck, and she buckled in. Then he shut the door and caught my hand as he walked me to my side of the truck.

All at once, it hit me. Maisie had been talking about Easter, which was two months away. My vision swam, and I covered my face with my hands.

"Ella," Beckett whispered, pulling me against his chest.

I gripped the edges of his coat and sobbed, the sound ugly and raw and real. "Easter. She's going to be here for Easter."

"Yeah, she is," he promised, running his hand down my back in sweeping motions. "It's okay to plan, you know. To look ahead to what life will be like for the four of us once she's healthy. It's okay to believe in good things."

"I've been stuck for so long. Just living scan to scan, chemo to MIBG. We didn't even buy presents until the week before Christmas because I couldn't see that far into the future. And now I can see a couple of months out." Sure, there were weekly scans, but a couple of months felt like an eternity, a gift of the one thing we'd been denied—time.

"We'll just enjoy it and take advantage of every minute she feels great."

"Right," I agreed with a nod, but with the word "remission" being tossed around like a beach ball at a concert, I felt the gut-wrenching longing for more. I'd always pushed thoughts of Maisie dying to the side, but I also hadn't thought about her *living*. My world had narrowed to the fight. My infinity existed within the confines of her treatment, never looking too far ahead for fear it took my eyes off the battle of the moment. "I think I'm getting greedy."

"Ella, you're the least greedy person I know." His arms tightened, grounding me.

"I am. Because I've been begging for weeks, and now I see months and I want years. How many other NB kids have died while she fought? Three from Denver? And here I am seeing this light at the end of the tunnel and praying it's not a freight train coming our way. That's greedy."

"Then I'm greedy, too. Because I'd give up anything for her to have the time. For you to have it."

We headed home with Maisie singing along to Beckett's playlist. Her earlier worries shoved aside for another day and another test.

My worries lingered. Wanting something that was so out of reach had been a distant thought, and now that it was a real possibility, that want was a screaming need that shoved everything else aside and demanded to be heard.

I didn't just want these few months.

I wanted a lifetime.

For the first time since Maisie was diagnosed, I had real hope. Which meant I had something to lose.

Two weeks later, my back hit the wall in my bedroom, and I barely noticed. My legs were around Beckett's waist, my shirt lost somewhere between the front door and the stairs. His fell somewhere between the stairs and the bedroom.

His tongue was in my mouth, my hands were in his hair, and we were on fire.

"How long do we have?" he asked, his breath hot against my ear before he trailed kisses down my neck, lingering on the spot that always brought chills to my skin and fever to my blood.

"Half hour?" It was a rough guess.

"Perfect. I want to hear you scream my name." He carried me to the bed, and a few seconds and some shedding of clothes later, we were both blissfully naked.

We were experts at quiet sex, the kind where mouths and hands covered the sounds of orgasms, where you stole showers or middle-of-the-night sessions to avoid the inevitable kid interruptions. We'd long since moved the bed's headboard off the wall.

But having the entire house to ourselves for a half hour? It was an excuse to be downright hedonistic.

He moved over me, and I cradled his hips between mine as he kissed me to oblivion. No matter how secretive he might be about his time in the military, he was an open book while we were in bed. Our bodies communicated effortlessly, and we somehow managed to get better at it every time we made love. The fire I'd half expected to fizzle out only burned brighter and hotter.

"Beckett," I groaned when he took a nipple into his mouth and slipped his hand between my thighs.

"Always so ready. God, I love you, Ella."

"I. Love. You." Each word was punctuated by a gasp.

The man knew exactly how to bring me to the brink with nothing more than a few—

Ring. Ring. Ring.

I forced my head to the side, where I saw Beckett's cell phone illuminated on the floor next to his jeans.

"That's. You."

"I don't care," he said before he kissed me. Between his tongue and his fingers, I was already arching up to meet him, desperate to make the most of our time alone. These were the moments when nothing else mattered, where the entire universe melted away and nothing existed outside our bed—our love.

Ring. Ring. Ring.

Damn it. I looked again and made out the letters on his screen. "It's the station, and if they've called twice…"

Beckett growled his annoyance but leaned over the bed to retrieve the phone. "Gentry." He put his mouth to my belly, and I ran my hands over the broad expanse of his shoulders. "Don't care. Nope."

His tongue trailed back up to the curve of my breast, then abruptly stopped.

He sat up on his knees, and I knew before he said a single word that he was leaving, because he was already a million miles away.

"I'll be there in ten." He set the phone down and gave me the look—the one that said he wouldn't go if they didn't need him.

"It's okay," I told him, already sitting up.

He put his hand on my knee. "I wouldn't go if they didn't—"

"Need you," I finished for him.

"Exactly. There's been a rollover near Bridal Veil Falls, and a ten-year-old girl is missing. She was thrown from the vehicle. It's…it's a kid."

Kids were the one demographic he never turned down. Even if he wasn't on call, if it involved a child, he went in.

I leaned forward and kissed him softly. "Then you'd better go."

"I'm so sorry." His eyes raked down my body. "So. So. *So* sorry."

"I know. I love you. Go save someone's little girl." I shooed him out the door with Havoc, and five minutes later, I stood fully dressed in my bedroom.

With an empty house.

The options were endless. I could read a book. I could watch something I'd DVR'd months ago. I could even take a bath. Sweet, blissful quiet.

Instead, I chose laundry.

"I'm going to start a nudist colony," I muttered as I grabbed Maisie's basket and headed down the steps.

My phone rang midway, and I did the basket-to-hip shuffle to get it answered. "Hello?"

"Mrs. Gentry?"

As lovely as that sounds— I shut that thought down.

"No, I'm Ms. MacKenzie, but I do know Beckett Gentry." I made my way to the small laundry room and tossed the load in. If we ended up living here after Maisie was cured, then the first thing on my list was to ask Beckett to install a new, bigger washer and dryer.

Holy crap, I'd just made plans not only for Maisie to live but for Beckett to still be with me. Wasn't I just the optimist today.

"Ms. MacKenzie?"

The optimist who had completely ignored the phone for her daydream.

"I'm here. I'm so sorry, what were you saying?" I poured soap in and hit start, then got the heck out of the laundry room so I could hear the woman.

"My name is Danielle Wilson. I'm with Tri-Prime." Her tone was all business.

"Oh, the insurance company. Of course. I'm Maisie

MacKenzie's mom. How can I help you?" Man, those dishes needed to be done, too. What the heck had the kids concocted with Ada this afternoon?

"I'm calling in reference to the letter I sent to Sergeant First Class Gentry's commanding officer. The same one copied to you as well." She was certainly annoyed.

I thought of the small stack of insurance envelopes on my desk that detailed the paid claims. "I'm so sorry, I actually haven't opened those in a couple of weeks. I'm usually way better about it." But knowing we had a couple of months off treatments made me feel all reckless about not opening cancer-related mail. I felt like Ross in that episode of *Friends*, telling the mail that we were on a break.

Then what she said hit home.

"His commanding officer?"

"Yes. Captain Donahue? We sent him the letter last week as well, in way of notification."

Beckett was out. He said he was on terminal leave when he got here in April, and it was already the first week of March. I didn't know much about the army, but I didn't think terminal leave lasted a year. Oh God, had he lied to me?

"I'd like to schedule a time to come out for a preliminary interview. Next week is available. Say noon on Monday?"

"I'm sorry, you want to come to Telluride?"

"That would be best, yes. Does Monday work, or would Tuesday be better for you?"

She wanted to come to Telluride in two days.

"Monday is fine, but can I ask what this is about? I've never had an insurance company visit before."

What she said next stunned me to silence. It kept me motionless until the kids came home with Ada. Then quiet through dinner and baths. My mind went in ten

thousand different directions as I got the kids to bed...
and didn't stop for hours.

It was after ten p.m. when Beckett walked through
the door, using the key I'd given him seven months ago.

He was exhausted, with streaks of dirt running down
his face. He stripped off his Search and Rescue jacket,
hanging it on the rack by the door, and Havoc stopped
by for a little rub before she headed toward her water
dish.

"Why don't I have a key to your place?" I asked.

"What?" He stopped abruptly when he saw me
sitting at the dining room table amid the open insurance
papers.

"I gave you a key to my place, and you sleep here
most nights now. It just seems so symbolic, you know? I
let you all the way in, and you keep everything locked
up so damn tight. I only get to visit when you open the
door."

He sat in the chair around the corner from mine.
"Ella? What's going on?"

"You still have a commanding officer? Donahue?"

The way his expression faded to blank told me that
answer. Ryan got the same expression whenever I'd
asked him something about the unit.

"Were you going to tell me that you didn't get out?"

He took off his ball cap and pushed his hands
through his hair. "It's a technicality."

"I kind of view being in the military as a pregnant
thing. You are or you aren't. There's no halfway
technicality." The dark, angry doubt I'd kept at bay
started to cut through my chest, working its way to my
heart. "Have you been lying to me this whole time? Are
you still in? Are you just waiting until I don't need you
anymore to go back? Am I still just a mission to you?
Ryan's little sister?"

"God no." He reached for my hand, but I pulled it

back. "Ella, that's not what's going on here."

"Explain."

"*Someone* showed up right after I got here, asking me to return, and I declined. After what happened, I wasn't really fit for returning, anyway, and Havoc might obey you guys, but she won't take working commands from any other handlers."

"Ah, another woman you've ruined for any other man," I said, saluting him with my bottle of water.

"I take that as a compliment." He leaned over the table, resting his elbows on the dark, polished wood.

"Don't."

"This…guy offered me a technicality, to take a temporary disability. It would allow me to keep everything army-wise the same without actually showing up. I could go back whenever I wanted if I just signed a set of papers that started with a one-year enrollment and could be renewed up to five. He completely worked the system, doing whatever he could to give me an easy way back in."

"And you accepted." I couldn't even look at those eyes. The minute I did, he'd convince me he was staying, when all evidence proved to the contrary.

"I declined."

My eyes shot up to his.

"But the night I realized I could put Maisie and Colt on my insurance, I knew I had to sign it. It was the only way to get them covered at 100 percent."

"When did you do it?"

"The morning I went to see Jeff. It was exactly one day before the offer expired."

"Why didn't you tell me?" A tiny bit of my suspicion faded.

"Because I knew you hated everything that we did, the lives we led. That you'd see me signing those papers as my getaway car for when I was done *playing house* here in Telluride. Am I right?" He leaned back and lifted his eyebrow in question.

"Maybe," I admitted. "Can't blame me, though, can you? Guys like Ryan, and you…and…" *Chaos*. "You all have the constant need for the rush. Ryan told me once that the time he felt most alive was in the middle of a gunfight. That everything in those moments happened in vivid color, and the rest of his life faded a little because of it."

Beckett played with the brim of his hat and nodded slowly. "Yeah, that can happen. Once you have that level of adrenaline rushing through your system, that heightened sense of life and death, the normal day-to-day stuff feels like it's just a little below. Like life is the monorail at Disney, and combat is the roller coaster—the highs, the dramatic lows, the twists and turns. Except sometimes people die on the coaster, and it makes you feel even luckier to get off, and a hell of a lot guiltier."

"Then why wouldn't I expect you to go back to that? If we're the monorail, you've got to be bored, and if you're not, then you're going to be."

"Because I love you." He said it with such incredible certainty, the way someone said the world was round or the oceans were deep. His love was a foregone conclusion. "Because kissing you, making love with you? When we're together, you eclipse all of that. It's not even in the background, it just doesn't exist. Combat never bothered me before because I had nothing to lose. No one loved me, and I cared only about Ryan and Havoc. I couldn't leave you. I couldn't go across the world and worry about you, about the kids. I couldn't go into combat with the same effectiveness because I'd know that if I died, you'd be alone. Get it?"

"I'm your kryptonite." That didn't sound so flattering.

"No, you gave me something to lose. Other married guys, they're okay, but maybe it's because they didn't come from such messed-up childhoods. Love for them was the monorail. You are the first person I've ever loved, and the first woman who has ever loved me. You're the roller coaster."

Well, if that didn't just pop a pin into my anger bubble and burst it.

"You should have told me."

"I'm sorry. I should have told you. But we were getting so close back then, and I wanted you so badly that I didn't want to risk it." He sat up straight and took my hand, looking into my eyes with such an intense expression on his face that chills ran down my spine. "If I ever hide something from you, it's because I'm terrified to risk losing you. That whole roller-coaster thing? I've never felt like this. Never had my heart leave my body and belong to someone else. I don't know how to have a relationship, and I'm bound to screw this one up."

I brushed my thumb over the underside of his wrist. "You're doing fine. We're doing fine. Come to think of it, this is my longest relationship, too. Just don't keep things from me, okay? I can always deal with the truth, and lies…" I swallowed the lump in my throat. "Lies are my hard limit. I have to be able to trust you."

And I still did, even though he'd hidden this detail from me.

"There are things about me that would change the way you look at me."

"You don't know that."

"I do." He was so certain.

"Try me."

The muscle in his jaw flexed, and he looked like he just might —

"How did you know about my commanding officer?" *Or not.*

Disappointment flooded my stomach. "The insurance company called. They're sending someone out on Monday to interview us."

"What? Why?"

"I guess the amount of Maisie's bills tripped some internal alarm with her recent enrollment. They're investigating us for insurance fraud."

His eyes closed slowly, and his head rolled back. "That's just fantastic."

"Beckett…"

He pushed back from the table and took his hat, tugging it on. "I think I'm going to sleep at my place tonight. It's not you, just the rescue, and I need…"

"Did you find the little girl?" I asked, shame lowering my voice because I hadn't thought to ask before now, too consumed with my own drama.

"Yeah. She should make it, but it was close."

I breathed a sigh of relief. "Then I'm glad you went in."

How different this conversation was from the one we'd had a few hours before when he'd left.

"Me, too."

"Stay. Please stay," I asked softly. "I know sometimes you get nightmares after you do rescues. I can handle it." If I wanted any future with this man, I had to prove to him that I wouldn't turn away when he showed the parts he purposely kept hidden. "I told you, there's nothing that would make me look at you differently."

"I killed a child."

He said it so quietly that I almost didn't hear him, but I knew he wouldn't repeat it even if I asked. So I sat as still as possible and simply watched his face.

"It was a bullet ricochet. She was ten. I killed her, and our objective wasn't even at the location we'd had intel for. I killed a child. Still want to sleep next to me?"

"Yes," I answered quickly, tears prickling at my eyes.

"You don't mean that. She had brown hair and light

brown eyes. She'd seen us coming and was trying to get her little brother out of the way." He gripped the back of his chair. "I still hear her mother screaming."

"That's why you go for every child rescue, no matter what."

He nodded.

Maybe it was part of the reason he was so determined to save Maisie, too.

"It wasn't your fault."

"Don't ever say that to me again," he snapped. "I pulled that trigger. I knew the risks. I killed that child. Every time you see me with Maisie or with Colt, think about that, and then you decide how much you really want to know about how I've spent the last decade."

My heart broke for him, for that little girl and her mother. For the brother she'd tried to pull out of the way. For the guilt Beckett carried. I wanted to tell him that he couldn't scare me. That I knew who he was down to his soul, and he was a phenomenal man. But the look on his face told me that wasn't an option tonight—he wasn't ready for anyone's absolution.

In case no one ever told you—you're worthy. Of love. Of family. Of home.

Ryan's words from his last letter to Beckett hit me. He was the only person who might have known Beckett better than I did, and I had a feeling that while I knew all the beautiful sides of Beckett, Ryan had known the shadowed ones.

I stood and held out my hand, waiting for him to make his decision.

After what felt like a lifetime, he took my hand and went upstairs with me. Once he'd showered, and we lay together in the darkness of my bedroom, Beckett pulled me against him, holding my back to his front.

"I didn't give you a key because you own the cabin, Ella. I figured you already had one. Maybe I should have told you to use it whenever you wanted, but I guess I thought you knew."

"Knew what?"

"You gave me your key when we reached the point in our relationship where you trusted me, then I was allowed access to you."

"Right."

"I had to earn your trust. But you've had mine since day one. You already had a key to me. I know the attic door is a little jammed, but just give it some time."

I turned in his arms, remembering every time he'd asked if he could help me. The day he'd found Colt at his house. The night I'd walked in to read Ryan's letter...and then again the night of the adoption. When he'd first come, I was the one who'd shut him out.

"I love you."

"I know, and I love you," he told me. Then he spent the next hour showing me with every touch of his hands and kiss from his mouth.

Like I said, we were experts at quiet sex.

Mind-blowing, earth-shattering, soul-shaping sex.

CHAPTER TWENTY-ONE

Beckett

Letter #21

Chaos,

It's Christmas. Huh. Have I really become that person, so sad and consumed with worry that even writing Christmas somehow looks depressing?

It shouldn't be. Maisie is here and, since it's been a week since her last chemo treatment, she's actually perking up. Her hair is completely gone now. It left right after the second chemo treatment, her birthday, to be precise. Once it started, she told me to take it all off. She said it was easier to be sad all at once than a little bit every day.

My six-year-old is incredibly wise.

So it's Christmas, and while my kids play with their new toys, I want to concentrate on what's good.

First, thank you for the robe. It's so very soft, and I love it. I'd ask where you found it, but that would probably mean telling me things you're not allowed to. I hope your present got there, too.

Second, you'll be here soon. I have to admit, I'm way more excited for that than I should be. I feel like I already know you so well, and getting to see you face-to-face is just that—seeing you. I met you twenty-one letters ago. How amazing it is to meet someone through their words before their face, to find their mind attractive, and then

*see if the body follows. Not that I'm judging
your body. I'm sure it's great, since you do what
you do. I mean, it's fine.*

   Stupid. Freaking. Pen.

   *I'm just saying that I have to admit that I'm
attracted to who you are as a person. Is that
weird? I hope not. More people should meet like
this, to really understand a person before they
see the outer packaging. And I know it's just
been letters, but I have this crazy feeling that you
understand me, probably better than anyone
here.*

   So get here.

   ~ Ella

"Behave," I told Havoc when we heard knocking.

I opened the front door to find Ella standing there,
binder in hand, her face tense. It was Monday, and the
insurance lady was due in ten minutes. We'd moved the
meeting to my house, hoping to not worry Maisie.

Plus, since I was the one on the insurance policy, I
was really the one she was investigating.

"Coffee?" I asked as Ella walked in.

"I'm shaking enough as it is." She slipped out of her
coat and hung it on the coat rack, revealing a pair of
jeans that her curves fit perfectly and a blue top that
matched her eyes. Damn, she looked good. Healthy. The
shadows under her eyes were fading, and her skin had a
gorgeous glow to it.

I couldn't wait to see how the light warmed her skin
through the stained-glass window I'd just had installed
at the new house—the one I hadn't yet told her I'd been
building the last six months. That was a secret I was
happy to keep. Two more weeks and it would finally be
ready to move into. Then she'd have this cabin back for

business and wouldn't feel like I was pressuring her to move in together.

The fact that the house was next to Solitude and big enough for everyone was just a perk.

"Don't worry. We didn't do anything wrong. I promise. This is just a cursory visit."

"She drove here from Denver, Beckett. Are you sure we don't need Mark? There's nothing cursory about this. It's inconvenient to her and invasive to us."

"Well, there is that," I said, putting my arms around her. "We'll call Mark if we have to, but I honestly think there's nothing to worry about."

When the door sounded again, I sighed. "Looks like she's early. Yay."

I left the warmth of Ella's arms and opened the door to find— "Whoa. What are you doing here?"

The firm set of Donahue's mouth told me it wasn't by choice. "I was summoned. Apparently this is easier for security purposes than random visits to our 'office.'" He held up air quotes.

"Come on in."

He walked inside, adding his coat to the rack, and then pulling up a little short when he saw Ella.

"Ms. MacKenzie," he said with a little nod.

"You were at Ryan's funeral." Her voice had gone soft.

I took her hand. "Ella, this is—"

"Captain Donahue," he answered truthfully. "I already know the insurance demon told her."

"Well, it's nice to see you again. I'm sorry I wasn't more personable at Ryan's funeral. I was a little…out of sorts."

"You were grieving. It's understandable. Besides, Chaos told me so much about you that I already felt like I knew you."

He couldn't have shocked me more if he'd punched

me in the nuts.

"Chaos," Ella said that name like he was a freaking saint. "You knew him. Right. Same unit."

Donahue's eyes flew to mine, and I gave the slightest shake of my head, imperceptible to anyone else but someone who'd worked with me in situations where that movement was life and death.

Like right now.

He instantly gave Ella a reassuring smile. "Good guy. Crazy about you, I can say that." This time his glance at me was definitely a little disapproving. "Gentry. How about we get some coffee."

That was not a suggestion.

"Sounds good."

"I'll wait here. I think I see her car pulling in," Ella said, her face almost against the door's glass pane.

"What the hell are you doing?" Donahue asked as I made him a cup of coffee.

"What Mac asked."

"And she doesn't know?"

"Nope. And it needs to stay that way." After the machine stopped hissing, I handed him the cup. I knew he liked his coffee like he liked his women, black and strong.

"You adopted her kids, and if my spidey senses are right, you're sleeping with her, and she doesn't—"

"The minute she knows, we're done. You know what happened. She'll kick me out of here so fast I'll get whiplash. How the hell am I going to help her then? I hate it. But this is the way it is. The longer I waited to tell her, the deeper it got, and now we're here."

The door opened and shut, followed by the sound of two pairs of feminine steps headed our way.

"Damn it, Cha—" He shook his head. "Gentry."

"Well, gentlemen. It's nice to see you're here and ready to start. I'm Danielle Wilson, and you must be

Samuel Donahue and Beckett Gentry." She looked to be in her midforties, with a sensible suit and minimal makeup. Her brown hair was pulled into a severe French twist, and a pair of glasses hung from her necklace.

My instincts told me she was out for blood. My blood.

"Coffee?" I offered.

"No, thank you. Shall we get started?"

We all gathered around the dining room table. Danielle sat at the head, spreading out folders and notebooks like she was prepping to study for finals. Ella sat next to me on one side, her hand firmly tucked in mine, and Donahue took the other side, leaning back in his chair and sipping his coffee.

Guy had always had a hell of a poker face.

But why would she have summoned him?

"Let's get started. Mr. Gentry, would you please tell me how it is that you came to adopt Ms. MacKenzie's children?" She put her glasses on, took out her pen, and braced it above a yellow steno pad.

Old school.

"I served in a unit with her brother, Ryan. He asked in his last letter that I come to Telluride and take care of his sister, Ella."

She nodded, writing quickly. "May I see the letter?"

"No," Ella answered. "That's private and none of your business."

Danielle leaned forward, locking her hawklike eyes onto Ella. "Your daughter was adopted in July and has since cost our company over a million dollars in care for a condition that was previously known—and immediately treated with a therapy that wasn't approved by your previous provider. Unless you'd like to pay those bills, I suggest you get me the letter."

Oh, this woman was a piece of work.

I arched my hips and took the letter out of my back

pocket, sliding it across the table to her. "You can't keep it."

"You keep it on you?" she asked, looking over her glasses at me.

"I do. When your best friend asks you something like that, you tend to keep it close."

She opened the letter and read it over, then snapped a picture with her phone.

I felt violated, like she'd just taken a picture of Ryan's naked soul without his permission. *It's what he would want. He wants his family protected.*

And so did I.

"Interesting. So did the unit sanction this mission?" she asked Donahue.

"I'm not sure what unit you're referring to," he answered with a shrug.

"I'm well aware of what you do, Captain Donahue. I followed your paper trail, and the deal you made with Mr. Gentry to keep him in that little disability loophole. Did you plan this all out? Keep him on temporary disability so he could pony up the insurance for the little sister here?"

Donahue took a sip of his coffee, and I was shocked it didn't ice over, he was that cool. "No, but if that was a benefit of my offer, I'm happy to have helped. Gentry was offered temp disability because I have the power to offer it, and he was unfit to return to duty."

"And those reasons were…" She looked up at him.

"Above your pay grade. Look, I agreed to come here for the benefit of Ella and Beckett, and I have no problem clearing up whatever issue you think there is. But you don't have the clearance to know…well, almost anything. All that you get to know is that I was authorized to offer him temporary disability in the hopes that he would heal enough to return to active service any time in the next five years. Proper paperwork was filed, and he remains eligible for healthcare. That's it. That's all you get from me."

She adjusted her glasses and set her sights on Ella and me. "So you randomly show up in Telluride to fulfill your dead buddy's letter request and adopt her kids."

"Not random, but yes. I fell in love with the kids, just like I did with Ella. When you love someone, you want to protect them. They didn't have a dad in their lives, and I wanted to be that for them."

"But you could have simply married Ms. MacKenzie and achieved the same thing, right?" Her gaze flickered between us.

"Then that would have been fraud," I said as Ella's hand tightened in mine. "That would have given you a case, though if you went after every young girl who tag-chased GI's for benefits, you'd be too busy to show up here."

"I don't really believe in marriage," Ella added.

What. The. Hell?

"You don't?" Ms. Wilson asked, clearly not believing her.

"Nope. I was married to Colt and Maisie's biological father. He walked out as soon as he knew they were twins. Divorced me shortly after. Marrying Beckett would have been absolute fraud when I don't have any faith in that institution. After all, what is it when vows mean nothing and a piece of paper binds your life to someone's as easily as the next one dissolves the bond? It doesn't mean anything. But adoption does. He has an amazing bond with my children and shares just as much of the parenting duties as I do. He takes Maisie to treatments, he takes Colt to soccer and snowboarding. He built a tree house for them and packs lunches in the morning. Does that sound like fraud to you?"

An awkward silence descended as Ms. Wilson feigned looking over her notes. None of this made any sense. Sure, Maisie's bills were astronomical, but people adopted kids with high levels of needs every day.

"If we're done here—" Donahue started.

"I'm not satisfied." The tone of her voice, the way she flat-out glared at Donahue, made me lean forward and scan the details of her face. This was personal.

"How did you know about the unit?" I asked.

"My best guess is she found out from her sister, Cassandra Ramirez." Donahue stared her down.

Ramirez. He'd gotten out after he'd lost his arm. From what I'd heard from the guys before I left, the transition hadn't been easy. In that regard, Ella was right—guys like us didn't give up the adrenaline rush without a fight. I had search and rescue. Ramirez... didn't.

She swallowed and tapped her pen on the paper a few times before looking up. "Yes, I'm Cassie's sister. But that has nothing to do with this investigation."

Bullshit.

"Sure it does," Donahue said with a shrug. "You want justice for what happened to him. For the fact that he had to quit before he was ready, and I couldn't give him the same deal I gave Gentry. Not the money—his medical retirement covered that—but the hope of coming back. That's why you're here. It's not for Maisie, or Beckett, or Ella. It's for me."

She cleared her throat and stacked up her folders. "That has nothing to do with this. At all. And I'm sorry, but unless you can provide me with proof that you had any established relationship to this child before her diagnosis, I'm going to recommend your case be reviewed and that all current treatments are put on hold while we investigate further."

"You can't do that!" Ella snapped. "They are his children by law. He cares for them, supports them, and acts as their dad in every single way."

"Funny, because when I happened to run into Colton earlier at school, he told me he didn't have a dad. And when I asked him about you, he said you were his uncle's best friend and his mom's boyfriend, but never once mentioned being adopted by you. Why would that be?"

"You spoke to my child without my consent?" Ella flew across the table, and it was all I could do to get my arm around her waist and haul her back.

"Calm down. It certainly wasn't part of my investigation. I happened to go by the school to get a few more facts on when Margaret was pulled from school and the emergency contacts changed for Colton, when I happened to see him."

"Liar." Ella seethed.

"You overstepped," I said as calmly as possible. "This entire investigation is an overstep, and when we shut you down you can bet we'll take it higher than you are."

"There is a little girl's life at stake." Ella spoke in an even tone, but her hand had mine in a death grip. "And you only care about getting back at Donahue."

"I care that the rules are followed, which these men should have no trouble respecting. The truth is that this man adopted the two children of his now-girlfriend, one of whom needs millions of dollars in treatments, and you haven't even told the kids they're adopted. It smells really bad. If it turns out a full Tri-Prime investigation isn't needed, you'll have my full apologies, of course. We're cracking down on fraud this year."

She was on a witch hunt, and even though what we'd done was perfectly legal, and in no way fraud, she was going to twist it up and throw us into hell while they "investigated." They could pause the payments on Maisie's treatments, scans, the upcoming radiation…all of it. Even though we'd be found innocent of any wrongdoing, it would be tied up long enough for Maisie to feel the ramifications.

Unless I could prove that I knew the kids before the diagnosis.

A dull roar filled my ears as Ella and Ms. Wilson exchanged words. I'd lose Ella, but I'd known that the moment I'd shown up in Telluride. The time I'd had with her was a gift that I'd had no right to. Hell, I'd stolen it. She didn't really know the man she was in love with, because I hadn't told her.

Three things. Three reasons. That's what I used to make decisions now, used to quell my need to jump first and regret later.

Ella deserved the truth.

Maisie deserved to live.

My love for the kids wasn't fraud.

Decision made.

"If you'll wait here a moment," I said above the fray, excusing myself from the table. I took the stairs two at a time and retrieved the box I kept buried under a stack of underwear in my nightstand.

Evidence in hand, I came down the stairs slowly. Ella and Ms. Wilson were still arguing, but Donahue turned toward me. He took in the box and my expression.

"Are you sure?" he asked quietly.

"It's the only way."

He nodded as I walked by him to stand next to Ella. The conversation stopped, and all eyes were on me.

"I love you. I've always loved you," I told Ella.

"I love you, too, Beckett," she responded, her eyebrows drawn together in confusion. "What are you doing?"

Kissing her was the first thought in my mind—taking that last second with her so I could memorize everything. But I'd taken enough from her already.

"I should have told you, and I know this is about to cost me…you, but I can't let another kid pay for my mistakes, especially not Maisie."

The box made a soft scratching sound as I slid it down the table. Ms. Wilson took it and lifted the square lid. "What exactly am I looking at?"

She pulled the evidence of my sin onto the table, and Ella gasped.

"Why do you have my letters? *His* letters?" she whispered.

I kept my eyes on Ms. Wilson, unable to man up enough to watch the love die in Ella's eyes when she caught on.

"You said you needed evidence that I knew the kids before the diagnosis, that I had a relationship with them. You'll find letters in there dating before the diagnosis, as well as pictures drawn by the kids and little notes. I knew the kids, loved them, and loved Ella before Maisie was diagnosed. You have no reason to investigate. If this was just about Maisie's treatments, I wouldn't have adopted Colt, too. The truth is that I wanted to be their dad."

Ms. Wilson sighed, thumbing through the letters. "I'm going to need to step outside and make a call." She snapped a couple pictures of Ella's letters and the kids' pictures, gathered her notebooks, and walked out the front door.

"Ella—" I started.

"Don't. Not one single word. Not yet." Her knuckles were white and so were the tips of her fingernails where they dug into her biceps.

Donahue sent me a look full of so much sympathy that I nearly crumbled right there.

Minutes passed. The only sounds amid the tension in the room were the ticking of the clock and the rending of my heart roaring in my ears, consuming every thought. Would it be enough? Had I just given up everything…for nothing?

The front door opened, and Ms. Wilson walked back in, a faint stain of blush on her cheeks. "It appears I have been mistaken. I'm...sorry"—she choked that word out—"to have inconvenienced you. While the situation still remains a very...gray area, you didn't do anything that would justify canceling the policy, and my supervisor has decided that the investigation is now complete."

I almost sagged in relief at our win, no matter what it had cost.

"Don't sound so disappointed. You get to help the good guys today." Donahue pushed back from the table. "I'll walk you out."

Ms. Wilson stood, then gave me a forced smile. "My brother-in-law said you were one of the good ones, if that counts for anything. He said you and the dog were perfectly matched, like nothing he'd ever seen. Even your names meant the same damn thing. It was nice to meet you, Mr. Gentry. Ms. MacKenzie." She turned to where Havoc sat at my side. "Havoc, right?"

"This way, Ms. Wilson," Donahue called out. He locked eyes with me as she walked toward him. He knew I was about to have my hands full. "That offer stands. You can always come back."

I nodded, and they left, the door shutting with an ominous, echoing sound behind them.

"How could you have hidden those from me? Why do you have his letters?" Ella asked, rising from her chair and backing away from me toward the box.

"Ella."

She put her hands on either side of her head and shook it. "No. No. No. Oh God. The tree house, the same lettering on Maisie's diploma. Havoc. It's not a coincidence, is it?"

"No." All of my life I'd been able to compartmentalize, to turn off my emotions. It was how I survived all those years in foster care, how I existed in special ops.

But Ella had changed something in me. She'd opened my heart, and now I couldn't shut the damn thing down. This pain was excruciating, and it was just the beginning.

"Say it. I'm not going to believe it unless you say it. Who are you?"

My eyes squeezed shut, and my throat closed. It was all I could do to draw a breath. But she deserved the truth, and now Maisie was protected. I'd done all I could to honor Ryan's request, and the consequences to my heart didn't matter. I straightened my spine and opened my eyes, taking in the pleading, terrified look in hers.

"I'm Beckett Gentry. Call sign Chaos."

CHAPTER TWENTY-TWO

Ella

This wasn't happening. I simply refused to believe that any of this was real. But those were my letters on the table, along with the pictures and notes the kids had sent to Chaos.

Beckett.

I looked again, just to make sure I hadn't lost my mind. Nope. Just my heart.

"How? Why? You told me he was dead!" The words flew out without any pause for him to explain. Maybe it was because I honestly didn't want to hear it. I didn't want my tiny little glass bubble of contentment to shatter.

"I never said that. I told you that knowing what happened to Ryan—to me—was only going to make you hurt worse than you already did." His hands gripped the back of the chair. Lucky for him, having something to hold on to when I was in free fall.

"How? When you're *alive*!" I shouted. "How could you let me think you were dead? Why would you do that to me? Is this all some kind of joke? God, the things you knew about me when you showed up…why, Beckett?"

Sensing the tension, Havoc got up, but it wasn't Beckett she sat next to, it was me.

"It isn't a joke—never was. I didn't tell you because I knew once you figured out who I was, what had happened, you would throw me out. Deservedly so. And when you inevitably did, I wouldn't be able to help you. I wouldn't be able to do the one thing Ryan asked of me, which was to take care of you."

"My brother. All of this was for my brother? Did you sleep with me for him, too? Just to keep me close?

Make me fall for you?" *How much of us was a lie?*

"No. I fell in love with you way before Ryan died."

"Don't." I backed up, needing distance and air. Why was there no air? My chest hurt so badly that the simple act of breathing took concentration.

"It's true."

"It's not. Because if you'd loved me then, you never would have let me believe you were dead. You wouldn't have left me alone at the worst time in my life, and then shown up a few months later as someone else. You lied to me!"

"By omission, yes, I did. I'm so sorry, Ella. I never wanted to hurt you." He looked convincingly sincere, but how could he be when he'd been lying to me for eleven months?

"I mourned you. I cried, Beckett. Those letters were special to me, *you* were special to me. Why would you do that?"

He stood there silent and stoic, and my disbelief and shock transformed into something darker and more painful than I'd ever imagined.

"Tell me why!"

"Because I'm the one who got Ryan killed!" His roar was guttural and raw, as if the admission had been ripped from him unwillingly. The silence that followed was louder than either of our voices had been.

Havoc abandoned me, taking her place at his side. Havoc and Chaos. How very perfect they were for each other.

"I don't understand," I finally managed to say.

Beckett bent slightly, rubbing Havoc's head in a way I'd seen him do hundreds of times. It wasn't for her, but to soothe him. She was his working dog and his therapy dog all in one.

"Do you remember when I told you that I killed a child?"

"Yes." I wasn't likely to forget something like that.

"It was on the twenty-seventh of December. That intel didn't pan out, and I lost it. You tell yourself that you're the good guy. You're there to stop the terrorists, to give the civilians back the country they deserve, that we're keeping our country safe. But seeing that little girl die at my hand…it broke something in me. I couldn't stop thinking about her, about what I'd done, or what I could have done differently." He rubbed his hands over his face but pulled it together.

My stupid heart swayed toward him, despite everything he'd done. I'd seen firsthand what those nightmares did to him. The rest of him might be a lie, but I knew this was true.

"The next night, new intel came in, and we had orders. Half of the squad was tasked to go, me included, but the thought of putting my hand on my weapon literally made me vomit. I knew I was a danger not only to myself and the mission but to my brothers. I went to Donahue and pulled myself off the line. I know that sounds simple, but it's not. It's admitting to your brothers that you don't belong with them—that you're broken. Donahue agreed and said I needed a few days of downtime to get my head straight."

"That's understandable," I said softly.

"Don't do that. Don't pity me. Because when I pulled myself off the line, there was an empty slot, and Ryan took it."

I breathed through the pain like I'd learned to when Mom and Dad died. All I'd wanted since those men showed up at the door was my brother back, but I would have settled for knowing what happened to him. Now that door was cracked open to the truth, and I was torn between longing to know and the clawing need to slam it shut and continue on in ignorance.

"He took your place." Just saying the words sent a

torrent of emotion coursing through me. Pride that Ryan had stepped up. Anger that he'd put himself in harm's way one time too many. Gratitude that Beckett had lived. But the sadness overwhelmed it all. I missed my brother.

"He took my place." Beckett's jaw flexed as he drew a shaky breath. "During the mission, he was separated from the rest of the squad. They acquired the target, but Ryan was gone. Chatter indicated capture."

My eyes burned with the familiar sting of tears. Keeping them closed, I brought a memory of Ryan to mind, laughing with the kids by the lake, skipping rocks. Giving up on teaching them finesse and just going for the splash contest. Alive. Healthy. Whole. I gripped that mental picture so tight I could almost feel the water on my skin. Then I opened my eyes. "Tell me the rest."

He shook his head as his fists clenched. "You don't want to know the rest."

"You lost the right to tell me what you think I need. Now finish it." This was like Maisie's mega-chemo, right? Blast out everything in one powerful, excruciating procedure, and then rebuild.

"God, Ella." He looked up at the ceiling and then down at my letters before dragging his gaze back to mine. "He was tortured. It took us three days to find him. When they told me he was missing, I pulled myself together, and Havoc and I went hunting. Radio chatter, sources…they all came up blank after that first night. I even searched the internet, thinking if they'd killed him, they would have posted it online." He hissed. "Sorry, that didn't need to be said."

"It all needs to be said."

He nodded. "Okay. We finally got some intel off a group of kids, goat herders a little ways outside the town. We rode out, but by the time we got there, the compound was empty. Havoc…she found Ryan about fifty yards away."

"He was dead," I guessed.

"Yes." His face contorted, his eyes darting from side to side, and I knew he was lost to the memory. "Yes, he was dead."

"Tell me."

"No, it won't help you sleep, Ella. Trust me, it's the stuff of nightmares. The stuff of my nightmares."

Did I really want to know? Would it help in any way? Would I regret passing up this one chance I had? "Give me the basics." After this, I might never see Beckett again, and no one else in that unit was going to tell me anything.

"Basics? There was nothing basic about it." His expression shifted every few seconds in the set of his mouth, the puckering of his forehead, the tension in his jaw. "We found him stripped of his uniform—down to his boxers and tee. They'd…worked him over something awful."

The first tear escaped, streaking my cheek with fresh, ugly grief.

"Ella…" The anguished whisper was nothing like I'd ever heard from Beckett.

"Go on." I blinked, sending another stream of wetness down my face without bothering to wipe it away. If Ryan had endured all of that, then I could cry for him without the social niceties of clean cheeks. "They wouldn't let me see him. They said the remains weren't suitable for viewing."

"He'd been shot in the back of the head, and that kind of wound—"

"Executed."

"Yes. That's our best guess. They did it in a hurry when they heard us coming, and…left him as they escaped into the hills."

I nodded, the motion sending wetness onto my shirt. "What next?"

He pulled out the chair and collapsed into it, deflated, with his hands over his face.

I should have felt guilty for putting him through this—making him tell me. But even after what he'd put me through with his lies, all I felt was an unexplainable connection to the man I loved, who had been there and recovered my brother. In a strange, horrible way, that pain connected us in a bond I was both terrified and desperate to sever.

"Please, Beckett."

His hands fell listlessly to his lap as he slouched back in the chair. When he looked at me, misery was etched in every line of his face and deadened eyes.

"He was gone, but warm, and I flipped him over, thinking I could start CPR, but I couldn't. There wasn't…" He shook his head. "I can't. I just can't." His eyes shifted like he was pushing fast forward in his mind. "The helo came, and we evac'ed him. I took his dog tag—I'd known he'd wanted you to have it—and sat with him all night before the plane came, and then Jensen brought him home to you. I was deemed too valuable to the mission to be given leave—especially now that our objective had changed to Ryan's killers."

"Did you find them? I don't know why that seems important; it's not like there's really any justice in war."

"Yes. We did. And do. Not. Ask." His eyes turned hard and dangerous, and I saw him again—the man who was capable of compartmentalizing everything. I saw the storm in his eyes, the way his fists balled. This was Chaos.

And at one time, I'd had true, deep feelings for him.

"Did you get the other letters? The ones I sent after?" I needed to know. They'd never been returned. Those letters had been testaments to my pain. Had he read them and simply turned away?

"Yes. But I couldn't bring myself to read them.

Couldn't make myself lift a pen and tell you what happened, not that I was even allowed to. I'd fallen for you, this incredible woman I'd never even met. I'd never felt love before, not in that way, and all I wanted to do was protect you."

"By ghosting me? By making me think you'd died alongside my brother?"

"By not doing anything that would bring an ounce more of pain into your life. I break everything and everyone, Ella. That's why they call me Chaos. It was given to me long before the military, and once I came to your brother's defense in a bar fight and the nickname came to light, it stuck there, too. Rightfully so. I bring destruction everywhere I go. I hadn't even met you yet, and I'd already cost you Ryan. The last surviving member of your immediate family died because I couldn't get my shit together long enough to do my mission. I am the reason he's dead. Did you want to keep writing to the man who got your brother killed? Should I have lied to you then, instead? You don't give second chances when it comes to your family, remember? Even if I told you the truth, and you somehow forgave me, then keeping up with our letters, knowing I had caused his death, and that I might be the next notification you got? I couldn't do it. You deserved to cauterize that wound and move on."

"Move on?" I paced back and forth along the end of the table, my energy suddenly too much to contain standing. "My daughter had just been diagnosed with cancer, my brother was dead, and I had no one. Ryan left me because he had to. You *chose* to."

"It was far better for you to think I died than to know the man you'd been so kind to befriend was responsible for Ryan's death."

"Go to hell." I turned and headed toward the door, only to stop before I made it out of the great room.

"When did you decide to come here? To carry on the lie?"

"Donahue gave me Ryan's letter right before I was due to get out. He keeps all of our last letters. I had already chosen to stay in—there was nothing else for me. But I read the letter, and I knew I had to come. Even if it shredded my soul to be this close to you and never tell you who I was, or that I loved you, I had to come. I was the reason he was dead. I couldn't very well deny my best friend the only thing he ever asked of me."

"So you decided to lie." He'd invaded my life, my heart, every molecule of my existence under false pretense. "Knowing what my father had done, what Jeff did, you still chose to lie to me."

"I did."

I leaned against the wall, my heart demanding I walk out the door and save whatever was left of it, while my brain fought to get every answer I could before the heartbreak consumed me. Even Jeff walking out hadn't hurt this bad, because I hadn't loved him like this.

I loved Beckett to the depths of my soul, in a way that consumed even the smallest bits and shadowed places I'd kept hidden from everyone else. Even the love I had for my kids connected to the way I loved Beckett, because he loved them, too.

"Did you ever think about telling me?" I turned my head slowly, somehow finding the strength to look at him.

"From the first moment I saw you," he admitted, having moved to lean against the end of the kitchen counter, the same one we'd made love on for the first time. "It was always on the tip of my tongue, especially when you asked about Chaos. I saw the pain you were in, and part of me wondered if maybe you'd fallen for him the same way I had for you."

"And still you let me believe he—you were dead." I didn't answer the implied question.

"I would get so jealous of myself, wondering why you had opened up to me when I was just a letter, but the real me had no chance. I knew from the beginning that telling you would lead to the moment we're having right now, when you would inevitably kick me out of your life, and that meant I couldn't do what Ryan asked and what you needed. The lie was the only way to help you. So I accepted that I would never be more to you than the guy your brother sent."

"And then I fell in love with you." Foolish, stupid, naive heart.

"You gave me a glimpse of the life I never thought I could have. You showed me what it meant to have a family and people who show up, and I did my best to show up for you. I can't thank you enough for the last eleven months, and I can't begin to explain how immeasurably sorry I am for what I've done to you, and what I've cost you. Ella, you're the last person I would ever want to hurt."

"But you did." That hurt was an avalanche headed my way. I felt the rumble in my soul, saw the chilled powder descend over my common sense, even heard the warning sirens in my head. I'd fallen in love with this man, and he'd lied to me every day for the last eleven months.

Jeff promised he'd love me forever. He pretended to be something he wasn't, and then he walked out.

Ryan promised me we'd always take care of each other. He joined the military and came home in a box.

My father promised he was just going TDY for a week or two...and never looked back. Never even asked for visitation.

Beckett...Chaos. What else had he lied about? Could I believe anything he'd said in the last year? Had he lied to the kids? Was he even telling me the truth now? Or just what he thought might earn him my mercy? Could I believe anything he'd ever tell me again?

"I am so very sorry. Forgiveness, or even understanding, isn't something I'm expecting from you. I'm in no way worthy of it, or you. I never was."

My heart started screaming. I was near the end of whatever strength I had and needed to get out of here before I had a complete breakdown. The look in his eyes kept my feet glued to the floor. There was no plea, no terror over what was happening to us, just sorrowful acceptance. He'd always known we would end up here. He put us through it anyway.

Was there any way to come back from this? I loved this man, and he loved me. That was worth fighting for, right? But how toxic would we be if we ever found a way past it? I would never forget what he'd done—it would always linger over us like an ominous cloud, raining down poison.

"I need to ask you one last question."

"Anything," he answered. How could a face so beautiful mask so much deception?

"Everything you did—the adoption, our relationship, Maisie's graduation, Colt's tree house—was that because of Ryan's letter?" My breath caught in my chest, waiting for his answer. As much as he'd hurt me, I needed to know that we were real, that I hadn't been that stupid.

"No. Ryan's letter got me here. I wouldn't have come without it. But the rest, Ella, that was all because I love you. Because I love Colt and Maisie. Because for this brief, shining moment, you were my family, my future, and it looked a lot like forever. I didn't do all of that for Ryan. I did it for you. For me."

The ten feet between us stretched endlessly and yet felt like nothing as I debated my next move. There were equal parts of love and lies between us, but my anger over his betrayal overshadowed it all.

I still loved him—both sides of him—but I'd never be capable of trusting him again. Without trust, what good was love? How could you build a life with someone if you had to question the truthfulness of everything they said and did?

"It's not enough." Once the words were spoken, I felt their truth ring in my soul. "You've looked me in the eye for nearly a year and lied to me. I shared everything I had with you—my heart, my soul, my body, and even my family—and you couldn't even be truthful about who you are. I don't know how to even process that. I don't know what parts of you—parts of us—are lies or truths. I want to be strong and say that we'll get past it, because we love each other so much, but I don't think that's possible. Not now, anyway. I don't have enough strength left in me for this. Ryan's death took it. Maisie's diagnosis took it. I should have known you'd take it, too, but I trusted you, and now I don't have anything left to give."

My hand along the wall steadied me as I walked toward the front door. The sunlight streamed in through the glass pane, beckoning me like a promise—if I could just get out of here somewhat intact, I'd be okay. Because I had to be. I had Colt and Maisie to take care of. I didn't have the luxury of falling apart like some lovesick girl.

I didn't have the luxury of forgiving Beckett.

"I understand." His voice came from right behind me as my hand gripped the door handle. I felt his nearness, that palpable electricity that had always sparked between us, and knew if I turned he'd be right there. "If you need anything, I'm still here."

My eyes burned again, but this time it wasn't grief over Ryan, but Beckett. The feeling was similar, knowing I'd lost the person I'd loved most.

"I think it would be best if you left." I spoke directly to the door. Beckett remaining in Telluride would only give me time to fall right back into him—and I couldn't survive another lie. I couldn't be strong for my kids when Beckett brought me to my knees, and they came first. Always. "I'll have your things boxed from my place and sent over. I don't ever want to see you again."

As surely as if I'd cauterized the wound with a branding iron, every nerve in my body cried out with pain, sharp and nauseating. Without waiting for his response, I walked out of the cabin and didn't look back.

CHAPTER TWENTY-THREE

Beckett

Letter #22

Chaos,

Ryan is dead. But I'm sure you already know that. I honestly feel like I'm just writing it out so it feels real.

Ryan is dead.

Ryan is dead.

Ryan...

Nothing about it feels right. His body is still in Dover, being prepared for burial, and they've already told me that I can't see him. In that way, I'm hoping it's all a cruel joke, that he's not really in a box. That I don't have to figure out where to bury my brother.

My mom. My dad. My grandmother. Ryan. They're all gone, and yet I'm still here. Is Maisie next? Is this what life really is? One tragedy after another? Or is this simply the way my life is going?

Colt and Maisie are devastated. Colt refused to speak yesterday after I told him, and Maisie hasn't stopped crying. I, on the other hand, haven't started crying. Not yet. I'm terrified that once I start, I won't ever stop. I'll just be this saltwater fountain who leaks misery.

Ryan was my best friend. My safe harbor in a storm. And now I feel like I'm out on this endless ocean in the middle of a hurricane, and the waves are just waiting to capsize me and take me under.

I know this sounds crazy, but the only person I want right now is you. You're the only person I've been completely honest with these last few months. You're the only person who might understand the debilitating, soul-crushing grief that I can't even begin to fathom. Because I know, as much as you swear you don't know what family is, Ryan was your brother. He was your family.

I'm just hoping you come for his funeral, because I know he would have wanted you here. I know I do. And if you can't come, then I hope you're not changing your plans. Please come to Telluride. Even if it's just to get a cup of coffee with me. Please come.

~ Ella

I read the letter for the hundredth time or so, and then put it back into my nightstand drawer. I'd avoided that letter, and the two that had followed, for the last sixteen months, and now it was all I wanted to read—to hear her voice in my head.

If I'd read it when she'd sent it, instead of hiding it away, I would have come. I never could have denied her, and everything would have been different. Then again, Ryan would still be dead because of me, so maybe not.

I came down the stairs of my new house to find Havoc napping in the sun that came through the floor-to-second-story windows in my great room. I'd had a section of the trees cleared so I could see the island that perched in the middle of the tiny lake. Luckily, with the angle my house was at, I couldn't see Ella's house.

Maybe I was torturing myself keeping Ryan's grave in sight, but knowing Ella was this close and so damn far was way worse. It had been over a month since she'd walked out of my cabin. My things had arrived that afternoon. My entire role in Ella's life came down to four moving boxes.

As breakups went, I'd expected screaming, shrieking, throwing things at me for what I'd done, but her stoic silence was worse. She'd accepted that we were done, and now I had to move on without her and the kids.

God, I missed the kids. Falling for Ella had tied me to them in a way that was both a blessing and a curse. A blessing for all they taught me, for the love I hadn't realized I'd even been able to feel. A curse because Ella cut off all my access, as was her right. She didn't trust me, and that extended to the kids. Her heart was broken over me, but my heart was shattered over the loss of all three of them.

I sighed at the sight of my empty living room. I really needed to buy some furniture. I had the bedroom covered, and most of the kitchen stuff was being delivered daily, thanks to Amazon.com. But the rest of the furniture just didn't seem important, because this was my house but for some reason didn't feel like my home.

My phone rang as I opened the fridge to figure out some lunch.

"Gentry," I answered, wondering who had gotten themselves lost this time. As spring came to the area, more hikers were showing up and getting altitude sickness, or lost, or breaking their bones in inconvenient locations.

"Mr. Gentry? I'm so sorry to bother you. This is Principal Halsen over here at the elementary school. I happen to have Colton in the office."

My stomach lurched. "Is he okay? Is he hurt?" Why were they calling *me*?

"No, no. Nothing like that. He actually got into an altercation today with a classmate and needs to go home."

"A fight?" No way. Not Colt. Sure, the kid got fired up, but I'd never seen him get violent unless it was over Maisie.

"Yep, a fight."

"Whoa. Did you call his mom?"

"We tried, but she's not answering, and Colt told us that she's in Montrose for one of Margaret's therapies. I was hoping you might be able to come pick him up."

I pulled the phone away from my ear and checked the number, just to make sure I wasn't being pranked. "Pick him up?" I asked slowly.

"Yes. Policy demands that he go home for the day, and you're the second name on his emergency contact sheet."

Shit. Ella hadn't updated the kids' information yet. Which meant I might get to see Colt. I slammed the door on my excitement. Ella didn't want me to see him, and I had no right to. "Is anyone else on the list?"

"Only Ada and Larry, and from what I'm being told, they're on vacation in Glenwood Springs for a few days."

Which left me.

"Yeah, I'll be there in twenty minutes."

He thanked me, and we hung up.

I hesitated for a second, my finger hovering over Ella's name on my contacts list, but I manned up and clicked the phone icon. It went straight to voicemail, not that I was surprised. I'd tried to call a few times that first week and had the same result. Ella was done with me. She'd told me that lies were her hard limit, and she meant it.

"Hey, Ella, it's Beckett. Look, the school just called, and I guess Colt got into a fight and needs to be picked up. I'm the only one on his list, so I'm going to grab him. Let me know if you want me to drop him at the main house at Solitude or bring him up to Montrose. If I don't hear from you, I'll just bring him back to my house. I know you don't want me to see him, but this is a little out of my control, so I'm hoping you'll understand. Thanks." I hung up and rested the phone against my forehead. Even hearing the message on her voicemail was torture.

I left Havoc sleeping in the sunshine and headed out, driving along the dirt road that cut through the property. Within twenty minutes, I pulled up to the school. With all the butterflies in my stomach, I would have thought I was the one about to get it from the principal. Instead, I was about to get it from Colt.

I walked through the doors and signed the clipboard, then looked up at the receptionist. "Hi, I'm Beckett Gentry, I'm here to pick up—"

"Colton MacKenzie," the young woman said with a smile. "I know who you are. We all do." She nodded toward a few other women who gathered around the desk behind her.

"Ah, okay. So, can I get him?"

"Oh, sure! I'll buzz you in."

The buzzer sounded, and I walked into the school. The last time I'd been here had been with Ella for Colt's first grade play a couple of months ago. As recent as it felt, it also seemed like someone else's memory.

"This way," the receptionist said, tucking a strand of hair behind her ear and giving me a flirtatious smile. "I'm Jennifer, in case you don't remember."

"Jennifer, right. We met last year, right?" She led me into the administration offices.

"Yep! When you came in for search and rescue with your dog. I may have slipped you my number when you signed in."

"Yes, I do remember that." I tried to force a smile. Ella and I hadn't been together then, but it hadn't mattered, and I hadn't called Jennifer. "I'm sorry for not calling. I hope there are no hard feelings."

Jennifer touched my arm just outside the principal's door. "None. I was so sorry to hear that you and Ella broke up. If you ever need anything, or just want to talk, I'm happy to give you my number again, just in case."

Oh boy. She looked so hopeful, and uncomplicated, and not Ella.

"Thanks, I'll...keep that in mind." It was the best I could do without offending her.

"You do that." She smiled again. *A lot of smiling.* I bet she was happy most of the time. That she wasn't fighting to keep her kid alive, or dealing with the death of her brother and the betrayal of the man she loved. She was all shiny, like a new penny.

But in the last eighteen months, I'd learned that I liked a little bit of tarnish. It gave depth to the lines and made the shiny parts all the more eye-catching. Ella was beyond beautiful for what she'd been through. Tragedy hadn't broken her, it had refined her.

Jennifer knocked and opened the door to the principal's office, and I entered, my eyes immediately locking onto Colt's.

His flew impossibly wide.

"Principal Halsen," I addressed the administrator, who motioned to the empty chair beside Colt.

I took it, sitting next to a very rigid Colt. Every line of his little body was tense, and his mouth was all pursed up. His hand gripped the armrest, and I reached over, giving him a reassuring squeeze. His posture softened the slightest bit, but it was enough.

"Mr. Gentry. I'm so sorry to call you in here, but in this kind of incident when there's violence, we do need to send him home."

"Can you tell me what happened?" I asked Colt.

"He attacked a classmate—"

"I'd like to hear it from him, first, if that's okay," I

interrupted Principal Halsen.

"We were on the playground, and Drake Cooper wouldn't leave Emma alone. She doesn't like him." Colt kept his eyes forward. "She told him to leave, and he wouldn't, and he tried to kiss her."

Drake. Recognition hit me. Letter number three.

"Is this the same kid who went after Maisie with that kiss-tag stuff?" I asked. It was the first time I'd ever used something only Chaos would have known. Of course, Colt didn't know that, didn't realize that as I sat next to him. I felt an odd merging of the guy who had written those letters and the man who had adopted Colt.

"Yeah. I guess he didn't learn."

"Guess not."

Principal Halsen gave me a disapproving look, which I blatantly ignored.

"So I pulled him away and hit him," Colt finished with a shrug. "He tried to hit me back, but I dodged."

"Nice," I said with a nod.

"He's slow." Another shrug.

"Mr. Gentry, as you can see, your son instigated violence in an unprovoked attack. He'll be sent home today and suspended tomorrow. We have to send a message that this kind of violence isn't tolerated."

"I'm not his son," Colt whispered.

Yeah, you are.

"Right, sorry, Colt," Principal Halsen corrected and sent me another pointed look. He knew about the adoption from the records point of view.

"I have no problem with taking Colt home or him being suspended. You're right, he did swing first. But my question is what you're going to do about Drake."

Colt's head swung toward me in shock.

"I'm sorry?" Principal Halsen asked.

"My guess is that you've told Colt he's purely at fault

here, right? After all, he swung, he did what you thought was escalating violence."

"He is in the wrong."

"Maybe. But so is Drake. And he was already in the middle of an act of violence, which Colt stopped."

"I'd hardly call playground antics like that violence," Principal Halsen scoffed. "Drake has been told that his actions are unacceptable. But you know how little boys with crushes are, I'm sure."

I glanced at Colt, who had the same look on his face Ella did when she was about to blow a gasket.

"Actually, I do. They act like Colt and protect the girls they like. What the other kid did, whether or not you see it, is wrong. And sure, you can brush it off as a playground antic, like I'm sure you've done for the last thirty years you've been at this school. The problem isn't this one time; it's the pattern. You did nothing last year when it was Maisie. Now we're here, and that kid is another year older. So sure, I can take Colt home and give him a stern talking to about when it's appropriate to use force. But I'll probably end up showing him how to throw a better punch, because one day that other kid will be sixteen, and it won't be just playground kisses he's taking by force."

Principal Halsen dropped his jaw, and I stood. "Thank you for bringing this to my attention. I'll be sure his mother takes appropriate action. Colt? Ready to go? I think ice cream is in order."

Colt nodded, scooting off the chair and swinging his backpack over his shoulder. We walked out of the office, through the double set of doors, and into the brisk March air. Colt was silent as we climbed into the truck and he buckled into his booster seat.

I hadn't removed it in the last month. That action seemed more permanent than when Ella had walked out of the cabin.

"Your mom hasn't called," I said as I checked my phone.

"She's in Montrose with Maisie," Colt answered.

"Yeah. Who is taking care of you since Ada and Larry are on vacation?" I pulled out of the parking lot and headed toward Solitude. Traffic wasn't too bad this time of day, but as soon as the sun went down, it would be mayhem as usual during tourist season.

The fact that I'd now lived somewhere long enough to recognize there was such a thing as tourist season was a revelation.

"Hailey."

"Okay, want me to run you by the main house?" I looked in the rearview mirror, but he was staring out the window. "Colt?"

"I don't care."

I'd never had three words cut me that quickly before. Of course he was mad at me. He had every right to be. "Well, I left your mom a message that if she didn't call me back, I'd take you to my house. Is that cool? Or would you rather go to Hailey?"

This was a catch-22, and I knew it. More than anything, I wanted a few hours with him. I needed to know how he was, what was new in his life, if he'd made the spring league soccer team. I missed the twins just as much as I missed Ella. But I also knew this was against Ella's wishes, and I couldn't just steal these hours.

"How far away do you live?" he asked, still watching the scenery go by. "I can't get on a plane or anything. Mom would be really mad."

My heart lurched. "Bud, I still live in Telluride—"

"You do? I just thought…" He shook his head. "I guess we can go to your house, that way you didn't lie to my mom. She gets really mad if you lie."

I knew Ella was the kind of mom who wouldn't go into that much detail of why we weren't together anymore, but those words hit home just the same. "You sure?"

He nodded. "Hailey's working, and the sub cook doesn't like kids around. Ada doesn't like her, anyway. And if it's okay, I'd really like to see Havoc." His tone was flat, as if he'd been deciding between broccoli and cauliflower on his plate.

"Yeah. She'd like that, too. So would I. I miss you, buddy."

"Okay." He scoffed.

"I do, Colt."

He didn't respond, and continued the silent treatment until we pulled onto the dirt road that began just on the edge of the Solitude property.

"Where are we going?" he asked.

"My house."

He leaned toward the window, checking out the property. "You live back here?"

"I do." We pulled into the small clearing where the house was built, and Colt's head swiveled.

"You live on the other side of the lake?"

"Yep. Pretty cool, right?" I pulled into the garage and killed the engine.

"Sure." Colt grabbed his backpack and was to the house before I was.

I opened the door, and he flew inside, dropping to his knees where the mudroom met the kitchen and throwing his arms around Havoc.

She whined, her tail thumping on the floor as she laid her head on his shoulder, then the other. "I know. I missed you, too, girl," Colt said, rubbing behind her ears. "It's okay."

I don't know who was killing me more at the moment: Colt with his soft words or Havoc with her whines. She'd been the same way when Maisie came home from mega-chemo in December.

"I've got ice cream in the freezer," I offered.

"Nah. I'm good. Let's play!" He ditched his bag after grabbing his jacket, and Havoc led him out the front door, her Kong already in her mouth.

I followed and sat on the front porch steps as Colt threw the toy on the shore of the lake. He was only thirty feet away, but man, he'd frozen me out so efficiently that it felt like miles.

After a few minutes, I walked toward them.

"You like it?" I asked.

"You can't see my house from here," he said with another shrug.

"Nope, it's behind the island."

"Is that why you forgot about me?" He flung the ball down the shore.

Yeah, I wasn't going to survive a few hours with him at this rate. Ella would find me dead, Colt holding the shredded remains of my heart.

"I never forgot you, Colt. That would be impossible."

Havoc brought him the Kong, and he threw it harder, the motion more anger than exercise. "Yeah, right."

"Colt." I dropped to my knees and turned him toward me, then took a huge breath to steady myself. He had twin tear tracks down his cheeks. "I did not forget you."

"Then why haven't you seen us? One day I went to school, and when I came home, Mom said you guys weren't friends anymore, and that was it."

"Bud, it's complicated." I put my hands on his shoulders.

"That's what grown-ups say when they don't want to explain stuff." He blinked, and another set of angry tears dropped.

"You know what? You're right. Relationships between grown-ups are really hard to explain, but I'll try. I messed up. You got that? Not your mom. This isn't her fault, it's mine. And I messed up so big that we broke up."

"But you didn't break up with me!" he shouted. "Or Maisie! You just disappeared! And when I snuck out to see you, you were already gone. You left without a goodbye, or a reason."

"I'm right here," I promised, my throat tightening, nearly choking my words.

"But I didn't know that! You said you loved me and that we were friends. Friends don't do that."

"You're right. Colt, I'm so sorry." I put every ounce of emotion I had into my words, hoping he'd realize how true they were. "I have missed you every single day. There hasn't been a minute when I haven't wanted to see you, or talk to you. What happened between your mom and me doesn't mean that I don't love you and Maisie. It's just…" Why weren't there words for this? Why couldn't I explain things to him without placing blame on Ella? It wasn't her fault. It was mine.

"Complicated," he finished.

"Yeah. Complicated."

His anger faded, his mouth drooping into a profound, lip-trembling sadness. "I just…I kind of thought you were my dad. Or maybe you would be one day. And then you were gone."

This time his tears destroyed me. I yanked him against my chest, wrapping my arms around him. "Me, too, Colt. Nothing would have made me happier than to be your dad. You are the best little boy I could have ever imagined having. This isn't your fault. It's not your mom's fault. It's my fault. So if you want to be mad, that's okay, but you have to be mad at me. No one else. Promise?"

"I don't want to be mad." He cried into my shirt. "I want you to fix it!"

"I wish I could. But there are some things too broken to fix."

He pulled back and glared at me. "Maisie was really broken, and you and Mom fix her. And she gets sick, and she cries, but Mom says she'll get better if she fights, and then it will all be worth it."

"I know." I was usually really good at kid logic, but he was stumping me here.

"So you can't be more broken than Maisie and not try to fix it. You don't see Maisie giving up, and it's been forever." He dragged out the last word. "You and Mom broke in a day."

"I really wish it was that simple, Colt."

"So does Maisie. But she's brave enough to try."

I was seriously getting schooled in relationships by a seven-year-old. "You know who you sound like right now?"

He raised his eyebrows but didn't answer.

"Your Uncle Ryan. Just like him."

He looked out at the island and back to me. "Okay. So are you going to try to fix it? Or are you giving up?"

Everything to Colt was so easy. He hadn't seen the worst of humanity yet, what people were capable of doing to one another. Hadn't seen what I'd done to his mom. Didn't know that I'd cost him his uncle. I loved Ella even more in that moment for not turning them against me.

"I can try, buddy. For you and Maisie, I can try." I'd respected Ella's wish to disappear. Having taken away all her other choices, that seemed like the best way to honor her. Besides, it wasn't like I deserved a second chance. But what if I'd made a mistake? What if I should have pushed?

She would have pushed you right back.

"Good. Apologize. Girls like that." He gave me a nod and a pat on my shoulder.

"I'll keep that in mind. Anything else?"

His forehead puckered for a moment, and then he

gave me a smirk. "They like it when you fight for them, too."

Man, I loved this kid.

"Emma's the one, huh?" From what I remembered of Colt's birthday party, she'd been cute, kind, and smart, with big brown eyes and curly black hair a few shades darker than her complexion.

"She's got pretty skin." He nodded for emphasis.

I joined in on the nod, managing not to chuckle. "You tell her that?"

"No!" He looked around for a second, pondering. "Maybe when we're twelve."

"Playing the long game, gotcha." I stood as he turned and threw the Kong for Havoc again, who had been waiting patiently. "I think what you did for her today was pretty awesome. It's always good to protect smaller people. Maybe less hitting, though."

He nodded. "I got really mad."

"Yeah, I get that, too. But that's a big part of being a man, knowing your strength and controlling your anger."

"I'm seven."

I almost laughed, realizing I'd been in his life long enough to hear him preach *I'm six.*

"Not for long. You could have just pulled him off, and the result wouldn't have been as satisfying but just as effective. Plus, no principal time."

"I'll keep that in mind," he said, echoing my words from earlier.

"So what do you think about the house?" I'd built it for him, for Maisie…for Ella. Ironically, we'd broken up right before I could surprise her with it.

Or maybe I just should have told her from the beginning, like everything else.

He looked up at the house, his brows drawn in appraisal. "It's good. I like it."

"I'm glad to hear it."

"It needs a tree house." He pointed over to a gathering of pine trees. "Right there would be good."

"Noted."

"And a zip line."

"Not going to give up on that one, are you?"

"Never!" He took off, chasing Havoc down the beach as my phone rang.

Ella.

"Hey," I answered.

"What happened to Colt?" she asked, her voice pitched. "I'm so sorry, I don't have service in that wing of the hospital, and I missed all the calls and now school is closed. What a mess."

Her voice slid through me, soothing and cutting in one graceful move. "It's okay." I cleared my throat, hoping to clear the gravel sound out.

"I can't believe you went all the way there. How far away were you?"

"Maybe ten minutes?"

"Wait. You're still in Telluride?"

"I told you I wouldn't leave."

Her breathing pattern changed multiple times, like she would start to say something and then change her mind.

"So, Drake tried to kiss Emma," I said, "and Colt went after him."

She groaned. "What a jerk. Drake, I mean. Not Colt."

"Yeah, I know. I might have caused a little drama with the principal, though. I told him it was partially their fault for not putting a stop to it when it happened with Maisie."

"Right? They let that kid get away with murder. Wait, how did you…?"

I heard her slight intake of breath as she realized how I knew.

"Your third letter." I felt the tone of our call change as my sins barged in between us, but I didn't back away from it. "I told Colt it was great to stand up for the girl you like, but maybe a little less hitting."

"Yeah. True."

Silence stretched between us, sad and heavy with the things we'd already said last month.

"So, he's playing with Havoc right now, but I can take him to Hailey if you want. He's suspended tomorrow."

"Crap, I'm not due home until tomorrow afternoon, and Hailey's watching him while Ada and Larry are away, but she's working all day tomorrow. I don't mind him at the main house, but—"

"But the cook subbing in for Ada isn't a big fan of kids. Colt told me."

"Yeah, she's kind of mean. But really good, too." She sighed, and I could picture her smoothing her hair back, her eyes darting from side to side, trying to figure out what to do.

"I can keep him with me. I have the room, and I'd love nothing more than to hang out with him. But I understand completely if you don't want that, and I'd be willing to bring him to Montrose, too." *Or slice my heart open and bleed out, whatever you'd like.*

A few seconds of silence passed, and I almost took it back, hating that I'd put her in that kind of position.

"That would be nice, and I'm sure he'd love it. He's really missed you." Her voice dropped to a whisper. "Maisie, too."

"I've missed them, too. It's…it's been hard."

I've missed you every second, so much it hurts to breathe.

"Yeah."

More silence. I would have given anything to see her in that moment, to hold her, to fall at her feet and make whatever sacrifice she demanded.

"Look, I'll call Solitude and let Hailey know, and I'll be there around five tomorrow. Is that okay?"

"No problem."

"Thank you, and I'm glad you're still here, I mean there. In Telluride. Okay. Bye, Beckett."

"Ella." I couldn't bear to say goodbye, even if just for a phone call.

The line went dead, and I looked over at Colt. I had twenty-four hours with him. I did what any rational man would. I called in to work and made the most of every minute.

CHAPTER TWENTY-FOUR

Ella

Letter #2

Ella,

These cookies are the best thing ever. I'm not lying.

First, don't let the judgy PTA ladies scare you off. Though I'll admit, I've been to war. A lot. And those women still intimidate me, and I don't even have kids, so I will simply throw you the Hunger Games salute and wish you the best.

Yeah, we watch a lot of movies over here.

You asked about the scariest choice I've ever made. I'm not sure I've ever really been scared of a choice I've made. Being scared means you have something to lose, and I've never really had that. Without going into my background too deeply, I'll simply say that I don't have family outside of this unit. I don't have anyone waiting for me to come home from this trip, either. Even joining the army was a no-brainer, since I was eighteen and on the verge of getting kicked out of the system.

I get scared on behalf of the other guys. I hate seeing them get hurt, or worse. I get scared every time your brother pulls some reckless crap, but that's not my choice.

But I will tell you the biggest choice. I bought a tract of land, sight unseen, simply because it came recommended to me. The owner was in a bind, and I took the plunge. I have no idea what to do with it, either. My investment guy—yes, I have one of those so I don't die broke—told me to hold on *to it and sell it to developers when I want to retire. Your brother said to build a house and settle down.*

Now that scares me. The idea of settling somewhere, not starting over every few years, is a little terrifying. There's a peace that comes with being such a nomad. I start fresh when I move. A clean slate just waiting for me to mess it up. Hey, I warned you, I'm crap with people. Settling down means I have to work on not alienating everyone around me because I'm stuck with them. That, or I become a mountain hermit and grow a really long beard, which might actually be the easier choice.

I guess I'll let you know when I figure out which decision to make.

Your place sounds great, and I have the ultimate faith that you made the right choice mortgaging it for improvements. Like you said, nothing ventured, nothing gained.

What the heck do you put in these cookies? Because they're seriously addicting. I might curse you after I run a few extra miles, but these are so worth it.

Thank you again,
~ Chaos

"You're sure this is the right way?" I asked Maisie as we pulled onto the dirt road. "We're really close to Solitude."

Telluride. Beckett was still in Telluride. He hadn't left. Hadn't moved on like I'd so foolishly assumed.

"That's what the lady says from the GPS pin he texted you," Maisie answered, waving the phone with the Google Maps app open. "Do I really get to see Beckett?"

The hope in her voice was brutal.

"Yeah, for a few minutes." I tried to keep my tone light but failed miserably. Maybe it was the exhaustion from two weeks of hospitalization with Maisie for the radiation. Maybe it was hearing that another kid Maisie had met in Denver passed last week. Maybe it was Beckett.

Or maybe my heart was simply broken by all of the above.

"I miss him," she said softly.

"Me, too, love," I answered without thinking.

"No, you don't. If you missed him, you'd call him. You'd let us see him." Her tone was anything but understanding as we wove our way through the woods.

"Maisie, it's not that easy. Sometimes relationships just don't work out, and you might not really understand that until you're older."

"Okay."

Man, I was in for it when this sassafras became a teenager. Then I smiled, realizing she had a shot at becoming a teenager now.

Because of Beckett.

But the lies were woven in with the love, and that was the killer. The lies didn't wipe out everything he'd done for me, for us. They didn't wipe out the way it felt when he kissed me, the way my body fired on all cylinders when he was in a room. They didn't wipe out the way he loved the kids, or the way they loved him.

But that love didn't wipe out the lies, either, or my fear that he'd tell more.

And there was our impasse.

It wasn't that I couldn't see past what he'd done to understand *why* he'd done it. It was simply that I couldn't afford to trust him.

"Oh my God," I whispered as we came upon the house. I looked at the lake, just to be sure, then back at the house. I would have asked Maisie if she was sure, but Colt came running out of the house with Havoc on his heels, and that answered the question.

Beckett owned the twenty-five acres I'd sold off two years ago to that investment company.

The house itself was beautiful. Built in the log-cabin style, which matched the ones in Solitude. It was two stories with multiple A-frame rooflines and stone pillars. It was classic, rustic, and modern, all in one style. The definition of Beckett.

Colt threw open Maisie's door. "There you are! I missed you!"

"Me, too!" she said, and the two locked in a hug.

"Hey, honey," I said when they broke apart.

"Hi, Mom!" Colt threw me a grin over the back of the seat. "We made dinner, come on!"

"Oh, Maisie doesn't feel too well." I immediately panicked at the thought of spending any more than a few minutes with Beckett.

"We figured. So we have chicken, and rice, and saltines, if you need them, Maisie. Come on, you have to see the house!" Maisie jumped down, more agile than I'd seen her these last two weeks, and the two were off like a shot.

"Well, I guess that settles that," I mumbled to myself. The urge struck to check my hair and makeup, and I shook it off. There was no need to impress Beckett. Funny, I'd used to think the same thing, because he'd loved me. Now it was because I wasn't supposed to care what he thought.

I threw a glance in the mirror and fixed my hair with a couple of quick tugs…because I did care. *Damn it.*

"Don't be a chicken," I lectured myself as I got out of the Tahoe. I left him, not the other way around. So why did it hurt this much? Why was my heart galloping? Why did I crave the sight of him almost as much as I avoided it?

Ugh.

I was twenty-six years old with my first real broken heart. When Jeff left, the twins and my own stubbornness had eased the ache and distracted me. But Beckett? There was no distraction for Beckett. He was in my thoughts, my dreams, my voicemails that I refused to delete, and the letters I wouldn't throw away. He was freaking everywhere.

My steps were slow as I made my way into the house. The inside was just as beautiful, with dark hardwood floors and high ceilings. It was exactly the house I would have designed for myself. But it wasn't mine, and neither was he.

Wait. Where was the furniture? There were no pictures on the walls, no signs that he'd even really moved in. Was he leaving after all?

"Hey," he said, coming around the corner.

Crap, he looked really good. Jeans and a long-sleeve baseball tee with Colt's soccer team logo on it were bad enough, but his hair was a little longer and perfectly mussed, and he'd had the nerve to grow a really sexy layer of scruff.

"Hi." Of all the words we needed to say to each other, that was all that came out.

"The kids are off exploring." His eyes drifted toward the ceiling as the sound of running feet came through. "Look, Colt wanted to make you dinner. I told him it probably wasn't a good idea, but he was adamant, and I figured you could just take it with you if you didn't want to stay."

"You live on the back twenty-five of Solitude that I sold two years ago."

"Yes." He said it so easily.

"This is where you went?"

"After we broke up?" he clarified.

I nodded slowly. "When you checked out, and Colt

told me your stuff was gone, I asked Hailey if you'd left any forwarding information."

"I didn't."

"I know. That's when I assumed you'd gone back to the army." Like two of the other men I'd loved.

"I didn't leave any forwarding information because I figured you'd call the station. It never occurred to me you'd think I'd actually leave you and the kids after I promised you I wouldn't." He sighed, rubbing his face. "Then again, I did lie about who I was, so..."

He was right. We both knew it.

"I didn't like the way we'd ended things. *I'd* ended things," I amended.

"Neither did I," he answered softly.

"You didn't call."

"I tried that first week, but you didn't answer. I figured you meant it when you told me you didn't want to see me again."

"I'm sorry. I never should have said that. I tend to... overreact when it comes to lies, and..."

"And build a fortress around the kids," he finished my thoughts, reciting my own words from our letters. "I understood, and I deserved it. It's not like you didn't warn me in your first letter, right?"

God, the man knew me so well, and I hated the feeling that I didn't know *him*.

"You don't have any furniture."

His eyebrows rose at my change of subject. "Just in the bedroom and the kitchen. Not that I mean to imply anything. I just needed a bed. For sleeping. Just sleeping." His shoulders rose, and he tucked his thumbs into his jeans. "And the kitchen, of course. For eating. Because it's a kitchen."

The way we both awkwardly navigated the conversation would have been funny if seeing him didn't feel like he'd just ripped my heart out and watched the final beats.

"Why? Why don't you have furniture?"

"Honestly?"

"Yeah. I think we have enough lies between us, don't you?" I winced. "That wasn't called for. I'm sorry."

"Feel free, I deserve whatever you want to dish out."

"The furniture?" I reminded him to get the heck off that topic.

"I bought what I needed. I'd always planned on letting you pick out the rest, and afterward…well, I didn't really care. I should probably get a living room set before football season, though. It's a little awkward to eat all those snacks in bed."

The kids raced down the wide steps that curved to the second story. "Isn't it great, Mom?" Maisie asked as she flew by with Colt on her heels. Man, that girl rebounded so fast. Havoc stopped by for a quick pet and then chased after them.

"Wait until you see the rec room!" Colt told her, and they were off down another hallway.

"Did she even say hi to you?" I asked with a small laugh.

"Yeah, I got a huge hug before Colt took her upstairs to see the bedrooms."

"How many are there?" Not that I needed to know.

"Six. Five here, and a suite above the garage."

"Wow. Big." I shook my head. "Please don't make a that's-what-she-said joke."

"Wouldn't dream of it." His smile was breathtaking and heartbreaking.

As usual, everything with him was so effortless and easy, but now it was excruciatingly difficult, too.

"Okay, it's none of my business, but *you* built this? You own the land I sold?" I'd seen it being built and kicked myself for selling the property every time I'd spied the construction crew. Luckily, the island hid it when I was home, so I'd been able to ignore it.

"I *had* it built over the last seven months or so. For you."

I forced my lungs to draw air when they were obviously averse to the idea. "For me."

"You said no lies." He threw a grin over his shoulder. "And it was the biggest choice I've ever made."

"You bought the back twenty-five two years ago? I thought it was an investment company."

"It was. Ryan asked if I'd be interested in an investment property. I agreed and gave it to my finance guy to handle, since we were overseas at the time. He'd been after me to diversify, so I did. Well, he did. I just signed the papers once we got back after that tour. I didn't realize they were your acres until I was already here."

"And you didn't tell me. Don't you see a pattern?"

"Nope. There are secrets, and there are surprises."

"You own the back twenty-five acres of my property!"

"Actually, only the back four acres. Go ahead and check with the county. I deeded all the land except four acres for the house over to you. Oh, and there's an easement for the road. Hope you don't mind."

"You gave it back?"

"Except the house. I mean, yeah, I built it for you, but for me, too. And it's cool if you want the house, but I come with it. Now come get some of this food. I can put it on plates and wrap it up if you don't want to stay. There's no pressure."

He turned around and started walking, so I followed him. The house really was spectacular. He led me to a large, modern kitchen that did, indeed, have a table and chairs. It opened onto a giant patio through a sliding glass door.

Freaking perfect house.

"You can't build me a house."

"Already did," he answered, walking around the island to where the food rested.

"It's not normal to build a house for a woman and not tell her." I came into the kitchen and leaned back against the dark granite counters. Good counter space, too. Perfect for— *Shut that thought down now.*

"Yeah, well, I had this stupid, romantic notion that I'd build it and prove to you that I wasn't leaving. And then when Maisie was cured, and everything leveled out, maybe you'd want to live here. With me. But I also know you love living on property, so I wasn't going to pressure you, and we really weren't ready for the move-in conversation." He piled food onto plates. "And we both know I'm not exactly good at the whole relationship thing. I'm probably fourteen for all the experience I have in that area." He gave me a teasing shrug.

"Is this really so easy for you?" Oh, that had come out really harsh.

The plates clicked against the granite as he set them down, then slowly turned toward me.

"No. It's not. It's impossible to see you, to be in the same room as you, and not want to drop to my knees and beg your forgiveness. It's all I can do to keep my hands off you, not to kiss you, touch you, remind you how good we are together and how much I love you. It's killing me not to take you upstairs and show you the bedroom I built just for you, if for no other reason than to get to sleep next to you. Every aspect of this feels like a knife is twisting in my gut, and the worst happened yesterday when Colt told me that I didn't love him. That he'd thought I was going to be his dad and instead went and forgot about him, and then said I was a coward for not fixing us. And you know what? He's right about the coward part. I can lie and say I know you don't want me to fight for you, that I'm not even worthy of a second chance, but the truth is that I'm too scared to do anything but breathe for fear I'll make it worse. I didn't lose just you, Ella, I lost them, too. There is *nothing* easy about this, and I'm doing my best to keep it light. So do you want these damn peas? Because the website I read said they're good to eat after radiation."

He'd sworn.

"Peas are good." It came out as a whisper.

"Excellent. There's whole grain rice, too. And lean chicken, since that's easier for her to digest." He plated the peas. "Do I get to know what comes next? Or just wait for the insurance statements?"

"We have blood work scheduled next week. If that's clear, then we start immunotherapy."

A relieved smile crossed his face, but it wasn't for me. "That's the last hurdle, right?"

"Maybe. Hopefully. I don't really want to hope."

"Hope is good. Feel it. Because we have no idea what's coming around the corner. You have to take the good when it comes, because the bad isn't going to give you a choice."

The kids ran into the kitchen, and Maisie slouched in one of the chairs.

"Maisie?"

"I'm fine, Mom."

"Just don't overdo it," I said out of habit.

"Stay or go?" Beckett asked me in a whisper so the kids wouldn't hear. He gave me the choice. He always gave me the choice.

"Beckett. Colt made the spring league soccer team," Maisie offered, swinging her legs back and forth in the chair. "Plus, Hailey broke up with another boy, and I turned down my make-a-wish again."

"Wait, you what?" Beckett asked, walking toward her. "Why? Don't you want to dress up like Batgirl for the day in Denver? Or be a mermaid in the Bahamas? Work on a movie for a day with Ron Howard?"

She shrugged. "I have everything I want, and the only thing I'd ask for, they can't give me, so they should give the wish to someone who needs it."

He crouched down. "What do you want?"

"It doesn't matter now. Are we going to eat?"

I didn't lose just you, Ella, I lost them, too.

His words hit me again, twice as hard as the first time. I'd loved this man—still did, if I was honest with myself—trusted him enough to let him adopt my kids. Then in a twist of irony, I'd cut off contact to spare my heart, and in doing so crushed the twins—the very thing I'd been scared he'd do. All because I wasn't capable of being around him and taking a full breath at the same time. He'd never been a danger to them, and maybe I was foolish, but a little distance had cleared my head, and I believed he'd always been honest with the kids. Hell, he'd been their dad in more ways than just the legal one. He hadn't abandoned them like Jeff. He'd built them a damn house and dropped what he was doing to go for Colt even though we weren't together anymore.

And although I'd cut him off cold turkey, he'd never once come at me with that adoption agreement to force the issue. He'd given me the choice.

And I'd chosen wrong.

I was wrong.

"We'll stay."

Beckett stood, sending me a look of pure shock. "You'll stay."

"It's just dinner."

His face twisted with emotion before he smoothed it out with a nod and a forced smile. "Yeah, let's eat. Colt, grab some drinks for the girls."

Colt cheered and then got to pouring lemonade from the pretty glass pitcher.

We ate, and it was normal and excruciating at the

same time. My kids lit up and never stopped talking, filling Beckett in on everything that had happened the last month. He listened and responded, his eyes dancing as he soaked up their every word.

I watched him quietly, dropping my gaze whenever he noticed, only to return. He was Beckett, but he was also Chaos, and with each bite I took, lines from his letters bombarded my heart, reminding me that the man sitting across from me was the same one I'd felt immediately drawn to. The same one who was sad, and lonely, and who didn't feel worthy of human connection—of family.

We finished eating, and I stood. "Colt, will you clear the table? I want Beckett to show me the upstairs."

"Yeah!" he said with an enthusiastic nod and then whispered something to Beckett that sounded a lot like "apologize."

Beckett nodded solemnly and then ruffled Colt's hair and gave Maisie a wink. Then he motioned for me to follow and led me up the stairs.

The stairs reached a landing, where the hall split in two sections with a bridge that crossed over the entry. "The kids'—the other rooms are that way."

"Show me the master."

He walked the opposite way and led me into a gorgeous master bedroom that had vaulted ceilings and massive windows. A king-size sleigh bed took up one wall, with silver and white bedding that I would have chosen myself.

"There's a bathroom through there with two walk-in closets and a washer-dryer set. There's a second set downstairs by the mudroom, because…well…kids get stuff dirty. Not that it matters, or anything. You can check it out if you want." He sat perched on the footboard of the bed.

"I don't need to. I know it's perfect."

"Well, if you didn't come up here to see the bathtub, what's up?"

"We're not getting back together." It flew out of my mouth.

"Well, let's not pull any punches."

"I'm sorry, I mean, I wanted that clear before I say what's next." I started pacing back and forth in front of the bed. Man, the carpet was really soft.

"Well, after that intro, I can't wait to hear it." He leaned forward a little, bracing his hands on the footboard. "But first, I'm supposed to tell you that I'm sorry. Again. Louder maybe, so Colt can hear. He's advised me that girls like it when you say sorry. So, I'm truly, deeply sorry for lying to you. For letting you think I was dead. For not reading your letters after Ryan died. If I had, I never would have stayed away when you asked me to come."

"You read the letters?" After everything, he'd finally opened them.

"I did. And I'm sorry. I should have responded. I should have come. I should never have kept it from you. I'm so incredibly sorry for the pain I caused you, and there aren't enough words of remorse to express how I feel about costing you Ryan."

I stopped pacing. "Beckett, I don't blame you for Ryan."

His eyes shot up to mine. "How can you not?"

"How can I?" I sat next to him on the wide edge of the footboard. "It wasn't your fault. If there were any chance you could have saved him, you would have. If there were any way you could have changed the outcome, you would have." I recited the words from memory.

"Ryan."

"Yeah, Ryan. What happened to you over there, that's not something anyone should have to go through.

You didn't intentionally kill that child. It was an accident. I know you, Beckett. You wouldn't hurt a child. Accidents are horrid, and awful things happen with no reason and no blame. It wasn't your fault. What happened to Ryan? That's not your fault, either. You're no more responsible for that than an African butterfly is a hurricane."

"It's not the same."

"It is. There are ten thousand ways to blame Ryan's death on someone. It's my parents' fault for dying, for changing his life that way. My grandmother for not putting up a bigger fight when he wanted to enlist. Terrorists for making him feel like he needed to get out there and do something. Me, because I prayed for so long that he'd come home without detailing what condition I wanted him in. But none of that matters. He volunteered to go on a mission, and my guess is that he would have volunteered to go even if you *had* been there, because that's who he was. He's the same as my father—it just took me years to see it. If you want to blame someone, you blame the men who pulled the trigger, because that's the only blame worth placing."

He dropped his head. I turned, took his beard-rough cheeks in my hands, and lifted his face to meet my eyes. "Sometimes bad things happen. And there's no blame to be placed. You can't reason with the universe, no matter how sound your logic is. If everything made sense, then Maisie wouldn't have cancer, and my parents would be alive, Ryan would be here. You never would have grown up the way you did. We are imperfect people made that way by an imperfect world, and we don't always get a say in what shapes us. I do not blame you for Ryan. The only person who does, is you. And if you don't let that pain go, it's going to shape the rest of your life. You have that choice."

"I love you. You know that, right? No matter what's

happened, or how badly I screwed this up, I love you."

I dropped my hands, swallowed the lump in my throat, and nodded. "I know. And I wish that love and trust went hand in hand with us, but somewhere they got separated, and I don't know if they can ever find their way back. I have to be able to believe the things you tell me, and that's broken. Maybe if Maisie weren't sick, and I was a little stronger...but I just can't. Not right now, at least. And I know that you love the kids, and they love you. And I was wrong to cut you off from them. I was hurt and made some lame excuses in my head. But the truth is that I could always trust you with them. I mean, you're their father." I gave him a side nudge.

"On paper."

"In reality." Something clicked in my head. "This is why you didn't press me to tell them about the adoption, isn't it? You knew the truth would come out."

"Yes."

"And you didn't want them in that position."

"Yes."

I stood and began pacing again. "Do you want a role in their lives?"

"God, yes. I'll take whatever you're willing to give me."

He'd said those same words after the first time we'd been together. He'd lived them since he arrived in Telluride, always given me the choice on how far I'd let him in. He'd never pushed his way in, never demanded anything more than I wanted to allow.

It didn't matter how badly he'd hurt me, Beckett was still the same guy I'd fallen in love with. The same man my kids loved and needed. The only thing that had changed was my perception of him—of us.

"Okay, then here's what we're going to do. We'll just act like we're divorced."

"We were never married."

"A minor detail. What I mean is that people who have one-night stands manage to share kids. You and I love each—loved each other. We can figure it out. If you're serious about staying—"

"I built a house, Ella. What more do you want?"

"Are you still in the military?" I knew the answer, of course. He couldn't get out, not while we needed the coverage for Maisie. But I also knew that once she was well he wouldn't be able to handle settling in one place now that we weren't together anymore, when all that kept him here was the kids. His nomadic soul would itch to move on.

"That's not fair."

"Yeah. I know." I sighed. "Okay, if you're sticking around…for now, then the kids can come over whenever they want. If you want to keep up the soccer stuff with Colt, we'll work that out. If you want to hang with Maisie on the weekends, or whatever, we'll see what works for everyone. You can have access to them, and them to you. We're adults, and they're kids. So we need to act more adultier than the kids. You need to speak up for your rights, and I need to give them to you. And I don't want to hide the adoption from the kids, so maybe once Maisie is out of the woods, if you're still here and everything, we should tell them that you're really their dad. I mean, that's what I'd intended before—"

I'd barely paused in my pacing, when I found myself enveloped by warm, strong arms and pressed against a hard, familiar chest.

"Thank you," he whispered into my hair.

He smelled so good and felt so right. Maybe if we stood here long enough, nothing else would matter. We could just freeze the moment and live in it, surrounded by the love we had for each other.

But we couldn't. Because he'd put me through hell

for over a year, and no matter how much I loved him, I wasn't sure I could ever trust him with my heart again, ever trust him to tell me the truth when it came to our relationship.

"You're welcome. And I'm sorry for cutting them off from you. You always joke that you don't have any relationship experience, but I don't either, really. I handled it all wrong. But I'm going to be better starting now."

"I'll be here," he promised. "I will show up for them and for you. I know you don't have any faith in me, and that's okay. I'll prove it to you. I'll earn back your trust one millimeter at a time. You won't regret letting me adopt them, I swear."

"I've never regretted that," I said, wrapping my arms around him for a hug and then stepping out of the security of his arms before I did something stupid like believe what he'd just promised. "Want to tell the kids?"

"Yeah." His face lit up like a kid on Christmas morning.

We found them at the cleared kitchen table, and they stopped their conversation immediately to look up at us.

"Did you fix it?" Colt asked.

"Not in that way, little man," Beckett said softly.

"Did you say sorry?"

"I did, but sorry doesn't fix the unfixable."

Then Colt glared at me.

"Nope." Beckett stepped forward and bent down. I always loved how he brought himself level to my kids. "You don't get to be mad at the person who got hurt, or judge them for it, because only that person can tell you how deep the cut is, got it? This is not your mom's fault. It's mine." He looked over at Maisie, who had tears in her eyes. "It's mine."

He stood back up and came to my side.

"So, we're not together," I reiterated. No good came from confusing kids. "But I know you guys love him, and he loves you. So from now on, as long as everyone is on the same page, you can come over whenever Beckett says it's cool. Soccer, treatments, phone calls, visits, we'll work it out."

Maisie's mouth popped open. "Really?"

"Really," I promised her.

Colt had been a silent ball of rage since I'd split with Beckett, but Maisie had been the most openly vocal and sometimes downright mean.

"So you're not together, but we get to keep him? He's ours?"

More than you know.

"That's what I'm saying."

The kids flew out of their chairs, hugging Beckett, then me, then back to Beckett, then each other. Then Maisie hugged Beckett again and whispered something in his ear. He gave her a smile that bordered on tears and said, "Me, too."

We walked the kids to my car, and they buckled in. Once the doors were shut, I turned to Beckett, who again had his hands in his pockets. For having a crazy amount of self-control, I'd picked up on that nervous tell easily enough.

"Thank you. For dinner, for taking care of Colt. For the land, and the house, even if it's not mine. The intention was spectacular."

"Thank you for them," he answered.

"What did she tell you?"

"Really want to know?"

"Beckett," I warned.

"She said that was her wish, the only thing she'd wanted was...me, in a roundabout way."

"She wanted a dad," I guessed. "You to be her dad."

"They're kids," he said with a shrug, but I knew how

much it meant to him.

"They're our kids."

"Look, I heard what you said upstairs loud and clear. I know that being together isn't an option. But as trite as this sounds, I'd really love if we could manage to be friends. Even if it's just for the sake of the kids."

Standing there, outside the house he'd built for me, I wished I'd never known. Wished he'd never lied or that we could take it all back. Wished he wasn't both of the complicated men I'd fallen for. But he was, and he did.

And despite everything, I still loved him.

"Yeah. I think we can manage that."

"I'll earn your trust back, no matter how long it takes," he promised again.

Even if I wasn't ready—wasn't sure I'd ever be—I wanted to believe that he could, and that desire lit a tiny kernel of hope in my heart.

It wasn't a bright enough fire to keep me warm, not like our love had.

But it was a spark.

"I need to learn to give out those second chances. Small steps. Good night, Beckett."

He nodded and stood on the porch until we pulled out of view.

SIX MONTHS LATER

CHAPTER TWENTY-FIVE

Beckett

Letter #23

Chaos,

It's been two days since we buried Ryan. You didn't come, and you haven't answered my letter. When I asked the guys from your unit if you were okay, at least I assumed by their haircuts they were from your unit, they told me they had no idea who I was talking about.

So yeah, they were from your unit.

If you're not answering me, and you didn't come to Ryan's funeral, then I'm left with one option that I can't bring myself to ask. Because I don't know if I could bear it.

You've become something I never expected, this silent support who never judges. I didn't realize just how much I've come to depend on you until you weren't here. And I'm terrified. You told me once that you're only scared if you have something to lose. And I think, maybe, we do have something to lose.

There's so much pain right now. So much that I feel like every second I'm awake, I'm at a ten on that little hospital chart. Scratch that, I'm at a nine. I can't be at a ten, right? Not when I have Colt and Maisie. But it hurts so much.

Ryan. I watched them lower him into the ground on our little island and still can't put all the pieces together to form a real picture. Everything feels hazy, like some nightmare that I can't wake up from. But at night I dream Ryan is home, and you show up at my door—a blurry figure I can never quite remember in the morning. Dreams have become the reality I want, and I wake up to the nightmare.

So I'm begging you, Chaos. Don't be dead. Please be alive. Please don't tell me that you were there with Ryan, that you met the same fate. Please tell me that you weren't buried somewhere at a funeral I was never told about. That I wasn't robbed of the only chance I'd ever have to stand within a few feet of you.

Please show up in a couple of weeks and tell me you're fine, that it was too painful to respond to my letters. Tell me you're broken up over Ryan. Just please show up.

Please don't be dead.

~ Ella

"You're sure about this?" Donahue asked through the phone.

"I am. You're holding the paperwork, right?" I unhooked Havoc's work vest and hung it in her locker, which was right next to mine.

"Yep." He sighed. "It hasn't been that long."

"It's September," I said with a laugh. "That means it's been eighteen months since I went on terminal leave." *Two years since I got Ella's first letter.* "You can't keep me on the bench forever, coach."

"I have three more years."

"Nah. It's time." I grabbed my car keys from the hook in my locker and glanced at the pictures that covered the interior door. Hiking with Ella and the kids last month. Camping this summer. Colt after he won his league semifinals. Maisie finally getting to swim in the lake a few months after she'd completed immunotherapy. Ella sitting with Havoc's head in her lap. Ella and I were still in the friend zone, but they were my family, and this was my home. Getting the full-time slot that opened up a couple of months ago meant my new insurance fully covered Maisie, so all the pieces were finally in place. "I miss you guys. Not going to lie. You were my first family. But I'm never leaving Telluride. We both know it. Hell, Ella broke up with me seven months ago, and I'm still here. I found a home. And besides, Havoc is getting fat."

She whined and tilted her head at me.

"It's okay, I like you with a little curve," I reassured her with a pat, well aware she had no idea what I'd said in the first place. "And it's only five pounds."

"Okay. If you're sure, I'll accept it. But if anything ever changes, you call me. Understand?"

"Yes, Sir. But nothing's going to change."

He sighed. "You're a good man in a storm, Gentry."

"Funny, that's not what you said when I was there."

"Can't have you getting a big head on me. Later."

"Later." There was a click, and the line was dead.

I slipped my phone into my pocket, and then shut our lockers.

Hers read, "HAVOC."

Mine read, "CHAOS."

Because under it all, I was still me, and once I'd quit fighting it, I realized I was okay with that.

"Hey, Tess said to haul you home if you need dinner," Mark offered as I hit the parking lot.

"I would, but Ella called earlier and said the kids want to have dinner, so I'm headed to her place. Tell Tess thanks."

"Sure thing. How's that going, anyway?" he asked, just like every other week. He'd become our not-so-silent cheerleader.

"Slowly, but going."

"Fight the good fight." He waved as we both got into

our vehicles.

Havoc settled into her seat, and I brought the truck to life. We drove home with the windows down, Havoc sticking her head out the window. It was an Indian summer, with temps still in the upper seventies, which meant the hikers were here later than usual for the season but, since Labor Day had passed two weeks ago, it was a little quieter in the lower portion of Telluride.

I hit a button on the dash, and Ella's voice filled my truck.

"Hey, you on your way?"

"Yep. Want me to grab the pizza?"

"That would be amazing."

"I'll be there soon."

"Okay. Drive safe." She hung up, and I smiled. Not together, but we were good. Sure, the sexual tension was still there, and I loved her—that was never going to change—but I was proving myself to Ella every day, and I couldn't help but hope that one day it would be enough to repair what I'd broken. But hey, I'd lied to her for eleven months, and I was only seven months into my penance.

Truth was, I'd wait forever.

In the meantime, it was like being married without the whole marriage part.

There were days I thought our second chance was within reach, and days she felt a million miles away. But neither of us dated anyone else, and I held on to that tiny sliver of hope that the times I caught her looking at me meant we were getting somewhere.

We had as much time as she needed.

I parked in front of the pizza shop and brought Havoc in with me while they pulled our order. The funny thing about putting down roots was that people knew me. Knew Havoc.

"Here you go, Mr. Gentry," the Tanners kid said,

handing me three boxes. "Hey, Havoc."

"Good game on Friday," I told him as I paid.

"Thanks! You coming next week?"

"Wouldn't miss it," I said as I backed out of the doors with the pizza.

I waved at a couple of people I recognized and put the pizzas in the space between Maisie's and Colt's booster seats as Havoc jumped into the passenger seat. The twins would turn eight soon, which meant I'd get a heck of a lot more space back in my truck. I eyed the smashed bag of Oreos in Colt's cup holder and rolled my eyes.

That boy was going to be the death of me.

A few songs on the radio later, I pulled into Ella's driveway and popped the doors. Havoc flew, racing to greet the kids.

"Beckett!" Maisie called out, running down the steps.

Her blond hair had grown back with a little curl to it and was now in a bob that lined up with the bottoms of her ears. Six glorious inches of non-chemo-treated hair. We were still holding our breath, watching her blood work and CT scans, but she'd come through immunotherapy with flying colors, and now it was a waiting game while her body fought on its own.

"Hiya, Maisie-girl," I said and hugged her with my free arm. "How was school?"

"Good! I aced another spelling pretest."

"Aren't you just the smarty-pants?" I placed a kiss on the top of her head as we walked up to the porch. "What about you, Colt?"

"I did not," Colt answered as he pushed his way in to hug me.

"Just a pretest, my man. We'll study, okay?"

He nodded and got the door open for us.

"I come bearing food!" I bellowed.

"Ah, the hunter-gatherer returns," Ella said with a smile as she came out of her office. "Good day?"

"It is now." My eyes swept down her white sundress, noting her tanned skin, curled hair, and mile-long legs. Damn, I missed her body. Missed the way she gasped in my ear, the way her back arched when I was inside her, the way we lost ourselves to each other. But we weren't there yet, so I told my dick to settle down and took the pizzas to the kitchen. "That's a beautiful dress. Anything going on?"

She'd been dressing up a little more lately. With Maisie going in for scans every week, then every other week, Ella had more time for herself, and it showed. Her skin glowed, her eyes were bright, and those were definitely not Yeti legs.

"Oh, well, David Robins did ask me out for tonight." She ran her hand down my arm and gave me a wide-eyed, way-too-innocent-to-be-serious bat of her lashes. Holy shit, was she actually flirting with me?

Now I was equal parts amused, aroused, and jealous as hell.

I didn't miss her little grin as the boxes slid from my hands onto the counter, but I caught them before dinner ended up on the hardwood floor. Oh yeah, my girl was teasing me.

Robins had asked her out every month since we'd broken up. Pretty soon I was going to show up at his house and ask him out with my fist. Stupid pretty boy.

"Oh?" I tried to ask all nonchalant after I stopped fumbling with the boxes.

"Well, I know Jennifer Bennington asked you out when you had lunch with the kids today. She's been after you since...what, the dawn of time?" She switched sides, running her hand along the small of my back before she looked up at me with a knowing little smirk. She never touched me this much. I didn't know what had gotten into her, but I'd take it.

"Don't poke the bear. You know I told her no today. Just like I tell her no every other time and will continue to tell her no."

She tugged on her bottom lip with her teeth and gave me a look I hadn't seen in seven months. That look was going to get her on this counter in about ten seconds if she didn't watch it.

"Ella?"

"What?" She danced around the other side of the island.

"Did you just twirl?" Something was up.

"Maybe. I'm in a good mood."

"Apparently." I grabbed four plates out of the cabinet. "So I'm guessing you're not eating with us," I teased, wanting to see how far she'd go with it.

"Why did you tell her no?" Ella asked, sliding up next to me. Her hair was loose down her back, and my fingers itched to weave through it and feel the strands against my skin.

"You know why." Yeah, we were good, but she was killing me. Slowly. Torturously. She looked up at me, so damn beautiful that my breath caught. I checked to make sure the kids were still outside before giving her a look of my own. "Because I'm still in love with you."

I told her at least once a week, let her know that I wasn't just in this for the kids. Warned her that I wasn't going anywhere, that our friendship was great, but I was coming after her heart. I was trying out that whole blatant honesty thing.

Her lips parted, and if this had been eight months ago, I would have kissed her. Would have done a hell of a lot more than kiss her once the kids went to bed. But it wasn't eight months ago, it was now.

"Well, I told David no, too." She smiled and spun away.

"And what was your reasoning?" Shit, now I was smiling, too. The woman drove me insane, but yeah, I still loved her with every bone in my body. How could I not?

"You, of course. We have dinner plans, right?" she said from the edge of the kitchen headed for the front door.

It wasn't a declaration of love. I hadn't had one of those from her since the night we'd agreed to co-parent. But I was nothing if not patient.

"Dinner!" she called out after opening the door, and there was a rumpus of feet, both two-legged and four-legged.

"I've got Havoc!" Colt grabbed her food and filled her dish.

Maisie took plates full of pizza to our respective places at the table. As I watched everyone take their seats and Ella put a glass of sweet tea at the top of my plate, I realized nothing had really changed in our relationship except the physical aspect.

She was still my first phone call when something went right.

I was still the one she leaned on when things went wrong.

She was at my side when I'd found out another member of my unit had died last month.

We still sat in the same places at the table.

I carried in Ella's plate and put it in front of her.

"Can I say grace?" Maisie asked as I sat.

"It's all yours." We joined hands—mine with Ella and Maisie, and Colt directly across from me—and bowed our heads.

"Our dear Heavenly Father, thank you for our day, and for everything you've given us. For our home, and our family: Colt, and Mom, and Beckett, and Havoc. And thank you for Dr. Hughes. But especially, thank you for making me cancer-free."

My head snapped up, my eyes flying to Maisie, who grinned at me, missing front teeth and all. She nodded, and I just about lost my shit. I turned to Ella, who had tears streaming down her face.

"No evidence of disease. We got the call today." Her smile was huge as she laughed. Pure, sheer, unfettered joy.

"No way!" Colt threw up his hands in the classic victory sign. At least I wasn't the last to know.

I pushed back from the table so fast that my chair crashed to the floor. Then I grabbed Maisie out of her chair and hugged her. She buried her face in my neck, and shudders wracked my body as I held her tight.

She was going to be okay. She'd made it. She was going to live.

"Beckett?" she asked.

"Yeah, Maisie-girl?"

"I can't breathe," she squeaked.

I laughed and set her down. "We finally get you to live, and now I'm killing you off with my ultra-awesome hugs."

"My turn!" Colt snatched his sister, and the two jumped and hugged.

"Hey," Ella said from behind me.

I turned around, and she reached for my face, wiping away tears I hadn't realized were there. Crossing the line, I wrapped my arms around her and pulled her close.

Much to my relief, she melted against me, her head fitting in that exact spot below my collarbone that was hers. She held me tight, her hands splayed on my back, and I rested my chin at the top of her head.

"She's going to be okay," I whispered.

Ella nodded.

We stood there for long minutes while Colt and

Maisie raced around the house shouting and laughing.

"Good surprise?" Ella asked, pulling back just enough to look at me.

"The best possible surprise. Ever." I cupped her cheek with my hand, letting my thumb caress her perfectly soft skin.

"Food!" the twins called out, breaking our little spell.

We pulled apart and sat back down to the best lukewarm pizza I'd ever had in my life.

"Let me do that," I told Ella, taking over the dishes a couple of hours later.

"Colt okay?" she asked, wrapping up the pizza.

"After I read *Where the Wild Things Are* for the tenth time, he was satisfied," I told her. "Maisie?"

"Off to sleep without a fuss. I think she's emotionally exhausted." She leaned back against the counter and watched me slip the plates into the dishwasher.

"Understandable." I shut the dishwasher. "I can't believe it's over."

"Yeah. It's so surreal." She looked off into space. "I mean, they told me the relapse rates, and they're high. Really high. So, it could come back. But if she makes it five years, then the chances—"

"Ella," I interrupted, stepping in front of her and taking her face in my hands. "Take the good. Feel the happy. This is the best kind of good, and you did it. You got her here."

"You got her here, too." Her voice softened, and she leaned against my hand.

"Okay, we got her here. So let's take the happy."

She rose up on her toes and kissed me.

My shock lasted all of a millisecond before I kissed her back. I moved my lips over hers, savoring each touch, because I never knew if I'd get it again. When her lips parted, I took full advantage and deepened the kiss.

Her back hit the counter as my tongue swept into her mouth. Then her hands fisted in my shirt, her whimpers sweet in my ear as the kiss turned explosive. Over and over again I took her mouth, kissing her until she was arched against me, her breasts pressed into my chest.

I ripped my mouth away and stepped back. "Ella." My breathing was erratic, my heart thundered, and I was pretty sure if I didn't readjust myself, I'd be losing my dick to boxer-brief asphyxiation in a matter of minutes.

"Beckett."

"What are you doing?"

"Taking my happy. You're my happy." She stalked forward.

"What does this—"

She interrupted me with a soft kiss. "Just be my happy, and let me be yours. We can sort it out tomorrow."

If I'd been stronger or a little less on an emotional high from Maisie's recovery, I could have walked away. I could have said no and made her lay out our relationship status. I would have been more careful with my heart.

Three things.

One. I loved her.

Two. She was all I wanted, ever. So if this was all I could have with her, then I wasn't turning her down. Hell no.

Three. I'd use tonight to remind her exactly why we belonged together so tomorrow all we'd be sorting out would be where we'd live.

I gripped her ass in my hands and lifted her against me, kissing her deep and hard. "Lock your ankles," I ordered against her mouth.

She did, wrapping her legs around my waist.

I kissed her up the stairs and down the hall, carrying

her through the house like she was my ultimate prize. I didn't stop when I shut the bedroom door and locked it behind us, or when I laid her in the middle of her bed.

She broke the kiss, fumbling with the belt on my jeans as I kicked off my shoes and stripped off my socks. Then my hands moved up her thighs, and my mouth followed, kissing every sensitive spot I knew she had.

"I missed this," I said against her skin.

"Me, too," she answered, her hands in my hair as I ran my teeth over her panties. "Beckett." Her hips rolled in my hands.

I made quick work of her little lace thong and had her dress over her head—bra following—within a minute max. Then she was naked, spread out before me with open arms and a smile.

Yeah, this was my happy, all right.

I removed the rest of my clothes and then covered her body with my own. "You're sure?" I asked.

"I'm sure." She pulled me down for a kiss, and our mouths met in a fury of need. There was nothing gentle about it—this was the result of months and months of denied need and heartache.

I kissed my way down her body as she wiggled beneath me. When I hovered over the apex of her thighs and gripped her hips, her fingernails grazed my scalp. "Please, Beckett."

If she said my name like that again, I'd be her willing servant for the rest of eternity. Especially if it meant in bed.

I set my mouth to her, and she bucked. I pinned her hips and relentlessly ate at her until she started calling my name again, her head thrashing on the pillow. I'd missed this taste, the way her legs tensed when she was close, the pull of her fingers in my hair as she lost her mind. I drove her upward with my tongue, giving her no pause, no chance to escape what I knew was coming quickly.

When she started to shake, I pushed even harder until she came apart under my mouth, muffling her cry with her own fist. She was the sexiest, most sensual woman I'd ever seen.

When her legs relaxed, I rose above her, taking a second to appreciate the glazed-over sheen to her blue eyes, her kiss-stung lips, and the flush in her cheeks. "You're beautiful."

Her smile was slow and somehow more intimate than what I'd just done to her.

"I'd almost forgotten what it was like between us," she admitted. "Or I told myself I remembered it wrong."

"Electric."

"Remind me again." She drew her knees up, and I hissed as my erection slipped through her wetness to land at her entrance.

"Pill?"

"Never quit, and there's been no one else."

"You've been it for me since the first letter. Just you. Always you." I sank into her until she surrounded me. *Home.* "I love you, Ella."

She pulled my head to hers, and our mouths were done talking. As urgent as her first orgasm had been, I took my time now, drawing out every stroke, every time we came together only to retreat again. I used every ounce of skill and stamina I possessed to show her the way I felt about her with drugging kisses and slow, deep thrusts.

She met me move for move, our bodies arching together in perfect partnership until we built to a frenzy. When her body tightened around mine as her second climax took her, it was with my name on her lips and my heart in her hands. I followed almost immediately, collapsing on top of her and quickly rolling us to the side so I didn't crush her.

"Are you okay?" I asked, brushing her hair from her face. I was more than okay. I was perfect. Content. Whole. Home.

She gave me a sleepy stretch with a smile. "Happy. Really, really happy."

"Me, too."

She rolled again so she was on top, grinning down at me, her hair a curtain that surrounded us. "I bet I can make you even happier."

Then we started all over again.

CHAPTER TWENTY-SIX

Ella

Letter #20

Ella,

 So Colt wants a tree house, huh? I bet your brother and I could handle that.

 Don't worry that your mind automatically goes to Maisie. I would worry if it didn't. What you're going through consumes just about everything. Hell, I think about you guys a ton, and I've never set eyes on you.

 But here, let's give you a little distraction. I promised a couple months ago that I'd tell you the story behind my call sign. So here it goes. Chaos. That whole state of dysfunction where everything blows apart without rhyme or reason, right? That's pretty much me. Exactly. Growing up, I got into trouble wherever I could, or sometimes it just found me. They called me Chaos, because when I showed up, destruction inevitably followed. Usually property, but sometimes people. Too many people. Someone gets attached, I can't let them in, and I go into self-destruction until they walk away. I'm old enough to see the patterns but not worried enough to really change them.

 So your brother and I go out to a bar right after selection, and he starts hitting on a woman. I don't see her face, just a body poured into a dress that shows pretty much everything. He assumes she's a prostitute—don't ask me why, because I have no clue—and then it turns out she's actually one of our instructor's wives.

Yeah, all hell broke loose. The guy lost it, the bar got tossed over because I jumped in, and once noses were broken and bottles stopped flying, I turn around and realize she's someone I grew up with. So she just looks at me and says, "As usual, walking, talking Chaos. You walk in, and it all goes to hell." Your brother and the trainer heard, and it stuck.

So yeah, that's the definition of me. I walk in, and it all goes to hell. Still sure you want me to come visit? Just kidding, you know I'll be there.

I hope you're getting presents wrapped for the kids and trees trimmed and all that. I'm loving the little battery-operated lights Colt sent and the tiny pink tree from Maisie.

Catch you later,
~ Chaos

I stretched, feeling deliciously sore in places I hadn't felt since—

A warm, strong arm draped over my waist and pulled me back into the curve of a very firm, male body.

Beckett.

I waited for the panic to rise, the oh-shit feeling when the mistake had already been made and you couldn't do anything but deal with the fallout, but it never came, because it wasn't a mistake. Just a sweet contentment and the ache of well-used muscles.

How many times had we lost ourselves in each other last night? Three?

I'd told him we'd sort it out today, and I meant it. This was my kids' dad, the guy who built not one but two tree houses, who showed up no matter how many times I doubted him.

And no matter the lies, the deception, and everything that had come to light, I loved him. That had never changed. And truthfully, I'd forgiven him long ago for the lie. Once I could step outside the hurt, I reread the letters. Saw the self-loathing he masked, the true feeling that he wasn't worthy of love and couldn't connect to people.

When he finally connected to Ryan, and then lost him, he went into a spiral. I just happened to get caught up in the vortex.

And as for the trust? He'd painstakingly rebuilt it over the last six months, never once wavering and always declaring his intent. That kind of relentlessness was impossible to ignore, and now that Maisie was cancer-free, it was time to figure out what Beckett and I were going to do about each other.

I could take a moment to be my own priority for the first time in years, and what I wanted was *him*.

"Mom! Come on, we're going to be late!" Maisie called from the hallway.

I craned my neck to see the alarm clock.

"Oh crap! Beckett, we're late!" I flew out of bed, running for the bathrobe I kept hanging on the back of my door but never used.

"What?" He shot up, the covers falling to his waist.

Good God, that man was gorgeous. Really, mouth-wateringly beautiful. *This is exactly why you're running late.*

"We have to go. It's already seven thirty! The kids have to be at school by eight or they miss the field trip!" I ran out into the hallway to find both kids dressed, baseball caps on, hiking shoes tied. "Good morning."

They gave me a grin that said they knew exactly who was in my bed.

Parenting fail.

"So, who is taking us to school?" Maisie asked with a

little bounce on her toes.

"Yeah? You, or Beckett?" Colt added, bouncing identically.

"Okay, we'll discuss this later. We need to get ready. Now."

"We already did!" Maisie said, looking entirely joyful.

"Breakfast?"

"Cereal," Colt said. "We knew you'd get mad if we used the stove."

"And we wanted you to sleep." Maisie held up her fingers and started counting. "Breakfast, done. Teeth brushed, done. Havoc fed. She slept with me last night, but she's a bed hog, so she has to go to Colt tonight."

And that is exactly what I got for letting Beckett sleep in my bed. The kids automatically assumed we were back together. Or maybe we were. There was absolutely no time to think about that right now. My moment was over, and the kids were back in the priority spot. The sorting-out had to be handled by Beckett and me later. At a table. With lots of clothes on. Tons of clothes. Maybe a parka.

"We have our hiking shoes, our hats, our pants, and fleece, and we lathered each other up with sunscreen. All we need is a lunch." She stopped counting.

"Lunch. I can do that…with the ten minutes I have." I ran into the bedroom to find Beckett already dressed, looking sexy as hell and sleep-rumpled. Sex was a lot like sugar—give it up and you stop missing it after a while, but you start back up and you're just jonesing for the next hit. And man, I wanted to hit that again. A lot.

"Kids okay?" he asked, tying his shoes.

"Oh, just jumping to assumptions, but other than that, they're fine. I might need a little tag team help." I dropped the robe and pulled on my underwear. "Beckett, concentrate."

"Oh, I am. Trust me." His eyes were locked on my ass. Bra on and snapped.

"We have ten minutes before they have to leave—"

"Lunches?"

"Exactly."

"On it," he said, already walking toward the door. He caught my shoulders as he passed me, keeping me from falling as I hopped around like a lunatic with one leg in my jeans. "Good morning," he said softly as he pressed a kiss to my forehead.

"Good morning to you," I answered, and he was out the door. Man, I liked this too much. Falling back into that sweet rhythm we'd had while we were together. Knowing those giggles I heard coming up the stairs were the result of happy kids on a hectic morning with their dad.

I slipped on my green, long-sleeve, boat-neck tee and ran down the stairs, socks and boots in hand. Then I paused at the threshold of the kitchen and watched the scene for a minute that we didn't have.

Beckett worked at the counter, rolling meat and cheese pinwheels, while Maisie filled their water bottles and Colt grabbed yogurts.

"I feel like I've been waiting for this day for forever," Colt said, throwing apples into brown paper bags. "A whole day of no school, just hiking for leaves."

"Well, it's kind of school," Maisie countered.

"You know what I mean." Colt tugged at her cap.

"Man, I wish I hiked all day for a living," Beckett teased, cutting the pinwheels.

"You do!" Maisie answered with a giggle.

"That's right!" he responded with a shocked face.

This was the picture of perfection, and I knew I could have it for the rest of my life...as soon as we had time to talk. Tonight, maybe?

"What about treats?" I asked, petting Havoc on my

way to the pantry. "M&M's sound good?"

"Yes!" the kids shouted as I tossed them in the field trip-required paper bags.

"Okay, is that it?" Beckett asked.

"I think we're ready," I told him. "Kids, grab your bags and hop in my car."

They both hugged Beckett and ran out the door.

We stared at each other across the kitchen island for a second, before he cleared his throat. "I feel like there are things that need to be said."

I walked around the island, rose on my toes, and pressed a soft kiss to his mouth. "I think so, too. How about later tonight?"

A flash of hope ran through those green eyes of his, and he smiled. "Tonight it is."

We walked out hand in hand, and he waved at the kids as we took off down the driveway. *They might be two minutes late. Okay, three.*

I parked the car as kids from the second grade filed onto the buses. "Okay, let's find Mrs. Rivera," I told the kids as we crossed into the crowd.

"I see her!" Maisie said, pointing ahead.

"I'm so sorry we were running late," I told her.

She smiled, the corners of her brown eyes crinkling. "That's okay, you made it just in time. Colt, Maisie, why don't you head into the bus with your class?"

"Bye, Mom!" Maisie said, pressing a quick kiss to my cheek.

"You coming, Colt?" Emma asked from the bus window above us.

"Yep!" he answered. That crush was still going strong, but she really was the sweetest little girl. Colt hugged my waist, and I kissed the top of his head.

"Have fun, and grab me a red leaf if you see one. The gold ones are everywhere, but the red ones are rare around here."

"You got it!" He waved and ran off, taking Maisie's hand as they climbed onto the bus.

I headed back to Solitude and got to work.

We had two weddings this month, and all the cabins were booked. The three we'd had built over the summer were nearly finished, if they could just get those hardwood floors stained.

The hours passed in a flurry of bookwork and guest relations until I realized it was almost lunchtime.

"Hey, was that Beckett's truck I saw coming from your way this morning?" Hailey asked, popping her head into my office.

"Maybe," I said without looking up.

"It's about damn time."

"It's none of your business," I told her, putting down my pen and looking up. I hadn't even told Beckett how I felt, and he deserved to hear it first.

"It should be. That man loves you, and yeah, I know he messed up pretty badly, but he's also darn near perfect. You know that, right? Because I'm out there in the dating pool, and if I had someone like Beckett that devoted to me and my kids, I'd be locking that down."

"I get the point."

"Okay, because he's gorgeous. I've seen the abs while he was jogging, and if your washer breaks, you have a great alternative."

"He has two washer-dryer sets at his house. I'll be fine," I joked.

"And he built you a house! I mean, is it the sex? Is it bad?" She leaned against my doorframe.

"I don't think Beckett knows the definition of bad sex." Which he'd proved again last night. Over and over. Even when we were frenzied and fast, our chemistry was enough to push me over the edge. The man sent me into a lust-crazed tizzy by simply existing.

"Seriously. Lock it down."

"Ella," Ada said from the doorway.

"Not you, too." I rolled my eyes as she walked in, Larry on her heels. "Look, yes, Beckett spent the night last night. And yeah, he's…Beckett—"

"Ella!" Ada yelled.

"Whoa. What's up?"

Larry yanked off his ball cap and ran his hand over his thick, silver hair. "I was listening to the scanner out in the barn."

"Okay?" The stricken looks on their faces finally registered. "Guys, what is it?"

"Search and rescue call. They called in Telluride, not just the county." The two exchanged a look that dropped my stomach.

"Beckett? Is he okay?" He had to be okay. I loved him. I hadn't decided what to do about him, but I knew I couldn't live without him.

Larry nodded. "Beckett was called in. Ella, the call was from the Wasatch trail."

My stomach hit the floor.

"The kids."

CHAPTER TWENTY-SEVEN

Beckett

Rotors spun above me in a familiar rhythm as the ground fell away. Havoc sat next to me, her ears back. She could handle helicopter rides, but she still wasn't a fan. I snapped my helmet and turned on the radio.

"Okay, we're in. What's the emergency?" We'd been outside, running a few drills, when the call came in. I heard Wasatch trail, and that was it, and I wasn't familiar enough with every hiking trail in the county to remember which one that was.

I'd grabbed my gear, thrown in Havoc's rappelling harness, and taken off at a dead run while they ran the helo up for launch.

"They've got a kid off the grid," Jenkins, the resident medic said through the comms.

"Lost?" A chill ran down my spine. Where were the kids today? Ella had signed that permission slip, and I hadn't asked.

"Yep. That's all we know. Report came in about ten minutes ago, said kid went missing."

I nodded and looked out the open doors as we passed over Bridal Veil Falls and headed up the pass. Absentmindedly, I stroked Havoc's head as we crept up the mountain.

"I think we can put down right there," the pilot said, and I looked over to see where he was indicating.

The small clearing intersected with the trail, which looked wide and well-traveled.

"Once we're on the ground, you two do your thing," Chief Nelson ordered from the bench next to Jenkins. "County is involved, but they know you're coming, since their dog can't ever find shit."

"Got it."

A kid. My blood started pumping furiously through my veins, just like it did before every mission I'd ever taken part in. This was that same adrenaline but a hell of a lot more scary.

"How much time went by before the kid was reported missing?"

"They don't know. Witness is in shock. If the kid slipped off the trail, it's pretty densely wooded after the cliff."

Holy shit.

"The kid could have fallen off a cliff?" I scanned the terrain, but we were too close to landing to get the full picture.

"Sounds like it. Wouldn't surprise me if this turns into a recovery effort."

My jaw locked. Not on my watch. I wasn't losing a kid to a freaking hike in Colorado.

"We'll wait here. Let us know what you need," the pilot called out as we unhooked and ditched our helmets.

I gave him the thumbs-up when he looked over his shoulder, then took hold of Havoc's leash, giving her the hand signal that it was time to go. She stayed at my side as I jumped the few feet to the ground and headed toward the team from County.

"The site is about a quarter mile up this trail," their chief said from the center of the circle. "Teachers and some of the students are still there, so be sensitive."

Teachers. Students.

I didn't wait for the rest of the brief, just broke into a dead run up the trail, Havoc perfectly paced with me. It was rocky and even on the path, but the drop-off to the south was anything but friendly. That was rough and rugged, but not too dramatic. Until the face became sheer. This was the cliff.

Shit, there was no way a kid was living through that kind of fall.

I increased my pace, nearly sprinting up the rest of the trail, passing a few uniforms from the sheriff's department until I rounded the corner.

Then I stopped so fast I skidded a little on the rocks.

Mrs. Rivera stood, shaking her head as she talked to a uniform. She was trembling, tears streaming down her face.

"Mrs. Rivera?" I called out, making myself move forward.

"Mr. Gentry, oh God." She covered her mouth.

"Where are my kids?" I tried to keep my voice level, but it came out as a strangled bellow.

She glanced over her shoulder, and I bypassed her, looking for the small group of students who sat against the mountain, their lunch bags still out, all startlingly quiet. My eyes raked over the fifty or so of them until—

"Beckett!" Maisie cried, her little body emerging from the crowd. She ran full throttle at me, and I caught her, hugging her tight. She sobbed into my neck, her frame shaking with each cry.

One down. I gulped a breath and let myself feel her heart beat as my hand steadied her back. She was okay. She was here.

"It's okay, Maisie-girl. I've got you," I said as I looked past her, still scanning the group.

Where the hell was Colt?

I looked again, and my blood ran cold. "Maisie." I dropped down to my knees so she could stand, and then I peeled her off my neck. "Where is Colt?"

"I don't know, and they won't tell us anything until the grown-ups get here." Tears raced down her cheeks. "There's another group over there." She pointed up the trail about forty feet at another assembly of students.

"Okay." I debated sitting her down with the class for

all of two seconds. Screw that. If we already had one kid over the edge, my daughter wasn't going to be next. "Come with me."

I hefted her into my arms, bracing her on my forearm as I hiked up the trail. As soon as we were away from the first group, I looked down at Havoc and let her off the leash. If any parents freaked out, they could kiss my ass.

"Seek Colt."

She sniffed Maisie, no doubt smelling Colt on her, and then put her nose to the ground, heading toward the small grouping of kids. A pair of uniforms addressed no more than ten kids, all in some state of tears except one.

Emma. She stood off to the side, her back to me, looking up the trail.

"Mr. Gentry?" Another teacher stopped talking to the kids and walked over, her lip trembling. "Oh God. We just stopped for lunch, and then when we started again, the trail...it just..." She started sobbing. "We. Got. Separated."

"Where?" I asked the uniform.

"Trail's out around the corner, but there's no sign of the kid. Some of the kids think they saw him on the other side."

I put Maisie on the ground and placed her hand in Mrs. Rivera's, who had followed us up. "Please keep her right here. Maisie, give me a couple minutes, okay?"

I forced a smile and stroked her cheek. *Stay calm. Don't let her see the panic.* I repeated it to myself as I waited for her to nod. She couldn't see this, couldn't experience it, and as much as I wanted her at my side to keep her safe, she needed the protection of distance.

Then I took off, ignoring the teacher and following Havoc to where I'd already known she would lead— right to Emma.

The little girl stood looking up the trail, a good ten

feet back from the edge of the drop-off. An officer kneeled at her level, speaking to her, but she wasn't responding. Her eyes were blank, her mouth closed but lax, and in her hands, she gripped a Telluride Search and Rescue cap that Havoc was currently alerting me to.

No. No. No.

I tried to shove the panic down the way I had countless times in battle, but this was different. This was my worst nightmare.

"She's not talking." Every line of the officer's face was tense.

"Give her some space and let me try."

He nodded, backing away just far enough to hear but not hover.

"Emma," I said gently as I dropped to her eye level and turned her toward me. "Emma, where did Colt go? How do you have his hat?"

Her eyes slowly shifted from the cliff to me. "I know you."

"Yeah, you do. I belong to Colt and Maisie," I said, trying to keep my voice even and calm, knowing if she slipped into shock any further, I'd lose any chance of getting information. "Can you tell me what happened?"

She nodded, the motions taking three times as long as normal. "We were eating lunch, right there." She pointed to the group. "And then we finished, so we walked in a line, just like we're supposed to. We weren't even close to the edge, I promise!" Her voice broke.

The officer next to us started taking notes.

"I know. It's okay." I took her hands in my own with Colt's cap between us. "What happened then?"

"We turned around to come back, because the other kids were slow eating. Then the ground just disappeared. It was gone so fast."

"Okay, and what then?"

More uniforms gathered behind us, and I waved

them off. She looked up at them and then at Colt's hat, shutting down.

I looked over my shoulder and saw Mark. "Blanket."

He took one from the new batch of officers and handed it to me.

"Keep them back. She's in shock, and they're making it worse." He nodded and started barking orders as I put the heavy material around her. "It's just you and me, Emma. Can you tell me what happened next?"

Her eyes rose to mine. "The ground left, and I started to fall. Colt grabbed my hand and pulled? I think? Or pushed. I was behind him, and then I was in front of him. It was so loud. Like ice cubes in a glass."

Landslide. It had to be.

"I tried to grab him, but it was done. Then I was at the edge, and he was gone. I had this." She lifted his hat.

My heart stopped. It ceased beating, and everything around me froze. Then my heart pounded, and the world sprung into life again, but felt twice as fast.

Colt. Oh my God, Colt.

"Some of the kids think they saw him on the other side. Is that what happened? Did you get separated?" *Please, say yes. Please.*

She shook her head slowly.

"Emma, did he fall?" My voice was high, strained by the giant lump in my throat.

She nodded.

For three heartbeats, I didn't think I was going to be able to get control. But I sucked air into my lungs and somehow back out.

"Thank you," I told her. Then I sprinted up the path, whistling for Havoc. She came up on my heels and then right beside me. The trail narrowed as we rounded the corner, and I skidded to a halt, grabbing Havoc's vest as she slid.

"Careful, it's a bad drop," one of the county guys

said, leaned up against the hillside. "I don't see any sign of the kid, though, which is good. He's probably on the other side of the trail like the teacher thinks. We're just waiting for the team to come up from the other side."

Five feet in front of us, the cliff-side portion of the trail had fallen away, and the rest looked ready to go. My heart climbed into my throat. "Stay," I croaked at Havoc.

Then I inched forward, bracing my hand on the hillside to keep steady. Peering over the edge, I saw a dramatic fall—maybe fifty feet—that ended in a steep, tree-covered slope.

"See? No sign of him. Teacher said he has on a blue fleece."

"It's bright blue," I answered, scanning the terrain below. "With the TSR logo on the back and Gentry labeled on the front."

It was the one thing he'd begged for before he went back to school, and the only thing he had of mine with my name.

"Oh, okay, then. Well, we don't see him. What does your dog say?"

I glanced back at Havoc, who was sitting perfectly still. Not alerting. Not anxious to get over the trail. She knew the same thing I did. "She says he's down there."

I took one last look at the terrain, trying to commit it to memory.

"Damn. Then it's about to be a recovery mission, because there's no way that kid's alive."

I spun, shoving my forearm into the guy's throat as I pinned him against the mountain. "You don't know that."

He gurgled.

Hands pulled me back. Mark. He let me go and squeezed my shoulder.

"What the hell is your problem?" The uniform rubbed

his throat.

"It's his kid," Mark answered.

The guy's expression fell. "Oh, shit. I'm so sorry. I mean, there could be a chance—"

I was Colt's *only* chance.

Grabbing Havoc, I left, sprinting back down the trail, careful to keep my balance on the rocks. Rolling my ankle could kill Colt.

I grabbed my walkie and pressed the channel. "Nelson, it's Gentry. That helo still running?"

A static-filled moment passed as I came up on the first class. Maisie sat with Emma, holding her hand at the edge of the group.

"It is," Nelson answered.

"Keep it that way. Havoc and I are on the way, and we need to get down that cliff fast."

"Roger."

Mark caught up as I dropped down to Maisie, who had stopped crying and now looked completely blank, her arms wrapped around her stomach.

I hugged her, curving my body to surround her as much as possible. "I'm taking you down, okay? And then Mark is going to get you to the station, and we'll call your mom."

"Beckett, you want me to leave?" Mark asked softly. "Don't you need my help?"

"I need you to get my little girl off this mountain," I said as I stood, Maisie shifting in my arms to hold onto my neck. "Hold on, Maisie-girl."

I jogged, balancing her weight, knowing every second counted, but there was no way I was leaving her up there. Ella's voice filled my head as I thought about every time she'd felt guilty having to leave one to take care of the other.

We rounded the next bend, and the helo came into view, along with a group of parents who stood behind a line of uniforms.

"Bad news. Travels fast." Mark's words came stuttered through heavy breathing.

"Beckett!" Ada called from the front of the group.

"Ada's here," I told Maisie. "Mark, change of plans, get on the bird."

Ada ran to the edge of the crowd, Larry not far behind her. They reached an officer who let them through after I nodded.

There was a general cacophony of shouting from the parents, no doubt wanting news, but the whir of the helicopter behind me blurred any words.

"Is everyone okay?" Ada asked. "Oh God, where's Colt? Why didn't you bring Colt back, too?" Her voice shot high in panic, and Larry put his hand on her shoulder.

"I need you to take her," I told Ada, but Maisie clung to my neck. "Maisie-girl, you have to let me go, okay?"

She pulled back, taking my face in her hands. "He's hurt. I can feel it." She touched her belly.

"I'm going to find him right now, but I need you to go to Ada, okay?"

"Okay." She hugged me, and I gave her a squeeze before handing her over.

"Where's Ella?" I asked as Maisie transferred into Ada's arms.

"It's Colt, isn't it?" Ada asked.

I couldn't say it. If I said it, the cellophane walls I had up would stop holding me together, and that wasn't an option.

"Where's Ella?" I repeated.

"She's in the ranger station right back there with a couple other parents." She motioned behind the crowd. "They're trying to get news from the county. Want us to get her? Someone has to tell her." Her face crumpled.

Flashing lights came into view. Good, the ambulance was here.

"No, just stay with her. It's...it's not good. She's going to need you."

Colt didn't have the time for me to wait for Ella. I looked at Larry, whose face was drawn and tight.

"What do you want me to tell her?" he asked.

"Tell her I'm going to find our son." Before I could lose it, I ran to the helicopter, Havoc with me. I deadlifted her into the bird and climbed in. Helmet on. Seat belt latched.

"Fly south," I told the pilot. "There's a section of the trail that's fallen away. We need to be dropped right beneath it."

"Roger." The pilot took off, and my stomach lurched as we rose into the air.

I leaned forward and clipped the sections of Havoc's vest I'd need to keep her safe.

"Slight problem, there's nowhere to land," the pilot called back.

"Can you rappel?" I asked Mark.

"In theory," he answered.

"Get us to where we can rappel," I told the pilot, then I turned to Mark. "Keep up."

He nodded.

"I need you to be ready, Jenkins."

"I'm steady." He assured me from the bench. "Backboard and litter is ready."

"You have the new report?"

He nodded.

"What time did it happen?"

He scanned through the clipboard and checked his watch. "Report came in forty-five minutes ago, and they called it in about ten minutes after."

He'd been down almost an hour. I set the timer on my watch.

"Radio back and get as many hands down here as we can get."

The helo steadied above the only clear ground visible. We looked to be a short distance from where the rocks would have fallen.

"We're ready," the pilot said through the comms.

I removed my helmet as Jenkins secured the line. Then I clipped Havoc into the slider and kept her between my legs as we shuffled for the door. Jenkins passed me the line, and I secured the slider that let me control her rate of descent. "I know you hate this," I told her as I made sure it was tight where it attached to the line a couple feet above her harness. "But our Colt is down there."

I gripped the line and her slider, gave her the knee signal she was all too used to, and we stepped out into nothing. She went completely still as I worked us down the line with her dangling between my knees.

We'd done this hundreds of times, but I'd never felt as urgent. Urgent caused mistakes, so I calmed my breathing and lowered us slowly, hand over hand, until we reached the ground.

Then I unhooked the slider and stuck it in Havoc's pack. Mark started down immediately.

I slipped Havoc a treat from her pack. "Good job. I know that sucks."

"How do you do that with a dog?" Mark asked after he reached the ground a minute later.

"A lot of experience." I leaned down to Havoc. "Seek Colt."

She started sniffing, and we walked in the direction of the slide. "How long will that take her?" Mark asked.

"Not sure. He didn't walk this way, so she doesn't have a path to go on. We'll have to get close enough for her to catch his scent in the air, or anywhere he's touched."

We hiked uphill, through patches of knee-high grass

and then under tall pine trees. I concentrated on my breathing and my footwork as Havoc walked ahead of us, searching. The less I thought about what we would find, the better.

"Colt!" I called out on the prayer he could hear us… that he was capable of hearing us.

"Colt!" Mark joined in. "Should we have brought Jenkins?"

"No. He needs to stay with the helo. When the other teams show up, he needs to be available, and if he's with us, and someone else finds Colt…"

"I get the picture."

"I'm a combat medic, which means I'm qualified to do just about anything besides surgery. Everyone in our…everyone is where I used to work." It was part of the training before you were selected as a tier-one operator. "Colt!" I tried again.

And again.

And again.

The *beep* on my watch signaled that it had been an hour and a half, and still no Colt. I looked up the mountain. We were out of the tree line, right beneath the slide zone, and there were plenty of rocks around us that all looked the same. I couldn't tell what was new and what had always been here.

We'd seen the helo drop a couple teams, and Mark had handled radio coordination, making sure we chose different grids. My grid was wherever Havoc decided to go, and they could all deal with it.

Havoc was sniffing like crazy toward the south, so we followed along the tree line.

"Colt!" I saw the bright patch of blue just as Havoc took off at a dead run.

I covered the ground quickly, jumping rocks, ducking pine tree branches as I ran. Havoc sat next to him, whining.

"Colt," I called, but he didn't respond. His upper half was clear, but his lower half was obscured by fallen foliage.

"Good girl," I told Havoc, handing her a treat from my pocket out of sheer habit before dropping to my knees next to him.

"Colt, come on, bud." His skin was pale, blood trickling from small cuts on his face. I put my fingers to his neck and waited.

Please, God. I'll do anything. Please.

He had a pulse, but it was rapid and thready. His skin was cold.

"He's bleeding somewhere," I told Mark as he dropped to Colt's other side. "We need to get these branches off him, but only the lighter ones. If it's heavy, wait for me."

Mark nodded and started pulling the smaller branches off Colt. "Rescue 9, this is Gutierrez and Gentry. We've found the male. Pulse is present but thready. Please send in medics ASAP."

Static came through Mark's radio as I unzipped Colt's fleece.

"Shit. Gentry."

I looked back to Colt's lower half, and bile rose in my throat, but I looked up at the sky and forced it back down. Colt's right thigh was pinned under a large, jagged rock roughly half the size of a car engine.

"Cut his pants around it. I need to see the skin." Not good.

"Gutierrez, this is Rescue 9. Please note we are midrefuel. On our way immediately."

Shit. Shit. Shit.

"Colt, you in there, bud?" I asked, stroking his face. "Can you wake up for me?"

His eyelashes fluttered. "Beckett?"

The sweetest sound I'd ever heard was Colt's voice

at that moment. He was alive and able to speak. *Thank you, God.*

"Hey!" I hovered over his face, locking his head in place as his eyes opened. His right pupil was slightly larger than his left. Concussion. "Hey, don't move, okay? I'm here."

"Where am I?" he asked, his eyes scanning from left to right.

"You had a really bad fall, so you can't move, okay? You might have hurt your neck. Mark is here with me, and the doc is on his way. Just don't move your head."

"Okay." He winced. "I hurt."

"I bet you do. Can you tell me where?"

His eyes shifted. "Everywhere."

"Gotcha." I looked down to where he was pinned. "Colt, can you wiggle your toes? Just your toes?"

"Yeah," he said.

I looked up at Mark, who shook his head with a pursed mouth.

Don't panic.

"Good job, bud. Can you do it again?" I hoped I sounded way calmer than I felt, because I was about to crawl out of my own skin.

"See? Toes are fine. They don't even hurt," Colt said with a little smile.

Mark shook his head again, and my soul crumpled into a little ball.

"Your legs don't hurt?" I asked.

"No, just everything else." His eyes started to drift shut.

"Colt. Colt!" I gripped his face. "You have to stay with me, okay? Wiggle your fingers."

All ten wiggled. *I can work with that.*

"I'm tired. Is Emma okay?"

"She sure is, but she's worried about you. You did great, Colt. You saved her." I took his pulse again. Shit, it was faster and lighter.

"We protect smaller people," he said with a weak smile. "I'm cold, Beckett. Is it cold?"

"Look under that rock. Is there blood?" I ordered Mark. I stripped out of my fleece jacket and draped it across Colt's chest. "Better?"

Mark crouched down. "I can't see. I bet we could get it off him."

"We need to tourniquet it first. There's every chance he's got a crush injury. It's been almost two hours, we can't just lift it off him. There's one in Havoc's pack."

"Shit, Beckett," Mark said softly. "Blood."

I grabbed the tourniquet and knelt next to Mark. Dark red blood oozed out from beneath the rock. "Where the hell is the helo? Tell them to get the basket here."

"Rescue 9, this is Gutierrez and Gentry. What's the status on getting that basket?"

"Gutierrez, this is Rescue 9. We're inbound with a five-minute ETA."

"Fuck," I muttered. There was no better word in this moment.

I dug just beneath Colt's thigh, enough to slip the tourniquet through, and then yanked it tight, securing it right above where the rock had him pinned.

"Don't move it," I warned Mark.

Then I knelt at Colt's other side. His lips were blue, his skin pale, clammy, and cold. His pulse was fast and weak.

"Hey, bud, I got your bleeding stopped. You just gotta hold on for the helicopter, okay?"

He gave me a small smile. "I get to ride in a helicopter? Cool."

"You do. Plus you're kind of a hero. Everyone's going to think you're cool, but I'll still think you're the coolest," I promised. "Anywhere else hurt?"

"No, nothing hurts."

I froze. *Shock. Bleeding out.* We'd stopped the bleeding in his leg, but there had to be a secondary bleed, if not a dozen of them after that fall.

He's hurt. I can feel it.

Twins. Just like he'd woken up when she had the infected PICC line.

"Okay, just keep talking to me, buddy." I took my fleece off him and lifted his shirt. Deep purple bruising discolored the entire left side of his chest. His belly was swollen.

I sat back on my heels and put my head in my hands. *Ryan. You gotta help me here. Please.*

"Where are we?" Colt asked, his voice soft.

I stood quickly and grabbed onto Mark's arm. "He's bleeding out internally. My guess is spleen, which means minutes. Run to the nearest place you can see the sky and pop smoke."

He was the very picture of anguish as he looked at Colt, but he turned and ran.

I hit my knees beside Colt, and then I lay down next to him, curling my body around him. "I love you so much."

He turned his head, and I didn't yell at him about neck injuries. There was no point. "I love you, too, Beckett." He opened his eyes, and I rested my forehead against his.

"I was thinking maybe we'd add that zip line to the tree house. What do you say?" I ran my fingers through his hair.

"Yeah. I think you should make it go into the lake. That would be cool, and Mom wouldn't worry about falling so much."

This was one fall we hadn't seen coming.

Havoc whined, curling up next to Colt's other side. She knew.

"You're absolutely right." I checked his pulse. So damn weak.

"I think I'm dying," he whispered.

"You're really hurt," I said, my voice choking on the last word. I didn't want to lie to him, but I didn't want his last minutes to be spent in terror. There was nothing we could do at this point. I was going to lose him.

Ella. God, she needed to be here.

"It's okay. Don't be sad. Tell Mom and Maisie not to be sad, either." He took several labored breaths. "I get to see Uncle Ryan."

I couldn't breathe. My chest only rose and fell with his, my heart syncing to his frail rhythm.

"Just hold on, bud. There's so much you haven't done yet. There's so much to do."

He looked at me, love shining out of his eyes. "I got to have you. Just like a dad."

Tears fell from my eyes, running down the side of my face to the earth below. "Oh, Colt. We were going to tell you. We were just waiting for Maisie to be okay, but I adopted you last year. You've had a dad for a while. One who loves you more than the moon and stars."

His breaths came slower and slower, each one a Herculean effort, but he still managed a smile. "You're my dad."

"I'm your dad."

"So this *is* what it feels like." He reached over, his hand cold as he laid it against my cheek. "I love having a dad."

"I love being your dad, Colt. You are the best little boy I could have ever been given. I'm so proud of you." The words barely came out.

His eyes closed as another breath shuddered through him.

I heard the sound of rotors in the background.

"I'm a Gentry," Colt said, managing to pry his eyes

open again.

"You are. A Gentry and a MacKenzie. Always."

"Always?" he asked.

"Always. I will always be your dad. No matter what. Nothing will change that." *Even death.* My love for him would cross however far God took him.

"Colton Ryan MacKenzie-Gentry. I got everything I ever wanted." His eyes closed, and his chest rose only half as high. CPR wouldn't help, not when he didn't have any blood to circulate.

"Me, too," I told him, kissing his forehead.

"Tell Mom and Maisie I love them." His words were slower, punctuated by partial breaths.

"I will. They love you so much. You have a mom, and a dad, and a sister who would do anything for you."

"I love you, Dad," he whispered.

"I love you, Colt."

His chest rattled once more, and then his hand fell from my face as he faded.

"Colt?" I felt for the pulse that wasn't there. "Colt! No!" I slid under him and sat up, cradling him in front of me, my arms wrapped around him as his head rolled back against my chest.

A primal scream ripped from my throat. Then another, until my body shook with sobs. Beside me, Havoc sat up and started to howl, the sound low and keening.

Take care of him, Ryan.

"Beckett," Mark said softly. When I looked up, he was kneeling next to me, his eyes full of unshed tears. My eyes rhythmically blurred, then cleared.

"He's gone." My arms tightened around his little body.

"I know. You did everything you could."

"I made him pinwheels this morning," I said, running my hand over his soft hair. "He wanted extra cheese, and I gave it to him. I made him pinwheels."

That was hours ago.

Hours.

And now he was gone.

"What do you want to do?" Mark asked.

I realized there were half a dozen guys standing around us. Jenkins kneeled down and did the same checks I had, only to press his mouth in a tight line and stand again.

Want? What did I want to do? I wanted to scream again, to rip everything in this forest to shreds. I wanted to pound the mountain down to rubble with my fists. I wanted to look at my little boy and hear him laugh, see him run on the deck of his tree house. I wanted him to grow up, wanted to meet the man he was supposed to become. But he was beyond my reach.

Want didn't matter when nothing was in your control.

"I need to take him to his mother."

CHAPTER TWENTY-EIGHT

Ella

The helicopter landed in the small clearing about thirty yards in front of me, and my heart sank. There were only two reasons they would land. Either they hadn't found Colt, or…

"Breathe," Ada told me. Larry had taken Maisie home. I didn't want her here, didn't want her on the front lines of a tragedy.

A group from County stood behind us, all watching. Waiting.

"If they found him, they would have airlifted him to Montrose," I said. Trying so hard to push down the fear that held my stomach in a vise.

"Beckett will find him. You know he will."

I'd seen the map, knew how far that fall was.

The door opened on the helicopter, and Mark got down first, then Beckett. He was wearing a long-sleeve shirt but no blue fleece.

He looked at me, and I didn't need to see his face from the distance. His posture said it all. "No." The sound was barely a whisper. *No. No. No.*

This wasn't happening. This was impossible.

Beckett turned as other members of Telluride Search and Rescue climbed down and then slid out a backboard, carrying it like pallbearers.

Then I saw Beckett's fleece.

It covered Colt's face.

My knees gave out, and the world went black.

The world came into focus as I blinked. Bright lights hovered above me, and I caught the sterile smell of hospital. Turning my head, I saw Beckett in a chair next to me, his eyes swollen and red.

Havoc slept under his chair.

"Hey," he said, leaning forward to take my hand.

"What happened?"

"You passed out. We're at Telluride Medical, and you're okay."

It came roaring back to me, the helicopter. The fleece. "Colt?"

"Ella, I'm so sorry. He's gone." Beckett's face crumpled.

"No, no, no," I chanted. "Colt." The tears started in a deluge, coming hard and fast as I let out a sound between a cry and a scream that didn't seem to stop. Maybe it paused while I took a breath, but that was it.

My baby. My beautiful, strong little guy. My Colt.

Warm arms surrounded me as Beckett crawled into bed next to me, and I buried my head in his chest and wailed. Pain wasn't strong enough of a word. There was no scale. No ten to be medicated. This agony wasn't measurable; it was unfathomable.

My little boy had died alone and cold at the base of a mountain he'd grown up under.

"I was with him," Beckett said softly, as if he could read my mind. "He wasn't alone. I got there in time to be with him. I told him he was loved, and he said to tell you not to be sad. That he had everything he wanted." His voice broke.

I looked up at Beckett, my breaths short and choppy. "You saw him?"

"I did. I told him I adopted him, that he had a mom and dad who would do anything for him."

He hadn't been alone. There was something in that, right? He'd been born into the hands of his mother and died in the arms of his father.

"Good. I'm glad he knew. We should have told him earlier." All that wasted time because I was so scared. All the days he could have had Beckett and known who he was to him.

"Was there pain?" He must have hurt so much, and I wasn't there.

"At first, but it faded really quickly. He didn't hurt at all when he passed. Ella, I promise you I did everything I could."

"I know you did." That was a given, even without knowing what had happened. Beckett would have died to save Colt. "Was he scared?" I started to cry again.

"No. He was so strong and so sure. He asked about Emma. He saved her, Ella. That's why she lived. He pushed her to safety. He was so brave, and he loved you and Maisie so much. That's what he said last. To tell you and Maisie that he loves you. And then he called me Dad, and he was gone. Just like that."

The sobs started again, uncontrollable and unstoppable.

This wasn't heartbreak. Or sorrow.

It was the utter desolation of my soul.

"There was nothing you could have done," Dr. Franklin said from across the table, flanked by other doctors.

I looked out the window and saw the barest hint of sunrise.

I didn't want it to be a new day. I wanted it to be the same day that I'd kissed him goodbye, hugged him before he got on the bus. I didn't want to know what the sun looked like if it wasn't shining on him.

"Colton had severe internal injuries, including a severed spine, ruptured spleen, and a tear in the aorta, combined with the laceration to the femoral artery. And those are just the things we saw on the ultrasound. Please believe me when I say that there was nothing you could have done, Mr. Gentry. If anything, your quick thinking on his leg gave you those minutes that you had."

"That's why it didn't hurt," Beckett said, his hand covering mine.

"He'd lost all feeling. It didn't hurt."

Tears slipped down my cheeks, but I didn't bother to wipe them away. What was the point when they'd just be replaced?

"If I'd gotten there faster?" Beckett's voice strangled the last word.

Dr. Franklin shook his head. "Even if he'd had that fall outside our ER, there's nothing we could have done. Not even Montrose. Injuries that severe? The time you had was a miracle. I'm so very sorry for your loss."

My loss.

Colt wasn't lost. I knew exactly where he was.

He didn't belong in the morgue. He belonged at home, sleeping, warm and safe in his bed.

"We need to go home," I told Beckett. "We have to tell Maisie." A fresh wave of tears fell. How was I supposed to tell my little girl that the other half of her heart was gone? How was she supposed to pick up and carry on as half a person?

"Okay. Let's go home."

Dr. Franklin said something to Beckett, and he nodded. Then somehow I put one foot in front of the other, and we headed for the front door.

I paused just before the doors. The twins were born here. I'd stood from the wheelchair in this very spot and carried them out in their car seats, ignoring the protests of the nurses, walking because I had to know I could do it on my own.

"Ella?"

"I can't just leave him here." My chest seized, and I struggled for a second before I could draw a breath. My own body didn't want to live in a world without Colt.

Beckett's arms surrounded me. "They have him. He's

safe. We'll take care of him tomorrow. For now, let's just get you home."

"I don't think I can move," I whispered. I couldn't make my feet budge, to leave Colt behind while I went home.

"Do you want me to help you?" he asked.

I nodded, and Beckett bent and picked me up, one hand behind my knees and the other bracing my back. I looped my arms around his neck and put my head against his shoulder as he carried me out into the morning.

Beckett drove us home in my car. At least I thought he did. Time lost all meaning and relevance. I was adrift on an ocean, just waiting for the next wave to pull me under.

I blinked, and we were inside, Ada fussing over something. Beckett sat me down on the couch and put a blanket over my legs. Ada said something, and I nodded, not caring what it was. A cup of coffee appeared in my hands.

The sun came up in defiance of my grief. Uncaring that my world had ended last night, it was determined to move forward.

"Mom?" Maisie walked into the room, clasping her blue teddy bear. She was dressed in purple pajamas, her hair sleep-mussed, and little pillow lines creased her face.

So similar to Colt's face. Would I ever look at her and not see him?

"Hey," I croaked.

Beckett appeared at her side.

"He's dead," she said as if it were fact, her face more solemn than it ever had been in any phase of her treatment.

My eyes flew to Beckett, but he shook his head.

"I knew last night. It stopped hurting. I knew he was

gone." Her face twisted, and Beckett pulled her against his side. "He said goodbye while I was sleeping. He said it's okay, and to check his pocket." Beckett sat her next to me on the couch, and I lifted my arm so I could hold her.

"I'm so sorry, Maisie." I kissed her forehead, and she tucked in even smaller.

"It's not okay. He wasn't supposed to die. I was. Why did he? It's not fair. We had a deal. We were always going to be together." She began to cry, which started my tears all over again. Her tiny body shook against mine as her tears soaked through my shirt.

I willed myself to find the right words, not to leave my daughter alone in her grief because I couldn't see a way out of mine.

"It's not fair," I told her as I rubbed her back, her little blue bear wedged between us. "And you weren't supposed to die. Neither of you were. This is simply what happened."

How could there not be a better explanation than that? What was the reasoning in an accident you couldn't see coming? Where was the justice in that?

Beckett took her other side, and we surrounded her with as much of us as we had to give. She needed it all. I may have lost my son, but she lost her other half.

After about an hour, she fell asleep, having turned to Beckett. He held her against his chest, his hands running over her hair, and I couldn't help but wonder if that was how he held Colt as he died. Then I shut the thought down and shoved it behind a door that I'd open when I was ready for the answer.

Ada came in, holding a Telluride Medical bag. "Did you want this? She said to check the pocket."

I reached into the bag and took out Colt's fleece. There was no blood, no tears, nothing to indicate the trauma he'd suffered. I located the first pocket and came up empty. The next one would be, too, if logic ruled. After all, just because they were twins didn't mean—

My fingers came across something thin and crinkled. I pulled it free, and my breath abandoned me.

It was a red leaf.

The sun shone beautifully the day we laid Colt to rest. It trickled through the leaves of the trees on the little island, dotting the ground in tiny spots of light. The breeze picked up, bringing a cascade of colors down, mostly gold from the aspens.

I stood between Beckett and Maisie as they lowered Colt's small white coffin into the ground. Maisie refused to wear black, saying it was a stupid color and Colt hated it. She wore yellow, the color of sunshine, and clutched Colt's pink bear.

She'd put her blue one in with him last night, saying that was the only way they could be apart. But watching the light drain from her eyes, I knew we weren't just burying Colt but part of Maisie as well.

Emma, the little girl Colt had saved, stood with her parents, tiny tears on her cheeks. I was immeasurably proud of what Colt had done and couldn't bring myself to wish harm on Emma; it wasn't her fault. But I still couldn't understand how God could exchange the life of one child for another.

Had it been Colt for Emma?

Or had I prayed too hard the last couple of years and accidentally traded Colt for Maisie with my desperate pleas for her to live?

The line of mourners began coming our way, wanting to express their sorrow. Why would I want to hear how much they missed him? I could barely breathe through my own pain, trying to absorb Maisie's, support Beckett's.

There just wasn't any more room for anyone else's grief.

"I can't," I told Beckett.

"Okay, I can handle this," he said and walked me over to the small bench we'd added to the island when Ryan had died. Maisie sat next to me as Beckett and Ada took the line, and Larry ushered them to the small rowboats we'd hired to take them back to shore.

"Now I'm like you, Mom."

"How, baby?"

Her eyes stayed locked on Colt. "We both have brothers out here."

Another wave of grief came for me, dragging me under waves so thick I couldn't breathe, couldn't see my way to the surface. How did anyone live through losing a child? Why didn't the pain simply stop my heart as it constantly threatened and send me with him?

Maisie's hand found mine, and air trickled into my lungs.

"We do." I finally found the strength to answer her.

"Beckett matches us, too." She turned her attention to where Beckett was nodding and shaking hands with the last of the line. "Both his best friends are here."

I swallowed for the thousandth time, trying to dislodge the permanent lump in my throat as I watched him. He stood strong and steady, handling what I couldn't, even though his grief matched mine. He was simply that strong.

Soon it was just Beckett, Maisie, and me sitting on the bench, facing the house Beckett had built for us.

"Are you ready?" Beckett asked. "We can stay as long as you like."

I couldn't bear to watch them pour dirt over my little boy, to block out the sunlight on his face. It felt too final, too wrong. "Yeah, let's go."

We walked past where the workers were adjusting Colt, and I stopped at Ryan's headstone, putting my hand on the smooth granite surface. "He's with you, now. And I know you never really wanted to be a parent, but you have to be, just for a little while. Until we get there. Make sure he plays. Teach him everything, anything he wants to know. Hug him, and love him, and then let him shine. He's yours for a little while."

My vision blurred, and Beckett took my arm. I turned to see Maisie kneeling at the edge of Colt's grave, her shoulders shaking. I moved forward, but Beckett stopped me. "Give her a second."

I heard it then, her little voice talking to him. I couldn't make out the words but knew it was just for the two of them, like so much had been while he was alive. Beckett stood silent, supporting me until Maisie was ready.

How do you say goodbye to the person who shared your soul? Who had been with you through every heartbeat of your life?

She stood up, tall and sure, then turned to us with a sad smile. Then, she wiped her eyes and stopped crying. "He's okay now. We both are."

And somehow I knew she meant it. She'd found her peace with the certainty that only a child could have.

It felt like a blink, but we were back in the house. Ada had organized the reception in the main house, so mine was quiet and empty, which was exactly what I needed.

I sent Beckett up to the house with Maisie, and simply sat, trying just to be. Havoc lay at my side, curling her head in my lap as I forced air through my lungs, concentrating on the simple mechanisms of living.

There was a knock at the door, and then Captain Donahue entered. "I'm so sorry to bother you. I can't imagine how you're feeling, nor will I pretend to know." He stood in front of me and then dropped to my eye level. So much like Beckett. "I know this might not be the time, but we're shipping out, and I don't know when I'll get back to Telluride. So this is for you."

He handed me a white envelope with Beckett's handwriting on it. It was addressed to me.

"What is this?" I asked, peeling back the paper.

"Don't read it yet. Now isn't the time. Some of the guys asked me to keep their last letters. I kept Mac's for Gentry, and I kept Gentry's for you."

"For me?"

He nodded. "I'm leaving it with you in case you start to feel lost or forget how much he loves you. Like I said, not for now. But for someday."

He left, but I didn't remember the act of him leaving, or anyone else returning. The steady rhythm of my breathing was all I could concentrate on, counting to ten over and over, trying to live through the pain. I sat there, drank the water that was handed to me, ate the food that was prepared, and faked a smile when Maisie said it was time for bed.

I pulled myself together enough to tuck her in. I brushed her hair behind her ear with my fingers and put my hand over her chest as she drifted off, the day taking its toll on her tiny body. The beat of her heart gave strength to mine, the knowledge that she was still here because I'd fought like hell to keep her alive.

But God hadn't given me that chance with Colt.

I found Beckett in the hallway, leaning in the doorway of Colt's room.

"It's like some kind of cruel joke," I said, startling Beckett. "Like this isn't real."

He turned back toward me. "I keep expecting to find him in here. Like I can tell Havoc to seek him, and he'll pop out from wherever he's hiding."

I nodded, my words failing me.

"Let's walk," he suggested.

I didn't object as we walked outside, the fresh air

stinging my raw, salt-wounded cheeks. Across the water, my son lay next to my brother, and I still couldn't grasp the reality of it all. The fog that had surrounded my brain since the fall began to clear with the breeze off the lake, leaving room for other emotions for the first time in days.

This. Wasn't. Fair. None of it. Colt deserved better.

"I fought so hard for Maisie," I said, bracing my hands on the wooden banister of my deck. "I kept saying that she needed me, and that Colt would be okay, but Maisie was dying. How damn stupid was that?" My voice broke.

Beckett leaned back against the railing and listened, like he knew I wasn't looking for a response.

"All of those treatments, and trips, and hospital stays, just trying to keep her alive from the monster inside her. All that fear, and joy when she went into remission. All of those emotions…and then this happens. He falls only a few miles from our house and dies before I can even say goodbye to him."

His hand covered mine on the railing.

"Why didn't I get the chance to fight for him? I should have had the chance. Where were his doctors? His treatments? Where were his binder and his timeline? Where the hell was I? Did I trade his life for hers? Is that what happened?"

"No."

"That's what it feels like. Like every worst nightmare I had about Maisie, preparing to lose her, just came true with Colt, but it's worse than anything I could have imagined. I've spent two years battling for Maisie's life, while making sure I made every moment special because it could be her last. I was so busy staring down the freight train headed for Maisie that I lost sight of Colt, and now he's lost. I lost him."

"He knew you loved him," Beckett said softly.

"Did he? I keep playing that morning over in my mind. We were in such a rush, and I hugged him—I remember that—but I don't think I told him that I loved him. He ran off so fast, and I didn't think anything of it. I thought I'd see him later. Why didn't I stop him? Why didn't we sleep in later? He would have missed the bus. Why didn't I hug him longer? It was so fast, Beckett. All of it. His whole life went by so fast, and I forgot to tell him I loved him."

"He knew."

I shook my head. "No. I missed his plays, and games, and projects, and months of his life because I chose Maisie, and he knew it. I always chose Maisie because I didn't know that he'd be the one to go. What kind of mother does that? Chooses one child over the other constantly?"

"If you hadn't, we'd be burying two children right now. Ella, this isn't your fault. You didn't trade Colt for Maisie. You didn't bargain him away, didn't lose him because you fought like hell for her. This was an act of...I don't even know. It was an accident."

"There's no reason! None. No war to fight, no way to battle what just happened. It was over before I knew it even began. I couldn't fight for him. I would have, Beckett. I would have fought."

Beckett wiped the tears I hadn't felt. "I know you would have. I've never met a woman who fights like you do. And I know it doesn't help you, but I fought. I did everything I could think of, and when that wasn't enough, I lay down and held him for the both of us. He was not alone. You did not abandon him. You never abandoned him. Not during Maisie's illness, and not the day of the field trip."

The pain overwhelmed my system. I couldn't imagine it ever lessening, or living with it day after day.

"I don't know how to breathe. How to get up

tomorrow."

He wrapped his arms around me from behind, resting his chin on top of my head. "We figure it out together. And if you can't breathe, I'll do it for you. One morning at a time. Minute by minute if we have to."

"How are you so sure?"

"Because a very wise woman told me once that you can't reason with the universe, no matter how sound your logic is. And that we can either breathe through the pain or we can let it shape us. So I'm sure that we'll take it breath by breath until the ache lessens just a tiny bit."

"It's never going to go away."

"No. I'm going to miss him every single day. Maybe we lost a little of our sunshine, but Maisie's here, and it might not be as bright without Colt, but it's not entirely dark, either."

He was right. I knew it in my head, but my heart still couldn't seem to see past the next five minutes.

"Captain Donahue stopped by. He wanted to say goodbye. I guess the unit is shipping out," I said carefully. If Beckett was going to leave, this would be the time. Now that Telluride was a painful place to be.

"I'll wish them luck."

"You don't want to go?" My chest drew tight, waiting for the answer.

He turned me in his arms so he could see my face. "No. I don't want to go. And it doesn't matter anyway. I signed the papers last week. I'm out."

"You're out?"

"I'm out. Besides, the full-time gig at Search and Rescue has some really good insurance." He gave me a little half smile.

"You're out. You're not leaving."

"Even if you kick me out, I'll still sleep at your back door. I'm never leaving you." The truth rang clear in his voice, his eyes.

I'd forgotten to tell Colt I loved him. I would never make the same mistake again.

"I love you," I said. "I'm sorry I haven't said it for so long. But I love you. I never stopped."

"I love you." He placed a kiss on my forehead. "We're going to be okay."

In that second, I didn't feel like we would be, but my brain knew he was right. Because for that brief second when he'd told me he'd chosen to stay, a flash of joy had streaked across my heart, only to be extinguished quickly by overwhelming grief.

But that flash had been there. I was still capable of feeling something other than…this.

So I took my happy and tucked it away. I'd bring it out again when it wasn't so dark, when there was room in my soul for it.

And for now, breathing was all I could do.

And it was enough.

CHAPTER TWENTY-NINE

Ella

Ella,

If you're reading this, it means I can't see you in January like we planned. I'm so very sorry. I used to say that I couldn't be scared while I was here, because I had nothing to lose. But the minute I read your first letter, that all changed.

I changed.

If I never told you, then let me say it now. Your words saved me. You reached into the darkness and pulled me out with your kindness and your strength. You did the impossible and touched my soul.

You're a phenomenal mother. Never doubt it. You're enough. Those kids are so lucky to have you on their side. No matter what happens with Maisie's diagnosis, or Colt's stubbornness, you are the biggest blessing those kids could ever ask for.

Do something for me? Contact my financial manager. His number is at the bottom. I changed my life insurance to Colt and Maisie. Use it to send them to college, or give them the start they need to find their passion. I can't think of a better use for it.

Want to hear something crazy? I'm in love with you. That's right. Somewhere between letter number one and twenty or so, I realized I was in love with you. Me, the guy who can't connect to other humans, fell for the woman he's never been in the same room with.

So if I'm gone, I want you to remember that. Ella, you are so incredible that you made me fall in love with you with only your words.

Don't keep your words to yourself. No matter what, find someone who wants to hear them as badly as I do. Then love.

And do me a favor—love enough for the both of us.

All my love,
Beckett Gentry
Call Sign Chaos

Three months later.

"Where do you want this?" Beckett asked, holding a box marked "kitchen."

"Probably the kitchen," I teased.

"Ha, ha," he fake-laughed as he carried it past me into the kitchen, setting it with the others.

"How many more do you have out there?" I asked from the great room.

"Just a few of the stragglers in the truck. Why?" He gripped my hips and pulled me to him. "Have plans for me?"

"Maybe," I said with a slow smile. Somewhere in the last month, I'd stopped faking the small smiles. The bigger ones were still purely for Maisie's benefit, but the tiny ones? Those were real. Those were mine.

"I like the sound of that." He lowered his head until our lips met in a kiss. "Would these plans maybe include the shower? Because I had this little bench built into it—"

An icy blast of air hit us as the front door flew open. We turned to see Maisie and Emma fly in, snow covering their hats as they stomped their way to the mudroom giggling.

"That zip line is the best!" Emma said as her boots hit the floor.

"Right? Wait until it's summer and we can do the other one that goes into the lake!" Maisie added.

The one Beckett had built a few weeks after Colt died. He did a million things like that—keeping Colt with him in his own way. Maisie was right, both of Beckett's best friends were on that island, and just as Ryan had a part of Beckett that I might never know, so did Colt.

Beckett kissed me again quickly and headed to the garage for another box.

"How about some hot chocolate, girls?" I offered.

"Yes, please!" they both answered at the same time.

I pulled the cocoa down and started, pausing to admire the view of the snow falling on the frozen lake. My heart gave that familiar warning, and I looked away from the island, concentrating on getting mugs for the girls.

I missed Colt every day. Every minute.

But the months had given me just enough time that every second didn't belong to my grief. And I knew that time span would only grow. It would never leave entirely, but at least I wasn't capsizing on that ocean of grief with every heartbeat anymore. The waves still came in. Sometimes they were predictable, like the tide. Other times they hit me with the force of a tsunami, sending me tumbling so deep that I felt like I was at day one again, instead of day 105.

The girls ran in, hopping on the barstools I'd bought to slide under the granite expanse. They laughed and talked about the upcoming Christmas play. I poured the cocoa and plopped a few marshmallows in before sliding them across the counter.

"Thanks, Mrs. MacKenzie," Emma said before taking a sip.

I didn't correct her about the Mrs., just smiled. "No

problem."

"Thanks, Mom!" Maisie said, sipping at hers.

Beckett walked in with another box and put it with the stack next to the kitchen table. Then he leaned back against the counter with me. "What is this language?" he asked, staring at the girls.

"Girl speak," I informed him. "They're discussing the guest list for Emma's birthday party next month."

Maisie's birthday had just passed. She was eight now, older than Colt would ever be. She would grow and mature and thrive, but Colt would stay forever frozen at seven years old. The day had been hard, but Maisie had invited her new best friend.

Turned out that when Emma and Maisie both lost Colt, they found each other. Even gone, he was still giving gifts to his sister.

"Cocoa, huh?" Beckett asked, stealing a sip of Maisie's.

"Dad!" she chided with a giggle.

God, I loved the sound of that just as much as she loved saying it. We'd told her after the funeral, knowing she deserved to know every day of her life that Beckett loved her so much he'd become her dad. He'd saved her life, but that was something we kept between the two of us.

Beckett kissed my cheek and started opening the boxes, laughing when he found one of Colt's toys stashed in one of the pans. I loved that about him, the way he could talk about Colt and smile through the pain. He kept him alive in more ways than one. Through the zip lines, the pictures he hung around the house, the framed red leaf. He was never afraid to say his name, and more than once I'd come home to find him and Maisie snuggled up on the couch watching video clips of Colt.

I had yet to make it through one without crumbling. Maybe one day I'd be able to smile at the sound of

Colt's voice. For now, it was simply a reminder of what I'd lost and how empty everything felt without him.

Beckett kept us moving forward at a pace that was uncomfortable but manageable. He never let me wallow too long, but never let me ignore the pain, either. He pushed my boundaries and then backed off, and if not for him, I might have chosen to simply stop moving at all.

Maisie kept my heart beating.

Beckett kept me living.

I made sure they both knew I loved them every day.

It had taken almost all of the three months, but I finally read Beckett's last letter, and that was what got me here, into this house he built for the four of us—that would now house three.

Love enough for the both of us. That's what he'd said in the letter. And it spoke to my heart in a way nothing else could. Because that's what Colt would have wanted. He would have wanted to move into this house and live our life with the guy we all loved.

The man who craved my words and owned my heart.

He'd signed that letter with his real name. The last words Chaos had spoken to me merged the two men I loved until I saw them both in the Beckett who was currently looking at my garlic press like it was a torture device.

"This drawer," I told him, opening the one at my hip.

"Eyelash curler?" he asked, dropping it in the drawer.

"It's for smoothies. Works great on strawberries." I shrugged.

"Liar!" He laughed, then went back to unpacking.

I glanced out the window at the island and took a steadying breath as that ache ripped into me. Then I grabbed the next box and started unpacking, item by item, merging my life with Beckett's. I moved forward because that's where Beckett and Maisie were, and that's what Colt would have wanted. After all, he was here, too, in every line of this house Beckett had built for him—for us.

I still heard echoes of his footsteps on the stairs, his laugh in the halls. There were even moments I swore I caught the scent of his sunshine-soaked hair, like he'd sneaked in for a hug and run off again before I could capture him fully. The bedroom Beckett kept for him was untouched except for the boxes we'd brought from my house. I wasn't ready to go there yet, and that was okay.

There were too many memories I wasn't ready to pack away. I'd taken one look at the helmet Colt had worn that first Halloween in the hospital and known I wouldn't be able to make it through a single box.

But Maisie had grabbed the helmet and smiled, remembering when she'd traded with Colt to wear it that night.

He'd worn her halo.

Like they'd known they'd eventually switch roles.

Like it had been planned all along, and I'd simply missed the signs.

"Do you think the lake is frozen enough to walk on?" I asked Beckett.

He gave me that look—the one where he knew exactly what I was thinking—and then glanced out at the snowy lake. "I was out there yesterday, and the temps are even lower today. You should be fine. Want me to go with you?"

I shook my head. "No, I'd like to go alone. I think I'm ready."

He simply nodded and then gave me the space I needed.

Methodically, I laced my boots, zipped my coat, and grabbed my hat and gloves on the way out. The air was brisk, the snow the light, shimmery kind that looked like freshly falling glitter as I crossed the lake.

I made my way up over the island to the center, where Colt and Ryan waited.

I'd never been here alone, never felt like I was ready, like I was strong enough. Maybe I still wasn't, but I was tired of waiting to feel like it. Maybe feeling strong enough came from being strong so often that it was the default.

Words deserted me as I knelt before Colt's stone, uncaring that the snow immediately melted through my jeans. There were so many things I needed to say to him, but none of them would leave my lips. So I stopped trying and simply bowed my head, letting the tears from my eyes take the words from my heart straight to him.

Finally, my throat produced a sound.

"I would have fought for you. I would have torn down the very stars, Colt. You are loved, not in past tense, but now, every second of every day, and that will never change. I see pieces of you in your sister, little glimpses of your soul shining out from hers. She carries you with her the same way we all do. I miss you so much that some days it feels like I can't carry it all, but then I see her and somehow make it through. You taught me how to do that, you know. When your sister was sick, and it felt like too much, like I couldn't be enough to pull her through, I'd look at you and realize that I had to be, because no matter what happened with your sister, it would always be you and me, kid. You taught me how to pick myself up and take the first step. I just never realized how badly I'd need the lesson. But I'm doing it. For you, and Maisie, and your dad. We should have told you about him sooner…should have done a lot of things, really."

I lifted my face to the sky and let the snow fall on my skin. My tears blended with the melting snow until the two were one, and my eyes dried.

The air burned my lungs as I drew it deep, freezing out the heavy, tear-clogged feeling I carried with me like a badge of survival.

Needing the break, I walked the few feet over to Ryan's grave.

"I never said thank you," I told him, brushing snow off the top of the stone. "For Beckett, I mean. I don't know how you knew, but you did. And I know you told me the letters were for him, and you told him the letters were for me, but you knew how badly we needed each other. You saved me through Beckett, Ry. You saved Maisie. I found a ring while I was unpacking in our bedroom. He hasn't asked yet, and I'm hoping he waits a while, but I know he's my forever, and I only have him because of you. So thank you for Beckett, and for your letter that brought him home to me. Now, kiss my boy, would you?" I pressed a kiss to my fingers and put it over his name. "He's only on loan, so be careful with him."

Then I walked back to Colt's grave.

"I love you, and I miss you," I told him. "There's nothing truer that I could tell you. And I wish I had been with you, but I'm so glad you had your dad, and now you have your Uncle Ryan. You were my greatest gift, Colt. And as much as I hate every day that you're gone, I'm so thankful for the days I had you. Thank you for being mine." Then I pressed a kiss to the same fingers and let them trail across his name, all twenty-one letters of it.

COLTON MACKENZIE-GENTRY

The walk back across the lake was quiet in a profoundly peaceful way. I'd done it. I'd found the strength to put one foot in front of the other and get there. And I'd continue to do so in every way, because I was strong enough.

A lot of that was due to the man standing at the edge of the lake, waiting for me to come home to him.

"You okay?" Beckett asked, wrapping me in his arms.

"Yeah. I think I will be, at least."

He brushed my cheeks with his glove-covered hands. "Yeah, you will be."

"Do you ever think about fate?"

His brow puckered. "You mean the way we lost Colt?"

"Yes. No. Kind of. I've been so angry with God for taking Ryan, then Colt when we'd just gotten Maisie in the clear, for taking him at all."

"Me, too."

"But then I was looking out at the lake, and I had this thought. Maybe he was always supposed to go. Maybe they both were. If Ryan hadn't died, maybe you would have come to visit, but you wouldn't have stayed. It wasn't in your nature back then."

Beckett didn't speak, simply gave me a small nod and waited for me to continue.

"But he did die. And you came. And you saved Maisie with the treatments, and you saved Colt's heart by being here when I couldn't. You made his every wish come true, and you taught him such incredible things. Because of you, he wasn't lonely. Because of you, he was doubly loved. I'm realizing that fate would have taken him whether or not you'd been here. Whether or not Ryan had lived, or Maisie had died. But without *you*, he would have been alone. No one else could have found him, could have given him the peace you did. Without you, I would have buried both of my children."

His mouth pressed into a line as he struggled to maintain control. "I couldn't save him. I would have given my own life if it meant he could be here with you. I've saved every child since…" He swallowed and looked away.

"With every call, you're trying to repent for a sin you didn't knowingly commit. I see your face every time you find a child."

"But I couldn't save yours. Couldn't save my own. How can you forgive me for that?"

"Because there's nothing to forgive."

The girls laughed as they ran through the snow, heading toward the tree house.

"You think?"

I took one look at Emma, her smile bright as she helped Maisie up the ladder.

"I know." Warmth raced through my chest. "Maybe you couldn't save the little boy who was always meant to go, but you saved her by teaching Colt." I motioned toward Emma.

Beckett's jaw flexed. "Fate, you think?"

"Fate," I answered. "And maybe it's not true for everyone, but it can be my truth. That's enough for me."

He pressed his chilled lips to my forehead. "I love you. I will always love you."

I rose on my toes and pressed my lips to his in a gentle kiss. "I love you. Now, forever. All of it."

Yes, I was capable of immense grief, but I was also capable of infinite love. And I would love my life again. Maybe not today, but one day. Because I wasn't done yet.

Life was short. Colt taught me that.

Life was worth fighting for. Maisie taught me that.

Letters could change your life. Ryan taught me that.

Love—when it was right—was enough to save you. Beckett taught me that every single day. And ours was more than enough.

And so was I.

EPILOGUE

Maisie

I dropped a bag of M&M's on the grass and tore open mine.

"Guess what?" I asked my brother. "Not going to ask? Fine, be like that. It's like you're going all teenager a few months early or something. It's been five years. You know what that means?"

I popped an M&M into my mouth and chewed.

"It means I'm still cancer-free. It means my risk of relapse is like…nothing. It means we win. But it means it's going to be a while until I see you. Remember when we made that deal? The night I got so sick? The one where you said if I died, you'd die, too, so we'd never be alone?"

I ran my hand over his stone, tracing the letters of his name.

"I broke it. I just didn't know I was breaking it. I always thought the cancer would come back and hold up my end of the bargain. But it didn't. And I hope you're not mad. Because life is okay. I mean, Rory is nuts. Our little sister is full-blown squirrel. Yesterday, she jumped the banister to the landing. I thought Mom was going to have a cow. And Brandon is such a good baby, so sweet and cuddly, and Havoc doesn't even mind when he tugs on her ears. And Emma and I have plans for next weekend, nothing big, but you know…plans. Mom and Dad are good. They still get all kissy in the kitchen when they think no one's looking. Kinda gross, but they're happy."

I reached the final letter of his name and sighed.

"Five years. And I still miss you all the time. Well, not all the time, since there's a bunch of times I feel like you're with me. But yeah, I miss you. Everyone does. But I'm going to have to break our promise, and I know how to make it up to you: I'm just going to have to be twice as awesome and live for the both of us. Okay?"

I stood up and grabbed the extra bag of M&M's so Mom didn't freak when she came out later.

"Just do me a favor. Hang around. Because I'm definitely going to need some help being that awesome if I have to make up for you being gone. I miss you, Colt."

I kissed my fingers and pressed them to his name, the same way Mom always did. Then I got in the boat and rowed back across the lake.

As of today, my future was wide open.

The cancer wasn't coming back.

I was going to live, and so was Colt—because I always carried him with me. Some bonds couldn't be broken.

"Maisie!" Dad called from the porch as I tied the boat off at the dock we'd built a couple of years ago. "You want to head out with me?"

"Yep!" I answered.

I didn't ask him where to; if Dad was headed somewhere, I was in. Because Colt would have been, and I had a promise to keep.

Twice the awesome.

Loved this read? Find a reading group guide available on our website: entangledpublishing.com/the-last-letter-reading-guide

ACKNOWLEDGMENTS

First and foremost, thank you to my Heavenly Father for blessing me beyond all measure and the health of my six children.

Thank you to my husband, Jason, for giving me quiet weekends in hotels in the crazy three weeks that I wrote this book. For loving me even when I'm bleary-eyed from three a.m. writing sessions and showing up as 100 percent dad on days I struggle to balance being an author and a mom. I love you. Thank you to my children, who show me every day just how much I have to learn about life, and who are handling more than they should ever have to as military kids. To my sister, Kate, because we finally get to raise our kids together. To my parents, who don't bat an eye when I dye my hair pink or get a new tattoo—who even in the face of cancer have always stood together with inspiring strength, unity, and overwhelming love.

Thank you to my editor, Karen Grove. For hours on the phone smoothing out the twists and turns of this book, for your guidance, your humor, your expertise, and your friendship. For the fourteen F*s you had to give. You're the reason this is our fifth year together, and I wish I had the words to adequately thank you for handing me my wildest dream.

Thank you to my wifeys, our trinity, Gina Maxwell and Cindi Madsen, who keep me at the keyboard on the days when self-doubt gets the best of me. To Molly Lee for being a constant source of friendship and understanding. To Shelby for putting up with my unicorn brain. Thank you to Linda Russell for chasing the squirrels, bringing the bobby pins, and holding me together on days I'm ready to fall apart. To Jen Wolfel for your advice, friendship, and beta skills. To KP, for sandy-toed beach talks in Mexico, Emilie, and the Inkslinger team for everything you do for me. To my phenomenal agent, Louise Fury, for always having my back and holding my career in your very capable hands. To Liz Pelletier for encouraging me to write this book and never being too busy to take a phone call or open your home for an impromptu slumber party.

Thank you to the courageous women whose experiences made this book possible. To Nicole and Darlene for sharing their stories with me, for helping me better understand the world of childhood cancer. To Mindy Ruiz for sharing your battle with me and dropping everything to read as a beta. To Annie Swink for having the strength to share Beydn's fight with me and carrying on his legacy. A huge thank you to Ashton Hughes, not only for a decade of friendship but also for sharing the details of David's neuroblastoma diagnosis and treatment, upon which Maisie's entire timeline is based. You are one kickass mom. Thank you to the countless mothers who blogged their children's fights with neuroblastoma—I spent nights reading your posts, holding my breath for your children, rejoicing when they were declared cancer-free or sobbing with you as they succumbed to their illness. You don't know me, but you touched me. Your child changed me.

Lastly, because you're my beginning and end, thank you again to my Jason. Nineteen years together, and you still give me butterflies when your boots hit the entry hall. I can't wait for this deployment to be over. Fifth and final, baby. Fly safe and come home soon.

**KEEP READING FOR A
SNEAK PEEK OF REBECCA YARROS'S
POIGNANT AND MOVING NOVEL
GREAT AND PRECIOUS THINGS.**

CHAPTER TWO

Willow

Think, Willow. Think.

This was Mr. Daniels. I'd known him my entire life. Alzheimer's or not, there was no way he was really going to shoot me, right?

Except there was this one troubling factor: he had no idea who I was. Oh, and he had a shotgun pointed at my chest. That was troubling, too.

"Mr. Daniels," I tried again, keeping my voice soft. "It's me. It's Willow. I live next door, remember?" If you considered a mile away next door.

The breeze whipped a loose strand of my hair across my face, but I didn't dare tuck it back beneath my hat. The sun had set precious minutes earlier, and it was already getting dark. What if he just couldn't see me?

"Be quiet!" he shouted, jerking the shotgun. His eyes were wide and wild but not evil. He simply didn't know me or the circumstances that had led him here.

I gasped in reaction, my heart jumping into my throat. What if he pulled the trigger? What if it went off the next time he jostled it like that? We were half a mile away from the Danielses' place and three-quarters of one above my parents'. My cell phone was in my pocket, but I had a feeling he'd shoot me if I reached for it. At this range, I'd be dead before they could get me to a hospital…if they found me.

At least there were other search parties out right now. They'd come at the sound of gunfire.

"There are cougars out here, you know," he snapped.

Like the one that had mauled his wife fifteen years ago on this very field.

"What are you doing here? You're trespassing!"

I didn't bother arguing the trespassing point, since technically, I was. But Dorothy had called in a panic, and I'd immediately headed out to look for Mr. Daniels just like I had a few times in the last month. The gun... Now that had been unexpected.

"I know there are cougars," I told him with a slight quiver in my voice. "You taught me what to do if I ever ran into one." I'd been seven years old when he'd pulled Sullivan and me aside for lessons. Naturally, Cam had played the cougar while Alexander watched in quiet judgment.

Cam. My chest tightened in that same physical ache it always did whenever he crossed my mind, even with the present danger. Heck, maybe because of the danger.

"I don't know you! Stop lying! What do you want here? Why are you on my land? Get out!" He jabbed the gun toward me.

"Okay," I said with a nod and backed up a step.

"Stop moving!" he screamed, his voice pitching high in alarm. "Don't speak!"

I halted immediately. He was slipping further and further into the episode, and my mind stopped fighting the possibility that he might shoot me, my muscles locking in paralyzing acceptance.

Movement to my left caught my eye, and I turned my head a fraction of an inch to see the shape of a man only a few arm-lengths away, approaching with hands up, palms out. Who was it? Where had he come from?

I couldn't make out his face beneath the baseball hat, but he was massive, dwarfing my five-foot-four frame as he put himself between Mr. Daniels and me. The broad expanse of his back blocked my entire view.

I didn't recognize him—which was odd, considering there were only about a dozen of us who usually came to search for Mr. Daniels, but there was something familiar in the way he held himself, the way his posture advertised submission but his energy felt 100 percent aggressive. I had the utterly illogical impression that this guy was more dangerous than the loaded gun pointed at him. At least, I assumed it was loaded. If it wasn't, at least it would be a not-so-hilarious story to tell Charity later.

For all that Dad accused my sister of being impetuous, Charity had certainly never had a shotgun held on her.

"What is this? Who the hell are you? How many of you are there?" Mr. Daniels questioned, panic rising. The shoulders in front of me rose as if he was preparing to— "No, don't speak! All lies! You claim jumpers are all full of lies!"

Well, that story changed quickly.

The man reached back, hooked his hand around my waist, and tugged me closer. I tensed, even though the violation of my personal space was nothing compared to the shotgun pointed at us. His arm was a vise, locking me in place with casual strength. Just like freshman year when— I cut myself right off. *There's no way.*

"Be careful," I said softly to the stranger. "He has Alzheimer's. He doesn't know what he's doing."

He pulled me tighter against his back, and the scent of mint and pine filled my nose as he started to shift in tiny movements so my back was to the trees and not the ravine. God, that smell… I knew it.

"We're just hikers," he said to Mr. Daniels, low and slow.

Certainty slammed into me with the force of an avalanche, knocking the breath from my lungs. My eyes fluttered shut as I swam through the flood of memories, desperately hoping I wasn't the one hallucinating right now.

"Cam," I whispered, letting my forehead rest against his back as I gripped a fistful of his coat.

"Are you okay, Willow?" he asked so softly I would have gone with the hallucination theory if I hadn't felt his deep voice rumble through his chest.

I nodded, the fabric of his coat soft against my skin. Maybe Mr. Daniels had already pulled the trigger. Maybe I'd never felt the impact. Maybe he'd killed me instantly. That was the only logical explanation for Cam's presence.

Because Camden Daniels had sworn the only way he'd ever come back to Alba was to be buried here. But he felt so real. So solid. Smelled exactly like I remembered. And if I were really dead, wouldn't it be Sullivan's arms around me? Not Cam's. It could never be Cam. Not for me.

I followed Cam's almost-imperceptible lead as he backed us away from his father.

Cam couldn't be here. He hadn't been here in years. And he definitely couldn't stop a bullet. But a feeling of safety drenched me anyway. It never mattered if the rest of the world saw him as a menace— Cam had always been my unlikely refuge, even when he earned every last bit of his reputation. He'd protected me for the simple reason that I'd been theirs all of my life.

The girl who tagged along with the Daniels boys.

The naive teenager who stayed behind when three brothers went to war.

The woman who shattered when only two came home.

Cam might be here now, but one misstep, and we'd both be buried next to Sullivan.

"Stop moving or I'll shoot!" Mr. Daniels shouted, and Cam obeyed. "Empty your pockets! You'd better not be stealing from me!"

"I'm going to let you go, and I want you to slowly back into the woods and then get the hell away from here," Cam ordered me softly.

I vaguely heard Mr. Daniels's agitated muttering in the distance.

"I can't leave you here," I protested.

"For once in your life, listen to me, Pika. I'm trying to save your neck. Alexander is coming up behind Dad, and help is on the way, but you have to go."

The nickname tightened my throat with a lump so big I couldn't swallow it down. "He doesn't recognize you, Cam. He'll shoot. It's been six years since he's seen you. He doesn't even recognize me, and I see him almost every day."

"He'll remember me."

"Yeah, that's what I thought, too, until he pointed a shotgun at me, you stubborn idiot."

"What was that?" he whispered. "I thought I heard a squeak, but my coat must have muffled it."

I would have pinched him in retribution under any other circumstance.

"He's not going to remember you," I argued, "and you'll just agitate him even more when you try to remind him who you are."

Mr. Daniels's muttering grew louder until he was shouting again. "You trespassers, trying to steal what's mine! You can't have it! Can't have it…"

Cam's heartbeat stayed calmingly rhythmic, his breathing deep and even. If I hadn't seen Arthur Daniels myself, I'd never think there was a gun pointed at us.

"You can't have it!"

A shot rang out, and birds scattered from the woods at my back. I froze, my grip tightening on Cam's coat.

His hand splayed wide over the small of my back.

"Cam!" I whispered as loudly as I dared. If he was hurt—if he'd come back only to be buried… I wouldn't survive burying another Daniels boy. I leaned to see around him, but Cam's grip tightened, trapping me firmly behind him.

"I'm okay," he replied just as quietly. "He aimed at the sky."

"I guess at least we know it's loaded." My heart slammed against my ribs, fear coating my tongue with a bitter, metallic taste.

"Way to find the silver lining."

A corner of my lips lifted slightly.

"There's one more shot in the barrel. Remember what I said. Back toward the woods slowly."

"No," I argued.

"Yes," he countered, and his hand disappeared from my back. "Now, Willow."

Ice rippled through my veins.

He stepped forward, and I let the fabric of his coat slide through my grasp, leaving me precious inches away from Cam.

"Dad," Cam called out. "I could have sworn you told me never to point a gun at a pretty girl."

I stood paralyzed, watching Cam walk forward like his dad didn't have a gun pointed at his chest.

"What?" Mr. Daniels called out. "I'm not your... Who are you? What do you want?"

There it was—a softening in his tone. If Cam could get through to him, they both might live through this. But the odds of that happening were so small they almost weren't worth mentioning.

"It's me, Dad. Camden. And you looked about ready to shoot Willow, so I figured I should step in. You don't want to hurt Willow, do you? Little Willow? Our neighbor?"

"Willow? Who's..."

The farther Camden walked, the more his dad came into sight. I needed to move, needed to get back into the woods so this all wouldn't have been in vain, but the idea of leaving him here to face his dad alone was simply unfathomable.

Sullivan had been alone. I couldn't reach him. Couldn't hold him. Couldn't brush his hair out of his eyes one last time.

I wasn't leaving Cam.

"Come on, Dad. Put the gun down. We'll go back to the house, and I'll cook you up some chicken exactly how Mom made it, okay?" Cam kept his arms outstretched, his palms facing his Dad.

"Get off my land! You can't have it!"

Another shot fired, and I screamed as Cam's body flew backward, landing in the field with a sickening *thud*.

"No!" The denial ripped from my throat as I sprinted across the uneven ground to where Cam lay on a patch of winter-brown grass.

"Willow!" Xander shouted from behind his father, already gripping the shotgun.

"Call 911!" I didn't spare more than a cursory glance as my knees slammed into the unforgiving ground next to Cam. How the hell were we going to get him down the mountain? Could a helicopter land up here?

His jacket was shredded, tiny feathers spilling free all over his chest and blowing away in the wind.

But they weren't red. Yet. Neither was the grass beside him, right? But it was already so dark.

I reached for his coat, but his back arched, and I scanned up to his pained face—God, I'd missed this face—then took the scruff-softened angles between my palms without thinking. Motion in my peripherals told me that the other searchers had arrived. Too late. Too late. Always too late.

"I'm here," I told him, looking into eyes so dark they swallowed me whole. "We've got this," I promised when I had no right to, forcing optimism into my tone with an exaggerated nod and a shaky smile. "Help is coming."

His eyes were wide as he struggled for a breath that wouldn't come, his fear palpable as his gaze dropped down my frame and over my white coat, frantically searching.

"I'm okay. I'm not hit. You are," I assured him. Idiot.

Like that would comfort him. "I need to see how bad it is."

His hands reached between us, fumbling at his coat.

I jolted back, gently brushing his hands out of the way. "Let me."

He's okay. He's okay. He's okay. You can't take him, too. Do you understand? You took Sullivan. You can't have Cam.

Cam's lungs wheezed as the first stream of air made its way in. My eyes flew to his, finding them already on me, his brow slightly furrowed as he struggled for more air.

I unzipped his coat in one long pull and steeled myself for whatever lay underneath.

"Jesus, Cam!" Gideon cursed as he hit his knees on Cam's other side.

"Arthur shot him." My shaking hands opened his coat, revealing an expanse of dark fabric with several holes ripping apart the weave where the buckshot hit him. Where was the blood? "It's too dark! I can't see!"

"I'm. Fine," Cam forced out with a rasp of breath.

A *click* sounded as Gideon powered on his flashlight.

"Shut up," I ordered. "Stupid man can't even tell when he's been—" Light shone on Cam's chest and reflected back on tiny bits of shiny metal like a lone constellation in an otherwise dark sky. "Wait. What?"

"Son of a bitch!" Gideon laughed, shaking the flashlight with heaving breaths as he looked over his shoulder. "He's fine!"

"I. Said. I'm fine," Cam growled.

"How? You're shot…" And I could see the bullets. Defying all logical thought, I dipped my finger into a tiny hole and felt cool metal pressing back. I let my fingers trail down Cam's hard—too hard—chest.

"Pika, stop." Cam captured my hand, then flattened it, pressing my palm against the unnaturally hard surface of his chest. "I'm okay. Just had the wind knocked out of me." He let go of my hand and unsnapped a clip up by his shoulder and another at his side. Velcro ripped. A giant piece of... *What the heck is that?*

"Nice. What's that rated?" Gideon asked, nodding toward a slab of armor as it fell to the side, baring Cam's Black Flag T-shirt.

His very clean, very white, very intact T-shirt.

I blinked, then blinked again, convincing my brain that my eyes told the truth and this wasn't something I dreamed up out of desperation. There were no bullet holes. No blood. No damage.

"It's a four," Cam said, his voice returning to full strength. He ran his hand over his chest and abdomen, then gave a sigh of relief, letting his head fall back to rest on the ground.

"Nice. And you carry it around?"

"Funny thing about having all of your belongings in your car," Cam answered with a wry grin.

"You're prepared for your dad to randomly shoot you?" Gid scoffed.

"Something like that." Cam winced as he sat up.

"You're okay." My butt hit the unforgiving soles of my hiking boots as I rocked back, sitting on my heels. The voices behind me registered as white noise even as they became louder, everything buzzing in my head except the fact that Cam wasn't shot, or bleeding, or dying.

"I already said I'm fine." He pulled back his shirt and glanced down his collar. "I'll probably have a nasty bruise, but it's too dark to see."

"I'm just saying it's a good thing you were here," a voice said at my left. "The way you got that gun away from him was...that was heroic, Xander."

Sgt. Acosta stepped into my view, patting Xander on the back. The two were the same age, but Acosta looked way more comfortable with his sidearm than Xander did holding Arthur's shotgun.

"No, I didn't do anything," Xander argued, dropping

down to Cam's eye level. "Cam took the brunt of it. Are you okay?" he asked after glancing at the body armor.

Cam nodded and got to his feet.

"Yeah, if the brunt means aggravating your dad into shooting him." Acosta laughed, and my fingernails bit into my palms.

My mouth opened to tell Acosta that Cam had most likely saved my life, but a swift shake of Cam's head in my direction had me shutting it. He'd always been content to let others think the worst of him, and I guess nothing had changed.

"Let's just get him home," Cam said to no one in particular, clipping the vest back in place and staring straight ahead. His tone was one I'd heard often growing up—shutting down the conversation, letting me know he'd disengaged from whatever would have had the chance to touch him emotionally.

With the danger passed, I greedily drank in the sight of him. He was bigger—not taller, of course, but thicker, harder—and the same went for his presence. He had an edge to him that had been missing when he'd left Alba a decade ago, and those impenetrable walls he'd always kept felt even more impossible to breach. But his eyes— Those carried the same grief I'd echoed in mine when I'd seen him last.

He and Xander walked forward, pausing to no doubt discuss what was going on with their father as Art stood with Captain Hall, getting a quick field exam. Mr. Daniels was shaking his head, as if trying to explain the situation.

It had been tragic when Mrs. Daniels had died. Heartbreaking to bury Sullivan nine years later. But watching Arthur Daniels these last two years felt like burying a piece of him at a time, and it was torturous.

"Don't see much of you around town, Willow. You still playing with your paints?" Robbie Acosta asked, smirking down at me as Gideon joined the Daniels brothers.

"You still pretending there's enough crime here to warrant your job?" I retorted, my voice saccharine sweet. My graphic design business kept me more than financially comfortable, but no one ever took note of that. It was always the painting—or lack thereof—that people wanted to bring up.

Guess it was more fun for them to pick at my scabs than examine their own.

"Whoa." Robbie put his hands up like he was under arrest—like Cam had when he'd appeared in the field ahead of me. "Put your claws away, Willow. I'm just teasing."

"Yeah. Not in the mood." I kept my focus entirely on Cam's back. An all-too-familiar ache invaded my chest. When had he gotten home? How long was he here for? What—or rather whom—was he going to break this time?

"You need to get out more, especially if the only time you're social includes a man with dementia and a loaded gun," Robbie said, his voice pitching higher than I'd ever heard in high school as he rubbed the back of his neck. "You know, maybe I could take you to dinner?"

"I'm sorry?" I asked him, my head tilted to the side in genuine confusion. "You want to take me to dinner?"

"Yeah." He shrugged with a sheepish smile.

"You…you don't like me," I said slowly, shaking my head.

He'd always gone for the prom queens—the girls who had perfected their makeup by middle school. The ones in Buena Vista, where we'd gone to school, who were styled and Instagrammed. I was twenty-five and didn't even have a personal Instagram account…or any interest in Robbie.

"I mean, you're single. I'm single. Makes sense, right?"

"Sure, if humans were an endangered species or something." I immediately regretted my brash words when he looked away. "You know there's life outside Alba, Robbie. You don't have to date within town limits just because you're all grown-up now."

"True," he admitted with a cringe. "Oh man, I bet you're not ready yet, huh? Shit, that was a dick move."

"What, asking me out after Art Daniels pulled a gun on me?"

He blinked. "No, I mean, maybe you're not ready to date yet…" His eyebrows rose.

Seriously.

"Oh. I'm okay, really. Not that I don't miss Sullivan, but it's been six years." Time moved slower in small towns, I supposed. I'd healed my heart in the years I'd spent at college, but everyone here acted like we'd buried him last week.

Guess I was still supposed to be traumatized.

"Right. Good for you, keeping strong," he said with a nod and a pat on my back before answering a summons from the group at the edge of the tree line.

It was too dark to make out who they were, but my bet was the usual suspects—sans Dad. Had Dad been here, he would have gone ballistic.

Xander headed for Mr. Daniels, and I found myself drawn to Cam's side just like a million times before.

"I still can't believe you're here," I said before I thought better of it. *Mouth, engage filter.*

"Me, either." His eyes stayed locked on Xander and his dad. "What were you doing out here?" he snapped.

"Looking for your father." I bristled at his tone.

"Well, you sure as hell found him."

"I help search all the time. It's no big deal."

A muscle in his jaw ticked.

"And how many times has he pulled a gun on you?" His gaze swung slowly to mine, and the darkness was suddenly more of a blessing than ever. I saw enough in those eyes to know he was pissed.

"Never. And I'm sure Xander will lock up the guns and it won't happen again."

Cam scoffed. "Yeah, okay. He could have shot you."

"Well, he did shoot you." I poked his armor-plated vest.

A ghost of a smile passed over his lips, and I nearly crowed in victory.

"Looks like he's about ready to go," Cam noted as Mr. Daniels shook off Gideon's offered arm to help him across the uneven terrain. "Still stubborn as ever," he muttered as his father approached.

"Must run in the genes, or did you not remember me warning you that he wasn't going to remember you?" I teased, trying to lighten the mood. Cam had always done better if he could turn the hurt into something laughable. Not that this was.

"Remember him?" Mr. Daniels answered instead, stopping just in front of Cam. He was only a couple inches shorter than his son but had the kind of presence that made him larger than life. "I shot you."

"You did." Other than the clenching of his right fist, Cam showed no emotion. Guess that hadn't changed, either.

"Art," Captain Hall said as he clapped Mr. Daniels on the shoulder. "Not sure if you can see in all this dark, but this is—"

"I know exactly who it is," Mr. Daniels seethed.

I mentally prepared myself for what this episode of dementia was going to gift us with.

Cam cocked an eyebrow as Mr. Daniels glared.

"This is the son of a bitch who killed my Sullivan."

I gasped, sucking in air as I reflexively stepped close enough to Cam to brush my arm against his. He may as well have been a statue for all the reaction he showed. "Mr. Daniels—"

"I don't know why the hell you're here, but you can see yourself right back out." He cut me off, effectively dismissing the son he hadn't seen in six years.

Then he turned his back on Cam and walked toward the tree line, Captain Hall at his side.

"Cam," Xander called softly. Whatever he saw in Cam's eyes led him to shake his head and walk away, following his father.

"I'm so sorry. He doesn't know what he's saying," I whispered around the lump clogging my throat.

"Sure he does. And he's right." He looked down at me with a vacant-eyed smirk that sent me straight back to high school. He'd always been able to put a million miles of distance between us—between anyone—with a single look. "Told you he'd remember me."

He walked off toward his family.

"Cam!" I shouted in a desperate attempt to keep him here just a little longer—the Camden who had stepped out in front of his father's gun to shield me. But his transformation into cold, zero-fucks-given Camden was already underway.

"Go home, Willow."

And now complete.

I watched him disappear into the trees and battled the bone-deep urge to follow. So much for the idyllic homecoming I'd foolishly let myself fantasize about over the years.

But he was here. He was home.

And I desperately wanted to know why.

Intrigued? Pick up *Great and Precious Things*
wherever books are sold.

How to Lose a Guy in 10 Days *meets*
Accidentally on Purpose *by Jill Shalvis in this
head-over-heels romantic comedy.*

the aussie next door

by USA TODAY bestselling author
Stefanie London

American Angie Donovan has never wanted much. When you grow up getting bounced from foster home to foster home, you learn not to become attached to anything, anyone, or any place. But it only took her two days to fall in love with Australia. With her visa clock ticking, surely she can fall in love with an Australian—and get hitched—in two months. Especially if he's as hot and funny as her next-door neighbor...

Jace Walters has never wanted much—except a bathroom he didn't have to share. The last cookie all to himself. And solitude. But when you grow up in a family of seven, you can kiss those things goodbye. He's finally living alone and working on his syndicated comic strip in privacy. Sure, his American neighbor is distractingly sexy and annoyingly nosy, but she'll be gone in a few months...

Except now she's determined to find her perfect match by checking out every eligible male in the town, and her choices are even more distracting. He doesn't want to, but he's going to have to intervene and help her if he ever hopes to get back to his quiet life.

AMARA

an imprint of Entangled Publishing LLC